Love
is
Worth
Fighting
for

Book Three in The *Meraki* Series

Effie Kammenou

Copyright © 2022 by Effie Kammenou
All rights reserved.

Printed in the United States of America

First Edition:

10 9 8 7 6 5 4 3 2 1

ISBN 13: 978-0-578-28251-0

Library of Congress Cataloging-in-Publication Data TXu 2-310-653

Kammenou, Effie. Love is Worth Fighting for

Cover Design and inside formatting by Deborah Bradseth of Tugboat Design
www.tugboatdesign.net

Author photo by Alexa Speyer

Meraki

A small Greek word with a complex definition. In essence, it means to put your soul into something—anything done with great passion, absolute devotion, and undivided attention—a labor of love.

In dedication to my sweet angel, Mia.
You are a blessing and a joy to all of us.

A note to readers

When I began writing *The Meraki Series*, I had mapped out in my mind who the main characters were and how I wanted their stories to unfold. However, I had no idea that *Love is What You Bake of it* would publish when much of the world suddenly went into lockdown due to an unforeseen pandemic.

During this period of isolation, I wrote *Love by Design*, never thinking that we would still be hostage to this virus by its release day. Both of these books brought some levity to a dark period for readers, though there were some serious aspects to the story.

I had always planned to solve the mystery of the missing grandfather in this third book in the series. What I hadn't expected was for COVID to drive my plot, changing the course of events for these characters, just as it had in our own lives.

The characters traveled to beautiful locations in both *The Gift Saga Trilogy* and earlier books in *The Meraki Series*. Unfortunately, in keeping this book realistic to the times, there was only one brief but necessary trip to Athens, Greece.

Regardless of these limitations, all your favorite characters are back to push Krystina along in her quest for love and to make sure everyone around her finds it as well.

Thank you for reading and supporting me all these years to continue writing. I couldn't do this without your loyalty and encouragement.

Xoxo,

Effie Kammenou

Acknowledgements

To my husband, Raymond, and my daughters, Eleni and Alexa, for your never-ending love, support, and encouragement.

To my sisters, Kathy and Jeanine, who inspire me with their compassion and kindness.

To Valerie, a most trusted beta reader—the first set of eyes on my manuscripts. Thank you for your suggestions.

To Deb, writer and beta reader. I value and respect your opinions and suggestions.

To Marisa and Chris Raptis, who helped me brainstorm the historical aspects of the subplot in this series.

To Aphrodite Papandreou, who supplied me with much-needed facts and shared personal accounts of a tumultuous time period in Greece.

To my editor, Katie-bree Reeves of Fair Crack of the Whip Proofreading and Editing, a master at her craft and a pleasure to work with.

To Deborah Bradseth of Tugboat Design, for this incredible cover and all my other equally beautiful past covers.

To all my friends and family, too many to name, who support and inspire me every day—you know who you are. You may have even found traces of yourselves within the pages of my books.

To my parents. To my father, who amazes me every day. I pray I have inherited his longevity and sharpness of mind. And to my mother, forever in my heart as the tenth anniversary of her death approaches. If not for her, my first book would have never been written. I truly believe she sent me on this creative path. I know she is smiling down from above as she watches her family grow and flourish.

Love
is
Worth
Fighting
for

To love at all is to be vulnerable. C.S. Lewis

Chapter 1

Krystina

December 2019

"I'll bring you another one, sir," Krystina said as politely as she could stomach to one of the rudest customers to walk into her sister's café. On top of hearing the agitated man's litany of complaints, she also noticed Loukas hovering close by, wiping down a table for much longer than needed. This annoyed Krystina almost as much as the man she wanted to 'accidentally on purpose' douse with hot coffee.

"Are you okay, Minnie?" Loukas asked.

Muttering a string of inaudible curses under her breath, she rounded on him. "I've been better," she snapped. "And your name-calling isn't helping my mood."

Krystina stomped over to the coffee station to remake the vanilla soy latte with two tablespoons of stevia, precisely to the man's liking.

"Way to kill a cup of coffee," she muttered, pouring the soy milk over the espresso shot. Two more hours and she was out of here. Not that she didn't like helping out her sister or the generous tips she usually made, but this place was her sister Kally's dream, not hers.

At seventeen years old, Krystina had her own aspirations. With a little over fifteen thousand followers, she was already on her way to becoming an Instagram influencer. Not to mention the list of subscribers to her blog, *Island-trotting with Krystina*. One day, she hoped to change the title to *Globe-trotting with Krystina*.

Today, she was heading west of her Port Jefferson village to the Bayville Winter Wonderland. Now, if she only heard back from Chynna, her best friend and 'Instagram boyfriend,' so to speak. She was supposed to be here by now.

"Here you go, sir," Krystina chirped, forcing a smile and setting down the replacement beverage. Then she pivoted and walked away in a dash. She certainly wasn't about to wait for another complaint to spew out of the jerk's mouth.

Pulling her phone from her back pocket, she checked for a reply to her several texts to her friend. Nothing. She tapped out one more before giving up. Ten minutes later, Chynna responded.

Chynna: *So sorry. Was sleeping. I'm sick*

Krystina: *What's wrong?*

Chynna: *Sore throat. Fever*

Krystina: *Can I bring u anything?*

Chynna: *No xoxo*

Krystina: *Call u tomorrow xoxo*

"Why the glum face," Kally asked Krystina. "If you're upset over that rude customer, don't give it another thought. It happens." She shrugged.

"No, it's not that," Krystina said, disappointed. "It's Chynna. She's sick, which I feel terrible about, of course. But she was supposed to be my ride and photographer today."

"I can help you out with that," Loukas offered, coming up beside her and draping his arm around Krystina's shoulder.

Krystina flashed daggers in her sister's direction at the evident amusement playing on her face before turning her anger toward Loukas.

"Hands off," she growled, shrugging out from under him.

"Listen, Minnie, I've got the wheels and a pair of able hands to snap the pics. It'll be fun." Flipping away the silky black hair falling over his topaz-blue eyes, he grinned. "What do you say?"

Krystina let out a long, contemplative breath. No matter what she did, he always seemed to be around—at school, church, the café … She couldn't even escape him at home. He was there now more than he was his own house. So, what was the point in trying?

"Okay. But here's the deal—no telling me what to do, how to pose, or what shots to take. No touching me like you just did. And absolutely no calling me Minnie," Krystina insisted. "Those are my terms."

"So many rules. What do I get out of this?" Loukas groaned.

"I'll pay for your admission into the park."

"I'd rather pay my own admission and forget all the dumb restrictions."

"Take it or leave it," she deadpanned, folding her arms over her chest.

"I'll be ready to leave when you are," he relented with a sigh.

When Krystina's and Loukas' shift ended, he drove her home to change. As they pulled into the driveway, Krystina noticed a disturbance two houses down—Loukas' home— an occurrence that was becoming increasingly common.

It wasn't unusual to find Manny, Loukas' father, outside screaming at his son or falling down drunk on the lawn. Whenever Manny was 'not himself,' as her parents phrased it, they'd insist Loukas spend the night with them. There had been instances when Manny had become violent with his son. A combination of grief and alcohol made him this way, she supposed. But this was not the man she had known all her life, and it certainly wasn't the father Loukas had grown up with.

Krystina diverted Loukas' attention, rushing him along. "Let's hurry up before it gets dark," she urged. Jumping from the car, she shuffled over to the driver's side. Grabbing Loukas' hand, Krystina dragged him to the front door of her home.

"I thought you said no touching," he said with a smirk.

"Extenuating circumstances," she answered quickly. "Don't get used to it."

With the contentious situation in his own home, Loukas spent more and more time with the Andarakis family. His house hadn't been much of a home since his mother had passed away four years prior. But before that, his family life had been very much like the one he now found comfort escaping to. In fact, Krystina's parents and Loukas' had been the best of friends.

The loss of Markella had been immeasurable to Krystina's parents. Her death led to grief so paralyzing that Manny Mitsakis had gradually drunk his sorrow away until there was nothing recognizable of the man he'd once been. In a sense, George and Melina lost both of their friends that day. And Loukas, who looked so much like his mother, had become nothing more than a painful reminder of her. The destruction of the relationship between father and son was the most tragic result of it all.

"Give me ten minutes, Loukas," Krystina said. "Go up to Theo's room and amuse yourself with a video game until I'm ready."

"You're full of orders today," he joked.

But as Krystina knew he would, Loukas complied. Her nemesis spent a good deal of his time in her brother's room during his absence when Loukas feared his father's wrath.

Once Loukas disappeared into Theo's room, Krystina ran into the kitchen to question her mother. "Mom, what's going on over there?" she asked in a whisper.

"Manny got into his car, apparently drunk," her mother replied in a hushed voice. "Thankfully, he didn't get too far. He crashed into his mailbox, swerved, and landed in the middle of his lawn," Melina explained. "Loukas didn't see?"

"No. I got him into the house in a hurry before he noticed anything," Krystina said.

'Hmmm." Melina cocked her head. "It's nice to see you being kind to him for a change."

"I'm not a monster," Krystina defended. "I know how bad it must be for him."

"I immediately called Max directly instead of the police station," her mother explained. "He and Leo are over there now."

Krystina stepped out onto her front porch. Her soon-to-be brother-in-law, Max, a village police officer, and his partner, Leo, were on Loukas' front lawn. Max jumped in the car and moved it back onto the driveway while Leo, a large and muscular man, trained in martial arts, had a stronghold on Loukas' father, forcing him back into the house. The man was incredibly drunk. But for his incoherent mumbling of complaint, he didn't even have the wherewithal to resist.

With a sigh, Krystina turned and headed back inside to get changed. Despite how much Loukas drove her crazy, she knew his father's actions hurt him. She hoped that by the time they left the house the drama would be over and Max and Leo would have left. With a bit of luck, this time Loukas wouldn't even know what had happened.

The weather was unseasonably warm for December on Long Island, which pleased Krystina. Instagrammable photos were more appealing in a cute outfit sans a heavy coat. But she was prepared to freeze if it meant getting the shots in just the way she wanted. Fortunately, Boreas, the Greek God of winter, decided to give her a break. So Krystina slipped on a pair of warm, chocolate velveteen leggings, most of which wouldn't show under her above-the-knee suede boots and an oversize angora sweater.

She touched up her makeup with a bit of lip gloss and cheek bronzer. Krystina's hair was lighter than that of both her sisters. Mousy brown, if you asked her. It was her one complaint about her looks. In her opinion, hair should be dark brown and lush, illuminated by a rich hue or alight with luminosity. Hers was neither, so she gave Mother Nature a helping hand, adding sweeping highlights to her long tresses in a technique hair stylists called a balayage. As a bonus, she'd been paid to promote the hair salon on her Instagram account.

Krystina walked into Theo's room to find Loukas deeply invested in the latest version of *Assassin's Creed*. "I'm ready if you are," she said in an almost tender tone. She sometimes had to consciously remind herself that Loukas dealt with more pain than the little humiliations he had subjected her to on occasion.

Loukas glanced up at her suspiciously, narrowing his eyes. "Sure," he said slowly, as if he was trying to figure out her angle.

Krystina stepped further into the room to coax him out of the game chair.

Loukas grabbed her by the wrist and, in one swift move, pulled her down onto his lap.

Yelping, Krystina reprimanded him. "I said no touching."

Finding herself practically nose-to-nose with him, she could feel the warmth of Loukas' breath grazing over her skin.

"You didn't rule out kissing though," he whispered.

She blocked his mouth with the palm of her hand.

Loukas grinned. "One day, my little Minnie Mouse, you're going to realize that I'm exactly who you need."

"In your dreams."

"Yes, it is," Loukas admitted. "One day, it will be in yours too."

Chapter 2

Krystina

"So what do you say?" Loukas asked, pulling into Krystina's driveway.

"Do I have the job? I think I took some killer photos."

"Beginner's luck," Krystina retorted. "I'll maybe consider you as an alternative when Chynna isn't free."

"Oh, how generous of you, considering the going rate for my services."

"I didn't ask for your help. You offered." She raised an eyebrow in challenge. "Actually, you begged. Whatever," she scoffed. "We can discuss the terms of your photographic duties later." Krystina read an incoming text. "It looks like my mom wants you to stay at our house tonight."

"What did he do now?" Loukas asked, his question laced with exasperation.

And just like that, his mischievous tone from moments before, when he had playfully needled Krystina, disappeared. Loukas hung his head, expelling a weary sigh. His words might have spit out bitterness but his posture revealed so much more—deep, deep sadness and emotional exhaustion.

Krystina knew his situation must be painful. But she didn't want him focusing on it.

"Nothing you haven't seen before," she said dismissively. Then, nervously, she chewed the inside of her cheek.

Glancing at him with uncharacteristic concern, she opened the passenger door. But before she could exit the car, Loukas gripped her wrist. "I'm not looking for your pity. You never gave it to me before. Just give it to me straight," Loukas insisted.

She hesitated before answering simply, "He's drunk."

"So what else is new?" Loukas stared out at the cold, starless night, shaking his head. "What else?" he repeated in a deadpan voice.

"Loukas." Krystina laid her hand on his arm but he shrugged it away.

"What else?" he asked again through gritted teeth.

"He got in the car and drove over your mailbox," she spouted out quickly.

Loukas slammed his hand against the dashboard, startling Krystina.

She exited the car at a loss for words, hoping he'd follow. But Loukas didn't join her as she ambled up the paved walkway leading to her front door. He had other ideas, slamming the door shut and heading down the street with purpose in his stride.

Realizing Loukas had not followed her, Krystina turned and ran to catch up, shouting after him.

"Relax! I'm not going after him. I'm just checking out the damage." He bent down, picking up the mangled remnants of an aluminum mailbox. "He did a damn good job." Then, standing, he kicked the flattened post with the toe of his Converse high-tops. "Even that can't be salvaged."

"Let's go," Krystina urged, tugging at his jacket. "I'll have my dad look at it tomorrow."

"You don't have to be nice to me, Minnie. I prefer sincerity over fake sympathy." Loukas picked up his pace, overtaking her as he headed back to the Andarakis home.

"Keep calling me Minnie and you won't have to worry about it," she called out, sprinting to catch up to him.

"Now that's more like it." He chuckled humorlessly under his breath.

Krystina wanted to retaliate with a snarky comeback. But something in Loukas' hard gaze told her that he needed to have the last word tonight. She had a sudden longing to hug him. To be the friend to him she once was. To comfort him and wipe the anguish off his face and from his heart. Instead, they slipped through her front door and quietly went upstairs, retreating to their rooms without another word.

Chapter 3

Loukas

The Andarakis household was quiet when Loukas and Krystina entered the darkened foyer. Then, as if he lived there, Loukas climbed the stairs, Krystina on his heels. When he reached the top of the staircase, he turned right, in the direction of Theo's room, while she, without uttering a single word other than a strangled good night, turned left toward her own bedroom.

Loukas was grateful Melina and George, Krystina's parents, had gone to bed. Although they were like a second set of parents to him, he wanted to dwell in his misery alone tonight.

The day his mother died, Loukas lost not only her but also the loving, attentive father he had always known. His family was no more. At thirteen, life as he knew it was over. Markella was the life force of their home—like the trunk of a tree, supporting its limbs and leaves. Once the trunk had withered, the limbs snapped, and the green leaves fell to the ground, swept away and discarded. And that is how Loukas felt now. Discarded and ignored by his father except when the man needed to take out his aggression on him. Manny Mitsakis couldn't bear life without his beloved wife. The man drank himself into oblivion to wash away the pain, forgetting he had a son who needed emotional support now more than ever before. Logically, Loukas knew the reason why his father acted this way. But emotionally, he needed the love of the only parent he had left.

Loukas flopped onto the bed in frustration. Staring up at the ceiling, he scrubbed the exhaustion off his face with the palms of his hands. Craving a sympathetic ear, he contemplated knocking on Krystina's door, but he quickly brushed the thought aside. There was a time, long ago, when they were as inseparable as glue on paper. And if it wasn't for 'panty-gate,' they probably still would be. Maybe. Okay, so he had acted like a jerk a time or two in front of his friends, almost ensuring their feud would continue longer than it should have. It was his biggest regret, and he'd been trying to make amends ever since. But the girl was as stubborn as she was beautiful. Still, he could never get her off his mind, and the little girl who had once been his closest friend was now the girl he wanted in a very different way.

Pulling his phone from his back pocket, he typed out a text. He knew exactly what he needed to clear his mind. The response came swiftly. Loukas wasn't surprised. There were still some people he could always count on without fail.

Motivation gets you going, but discipline keeps you growing.
John C. Maxwell

Chapter 4

Loukas

Rivulets of sweat ran down Loukas' face. His mop of dark hair was drenched, and every pore on his skin glistened with perspiration. When he'd texted Leo the night before requesting a workout to burn off his anger, the Port Jefferson Village constable and gym owner was happy to comply. He and Max, Krystina's sister's fiancé, had taken him under their wing, mentoring him and keeping a close watch on him after he'd had a close call with a group of boys selling drugs in the park. If it wasn't for Max and Leo threatening him to get his head screwed on straight, he might be sitting in a jail cell at this very moment instead of willingly being subjected to Leo's torturous idea of training.

"Are we done yet?" Loukas sputtered through breathy gasps.

"Done?" A deep, vociferous laugh rumbled from deep within Leo's chest. "We're just getting started."

Loukas doubled over, his lanky arms hugging his torso. Insisting they meet at six in the morning was bad enough, but the key had barely turned in the lock when Leo ordered him onto the mat, spouting off a list of drills—battle ropes, box jumps, burpees, shuttle runs, and jump rope.

"I didn't ask to come here for cardio." Loukas straightened, looking up into a pair of steely gray eyes. "I just need to punch the shit out of something."

"Have at it." Leo pushed Loukas in the direction of an eighty-pound punching bag suspended from the ceiling. "Ten interval rounds. Power shots, body shots. Start slow," he ordered, offering Loukas a pair of boxing gloves. "I'll signal when to pick up speed. Stay focused." Leo placed his hands on his hips, ready to command Loukas to begin. At six feet, three inches tall, he could be intimidating. With his imposing stature, muscular form, and bald head, Leo looked like a modern-day Mr. Clean. All he needed was the gold earring.

But Loukas knew better. The man was as compassionate as they came. And even though Leo was putting him through his paces, he knew his mentor had a reason. He wasn't about to admit that to him, though. So instead, Loukas mouthed off for not being allowed to release his aggression the moment he stepped into the gym. Then, without Leo's permission to begin, he slammed his gloved fist into the bag, releasing the pent-up rage inside him. But he didn't stop there. Loukas pivoted into a roundhouse kick, his foot landing against the padded wall.

"Pull a stunt like that again and we're finished," Leo grunted. "If you can't reel in your anger and show some discipline then I can't help you."

Chagrined, he replied, "I'm sorry."

"Are you ready to continue on my terms?" Leo asked.

"Yes." Loukas hung his head, afraid to meet Leo's eyes.

"Okay. Let's get started, and if you have anything left in you after that, I'll let you have a go at me," Leo promised with a cocky smirk.

Loukas' eyes flew up to Leo's. He smiled at his mentor with appreciation and nodded eagerly. "I'm ready."

"Remember. Ten intervals starting with power shots. And go!"

Loukas took his first jab at the bag. This was what he came here for. He dug in deeper with the second hit but Leo ordered him back.

"Focus," Leo shouted. "Build up. Don't hit so hard right away. Otherwise you'll never make it to the end. Work on precision. Think of the end game."

Loukas followed Leo's commands, channeling his anger and exhibiting hard, clean punches. Finally, Leo let Loukas go full speed and at full force during the last interval. When he called time, Loukas dropped to the floor, spent and emotionally drained. He lay face down on the mat, his hands over his head, the rise and fall of his back hinting that he was crying. Leo bent down, patting his back and offering him bottled water.

Embarrassed, Loukas shook his head but didn't lift it off the mat.

"Hey, it's just you and me here. Man code, right?" Leo gently prodded Loukas off the floor.

After taking a swig of water and regaining some composure, Loukas caught his breath to speak. "Same old story. My father." He spat the words out vehemently, removing the gloves and wiping his tears away.

"I figured as much." Leo sighed. "He was in a bad state yesterday. Did he give you grief last night?"

"Wait. You know?" Loukas glanced up at Leo in surprise.

"Melina called Max as soon as she noticed him driving erratically. He'd slammed into the mailbox. When we arrived, his car was in the middle of your lawn. We got there just in time before he had a chance to back up and drive off again.'

Loukas averted his eyes from Leo. Instead, he zoned in on a motivational poster on the adjacent wall. 'The pain you feel today will be the strength you feel tomorrow.'

Loukas tugged at his hair. "You should have thrown his ass in jail."

"He was practically incoherent," Leo said. "We dragged him into the house to let him sleep it off." He raised his hand, silencing Loukas' question. "Max took the keys to his car."

Loukas sighed with relief. He waited for a beat before speaking,

14

wondering if he should censure his father further or come to his defense.

Quietly, Loukas tried to explain. "You didn't know him before. He wasn't always like this. He used to be a good man."

Leo cuffed his shoulder. "I know, man. I've heard."

Loukas nodded imperceptibly, his stormy blue eyes brimming with unshed tears. "It makes the whole thing worse, you know? If he was always a bastard, I wouldn't feel like I've lost everything. He was so in love with my mother and was good to both of us. Sure, he drank socially, like everyone else, and my mom was always after him to quit smoking, but he was nothing like he is now."

"How was he last night? Did he give you a hard time?"

"I slept at the Andarakis' last night." He picked up his discarded gloves and fiddled with the straps. "For all I know, he's still flat out."

Leo slapped Loukas on the back. Then, rising to his feet, he urged Loukas to follow. "If you think you've pounded that bag enough for now, instead of taking a go at me, how about we work on some Jiu-Jitsu moves?"

Loukas jumped to his feet. His eyes twinkled with eagerness. As much as these sessions resulted from his pain, he enjoyed them. Learning new moves with Leo distracted him. And Jiu-Jitsu was quickly becoming one of his favorite fighting styles.

"Okay! Let's do this." The deep timbre of Leo's voice resonated with pride.

Loukas looked down at his shuffling feet. "Thank you, Leo," he said gratefully. This man, who owed him nothing, offered so much of his time. But more than that, he gave him a sense of belonging and worth.

"No need. I've always got your back," Leo said, his voice catching. Then, clearing his throat, he swung his arm over Loukas' shoulder. "Your choice. We can work on submissions or sweeps."

"Sweeps," Loukas replied without hesitation.

"Good choice. A sweep can change the flow of a match, bringing you from a defensive posture on your back to an advantageous attacking position."

For the next hour, Loukas focused on nothing but Leo's instruction. All thoughts of his father, his grief, and even his tenuous relationship with Krystina melted away, if only for the time being.

Chapter 5

Krystina

Christmas Eve 2019

Joyful exuberance electrified the Andarakis home. Furniture was pushed aside for dancing. Laughter and loud cheers echoed over the bouzouki music coming from the scratchy-sounding vinyl records playing on George's old stereo system.

No matter how many times Krystina showed her father how to get all his Greek songs and even more on Spotify, he stubbornly insisted on reverting back to his collection of worn-out records. *Parents!* But he was having fun with all his buddies. Each one took their turn on the makeshift dance floor, moving to the sound of the bouzouki, baring their soul through each improvised step of *Zeibekiko*.

When the song changed, *Yiayiá* shuffled in, a tray of shot glasses in hand and a white napkin draped over her arm. "For you, for you, for everyone!" she called, handing out the shots. "*Stin ygeía mas!*" She toasted to her friends' health.

"One more! Ouzo for everyone!" the spirited old woman insisted, refilling everybody's glasses. "Now drink up and let me see you show-offs balance the glass on your heads," she challenged.

Being the architect of the plan, she led the group of men at the head of the dance line while waving the napkin in the air as her feet moved in step to the tempo.

"Kally," Krystina urged, laughing along as she watched from the sidelines. "Go tell Mia and Nicholas to come over here."

"I will," Penelope, Nicholas' sister, offered. "He won't believe what your *yiayiá* has convinced my very proper *pappou* into!"

"I only hope I have half her energy at her age," Krystina giggled.

Soon, the younger generation all crowded together as they caught a glimpse of what their elders must have been like long ago. It was easy to forget that they, too, were once in their prime. And although many years had passed since, the memories of those days, to them, seemed like only a moment ago.

Krystina envisioned her *yiayiá* as a young woman. Full of fire. In love and about to marry. It wasn't too long after that when her grandmother had a child. The stories she told from her youth were so vivid. And when she recalled them in remarkable detail, it was as though she had just lived them, the last fifty years washing away like grains of sand on the shore.

Krystina turned to Mia and began to comment, but it was Loukas she discovered standing behind her.

"Where did Mia and Nicholas go?" she asked in surprise.

"Beats me." He shrugged. "They left just as I came over. Weird." He picked his arm up over his head, bringing his nose to his armpit. "Maybe I chased them away. Do I smell? I don't think I forgot my deodorant today."

"Gross." Krystina pulled a disgusted face. "Get away from me," she ordered, giving him a shove when he leaned in closer, urging her to take a sniff. "This isn't helping you to stay in my good graces."

His eyes widened in mock shock. "I was in your good graces?"

Grunting, she scowled at him, her brows furrowing so deeply they nearly touched in the center. Then, flipping her long tresses over her shoulder, Krystina turned and stomped away.

Busying herself by replenishing platters of food, she dwelled on how Loukas went out of his way to annoy her. He was always in her face. The little boy who had once been her closest friend had turned out to be the biggest and most annoying pain in her ass.

"Hi, Manny," Kristina greeted when Loukas' father stepped into the kitchen. He had pulled himself together enough to join the holiday festivities, and she was relieved to see he was still sober, although still a little disheveled.

"Would you like me to make you a plate of food?" Krystina asked. But as she drew closer to him, she was sure she detected the licorice scent of ouzo on his breath.

"Have you been drinking?" she questioned him, disappointment showing on her face.

"Just one, *koritsáki mou*," Manny pleaded, his cigarette bobbing up and down as he spoke. "I only had one ouzo tonight. I just needed a little something."

"When I came over the day after the car incident, we talked this through," Krystina scolded. "You promised to do better for Loukas. To do better for yourself." She looked around, keeping her voice low so as not to be heard. But the music was loud and everyone seemed too busy enjoying themselves to pay any attention.

She motioned for him to follow her, leading him to a quiet spot in the laundry room. "We made a deal. I expect you to hold up your end of the bargain," she whispered.

"You can't hold me to that. I was in a bad state when you forced me to agree."

"You listen to me." Krystina was furious. "I promised to keep this between us. Why? I have no idea. There is no shame in getting help. But if you don't go to some kind of counseling and stop drinking, I will have my parents call child protection services and report how many times you've struck your son."

"I would never hurt my boy."

"You have but you've been too drunk to remember."

Krystina was at her wit's end. She hoped her harsh methods didn't backfire on her. Common sense told her she should speak to her parents but, for some reason, Manny felt ashamed and didn't want anyone else to know about him seeking help.

"Manny," she said softly. "I love you. I can't remember a time when you weren't in my life. In my whole family's lives. But I don't recognize you anymore, and it makes me so sad."

"That was before," he admitted, glancing away from her. "You don't know what it's like to live with this grief and guilt."

"I miss her too." Krystina laid her hand on his shoulder. "You have nothing to feel guilty over. But you do need help. I'll pick you up at seven p.m. Thursday for the AA meeting, okay?"

Manny nodded, relenting, but he didn't meet her determined gaze.

"That means no drinking at all. Not even one little shot. You can't go on this way."

"I'm trying," he whispered, his voice cracking.

"You know I only want the best for you, right?" she added, her features softening slightly. She knew this was hard for him.

Rifling his fingers through his hair, he hung his head. "Right."

Krystina leaned toward him, planting a daughterly kiss on his cheek. "Come. Let me fix you a plate of food."

Just as she finished piling food onto Manny's dish, Krystina was startled by a lively commotion coming from the living room. Scurrying to see what had happened, she found her mother, *Yiayiá*, Kally, and several other women hovering around Mia.

"What's going on?" Krystina weaved her way between the cluster of bodies toward her sister.

Almost giddy, Mia extended her hand, showing off a large, blindingly brilliant diamond ring. "I'm engaged!" she squealed.

Speechless, Krystina's jaw hung open. There was a moment of silence. Then, suddenly, she embraced her sister in a delayed reaction, jumping up and down, shrieking with excitement. "I'm so happy for you!" Tugging Mia's hand in for a closer look, she sighed appreciatively. "That is the most gorgeous ring I've ever seen!"

Mia laughed at her over-enthusiastic reaction.

But then, sheepish, Krystina turned to Kally. "Oh, aside from yours, of course."

Now there were two weddings to plan for. The upcoming year would be epic with so many happy events to look forward to. Not to mention her milestone in graduating and all the festivities that went along with it. Krystina just couldn't wait. Then another thought occurred to her.

"Do I get to be your maid of honor? You'll be Kally's, so I should be yours," she blurted out rapidly in one breath. "It's only fair." She was so excited, she couldn't think straight!

Before Mia could do anything more than nod, Loukas came up behind her. "And when we get married, Kally can be your maid of honor. It's like the circle of life," he declared, proud of his analogy.

"She would be matron of honor," Krystina corrected smugly. "And it would happen over my dead body."

"Whatever it takes," he whispered in her ear, chuckling.

"Oh, buzz off. Don't ruin this perfect moment."

As the other women hovered around Mia to congratulate her, Krystina stepped aside, searching for Nicholas to tell him how happy she was over their engagement. Then, spotting him, she strode over in his direction, an idea taking form in her head. Of course, the rambunctious teenager had more on her mind. Common sense would have told her to table her requests for another time but, some-how, she just couldn't contain herself. Chalk it up to excitement or a lack of control, after her heavy conversation with Manny, Krystina just wanted to jump into the many things she had to look forward to.

"Nicholas!" Krystina hugged him with enthusiasm. "I'm so happy for you and Mia. To think, in just a few short months, I've gained two brothers-in-law."

Nicholas laughed, hugging her back warmly. "I'm glad you're pleased. So you approve then?"

"Um, yeah! I mean for a while there I wasn't so sure." She lifted her

21

eyebrows, shooting him a reproving glare. "But you totally redeemed yourself."

Nicholas cleared his throat, trying to conceal his amusement.

"No, but really, I think you and Mia are perfect for each other." She gave him another warm hug.

"And she seems to have disappeared. Do you know where my lovely lady is at the moment?"

Krystina pointed across the room. "You see that cluster of women over there? She's buried in there somewhere. Her hand is going to dislodge from her body with everyone tugging to look at that ring."

"I think that's my cue to rescue her," Nicholas said, walking away before Krystina had a chance to tell him what was on her mind.

Later, when she found herself standing by Nicholas's side once more, she jumped at the opportunity to approach him regarding her own interests.

Shifting her weight from side to side, she tapped Nicholas on the shoulder to get his attention. "So, Nicholas, I have something I'd like to ask you. Now that we'll be related and all, do you think I can come work for you? I mean, I don't want any special treatment or anything. I'm a really hard worker and good at what I do. Maybe I could be the brand ambassador on social media for your magazine? I have over fifteen thousand followers, you know?"

"You don't say?" Nicholas played along.

"Seriously! And then, later, I could work my way up to a social media management position."

"Since you haven't graduated high school yet, we can start by discussing a summer internship. However, as far as any positions go, they will have to wait until you finish university."

Pouting, Krystina slumped her shoulders. "As long as an internship doesn't mean fetching coffee for you and making document copies, I guess it will be okay."

"As much as I love your ambition, you need to learn to start from the bottom." Nicholas pointed to his distinguished grandfather, chatting away in the next room. "My *pappou*? Nothing was handed to him. He was a self-made man who worked hard to achieve success. He wanted the same for Penelope and me. We did everything from receptionist duties to mailroom errands. We made coffee and learned how to manage advertising. We even interned in the accounting department. And all before we were allowed to touch anything on the creative side."

"I suck at math. So don't stick me in accounting."

"You can summer intern in social media but you'll have to learn the rest of the industry too. That is, if you're truly dedicated." Nicholas glanced at his watch. "Let's table this for another day. I've been engaged to your sister for less than two hours and you're already hitting me up for a job." He laughed.

Kissing her forehead, he walked away to find his fiancée. Krystina rolled her eyes, throwing him a halfhearted thanks.

Ugh! He is so going to make me his gofer.

Chapter 6

Krystina

Christmas Day 2019

Sitting at the dinner table, Krystina paid no attention to the conversations around her. Lost in her thoughts, she daydreamed of the future. Exotic locales and exclusive, glamorous events occupied her imagination. With the right opportunities and connections—namely Nicholas—she could achieve it all. But, sigh, he was adamant she would have to learn it all from the ground up. It's not that she was lazy or believed anything was beneath her. It was just that she was simply eager to begin her life the way she pictured it in her mind. In the end, she would do whatever he asked of her to get there. Even if it meant running coffee errands.

With all these thoughts clamoring through her head, she hadn't noticed that her peers had left the dinner table. Suddenly, she was the lone Gen. Z, sitting with her elders as they regaled tales from their past she'd heard at least a hundred times.

Excusing herself from the table, Krystina searched for her siblings but found the rest of the house unusually quiet. She was about to look upstairs when she noticed smoke billowing skyward from outside the window, carried away by a brisk wind as it lifted remnants of dried leaves up into the air. The weather was tolerable for a late December day on Long Island—forty-six degrees Fahrenheit. Still too cold for her liking but better than the frigid temperatures she was usually cursed to suffer through at this time of the year.

She stepped onto the back porch only to find the entire group seated in folding chairs, huddled around the outdoor fireplace—Mia and Nicholas, Kally and Max, Theo, who had just arrived home from college two days before. And Loukas. That boy was ubiquitous. He was like gum on the bottom of her shoe. A red wine stain on a white shirt. The embedded crust at the bottom of a frying pan.

"No one invited me to the party," Krystina complained, grabbing a bag of M&Ms from their hoarded snack pile and ripping them open.

"I have a chair right here waiting for you, Minnie," Loukas offered.

Krystina narrowed her eyes. Walking over to the proffered chair, she dragged it as far away from him as she could without distancing herself from the rest of her peers.

"Now that we're all here, I have something I'd like to discuss with you," Nicholas declared, flipping his chair around to face his future family. "As you're all aware, Mia and I went to Athens for a photo shoot. While we were there, we continued to gather information on your grandfather's disappearance. With the help of an investigator, we learned that your grandfather had been imprisoned by the Junta for participating in the Resistance. We also discovered that once that dictatorship fell, he was released."

Last year, Kally had gone to Athens to care for her father's ailing parents. During that trip, she searched for information about her missing grandfather. Mia continued the investigation when she and Nicholas went to Greece on magazine business but they still hadn't been able to locate their grandfather.

Theo nodded. "He was jailed for almost five years you said, right?" He sighed. "I don't know how he survived it."

"He and his friend, a bar owner in Athens, both somehow made it out," Nicholas continued. "According to Kostas, your grandfather's will to survive was fueled solely by his love for your grandmother."

"Yet he didn't come back for her," Krystina pointed out, fishing through the bag of candy for a red chocolate to pop into her mouth. "It doesn't add up. That Kostas guy is full of it."

"Why would he lie?" Kally argued, shooting her sister a disapproving glare. "What do you presume would be his motive?"

"Krystina is onto something though," Max agreed. As a police officer, he sensed something was missing from the story.

"Yes, she is," Nicholas confirmed. "My instincts told me Kostas was holding something back from the start. Not only did his story have unexplained gaps, his body language was that of a nervous man. So I kept my investigator on the case."

Nicholas waited for a beat while everyone stared at him, anticipating what he would say next.

Suddenly Krystina was all ears. There was nothing she liked better than watching a mystery played out on TV, except for maybe a zombie movie. But now, this was real life. Her family's life! And they were embroiled in a mystery of their own, looking for a man who had been missing for decades. But then the gravity of the situation struck her. If for no other reason, she wanted these questions answered so her *yiayiá* could finally have closure.

"Panos—your grandfather—might work at that bar," Nicholas continued. "It hasn't been definitively confirmed as of yet but there's cause to believe he may have even been there the night I went to speak to Kostas."

"You have got to be kidding me!" Krystina shot up from her seat. Then, pacing back and forth, she looked for the first place to direct her anger. With the toe of her boot, she kicked a stack of firewood, the split logs tumbling around her.

"Whoa, reel it back, tiger," Max said with a hint of amusement.

"All these years, *Yiayiá* has been waiting around for him. Believing he'd come back to her one day. Having faith in the love they'd shared." Krystina's arms were flailing like a crazy person. "It's all bullshit!" She stomped over to Loukas. "Men suck," she accused, poking him in the chest. "Nothing but lying, annoying fleas who aim to humiliate you."

Loukas threw his hands up in surrender. "What do I have to do with this?"

She glared at him, snarling. "You know! Oh, you know what you did."

Krystina's sisters stifled giggles while Nicholas couldn't have looked more confused and horrified if his corporation had been subject to a hostile takeover.

"Let Nicholas finish," Max said on a sigh.

Shrieking when Max grabbed her by the waist, she sat down in a sulk, still glowering at Loukas.

"As I was trying to explain," Nicholas continued, "my investigator has reason to believe this particular gentleman, who not only works at the bar but also lives in one of the back rooms, is indeed Panos Nikopoulos. There must be a reason we don't yet understand as to why he hasn't contacted your grandmother. But there's only one way to find out—he needs to meet his family. Once he sees all of you, hopefully, he'll realize what he's missed all these years."

"You're going to bring him here?" Theo asked.

"I don't think he'd agree to that," Mia said. "And kidnapping is a felony," she joked.

"We need to go to Athens. The four of you," Nicholas stated. "You're his grandchildren. Max and I will go as well. My grandfather has arranged for us to use his private jet."

"What about me? Can I come along?" Loukas asked.

"No!" Krystina snapped. "You have nothing to do with this."

"There's plenty of room," Nicholas said calmly, shooting Krystina an admonishing look. "You are most certainly welcome."

"He doesn't even have a passport."

"How do you know?" Loukas challenged.

Krystina raised an eyebrow. "Well, do you?"

"No," he muttered.

"That's enough," Kally reprimanded sharply. "It's enough I put up with your bickering at the café. Keep this up and neither of you will be going."

"There are expediters," Nicholas said. "And we'll need to use one because we are leaving in four days."

Collectively, everyone began to argue at once.

Nicholas held up his hand to silence the group. "If Panos gets wind that we suspect where he is, he might leave. We have no idea what his motive was for abandoning your grandmother. The sooner we leave, the better."

"I'll just go straight to London from Athens afterward," Theo said. "No sense in coming back for a week or so."

"I'll ask Egypt to manage the café," Kally added.

"I'll have to clear this with Mom and Dad. I may be missing a few days of school." Krystina was worried they'd say no. Then what? Everyone would go off on an adventure without her and she'd be stuck on this island. Not that she didn't love it here but she was just as much a part of this as her older siblings were. Besides, whatever they discovered, good or bad, she wanted to know firsthand so she could help her grandmother through it.

Chapter 7

Krystina

Garments were strewn in every corner of Krystina's room. Outfits were tossed on the bed, shoes and boots scattered across the floor, and sweaters hung over the back of her desk chair. According to her weather app, it was warmer in Athens than in New York at this time of year, but it was still quite chilly.

They'd only be gone for a short while. But was this a 'jeans and sweater' kind of trip or would an opportunity arise for her to dress up and take photos beside Instagrammable landmarks she'd only dreamed of posing in front of? She just didn't know. Maybe she could even write her first off-island blog post.

A soft knock on her door broke her train of thought as she obsessed over her wardrobe dilemmas.

"*Po, po, po!*" *Yiayiá* exclaimed. "*Ti hália áhoume ethó?*"

"This mess is me trying to figure out what to pack in my suitcase." Krystina threw up her hands in defeat.

"You young girls have a way of complicating what is very simple." The old woman pushed aside a pile of clothing on the bed, finding a spot to sit. "I have something for you."

Krystina sidled up beside her, kissing her on the cheek affectionately.

Yiayiá reached into the pocket of her flannel house dress and pulled out an intricately carved piece of wood no larger than the palm of her hand.

Krystina wasn't quite sure why her grandmother was giving this to her, and as the confusion evidently crossed her face, the old woman smiled with delight. Then, gently, she pried open a set of tiny wooden doors Krystina had not even realized were there. Inside was a triptych—a three-paneled icon, aged and faded yet still beautiful in its antiquity. In the center was the largest of the three images— the *Theotokos*, the ever-virgin Mary, holding the Christ child in her arms. The archangels Michael and Gabriel were depicted in the two icons to either side, standing watch over the divine mother and son.

"I brought this *icona* with me on my journey to America," *Yiayiá* explained in her heavily accented English. "It kept your mother and me safe, and I prayed it would bring my Panos back to me."

She pressed the icon into her granddaughter's hand. "Now it's for you. For your protection."

"And for me to find out where my grandfather is?" Krystina asked.

Melancholy shadowed her *yiayiá's* usually bright spirit. "All these years, I believed that if he could come to me, he would. But now, to find out that he might be out there and not want me—" A sob strangled her words.

The truth in what they would find in Athens worried Krystina. If the outcome was something that would further hurt her grandmother, what would they tell her?

Krystina wrapped her arms around her *yiayiá*, rocking her as if she were an infant. "No," she said soothingly. "I know there is a reason. We just need to find out what it is. Please don't lose hope," she pleaded. "I've lived my whole life on the idea of your romance. On a love strong enough to survive anything."

Yiayiá tweaked Krystina's chin, squared her shoulders, and grinned, her mood changing back to the frisky woman with the optimistic nature. "That's right, *koukla*." Then, standing, she sorted through the clothing on the bed and began to fold. "Ah! Take this one." She held up a cocoa-colored cropped sweater, shimmying. "Bare at the shoulders with a little belly showing. Loukas will have romantic ideas before you even get off the plane."

"*Yiayiá*! Stop, just stop," Krystina squealed, jumping up and covering her eyes in embarrassment. "First of all, Loukas is the last boy on Earth I want to get 'romantic' with." She air-quoted. "And seriously, can we not talk about my love life?"

"What do you say? He's a pain in your ass? Panos was a pain in mine too." *Yiayiá* playfully slapped her granddaughter's behind. "But one day, that all changed, and he became my one and only love."

"Loukas is not my Panos."

Yiayiá chuckled knowingly, and Krystina raised an eyebrow at her mocking.

"The two of you are 'to piss in a pot.'"

"What?"

"'To piss in a pot.'" She shook her hands for emphasis.

Krystina furrowed her brow, trying to decipher what her grandmother was trying to say through her thick accent. And then it registered. "Oh!" She laughed. "You mean 'two peas in a pod.'"

"Yes! That's what I said."

"I suppose you did. But if he and I were in the same pod, we'd kill each other."

"That boy has tried everything to get your attention. Yes," she said, her eyes misting over as if she was watching the past play out before her. "The two of you are just how Panos and I once were. And like Loukas, he was very much on his own."

"You never told me that. He had no parents?"

"No, he had no one. And it wasn't until I found out his circumstances that I let my guard down. In the end, he helped me through the most difficult time in my life."

Yiayiá refocused on Krystina and palmed her granddaughter's cheeks with purpose, holding her gaze. "You know what Loukas has been going through. Be kind."

Krystina swallowed the lump in her throat. Had her years-long grudge over his silly childhood ridicule gone on for too long? Maybe it was time to forgive him and move on. But could she do that?

Chapter 8

Kalliope

Kalamáta 1961

The morning rush had just about ended at the taverna. Kalliope absentmindedly wiped down awning-covered tables outside the weathered doors to the entrance. Terra-cotta plants spilling with vibrant fuchsia geraniums complimented the bougainvillea creeping up the stone walls.

She would soon go home for the afternoon break and begin to prepare dinner for her parents, who worked tirelessly in the olive groves, before returning later for the evening shift.

Daydreaming of owning her own pastry shop or café one day, Kalliope was jolted from her thoughts when Panayiotis came up behind her offering her wildflowers that had obviously been pulled from the ground.

"For you," he said, holding out the handful of purple blooms.

"For me?" She eyed them with disdain. "For anyone, you mean. Those look like you pulled them off the side of the road."

"I did!" He grinned. "But I thought of you as I plucked them out of the dry dirt."

Kalliope set the pitcher down in frustration. "Why do you keep doing this? Haven't I made myself clear?"

"Very," he admitted. "How else would I have my fun if not to irritate you?"

"I'm *fun* to you?"

"No," he dragged out. "You're no fun at all. If anything, you're a killjoy and as cold as that fish I tried to offer you the other day."

A bilious rumble rolled from Kalliope's throat. Fisting her hands on her hips, she demanded, "Get out of here and leave me alone."

"Don't worry, I won't be bothering you again," Panos retorted with a scowl.

With a huff, she stormed inside only to find Demos chuckling.

"He's harmless, you know," he told her, drying his hands on his stained apron. "Good-natured, despite his circumstances."

"Good-natured!" Kalliope repeated, incredulous. Removing her apron, she returned to the kitchen. "I'll be back after *mesimeri*," she told Yannis, the head cook.

She was about to walk out the door but her curiosity got the best of her. Turning, she asked, "What circumstances?"

"Huh?" Demos grunted absentmindedly as he restocked the glasses on the bar shelf.

Kalliope pursed her lips in disapproval. He knew full well what she was asking. She could see the smirk he was trying to conceal. "That boy's circumstances," she explained impatiently. "You said 'despite his circumstances.'"

Demos tapped his hand on the bar, inviting her to come and sit at one of the high-top stools. "*That boy*, Panos, has not had it easy. His mother died in childbirth."

"How old was he?"

"*He* was the newborn."

"Oh, that's sad. He never had a chance to know his mother then." Kalliope leaned in, resting her elbows on the edge of the bar.

"His father did the best he could but he had to make a living. So he relied on his late wife's mother until she passed away. After that, it

34

was the kindness of neighbors who helped out, but often the boy was left on his own until his father came home from work."

Kalliope was beginning to think she could have been a bit nicer to Panos, even if he was a presumptuous, overconfident sort.

"If all of that wasn't enough, his father took ill and never regained his strength. So from the time he was thirteen, Panos had to find ways to earn money to support both of them."

"How is it then that he always seems to be in a good mood? Walking around whistling and waving to everyone like he owns the pier?"

Demos tapped the tip of Kalliope's nose, smiling. "Would you rather he was a miserable sort?"

"No, of course not!" she was quick to say. "It's just that it doesn't sound like he has much to be happy about."

"Some people take their misfortune and wear it like a coat, out there for the world to see. They view life as hopeless instead of realizing the future can change and that it holds infinite possibilities," Demos explained. "Then you have a young man like Panos. He chooses to be happy. He looks for the good things that surround him and focuses on the simple joys life holds while still doing what he needs to survive."

"He counts his blessings rather than his troubles."

"Exactly," Demos agreed. "And"—he tipped his head toward her—"he likes you."

Embarrassed, Kalliope slid off the chair. "Doubtful! He called me a killjoy. And said I was no fun. No matter," she said indignantly, waving off the thought. "I'm not interested."

Each morning, Kalliope's parents drove twenty kilometers from their village to work at one of the oldest olive groves on the Peloponnese Peninsula. The work was laborious, and it was up to their only child to keep the house and prepare the meals.

As she left the taverna for the afternoon, Kalliope stopped at an outdoor fish market. Pointing to the *barbounia*, she held up two fingers. "*Thyo, parakoló.*"

For a moment, Kalliope entertained the thought that if she had accepted the fish Panos had caught the other day, she could have saved money. But as quickly as the idea entered her mind, she brushed it away. Moving onto the vegetable cart, he popped into her thoughts again as she squeezed bright, yellow lemons and inhaled the fragrance wafting from potted basil plants. It wasn't just what Demos had told her about Panos that occupied her mind. It was images of his loose blond curls nearly covering his enigmatic gray eyes. Eyes that were as soft and gentle as a kitten's fur until his emotions shifted and a hurricane of darkness swept through them, overshadowing the fleeting kindness in their mystifying depths.

The two-bedroom home where Kalliope lived with her parents was tiny, nestled between other similar homes. The kitchen was located on the back end of the house with a door leading to a small patio for outdoor dining. As Kalliope unloaded her market bag, her mind drifted back to Panos yet again.

No one had ever come to her rescue the way he had, she realized, thinking of how he had stood up for her when the drunken patrons at the taverna got a little too fresh. Drizzling oil onto the fish, she wondered about him and the difficulties he'd lived through. Then, cutting a pair of lemons in half, she squeezed the juice onto the fish with more force than required, her thoughts shifting back to his presumptuous behavior. She hadn't asked for his help yet he'd inserted himself at every turn. It was perplexing. Panos was like a pestiferous gnat she had to keep shooing away. Worse, her mind was reeling! One minute she felt terrible for his troubles, and the next, she wished he would just disappear.

Adding a generous amount of oregano and a few basil leaves, Kalliope slammed open the oven door. "A killjoy," she muttered under her breath, throwing the pan into the oven with a bit too much force. A splash of oil splattered and the stove sizzled. Picking up a rag from the counter, she dampened it under the faucet and wiped up the mess.

"A cold fish!" Slamming the oven door shut, Kalliope seethed. She wasn't about to give that contemptuous young man another thought. She was glad to be finally rid of him.

For the next several days, Panos kept his promise. He hadn't bothered her by bringing her wildflowers or smelly fish, or any other ridiculous token gifts. In fact, Panos had not stepped into the taverna at all. If Kalliope hadn't known better, she would have believed he'd simply disappeared into the night's fog. But she did know better. Each day she spied him strolling past the taverna as if it didn't exist. And an involuntary twist in Kalliope's stomach worsened every time he walked by without so much as a glance in her direction.

Demos came up behind her as she watered the plants, her eyes darting back and forth, searching up and down the pier for his arrival. "The boy might be an optimist but he does have his pride." He raised a knowing eyebrow, not in judgment so much but in guidance.

"I guess I owe him an apology," she admitted, taking one last look around. Sighing at the empty pier, she stepped back inside with her drained watering can.

Kalliope had made a point of noting the time of day when Panos typically passed her way. So the next day, when the hour neared, she busied herself with wiping down the outdoor tables, even though they had already been cleared. Earlier, she'd made a pan of *bobota*, a Greek-style cornbread, to offer Panos as a peace offering. Made with simple ingredients found readily in her home, Kalliope thought the bread would make a tasty breakfast for this boy who had to fend for himself.

Suddenly her heart began to race when she spotted him approaching. What should she do now? Wave? Call out to him? What if he ignored her attempt to catch his attention? There was only one way to find out. With her heart racing, she lifted the bread-filled straw basket she'd placed on one of the bistro tables and, with determination, hurried to the other side of the pathway, stopping Panos in his tracks.

"This is for you," she stammered, pressing the offering into his hands. She didn't meet his gaze. Instead, Kalliope kept her eyes trained on the needlepoint flowers sewn onto the linen napkin covering the cornbread. "You were kind and I was rude," she continued, swallowing nervously. She wanted to peer into his gray eyes to gauge what he was thinking but kept them trained on the ground, too nervous to look. Would they reflect the gentleness of a kitten's fur or the fury of an impending tempest? Turning, she rushed away, not looking back even when she heard his voice faintly calling her name.

* * *

It had been two full days since Kalliope's encounter with Panos and she hadn't seen or heard from him. She had made an attempt at an apology on her own terms. 'I'm sorry,' never actually rolled off her tongue but she had admitted she was rude, so wasn't that the same thing? All in all, she got what she had asked of him. He had left her alone. And now, by way of her gesture, Kalliope's conscience was clear. So why was there an unsettling, gnawing feeling eating away in the pit of her stomach?

It was just about closing time at the taverna when Demos came into the kitchen carrying one last platter of dirty dishes. "The last table has been cleared," he said to Kalliope. "But I need you to wipe it down."

She nodded, picking up a dishrag as she exited the room. The place was completely empty, but for one other patron. She was startled to find Panos standing at the bar, waiting for her.

"I came to return your basket," he said, pushing it across the bar in her direction. "That was the most delicious *bobota* I've ever had. I ate it with breakfast, lunch, and dinner," he confessed, smiling.

Kalliope smiled shyly, showing a side of herself very unlike the defensive version of her character Panos had faced before.

Panos watched her for a moment. "Demos told you about me,"

38

he stated quietly. "He must have for you to favor me with sudden kindness."

Hearing him say that stung, and she was suddenly ashamed of herself. Kalliope opened her mouth to speak but she honestly didn't know how to respond. It wasn't just what Demos had shared; he had made her see how quickly she had judged the boy. Kalliope wasn't used to being the object of a young man's affections. Unless she counted the slobbering men with lustful eyes she waited on, but that certainly was in no way the same thing. This was different, and it made her nervous. Kalliope used her frosty behavior to conceal her awkwardness. She simply didn't know how to act around Panos.

"Yes, he did tell me about your mother." She eyed him with concern. "And how you had to support your father after he took ill. But, like I said, I was rude, and there was no excuse for that."

Panos said nothing for a beat. Then, assessing her with his stormy gray eyes, he ran his hand up and down the scruff on his jaw.

Kalliope couldn't bring herself to steal more than a fleeting glance at him. So instead, she kept her eyes focused on a knot in the wood of the bar top. Then, when he touched her hand, she jumped, her stomach dropping as suddenly as a diver jumping off a cliff.

Still she wouldn't meet his gaze until Panos placed two fingers under her chin, lifting it in a challenge for Kalliope to look straight into his eyes. That was all it took for her heart rate to speed up. Her skin exploded with a frisson of electricity. Every cell in her body had just awakened as though it had been dormant her entire life. He was so close. Too close. Kalliope was a bundle of nerves. She didn't know what she'd do if he leaned down and kissed her.

"Take a walk on the pier with me." Panos took her hand.

"I have to get home to cook for my parents," she stammered.

"I'll walk you home then."

And Panos did. He walked Kalliope home every night for the next week. Each day, she grew a little more at ease with him. Yet she never once invited him in to wait and meet her parents. Her mother, she was sure, would have insisted Panos stay for dinner. But, on the other hand, Kalliope was afraid of what her father would have to say.

One clear evening, when thousands of stars shone brightly above and the full moon reflected the ripples in the water like candles flickering in the dark, Panos steered Kalliope to the edge of the dock to take in the beauty before them.

Together they stood, side by side, staring out at the water, appreciating a precious moment of serenity. The fishermen had anchored their boats for the night, and passing foot traffic was minimal. So other than the whipping sounds of the wind gently smacking the sails of moored boats, it was peacefully quiet.

"I should head home," Kalliope said regretfully. "And you should too. Your father must need you."

Panos furrowed his brow in confusion. "My father passed away three years ago. I thought Demos told you."

"No, I'm so sorry." Kalliope mentally kicked herself for bringing it up. "He said your father took ill when you were still pretty young and that you had to find work to care for him." She covered her face in embarrassment. "He didn't mention your father had died."

Panos gently pried her hands away. "It's fine," he reassured her. "You did nothing wrong." He took her hand, leading her back to the path toward Kalliope's home.

Panos had been carefully respectful, never doing more than taking her hand in his. She imagined he was mindful of her father's reputation and the tyrannical picture she and Demos had painted of him. In actuality, her father was a hardworking, kind man who adored her and her mother. He was simply overprotective. Too much so.

Rough, callused hands scratched against hers, the hands of a laborer, and she didn't mind. In fact, she liked the feel of his skin. She surmised friction from the ropes as he pulled the boats into harbor caused a good many of his abrasions, just as his days in the sun lightened the tips of his mop of curls.

"Your parents work late," Panos noted.

"It's the harvest. They always work more hours this time of year," Kalliope explained. "Working in the olive groves is tiring. I try to help out as much as I can."

As they arrived on Kalliope's street, she noticed a gathering in front of her house. Worried, they picked up their pace, seeing half a dozen neighbors gathered together.

"What's going on?" she asked.

At once, they all descended upon her, frantically speaking over each other. "We've been waiting for you. It's your father," a gray-haired, middle-aged woman said, raising her hand, commanding the rest of them to fall quiet. "He collapsed in the groves. A heart attack, they say."

"*Baba*," Kalliope cried, shaking with fear.

Panos draped his arms around Kalliope. "Where is he?"

"The hospital," another woman said quickly. "My husband can drive you," she offered to Kalliope. "We have a truck he uses for work."

"I'm coming with you," Panos said, taking command and ushering Kalliope after the woman who led them to an old, rusted vehicle.

Kalliope stepped inside her father's hospital room. Her mother was at his bedside, holding his hand. She had a faraway, blank expression in her eyes. The tears running down her face terrified Kalliope.

She placed a gentle hand on her mother's shoulder.

"He's gone," her mother cried, suddenly breaking down into racking sobs.

Panos, who had waited for her outside the door, raced in when he heard a heart-shredding wail rip from Kalliope.

* * *

Kalliope's mother struggled to pull herself together. Even after the funeral, she remained despondent. She spoke to no one and spent a good part of the day sitting in her husband's favorite reclining chair. Kalliope had to practically force-feed her, and what little she ate was barely enough to sustain her strength.

Panos loyally arrived every evening after work, helping out in any way he could, often cooking dinner to give Kalliope a break.

Each day, despite her grief, she felt herself falling in love with Panos more and more. This boy, who had become a man before his time. This boy, who she had tried so foolishly to dislike. This boy, who had now become as vital to her as the blood pumping through her own veins.

At the end of one particular evening, they bid each other good-night, just as they had for the last two weeks. But this time, Panos took her hand in his and pressed a tender kiss to the inside of her palm. A rush of emotion washed over her when his lips grazed her skin. She was no longer afraid to meet his eyes. In them, she saw the truth in his soul.

On impulse, and with her heart pounding, she rose to her tippy-toes as Panos leaned in to kiss her forehead. Instead, at her elevated height, their lips touched.

His eyes sparkled. Softly, he pressed his lips into hers and whispered, "I love you so very much."

"I know," she breathed. "I know from the way you look at me, from the way you care for me, and from how you have been here for me through all of this. I love you too."

"Don't love me out of gratitude," he stated firmly. "I don't want your love because you're grateful. *Eísai i zoí mou.*"

"No." She shook her head, smiling. "Never from gratitude. You are my life, too. Always. I know that now."

* * *

Kalliope's mother died one month after her husband's passing. She dwindled away from lack of food and the will to live. Her heart was just too broken to go on. Now Kalliope understood fully the magnitude of what Panos had gone through, though he had been so much younger at the time of his father's death. Still, they both now found themselves in the same position—parentless at far too young an age.

One week after the forty-day memorial for her mother, Panos asked Kalliope to marry him. He'd waited a respectable time, he explained, but couldn't go on for another day without her formally by his side as his wife.

"You and me. Together, we can be a family. I want to live this unpredictable thing called life with you," he pronounced. "Only you. I'll stand by you, love you, and we'll support each other through the happiest and saddest of days." Panos took her hands in his. "I'm a simple man. I only have my love to offer you. But I humbly stand before you and ask you to accept me as your husband."

And that was that. The persistent boy with the haunting gray eyes, who had once offered her smelly fish and dirt-rooted flowers, was now hers for eternity.

Kalliope's Bobota-Greek Cornbread

Ingredients

1 cup cornmeal

1 cup flour

2 teaspoons baking powder

½ teaspoon baking soda

½ teaspoon salt

¼ cup granulated sugar

½ teaspoon cinnamon

1 tablespoon honey

1 cup warm water

Juice from 1 orange

1 tablespoon Greek olive oil

1 large egg, beaten

Syrup

— cup water

½ cup honey

¼ cup sugar

1 cinnamon stick

A strand of fresh orange rind

Juice of 1 orange

Method

Preheat oven to 350°

Grease an 8 x 8 inch pan.

Mix the cornmeal, flour, sugar, baking powder, baking soda, salt, and cinnamon in a large bowl.

In a separate bowl, whisk the water, orange juice, olive oil, honey, and egg. Add the wet ingredients to the cornmeal mixture, whisking until all the ingredients are well combined.

Pour the batter into the pan. Bake for 25-30 minutes.

Prepare the syrup while the cornbread is baking.

Add the water, honey, sugar, orange juice, cinnamon stick, and orange rind to a medium pot. Bring to a boil then lower to a simmer for 10 minutes. Cool slightly and pour over the cornbread once it comes out of the oven.

Spend time with your elders. Not everything can be found on Google.
Sofo Archon

Chapter 9

Krystina

Present Day

"Wow *Yiayiá*, just when I think I know everything there is to know about you, new revelations surprise me. It's like finding that last M&M stuck to the bottom of the box of candy and discovering it's my favorite red one."

"That good?" The old woman laughed. "Here." She pulled a hard candy wrapped in silver paper from her pocket. "Just for you."

"Cherry!" Krystina untwisted the wrapping and popped the candy into her mouth. "How did you know?" she laughed.

It was a joke between the two of them. Her grandmother would buy the bag of assorted candies at the Greek grocer and pick out the cherry flavored ones, hiding them from the rest of the family. Those she saved just for her youngest granddaughter.

"So the lesson here," Krystina said while sucking on the hard candy, "is that I should be extra understanding to Loukas because his situation at home is difficult?"

Yiayiá cupped her chin. "Yes. But you already do that in your own way, don't you?" She tipped her head knowingly. "You may not let Loukas see it but I know what you've been up to."

Krystina was caught out so she figured there was no use acting defensive about it. "I … well … after what happened, I'm just worried Manny will get in the car drunk again and harm himself or someone else, that's all. It has nothing to do with Loukas."

Yiayiá smiled, unconvinced. "You have my obstinance but you also have my heart. Don't deny what it's trying to say to you," she advised, patting Krystina fondly on her cheek. "I'll leave you to finish your packing."

Krystina fell onto her bed, right on top of her massive pile of 'maybe to pack' outfits. Right now, that was her biggest dilemma. She would ignore the churning in her stomach for the time being. All thoughts of Loukas had to be pushed aside. That's what her head and her pride told her to do. However, her heart was a completely different matter.

* * *

"How long do you think we're going away for?" Kally asked Krystina while dragging two suitcases into the limo that would be driving them to JFK Airport.

"A girl can't have enough outfits. And I have a checklist of Instagram spots I want to hit."

"You *do* realize this isn't a vacation, right?" Kally emphasized.

"Nicholas said there would be time for a little sightseeing," Krystina challenged.

Just then, Loukas came up the driveway carrying a duffel bag.

"That's it?" Krystina criticized. "That's all you're taking?"

"Five days." Loukas held up his hand, counting off each finger. "There's more in here than you think."

On the way to the airport, Krystina repeated the story *Yiayiá* had told her. Maybe in some way, the information could help them find Panos or reach him emotionally once they did. He was their grandfather yet it was odd to think of him as anything but a stranger. She

47

hoped that would change once she laid eyes on him. Maybe she would detect a familiar feature in the man who was connected so closely to her and her siblings. *Yiayiá* had mentioned Panos' eyes were gray. No one in her family was gifted with those. Krystina and Theo had hazel eyes like their father, whereas Mia's and Kally's were the color of milk chocolate.

Suddenly, this whole thing had become far too real. They were really doing this. A feeling of ambivalence came over her. What if he rejected them and had no interest in his family? Or worse. What if *Yiayiá* no longer meant anything to him?

"What else did *Yiayiá* tell you?" Loukas asked. "The more information we have about their past, the more leverage we'll have with him."

"Leverage?" Krystina scrunched up her nose in disapproval. "You make him sound like a business deal."

"Loukas is onto something, though" Kally said thoughtfully. "We have to play on his emotions. On his memories of *Yiayiá*. She was his one true love. That doesn't just fade away."

"The reason why Nicholas wanted all of you to approach him was to show him what he has missed all these years, right?" Loukas confirmed. "You guys are part of that leverage."

Max spoke up for the first time. Krystina could almost see him calculating all the possible outcomes in his mind.

"What if you all show up and he's not affected. To him, you're a bunch of strangers. The man has been through a lot of trauma. He could be completely emotionally detached," Max said on a worried exhale.

"If we can just find out his reason for staying away all these years, we might be able to figure out what to say to him," Loukas added.

"Why are you so invested in this all of a sudden?" Krystina narrowed her eyes suspiciously at Loukas. "I thought you were just along for the free ride." But the truth was that Loukas loved her grandmother like she was his very own, and Krystina knew it. But was he truly coming to help? Or was this just one more excuse to hover over her for his pestering pleasure?

"Minnie, I'm always invested in whatever you are," he whispered in her ear, draping his arm around her.

Well, that answered her question. Krystina shrugged him off and slid as far away from him as she could within the confinement of the car.

"Teenagers." Kally chuckled.

Chapter 10

Loukas

Six years earlier
Age twelve

Seventh grade was the beginning of so many changes for kids Loukas' age. Childhood whims were abandoned, or at least hidden, to avoid embarrassment. Girls experimented with their hair and makeup and wore more fashionable clothing to emulate their older role models.

All of this didn't escape the boys' attention, who were going through their own physical and developmental changes. Yes, it was an age of discovery, but how to wade in those murky waters was quite the mystery.

Teasing and pulling pranks was one way to get a girl's attention. That seemed a lot safer than outright telling her that he liked her and risking rejection.

Much to Loukas' dismay, the other boys in the neighborhood had suddenly become smitten with Krystina. His Krystina. They all agreed she was the prettiest girl in school. And at twelve years old, while most girls were being fitted with braces and training bras, the curse of Mother Nature's awkward stage skipped over Krystina.

If Loukas hadn't already nicknamed her Minnie, he might have called her Bambi instead. She looked like a fawn with her large doe-like eyes framed by her delicate features. Her light brown hair still held onto leftover golden childhood strands. Her slim body was all legs, and unlike most of her female classmates, she had long since graduated from wearing a training bra. Because of this, the boys all talked about her. And that is how Loukas knew his friends were suddenly mesmerized with the girl he'd always liked. Liked? Loved? Could he be in love at twelve?

Today, Loukas and his friends rode their bikes to Rocketship Park. Finding a grassy area, they formed a circle, sharing a bag of assorted candy they had bought in town at the Frigate candy store.

"Hey, Loukas, we want to talk to you about something," his friend Tommy said as he chewed on a gummy worm.

"Sure. What's up?" Loukas was only half listening. He was more interested in his rock candy.

"We want to pull a prank on Krystina. Just a little one," Tommy assured him.

"Leave her alone, guys. She's the only girl on the block. Give her a break."

"Yup, she is," Phillip agreed. "And we're curious about what she wears under her clothes. Aren't you?"

"No!" Loukas stopped chipping away at his sugary rock and frowned at his friends.

"Well, we are. And since you have access to her room, we want you to find out," Tommy said, shoving another piece of candy in his mouth.

Now Tommy explained the whole crazy scheme, and the other guys were pressuring Loukas to follow along. Krystina barely spoke to Loukas as it was, all because of some harmless teasing when they were small. But if she got wind of this, he'd never have a chance to regain her friendship or trust.

"What are you worried about?" Tommy asked. "Are you chicken? You're in her house all the time. It'll be a piece of cake."

"When everyone is out or at the dinner table or something, just pretend you're going to the bathroom," Phillip instructed. "Then go up and grab the goods."

"You want me to take it? I thought you just wanted me to look and tell?" Loukas asked. "That's insane. It's not right to invade her personal property." There was no way Loukas was going along with this. If she found out … Holy shit! Or worse, if he got caught, it wouldn't be just Krystina he'd have to contend with.

"You practically live there. She's like a sister to you," Johnny chimed in.

"She is not my sister," Loukas chastised defensively.

"Oh, I get it!" Tommy instigated. "You like her."

"So what if I do? All of you must, too, or you wouldn't be interested in her underwear," Loukas shot back.

"Either do this and be part of the gang, or don't and prove you're nothing but a pussy," Tommy threatened, giving him no real choice. At least not in the mind of a twelve-year-old boy.

* * *

The piercing sound of the school bell rang. It was the last period of the day. Classroom doors swung open and students stampeded down the hallway as if the building was on fire. Locks clicked open, sounding like orchestrated notes in a symphony, books thrown into lockers rivaled the beat of a drum, and for the crescendo, the metal doors slammed shut like the crashing of cymbals.

Pre-teen girls busied themselves chatting up friends while they hurried to the exit while some of the boys loitered about.

Loukas and his 'partners in crime' bolted for their lockers, chucking books and notebooks haphazardly into them. He had been troubled over what he'd done and worried whether it would get back to Krystina. He tried to convince himself it was all just harmless fun, but he knew better. Sometimes his friends were assholes, and now he wished he hadn't gone along with them.

Krystina and Chynna strode across the hall, happily making plans for the weekend. Before she even had a chance to open her locker, Tommy called out to her, crossing over to her side of the corridor.

"Hey, Krystina! It's good to know you finally gave up those Minnie Mouse panties," he jeered.

Krystina scrunched up her face in annoyance. "Shut up! What do you know about anything?"

"Let it go already, Tommy," Chynna defended. "You're such a jerk."

Loukas put his hands on top of his head, covering his face with the length of his arms in shame. Oh no! He hoped that was the end of it. Like an idiot, he had taken the dare, falling prey to peer pressure. The last thing he wanted was for Krystina to pay the price. If his friend continued with his taunting, Loukas knew he'd pay the consequences.

Johnny sauntered over. "I'm impressed," he added. "Trading them out for angel wings and PINK splashed across your butt."

Krystina's face flushed bright red. Was it from embarrassment or anger? Loukas wasn't sure. Turning, he banged his head against the cool metal.

"It's not Victoria's Secret anymore," Phillip mocked. "More like Krystina's secret is out of the bag."

Loukas turned back, covering his face with his hands and spewing a string of curses under his breath. Between his fingers, he witnessed Krystina's growing rage as his friends giggled hysterically. Her fists clenched and her lips formed a tight line. Chynna, patting her friend's back, attempted to calm her.

"Does the color of your thirty-two B cup bra match your panties today?" Tommy prodded. "I just want to have the full visual."

"Knock it off," Loukas shouted. "Leave her the fuck alone," he snapped, lunging at his friend.

Krystina walked over to Loukas, eyes blazing, nostrils flaring. "You did this," she accused with venom, smacking him hard across the face. "Stay out of my room and out of my life," she demanded, storming away.

Loukas made a move to run after her but Chynna blocked him. "Don't even think about it."

"I need to fix this." Loukas hung his head.

"You can't. At least not now," Chynna said. "You guys think it's harmless teasing. But it's not. Making fun of someone, whether it's about their underwear or"—she paused for a beat, looking down at her shoes—"a body flaw, is not nice. It's insensitive and mean. You have no idea how hurtful it is. Or what it does to a person."

Loukas got the sense Chynna wasn't only speaking for Krystina anymore. He'd heard the snickers and mockeries behind her back over the purple mark around her mouth. He had never contributed to the taunts, but even so, he was ashamed of himself for what happened today.

"I'm sorry," he apologized sincerely.

"You know, you don't always have to go along with the pack," she schooled him. "The world won't come to an end if you have a mind of your own." With that, she walked away, leaving Loukas feeling like total shit.

Chapter 11

Krystina

Present Day

Krystina hadn't been to Greece since she was a toddler, but with the amount of research she had done on Google and Instagram, it was as though she knew every inch of Athens. Travel influencers were her go-to for photo ops, great food, and shopping ideas.

Nicholas had booked the Hotel Grand Bretagne, just as he had the first time he and Mia had stayed when they conducted business for the luxury magazine he published.

The lobby itself was opulent, and Krystina immediately wanted to change out of her traveling clothes and into something fashionable so one of her sisters could snap some photos of her.

Waiting as the rest of the group stood at reception, Krystina sank onto a cinnamon-colored velvet, four-sided sofa in the middle of the ornately designed marble floor.

It took her a moment before she realized Loukas had aimed his iPhone in her direction.

"Stop!" she scolded, covering her face. "I look terrible. I'm a rumpled mess after sitting on that plane for hours."

"You look fine, Minnie," he said with a broad grin. "We're in

Greece! I thought you'd want to capture this moment."

"I'd like to capture the moment you give up annoying me."

"That's enough, you two," Theo reprimanded. "We can head up to our rooms now." He handed them both key cards. "You're bunking with me, Loukas."

"Freshen up and meet us on the Roof Garden restaurant in an hour," Kally directed, approaching them.

While the rest of the group perused the menu, Krystina strolled about the perimeter, taking in the open view of the Acropolis. Pictures didn't do the ancient structure justice, especially as it was, spectacularly illuminated before her. It seemed as if the light was emanating from the marble itself. She imagined the Goddess Athena wandering amongst the pillars of her temple, watching over her city with pride. Maybe it was by her hand that the Parthenon shone so brightly against the indigo sky.

Krystina broke from her reverie when Mia approached her, beckoning her to return to their table.

"I took the liberty of ordering for you. A *visinatha* martini," Mia said, passing the crimson beverage to Krystina. "Anything cherry-flavored has your name written all over it," she added with a smile. "I figured you'd love this."

Krystina's eyes lit up as she tasted it. "OMG! This is amazing." She moaned her approval with every sip.

Loukas drank his beer quietly, hiding his expression behind his glass while eyeing Krystina as she over-emphasized her pleasure for her drink.

"I think you chose well for her." Kally laughed.

Nicholas cleared his throat and Max concealed his smirk as they observed Loukas' reaction to Krystina's moaning.

"It's been a long day of traveling. Tonight, we relax," Nicholas said to them after they had all taken a sip from their drinks. "Tomorrow, we'll decide on an approach," Nicholas added. "The private eye I've had on the case has been watching the comings and goings of Kostas' bar. It seems the man we believe to be Panos is there every day. He rarely leaves the premises."

"Do you think he lives there?" Kally asked.

"It's a good possibility," Max said. "Perhaps he stays in a back room."

"The investigator is pretty sure it's Panos based on the description his friend gave me last time I was here. He has the same torture marks Kostas described. This man is missing an ear and has a pronounced limp," Nicholas added. "Brace yourselves. You won't find him in the best of health."

Krystina sighed. "*Yiayiá* won't care. She loves him no matter what. The love they shared is something so special. A disability won't change how she feels."

Kally and Mia nodded in agreement.

"She was in love with his goodness and beautiful soul," Mia said on a wistful sigh.

"Tomorrow, we'll show up unannounced. If we tip Panos off, he might run," Max explained.

"But why would he do that?" Krystina asked.

"That's what we need to learn," Theo replied. "We don't know why he has stayed away for all these years. But tomorrow we will try to find out."

"Once he sees the four of you, hopefully, it will play on his emotions, or at least his guilt," Max added.

"At the very least, he'll have to give you some answers," Nicholas continued. "Anything to help your grandmother understand what happened."

"There's one thing none of us considered," Loukas spoke up. "What if his experiences were so traumatic that he has no memory of the past?"

They all fell silent.

After a few moments, Max exhaled with a frown. "I considered that but I didn't want to bring it up. What's the point in speculating until we see for ourselves."

Kally nodded. "So tomorrow let's meet in the lobby at three o'clock and then we'll head for the bar to presumably meet our *pappou* for the first time."

Krystina worried her bottom lip between her teeth and blew out an apprehensive breath. She feared returning home to her grandmother without the outcome they hoped for. Tonight she would hold *Yiayiá's* icon in her palm and say a prayer.

Until three p.m. everyone is free to do as they please," Mia announced jovially to lighten the mood.

Loukas leaned over to whisper in Krystina's ear. "What are we doing tomorrow then?"

Krystina edged her chair an inch or two away, glowering at him. "I have no idea what *you* are doing. But I'm going there," she countered, looking out the floor-to-ceiling window at the view. High up on the mountaintop, the Parthenon looked as though it was a vibrant, three-dimensional mural she could walk up to and touch. And that's what she wanted to do—experience this wonder that has stood for over two thousand years all for herself.

"Alone?" Loukas asked. "I don't think that's a good idea."

Krystina looked around the table. Mia and Nicholas probably had their own plans, and she was sure Kally and Max did too.

"Theo?" Krystina started.

"Don't look at me," he said, holding up his hand. "I have a date."

"A date!" Krystina said with incredulity. "We've been in Athens for two hours."

Theo smiled smugly, shrugging. "What can I say? I'm irresistible."

"Watch out. Your head might explode from conceit."

Loukas' face lit up as he realized he'd won. "Just face it, Minnie. We were meant to be."

Krystina groaned out her frustration. "I need another one of those drinks. Maybe two."

Chapter 12

Krystina

After dinner, everyone retreated to their respective rooms. Krystina was the only one to have a room to herself. By the time she had showered, blow-dried her hair, and performed her skincare routine, she felt lonely. Jet lag should have set in, but with her stomach twisting with anxiety, she would never fall asleep.

Shrugging out of the monogrammed hotel robe, she pulled a pair of yoga pants and a t-shirt from her suitcase. After she slipped them on, Krystina went to see if her sisters were still up. She was about to knock on Mia and Nicholas' door when she hesitated. On second thought, what if they were otherwise occupied? Instead, she rapped on Theo's door.

"Miss me already?" Loukas smirked, opening the door to let her in.

Ignoring the question, she strode past him. "I came to talk to my brother."

"What's up?" Theo asked, exiting the bathroom. Toweling off the moisture from his dirty-blond hair, he gestured to the TV. "We were just about to watch a movie."

"Aren't the two of you tired?"

"Na, we slept on the plane," Loukas said.

"What's on your mind?" her brother asked.

"I don't know," Krystina answered, taking a seat in the corner chair. "I was so pumped over coming here. I tried to focus all my energy on the sightseeing we might do in between our main purpose for being here. But now, I guess I'm a little nervous. Not so much for all of us, but what if we only have bad news to report? How will *Yiayiá* take it?"

"There's nothing to lose at this point. All we can do is try," Theo said as he tossed his towel onto the bathroom floor. "And if the worst happens, we simply tell her we hit another dead end."

"Lie to her?" Krystina didn't like that idea. But what choice would they have?

"Sometimes a lie of omission is the kinder act," Loukas replied.

Maybe he was right. After all, wasn't she keeping secrets by not telling anyone about Manny's AA meetings? But she did it for Loukas so he had one less thing to deal with regarding his father. For all his teasing and past indiscretions, Krystina cared about him, not that she'd ever admit it to him.

"I suppose you're right," she agreed.

"Try not to dwell on it until we see what happens tomorrow. Do you want to stay and watch the movie?" Theo asked.

"No, I think I'll go back to my room."

"Before you go, there's something I've been meaning to tell you," Theo said, his expression suddenly turning serious.

"Is something wrong?" she asked, curious about the shift in his mood.

"No, no. Everything is great," he assured her. "But we only have a few days before I head back to school, and this is as good a time as any."

He pulled her onto the edge of the bed to sit facing him. If the news was so good then why was Theo acting so strange?

"I met someone."

A look of bewilderment flashed across her face. "Okay? You meet a lot of people. What's so special about this one?"

"Krystina." Loukas shook his head as if she were completely dense. "He *met* someone."

She looked back and forth between Loukas and her brother. Clearly Loukas already knew what Theo was talking about.

"You mean, like, you're in a relationship?" she asked, scrunching up her nose as if it was the most unlikely thing to ever happen.

"That's right," Theo confirmed, rocking back on his heels.

"So why are you acting all weird about it? I mean, I never thought you'd take the plunge and give up your harem," she mocked sardonically. "But hey! I'm happy if you're happy."

"Harem!" Loukas laughed.

"I wasn't that bad," Theo argued. "And I am happy, it's just … complicated."

"What could be so complicated? It must be pretty serious for you to commit to one girl," Krystina said. "Do you love her?" she asked, her eyes like saucers as they widened in surprise at her realization.

"Very much."

"Why do I get the feeling you're holding something back?" Krystina crossed her arms over her chest.

"I'm not sure our parents will approve of her. Dad definitely won't."
"Why?"

"A few reasons. For one thing, she's not Greek."

"Oh, yeah," she spluttered. "He'll give you a hard time about that." She eyed him suspiciously. "What else?" Krystina inquired. "You said for one thing. What's the other?"

"I think that's all you need to know for now."

"You're being awfully cryptic."

She turned to Loukas, who had a knowing look on his face. "You know?" she seethed. He was *her* brother. Hers! Why should he know before she did? She fixed Loukas with a scowl.

Loukas threw his hands up, playing innocent.

"Oh, come on!" She gave her brother a shove. "Is she a much older woman? Married?" She put her hand over her mouth and gasped. "She's your professor?!"

Loukas snorted.

"It's nothing like that," Theo said with a laugh. "She's a nice girl and the exact same age as me. Her name is Mackenzie." Theo grabbed his sister by the shoulders and looked her in the eyes. "I told you because we've always been close. But just don't say anything. Okay? I'll tell our parents when I'm ready, but for now, I at least wanted you to know."

"I won't tell a soul." She hugged her brother. "But wait! You said you had a date. Is she here?"

"No. I just said that. I had something I had to do and I didn't want to get into it with everyone."

"Oh, that's too bad. I really want to meet her. Promise me we can FaceTime soon when you get back to London."

"All in good time," Theo agreed, closing the subject. "Now, are you sure you don't want to stay for the movie?"

"I don't think so."

"Are you positive? Don't you want to see *Resident Evil* dubbed in Greek?" Theo tempted her.

She lifted her eyebrows and grinned. "Maybe I'll stay for a little while."

* * *

The next morning, Loukas knocked on her door. "Are you ready?"

"So you're actually coming with me?" Krystina asked.

"Did you have any doubt?"

"No," she replied with an aggravated glare. But truthfully, it was better than wandering the streets alone. "I found this great breakfast place on Instagram, and it's not too far away."

"Sounds good. I'm starved."

"After that we can head to the Parthenon. Did you know they have those jump-on jump-off busses that stop at all the landmarks?" Krystina asked with enthusiasm."

Her trepidation from the night before was somewhat allayed. At least for now. She was adamant to put it out of her mind until the hour came when they walked into the bar to find Panos. Then she wasn't sure what to expect or how she'd react.

* * *

"This is it," Nicholas said as their driver pulled up in front of a rundown building.

Half the letters above the entrance were missing and the walls were covered in graffiti. The idea that Krystina's grandfather might have been living here all these years made her sad. And to think he could have been with a family who would have loved and cared for him. With a woman who adored him more than life itself. At this point, Krystina just wanted to understand, yet at the same time, she was racked with anxiety over what they'd discover.

Nicholas punched Max's number into his phone. "I'll go in first and approach the man. Put the phone on speaker. When you hear me tell him I have some people I'd like him to meet, come inside before he has a chance to refuse." He opened the door and they watched tensely as Nicholas walked over to the building, entering through the weather-beaten doors.

Krystina's stomach twisted. She reached for her sisters, squeezing their hands for comfort. Her disheartening thoughts from the night before churned in the forefront of her mind. "What if he rejects all of us? Most of all, *Yiayiá*? What if there was no good reason for his disappearance other than he simply didn't want her anymore?"

Loukas wrapped his arms around her, and for once, she didn't object. "Have faith. Your grandmother always did."

Krystina nodded, leaning her head against his.

"Remember me?" They heard Nicholas say through the phone's speaker. "I was here a few months ago and spoke to Kostas."

Silence. They all leaned in closer to the phone, intently listening for the man's next words.

"Damn," Theo whispered. "I wish I could see his reaction."

"Kostas is not expecting you," the man they presumed to be Panos said abruptly.

"I know. I didn't come for him." Nicholas paused. "I came to speak to you."

Silence. Other than the clinking of glasses, they heard nothing for a beat or two.

"I don't know what a man like you would need from someone like me."

This time, Krystina detected worry in the man's tone.

"Don't you?" Nicholas challenged. "You are Panayiotis Nikopoulos, aren't you?"

Silence.

Then … "No. That man died long ago."

Krystina choked out a sob. "Oh no."

They could hear Nicholas sigh heavily. "I can only begin to imagine what you've been through, and I know you must feel like the man you once were is not the same man as you are today. But no matter what you believe, you still have a family. You have a wife who has been waiting decades for you to return to her."

Silence. Shuffling.

Not a soul in the car took a breath, waiting for the man's response.

"I am not the man she married," he replied stiffly. "She's better off without me."

Everyone in the car gasped. It was him!

"Isn't that for her to decide?"

"I couldn't be a husband to her." Panos lowered his voice to a whisper. "You understand me? You have no idea what was done to me in that hell to make sure of it."

A collective sob from the girls broke the silence in the car.

"Look at me!" Panos exclaimed in anger. "I'm missing an ear. I'm blind in one eye. And my right leg is disfigured."

"I understand how you feel," Nicholas said sympathetically. "And I'm not sure I wouldn't feel the same in your shoes. But I can tell you that if your granddaughter, Mia, became ill or had an accident that changed her appearance or her ability to live life normally, my love for her would never change."

Mia put her hands over her heart and sighed.

"Your Kalliope feels the same. I know she does."

"I never said I stopped loving her. It's because I love her so much that I keep my distance," Panos admitted morosely. There was a moment's pause. "She's doing well? My Kalliope?" The shaky timbre of his voice spoke volumes. It was evident his decision had come at a great cost.

"As well as can be expected without you by her side," Nicholas said. "Panos, I have some people I'd like you to meet who can better answer your question regarding your wife."

"That's it," Max said. "Let's go."

One by one, they slid out of the car. "You four go in ahead of us," Max suggested.

Krystina took her sisters' hands as they entered the bar, Theo stepping ahead to usher the girls in. Max and Loukas stayed a few paces behind, but it was clear they were a strong unit.

"I want you to meet your grandchildren," Nicholas said.

The man was stricken. Blindsided with no warning, he abruptly turned his back on them and lumbered away, disappearing into a back room.

Wide-eyed, Krystina's jaw fell. "Oh my God. What do we do now?"

"Just give the man a minute to compose himself," Nicholas suggested.

The group gathered in a huddle, whispering their reactions to each other. "He's obviously been through a great deal, but considering we were warned of his appearance, he doesn't look as bad as I'd expected," Kally stated.

Panos re-emerged, announcing his presence by coughing loudly.

The group fell silent, waiting for this estranged relative to speak first. Before he did, he looked each of them over. Was he trying to detect a connection between them?

Having met Nicholas before, Panos addressed him first. "Why did you do this? Don't you see that in the end this will only hurt everyone more?" He was clearly angry at being thrown into this situation.

At first, Krystina was taken aback by his reaction. But then, she realized she was mistaken. Watching his taut expression, his fidgeting step, and his wary eyes, she saw what she had missed at first glance. Sheer panic coated by anxiety and maybe regret was written all over his face. Maybe the man needed to understand they weren't here to attack him.

So Krystina was the first to bravely approach him. "*Pappou*? Can I call you that? *Yiayiá* told us all about you. We feel like we know you," she said with a shaky voice.

The man curiously looked from one child to another but remained quiet.

Kally moved forward next. "I went to Kalamáta to look for you but my search led me back here to Athens."

"If it wasn't for Nicholas," Mia said, walking over to stand beside her fiancé, "we would have never found you. But it was *Yiayiá* who gave us the information that led us here."

The man looked puzzled.

"Your letter and the copy of a publication you distributed during your time with the Resistance," Mia explained. "It helped our investigator find you."

"*Yiayiá* needs to know you're alive, at least," Theo said. "She's held onto the belief that you'll come back to her one day. That hope and blind faith keeps her going."

"You are all my Melina's children?" Panos asked softly, looking from one to the other. "My girl made a beautiful family." Tears filled his eyes.

"You could have been with us all these years," Kally said on a sob. "We love you just from hearing the stories of you and *Yiayiá*. We want to know you."

"Please tell your *yiayiá* I'm alive and not to worry. Tell her I'm truly sorry." His apology caught in his throat.

Leaning against the bar to brace himself, he continued, "Tell her I will always love her but I stayed away for her own sake. She should never doubt my love for her." Then, the emotion overwhelming him, he turned his back on them. "I need you all to leave now," he pleaded. "This is too much for me."

Kostas, spying by his office door, walked swiftly over. "I think that's enough for today," he decided. "Come on Panos. Go rest in the back; I'll cover the bar."

His knuckles white as he gripped the edge of the bar, Panos supported himself, hobbling wearily over to the only man he'd trusted in decades. Turning, he faced his grandchildren one last time and sighed. A deep sadness was reflected in his expression. His eyes fell on Kally first. "You look just as I remember her," he said softly. "But you ..." he addressed Krystina. "You have that same fire I saw in her eyes the first time we met." Without another word, Panos retreated into the back room.

Solemnly, they stood there, not knowing what to do next. Nicholas spoke up first.

"Let's go." He sighed. "There's nothing more we can do for now."

"Nothing more!?" Krystina exclaimed. "You hired an investigator, tracked him down, and now you say there is nothing more to be done?"

"What do you want us to do?" Mia argued. "Kidnap him?"

"There has to be a way to convince him to come home with us." Then, throwing her hands up in the air dramatically, Krystina began to pace.

"I'll leave Kostas our hotel information and my phone number," Max suggested as he pulled out a business card from his wallet. "If Panos has a change of heart, he'll know where to contact us," he explained, scribbling down the information and passing it to a wary Kostas.

When they returned to the hotel, everyone was in a quiet, contemplative mood. Even Krystina, who'd had designs on hitting a trendy nightclub, something she wouldn't be able to do in the States until she was twenty-one, suddenly elected to stay in for the night.

Instead, they gathered in the living room of Nicholas and Mia's suite and ordered room service. Platters of burrata with sundried tomatoes, eggplant-filled pasta, and grilled sea bass wrapped in fig leaves dominated the dining table. There was shrimp risotto scented with lemon and dill, and Greek salad with large chunks of feta cheese atop tomatoes and cucumbers. And that wasn't all. Waiting for them on a side table was an array of desserts Krystina couldn't wait to dig into.

"Well, do we have a plan B?" Krystina asked.

"I'm not sure what else we can do," Mia replied. "I don't think it would be productive to storm in on him again."

"Max left our information with Kostas," Theo added. "Panos knows where to find us."

"Is anyone else annoyed that we still have no answers as to why he stayed away?" Krystina asked.

"Oh, he was pretty clear about that," Max countered. "In his mind, he thinks his wife is better off without him."

"That seems so wrong to me," Kally said. "It wasn't his decision to make alone."

"We tried," Nicholas said. "That's all we could do. The man has been through unspeakable abuses for extended periods of time. None of us can even begin to understand what this has done to his mind. Forcing the issue is in no one's best interest."

They finished dinner and changed the conversation to lighter subjects over dessert. It felt good to laugh after such an unsettling day. Although, despite the fact that Krystina was cataloging the many places she wanted to visit, today's disappointing mission still gnawed at her. Then, to put it out of her mind, she had a brilliant idea!

"Since we're apparently giving up on doing what we came here for, can we go to your place in Mykonos?" Krystina asked Nicholas. "I heard it's fire!"

Nicholas pulled a bewildered face. "Fire?"

"Yeah. You know, lit!" Krystina rolled her eyes. "Excuse me. Let me say it how you'd understand. It's groovy, man."

"How old do you think I am!"

"Well, I don't know." Krystina shrugged. "A lot older than me."

"Keep it up," Nicholas scolded, pointing his fork at her. "You're not helping your case by insulting me."

"So we can go?" she asked, forking a chunk of cheese.

"No, not on this trip. But I'll tell you what I will do. As a graduation gift, you can stay at my place when school lets out."

Shrieking, Krystina jumped from her seat to hug Nicholas, nearly squeezing the life from him. "I have to text Chynna and tell her!"

"How about me?" Loukas asked. "I'm graduating too. I can volunteer as her bodyguard."

"You are not coming with me!" The ice in her tone could have frosted the Aegean. "Bodyguard," she scoffed.

"You have no idea what I'm capable of," Loukas defended. "I've been working out at Leo's gym. He's been training me. Soon I'm going to enter a competitive fight."

"Hold on," Max interrupted. "That's not why we had you train. And besides, you're nowhere near ready for that."

"It's just on an amateur level."

"Still." Max shook his head.

Krystina didn't like the sound of that. Loukas fighting? She didn't know he was even training. A sick feeling settled in her bones. Did

Max arrange this so Loukas could learn to protect himself from his father's abuse?

Something in her wanted to blurt out, 'You can come with me to Mykonos.' Anything to get him away from the life he'd lived these past few years. But the other part of her just couldn't bring herself to do it. Resentment and hurt still burrowed their way into her heart from his past betrayals, and she hadn't yet forgiven him. He had chosen his buddies over her one too many times, and always at her expense. She wouldn't allow opportunity for another repeat. And although he'd claimed to be sorry, his constant teasing told her otherwise.

An awkward silence filled the room for a beat until Kally changed the subject. "I've been playing with a new idea for the café. I'd love your opinions."

"I'd love to hear it," Mia said enthusiastically.

"I was thinking of doing a flight of lattes. That way, the customer doesn't have to choose just one flavor." She pulled up a website on her phone and showed it to her sister. "I'm going to order these miniature glasses. And I'll pair each beverage with a small pastry."

"Like a beer flight but with coffee instead," Loukas said. "I like it."

"Well, with your approval, it's a done deal," Krystina grumbled sarcastically. "And speaking of approval ..." Her voice grew excited as she smiled at Nicholas enthusiastically. "Have you thought about the job I asked you for?"

"Job?" He feigned confusion but she wasn't fooled.

"Social media coordinator?"

"Oh, that job," Nicholas said. "Well, like I told you before, when you get out of college, if you're still interested in working at the magazine, we can discuss it then."

"I meant now." Krystina pouted. "I'm a wiz on Insta and every other platform trending. Why can't I go on location with you and post about it?"

"Krys," Mia warned. "You're putting Nicholas on the spot."

"Do you have amnesia, or do you think I do?" Nicholas admonished her. "I said you could intern in the summer. But, in the meantime, if and only if school is out when we happen to go on location, may you come. However, there will be no missing school for location shoots. Clear?"

"Yes, yes!" she exclaimed, bouncing in her seat. "You're the best!"

"You've been awfully quiet, Theo," Kally said, turning her attention to her brother. "What's on your mind?"

"I've been doing a lot of thinking." Theo sighed. He seemed hesitant to continue. "Panos referring to us as Kalliope's grandchildren, as his grandchildren, kind of made me realize ... I'm not actually blood-related."

Krystina reached out to take her brother's hand. Kally and Mia were older when her parents went to Athens to confirm he was indeed their father's son. But she couldn't remember a time in her life when Theo wasn't in it.

It had been a difficult time for the entire family, she knew. Her parents had been separated, and Theo was the result of an affair during that period of time. Her father had given up all hope that Melina would take him back, and when she had, George had no idea he'd fathered a child. It wasn't until a few years after they'd reconciled when the boy's mother passed away and George found out he had a son.

"But you are our brother, and *Yiayiá* is just as much your grandmother as she is ours. She loves you dearly," Krystina said. "Sometimes, I suspect she secretly loves you the most," she added with a laugh.

"I know, and I love her too," he assured her. "And Mom." He paused, collecting himself. "She's always treated me and loved me like her own."

"It's not always blood that makes a family," Kally said, smiling tenderly at Max.

Max took Kally's hand in hers. "That's right. Kally will soon be Athena's mother, and look at them together. You would think they were mother and daughter from birth."

"That's true. I know all of that. But … I have questions." Theo was silent for a moment. "I spoke to Dad's parents about my birth mother last time I visited them," he said, looking for their reaction. "It's time I did a little more digging and found out more about her. "I'm going to see Dad's parents again tomorrow. I'd like to delve into her family history, and maybe they can guide me in the right direction."

Krystina could see the trepidation in Theo's eyes, as if he was searching for disapproval in his sisters' faces.

"How do you all feel about that?" he asked cautiously.

"I say go for it," Mia encouraged, and everyone nodded in agreement.

"Really?" He exhaled in relief. "I don't want you to think I'm distancing myself from all of you or dishonoring our mother in any way."

"Except for the fact that you've left us to study abroad, I would never think you were pulling away from us," Kally assured him with a warm smile.

"I love you like a brother, man," Loukas interjected. "But it's fine with me that you're taking off for London again. It gives me a chance to crash in your room when the mood strikes me. Right next door to Minnie." He grinned.

Grunting, Krystina threw her napkin at him.

* * *

The following day, Krystina was dressed and equipped for a day of sightseeing. Dressed in a flowing, white sundress that hit right above the knee; flat, nude sandals embellished with aqua beads; and a wide-brimmed, straw hat, she was Instagram-ready. For a summer day, not January. She didn't care if she froze as long as she looked good, though. Thankfully, it was unseasonably warm considering the season, but still brought along a jean jacket to keep her from getting too cold.

Knocking on the adjoining door, she called to Loukas. "Are you ready?" When she got no response, Krystina impatiently knocked louder. Then she tapped out a text to him.

"Hold on!" Loukas called through the door.

Krystina wanted to lash out at him for keeping her waiting, but instead, she was rendered speechless when he opened the door. The sleep had not yet been erased from his hazy blue eyes, and his mop of nearly black hair stood up in every which way.

Loukas was shirtless. And she couldn't help staring at his incredible six-pack. It took a minute for her to notice he was wearing low-slung boxers with pizza slices printed all over them. It would have been comical if he didn't look so … so … hot. Damn! When did Loukas get so ripped?

He was just the annoying kid from down the block. Her ex-best friend from childhood. This six-pack guy with the … hell, was it hot in here? Where did that V between his hipbones come from? She tried so hard not to ogle him.

"See something you like, Minnie?"

"No," she blurted, shaking herself from her stupor. "Not at all," she exaggerated, twisting her lips in an attempt to regain her feelings of frustration. "You were supposed to be ready to go by now."

"Go where?"

"Didn't you get my text last night?"

"I didn't look at my phone. Why didn't you just tell me what you wanted when you had the chance?"

"Ugh!" She shook her fists. "Are you or aren't you going to be my Instagram …" She didn't want to say 'boyfriend.' Instead she added, "Photographer."

He raised an eyebrow. "Photographer," he huffed. "Give me ten."

"Where are we headed?" Loukas asked.

"The Plaka and Monastiraki. I've seen some really incredible spots from some influencers I follow. But first, we have to go to Pittaki

Street," Krystina declared, her eyes lighting up. "The alleyway is always lined with different overhanging decorations."

"As long as we get something to eat along the way, I'm game."

"Oh, don't worry, there are cafés every step of the way."

Krystina squealed with excitement when they arrived at Pittaki Street. It looked just as she dreamed. She had seen photos of pastel umbrellas suspended from above and had hoped they would be here now. And they were! Krystina didn't know where to look first. The cobblestone street was lined with cafés, elaborately decorated flower shops, and trendy boutiques. But her eyes kept wandering to the colorful magic suspended above.

She handed Loukas her iPhone, and he snapped photo after photo of her against eye-catching backgrounds.

"I think there's a few you'll approve of," he said proudly.

She took the phone from him and scrolled through the shots. "You've gotten good at this," Krystina complimented.

"Let's get a selfie," Loukas said, pulling out his own phone. Then, resting his head against hers, he snapped a series of photos.

"Hey! Those are for your eyes only," she warned, poking him. "No posting them."

"Whatever," Loukas said, resigned." He stopped in front of a street food window and asked for two spits of souvlaki. "You want one?" he offered.

"No, thanks." She waved it away. "It's only ten-thirty in the morning."

She zeroed in on another little shop. "I want some of those!" Pointing to a stand selling chocolate-covered pistachios, she asked the vendor for a small bag.

"It's only ten-thirty!" he threw back at her with a laugh.

Ignoring him, she popped one in her mouth and moaned in food-gasmic ecstasy.

As they strolled along toward Monastiraki, Krystina took in

the view around her—the open markets, the food vendors, and the large church set in the open square—all with a stunning backdrop of the Acropolis outlined by the clear blue sky. As she observed the people around her, it wasn't difficult to distinguish the tourists from the locals. The pedestrians rushing about or diners scoffing down food at warped speed were most likely tourists, trying to fit in as much as they could in one day. But the native Greeks savored a coffee over lively conversation or sat alone with an appreciation for their surroundings.

Hours could be spent weaving in and out of shops or stopping by restaurant fronts to check out menus.

"Right now, in New York, it's like four in the morning, dark, and probably below zero degrees." She lifted her face and breathed in the air. "Everything feels so different here. Do we have to go home?"

"It feels different because it is different," Loukas said. "Don't you think if, let's say, that person over there"—he pointed to a middle-aged man carrying a bag of groceries—"came to New York, he'd feel the same way?"

"Maybe," she pondered. "Loukas, there's something else I want to do later."

"Whatever you want," he agreed. "We have all day."

"Yes, we do. I purposely left it for last, though," she said, skirting around the details.

"What are you up to, Minnie?"

"I want to go back to the bar and speak to Panos."

Loukas spotted a trashcan and discarded the souvlaki skewers. Turning, he looked at Krystina earnestly. "That old man made himself clear. You can't change his mind. Who he is today is the result of his traumas." Loukas looked down at the floor. "And all the shit life threw at him."

Krystina didn't argue. Loukas knew about that better than she did. "I understand. I know." Those words were for him as much as they were for her grandfather. "But *Yiayiá* lives on faith. She hangs onto hope. The way I see it, as long as there's a tomorrow then the possibility of a new beginning is promised. It's a decision each person needs to make. Stay in one place and nothing changes, or risk it all and maybe dreams come true."

Mesmerizing eyes locked with Krystina's. She couldn't decipher what she saw in those stormy pools, blue as the depths of the Aegean Ocean. Had she convinced him that her plan was just? Or had something else she said struck a chord? For some reason, she found it impossible to pull away from his gaze. Emotions she purposely kept dormant in the recesses of her soul were about to flood to the surface. The blare of a horn broke his hypnotic hold on her.

"If you don't want to come, I'll go on my own," she challenged.

"Not on your life," he affirmed. "Not in that neighborhood. I'll go with you, but prepare to be disappointed."

For the rest of the afternoon, they ate their way through narrow streets lined with tavernas and pastry shops and snapped photos of ancient ruins. Then, later in the day, they enjoyed a drink at a rooftop bar with a view so breathtaking it seemed to overlook the whole of Athens.

Carefree, Krystina put the task she was about to endeavor out of her mind until she couldn't stall any longer. She could always ditch the whole crazy notion. After all, no one but Loukas knew what she was about to do. And in what hair-brained scheme did she think her words would make enough of an impact to change the stubborn, old man's mind. No! She mentally scolded herself. She would not wimp out on this.

Snapping his fingers, Loukas roused Krystina from her internal battle.

"Who are you fighting inside that brain of yours?" Loukas mocked.

"Me! Half of me wants to chicken out and run home with my tail between my legs. The other half of me wants to shake some sense into the man until he relents."

"Chickens don't have tails."

"What?" Krystina's face contorted into a disgusted grimace. "What does that have to do with anything."

Loukas took a pull from his beer. "You can't chicken out and run home with your tail between your legs." He took his last gulp from the bottle and stood. "Chickens don't have tails. Never mind." He laughed. "You've always been a person to follow your gut. So let's go," he ordered.

She took the hand he offered and let him lead her down the uneven stone steps until they reached street level.

"I thought you were against me doing this."

"You were determined, and I know you. If you don't at least try, you'll regret it."

* * *

"I think we should pay the cab driver to wait for us," Loukas suggested as the driver turned onto the street where the bar was located. "There's no way a cab is passing through this neighborhood once he's gone, and I don't think we should walk around looking for one."

"Why here?" Krystina wondered. "They could have chosen to open a bar anywhere in Athens."

"You're assuming it was always like this. Or maybe this was all Kostas could afford."

"It makes me sad to think he could have lived comfortably with us for all these years instead of hiding away in this seedy alley in Athens." Krystina frowned at the litter and garbage strewn about, the graffiti splashing the walls, and the overall dreary contrast to the pulsating energy of the Athens she'd seen thus far.

With purpose, she stormed into the bar, Loukas on her heels. Greek tunes played in the background, old songs, the ones she often heard her parents listening to when they were in a nostalgic mood. Groups of men sat at mismatched wooden tables, some laughing and others arguing.

Scanning the room, she spotted Panos right away, tending the bar. Ignoring the knot in her stomach, she searched for her courage and marched up to the counter, waiting for Panos to finish serving the man seated on one of the rickety barstools.

The minute he saw Krystina, Panos stopped pouring and set down the whiskey bottle with a thump. Krystina's eyes met his with steely determination.

"You are a coward!" Krystina boldly leaned over the countertop.

"Krystina!" Loukas scolded, grabbing her by the arm.

Slapping his hand back, she continued, "With the courage it took for you to survive what you did and to make it out whole and alive, you're too spineless to face the woman who has been waiting for you for decades?"

Panos remained stony-faced but for an imperceptible flinch.

"You made a promise to her. How dare you tell her you love her then leave, never to return?"

"Because I'm not whole!" The words ripped deep from within what was left of his ravaged soul. "I'm not the man she loves. Not in body or mind. That man was destroyed long ago."

Krystina swallowed the lump in her throat. "I don't believe that." From her cross-body bag, she pulled out a black and white photo of her *Yiayiá* and Panos, happy in their youth, slamming it down in front of him. "This isn't you?" She pulled out another that included her mother as an infant. "Or this one?"

Outstretching his arm, Panos ran his finger gingerly over the images as if the contact alone might scorch his heart.

Krystina held her breath. She was getting to him. The hardness was gone from his expression, replaced by the years of sorrow reflected now in his darkening gray eyes.

"Don't you see?" She had to convince him. "You are the man in these photos, the same man who lived through a traumatic, horrific ordeal. But also, the man standing here today living a lonely existence. That is the whole of your life. The good and bad of it."

She scooped up the photos but Panos clapped his hand over hers. "You want them?"

He nodded.

"They're yours," she said. "Keep looking at them to remember who you left behind. Your family. I've spent my whole life hearing about you. To be honest, my mother has nothing nice to say. She told us you abandoned her."

"No, no," Panos whimpered, shaking his head.

"But *Yiayiá* would hear none of that. She said you would come back one day when you were able. She believed … believes," Krystina corrected, "… in her heart that her soul is tied to yours. She swears that if you were no longer on this earth, she would know."

Krystina repeatedly jabbed her pointer finger at him. "That's how much she loves you. She doesn't care if you have one ear or fifty scars. She doesn't care if you came back to her blind or mute or incapacitated in any way. She just wants you," she spat with resentment. Overcome with emotion, Krystina fought back the tears.

She turned to Loukas. "We should go now. I've said all I can."

Turning, she began to walk away before pausing by the door. She swung around to find Panos still watching her. "I hope you're happy here." She looked around the dingy bar with disdain. "If you're giving up the love of your life for this then I feel sorry for you. If someone loved me that unconditionally, I'd move heaven, Earth, and all the planets in the universe to be with him."

The only true disability is a crushed spirit. Aimee Mullins

Chapter 13

Panos

July 1974

Confusion blurred all of Panos' senses. The air smelled medicinal, not rank and stale. Softness enveloped him like a cloud of cotton. Squinting, the light shining from above was blinding. He had been denied sunshine for almost the entire five years committed to that hell hole, but that was the least of his pain. Panos had been reduced to a crumbling bag of bones, his spirit all but expunged from the repeated humiliations he'd endured.

As awareness of his new surroundings grew, he strung together fragments from what he now presumed was a rescue. Darkness and evil were replaced by white walls and an ethereal figure who had to be an angel of mercy.

"You're awake." The nurse checked the IV needle in his arm, her soft voice forcing Panos to refocus. "I'm going to check your vitals. How are you feeling?"

"Confused. Where am I?" Panos asked, his voice gravelly. In a panic, he remembered his friend. "Kostas?"

The middle-aged woman smiled softly, her brown eyes wrinkling at the corners. "He's right here."

She pulled apart the curtain dividing the room. His friend lay quietly in the next bed, sleeping peacefully for the first time in many years.

Panos sighed with relief.

"You should rest too. As much as you can."

Later that day, when Panos awoke once more, he found Kostas sitting upright, digging into hospital food as if it was a gourmet meal. And for them, compared to the slop they'd been fed, it was.

"My friend," Kostas croaked. "We made it out." He set down his fork. "I thought for sure we'd die covered by rats."

"We did," Panos answered blankly.

"It's going to take some time but we'll be okay." Kostas' face hardened. "We have to be. Otherwise, they win."

"You have a visitor," a young woman said brightly as she entered the room. She was in the same uniform as the nurse who had checked on him earlier, but in his estimation, she couldn't have been more than eighteen.

A soldier appeared, greeting Panos and Kostas warmly. A vague memory flashed through Panos' mind. His face. That voice. The frame of his body as he approached though the darkness. This man had swooped his weakened, broken body from captivity. At the time, he wasn't sure if the figure was his savior or the angel of death sent forth to mercifully put him out of his misery.

"*Kalimera*," the soldier greeted. "I'm happy to see you are both doing well."

Wondering why the man had come, Panos kept his face free from expression.

"My name is Stavros. Do you remember me or anything regarding your rescue?" He looked between both patients, searching for a sign of recognition. "Stefanos, another soldier in my squad, and I pulled the two of you out of the prison."

Kostas' smile grew slowly. Raising his fists in the air, he exclaimed, "*Elefthería!* Freedom!"

"Yes." Stavros grinned widely.

"Thank you," Panos said quietly, but his enthusiasm didn't mirror his friend's.

Stavros nodded, clearing his throat. "I came to see how both of you are recovering. But I also have another reason for being here. I'm not sure what type of work the two of you did before your imprisonment," he started, finally getting to the point. "But so much has changed, and I'm sure you'll need help starting over." He shuffled his feet. "I want to help. My father owns a bar. He's getting on in years, and it's too much for him. The neighborhood was once very nice but it's a bit rundown now. It still brings in a lot of business, though. He could use someone to help him run it. We could use both of you."

Panos and Kostas looked at one another questioningly.

"There are rooms in the back of the bar so you wouldn't have to look for a place to rent."

"We have no money to offer," Panos stated.

"I assumed as much. Your living arrangements would be part of your salary," Stavros replied. "That way, you can watch over the place most of the time, and my father can work as much or as little as he chooses."

Kostas looked to Panos for confirmation. Panos nodded in agreement.

"Are you sure?" Kostas asked. "What about Kalliope? What about America?"

Panos turned away at the mention of his beloved wife. Grief so deep and raw took hold of his entire being; it felt as though his heart was being strangled—squeezing, draining, pulverizing it until nothing was left but hopelessness and despair.

Panos held little gratitude for his liberator. He didn't mean to seem ungrateful but he wished the soldier had just let him die. Couldn't he see Panos was a shell of the man whose spirit had perished long ago? And now, here he lay, with nothing left but a feeble, mutilated body and a shriveled, hollow soul.

When he finally pulled himself together enough to speak, his gray eyes grew cold and dark. "What about her? The man she loves no longer exists. She's better off thinking I'm dead."

Chapter 14

Panos

Present Day

Fifty years of guilt and regret flooded Panos' soul. With the photos his granddaughter had left behind clutched in his hand, he lumbered his way to the back of the bar where his private room was situated.

The girl was right. He was a coward. Frightened of what his beloved's reaction would be when she laid eyes on his disfigured body. Terrified she'd recognize his change in spirit and reject him.

But the guilt was worse. He lived in his own personal hell, knowing their separation could have been avoided. Panos had not included her in his decision. She was his wife and he gave her no voice. In the end, his contribution to the Resistance did nothing to stop the dictatorship. Thankfully, they had fallen by their own hand.

Sitting on the edge of his bed, Panos lovingly ran his fingers over the pictures. He remembered the joy in loving Kalliope and the family they had become. He stole that joy from himself and from his wife. He missed a lifetime of milestones. Lost out on the chance of watching his Melina grow into a young woman and eventually have a family of her own.

He did this and he'd paid the price all these years; the loneliness and longing suffocating him as if the oxygen had been removed from the atmosphere.

Panos couldn't change his present condition, but he might be able to make his Kalliope understand what had led to his decision. Perhaps the truth would finally set her free. Even though he now knew she had never actually forgotten him. She had never moved on as he thought she might. And if his heart hadn't been broken enough before, it shattered a little more knowing she still waited in faith for him to return to her one day.

Wearily, Panos rose. He went to his chest and opened the middle drawer. Pulling a stack of letters from underneath a pile of clothing, he whispered, "It's time." The envelopes, tied together by a blue ribbon, were organized in chronological order. The oldest were more yellowed and frayed than some of the others, for they had been hidden for safekeeping during the days of the Resistance. Now they would finally be delivered to their rightful hands, and finally read as they should have been so many years ago.

Chapter 15

Loukas

Present Day

"I'll have another one of these," Krystina told the bartender.

"I think you've had enough," Loukas argued.

When Krystina stormed out of Kostas' place, she asked the cab driver to take them to a bar where people her age liked to hang out. Loukas had urged her to return to the hotel but Krystina was unwavering. Now she was clearly upset and drunk, and Loukas knew he had to get her home soon before she did or said something she regretted.

"Don't tell me what to do," she slurred, pointing a shaky finger at him. "You're not the boss of me. I have more relatives than I can count ordering me around." Flinging her hair behind her shoulders, she leaned her elbows against the bar.

Loukas knew only too well what it was like to be disappointed by a family member. The day his mother had unexpectedly passed, he had lost not one but two parents. His father was never the same again.

It was Krystina's parents who nurtured Loukas and gave him the love and support his father was incapable of providing. And now, for the first time in her life, Krystina felt the stabbing pain that rejection had on the soul, and he would have done anything, given everything he owned, to take that pain from her.

"Love sucks," she sneered. "I'm never falling in love," she stated firmly. "But I do want to dance," she declared suddenly, lighting up as the DJ amped up the tempo. She draped her arms over Loukas. It was rare for her to throw herself at him in this way. No, not rare. It had never happened before. The blood in his veins thrummed, each life-giving cell coming alive from their close proximity.

The tune blaring throughout the crowded bar was upbeat, yet oblivious to the pace of the music, Krystina swayed slowly as if dancing to a ballad. Loukas was sure that without his hands supporting her waist, her languid body would fall to the ground.

Panos had not only renounced his commitment and vows to Krystina's grandmother, but by doing so, he had also divorced himself from his entire family. From Krystina, who had bravely stood before Panos, pleading with him, even shaming him to come to his senses, until she saw her efforts were futile.

Standing behind her at Kostas' bar, Loukas didn't need to see her face to feel the hurt and anger emanating from her.

Those last words she had declared to the man whose blood ran through her veins yet who would forever be a stranger had shredded Loukas. *If someone loved me that unconditionally, I'd move heaven, Earth, and all the planets in the universe to be with him.*

Me! Loukas wanted to shout. *Look into my eyes. I'm right here.* He couldn't remember a time when he didn't love her. She had always been there. Had always been his from the time they were small enough to speak.

It didn't matter if Krystina ignored or insulted him. Loukas would always stand by her, even if only from a distance. But tonight, he was bound to be her keeper, lest she found herself unconscious and lost on the side of an unfamiliar road.

With her arms wrapped around his neck and her head resting on his shoulder, Loukas pulled her in tighter. A sweet torture but he'd revel in it. For he knew she would not allow him to caress her in this way if she were sober. Or allow him to run his fingertips along the length of her back. Or rub his cheek against hers.

How he wanted to kiss her—to have his lips pressing against that sassy mouth of hers. The present circumstances might allow it. But he wouldn't do that to his Krystina. Not again. The next time he kissed her, it would be her idea.

Make no mistake, adolescence is a war. No one gets out unscathed.
Harlan Coben

Chapter 16

Loukas

Five years earlier
Age thirteen

Evaporating pool water drifted into the atmosphere. At seven in the evening, the sun had not yet set on this summery August day. Phillip, Loukas' neighborhood friend, had just finished vacuuming his pool while Loukas set out snacks and drinks for a small party.

It was fortuitous for Loukas that there was a boy from his grade living in just about every house on the block. But unfortunately, it was not so lucky for Krystina, who had to put up with their childish pranks and ridicule.

Loukas had been pressured into going along with his friends' jabs. And as a result, it had fractured his already splintering friendship with Krystina. But tonight, he had a plan. He was going to show her how much he truly cared for her. And all it would take was a game of Truth or Dare combined with Seven Minutes in Heaven.

"Do you have the two bowls with the names?" Loukas asked Phillip.

"I do. But I think you're making a mistake."

"I won't be any worse off," Loukas said, tossing a pool float into the water. "You got me into this, man. Now help me fix it."

"Who said you had to follow along?"

"I suppose you and Tommy meowing and calling me a pussy put no pressure on me at all."

Philip shot him a mock innocent expression.

"Cut the crap. You owe me."

"And what if she takes the dare?"

"Trust me, she won't." Loukas was confident of that. "I'll go first. You make sure to have the bowl with her name on every paper. Just don't forget to switch the bowls after."

"Yeah, yeah, I got the drill."

Less than an hour later, girls and boys, barely in their teen years, splashed about the pool—chasing one another, diving, floating, and flirting. They would all enter the eighth grade in a month, and a year from then, high school. Every day was a new discovery—a time of growth. The boys no longer wanted to hang out with only boys, and the girls had revolving crushes on each one of them.

But for Loukas it was different. He had always chosen Krystina. Although now his feelings were different than before. He no longer thought of her as just his best friend. What he felt was so much more; so much deeper. At thirteen years old, Loukas knew, indisputably, that Krystina was meant for him. The loss of her friendship and trust had gutted him, and he would do anything to gain it back. Without her, Loukas felt there was something missing from inside of him.

When the sun had finally set, and the only illumination came from the golden half-moon and a single patio lantern, the entire group formed a circle on the grass, blanketed by their beach towels.

"So this is how it works," Phillip explained the rules, holding up a plastic bowl filled with folded papers. "Loukas has volunteered to go first. He'll pick a name from the bowl and offer that person a kiss or a dare. If the person takes the dare but refuses to follow it through they have to take the kiss, which will be played out as Seven Minutes in Heaven. In there." Phillip pointed to the pool cabana.

"I don't want to play this game," Chynna whispered to Krystina.

"Everyone who stays plays," a girl named Tiffany, who was sitting next to Chynna, said in a belittling tone.

"You don't have to do anything you don't want to do," Krystina told her friend, sneering back at Tiffany.

"I'll stay," Chynna agreed, lowering her head. She was a sweet girl, often intimidated by the others. Petite with silky black hair and large, almond-shaped eyes, she was adorable, but for the one thing that separated her from her peers—the port-wine stain surrounding her mouth. It was a birthmark she had lived with her whole life but she often felt self-conscious about it, especially when people stared at her.

"Now that we've settled that, go ahead, Loukas," Phillip commanded.

Loukas dug into the bowl, exaggerating his movements as he swirled the papers around, mixing them as if it would make a difference. Finally, he drew a paper and slowly unfolded it.

"What do you know! Krystina."

Their eyes met and she glared at him. Angry, fiery flames lashed against the backdrop of her hazel eyes.

He shrugged his shoulders noncommittally. "It's fate." He stroked his chin, pretending to think up a dare. But in actuality, he already had. One he was sure Krystina would pass on.

"Kiss or dare? You can either kiss me or strip down to nothing and dive in the pool."

"That's dirty, Loukas, and you know it." She stood, fisting her hands. "I call that against the rules."

"There are no rules," a boy named Jared called out.

Loukas extended his hands, palms up in a shrug. "What will it be?" he asked smugly.

She narrowed her eyes, shooting arrows at him. And Loukas could tell they weren't Cupid's arrows. Her grunts and stomping feet scared him a little, and he wondered if he'd just made a colossal mistake.

"Turn out all the lights," she ordered Phillip. "Chynna, come to the edge of the pool with my towel and hand it to me when I come up from my dive."

"What?" Loukas felt like an idiot in front of everyone as they all snickered at Krystina's choice. Was kissing him that horrible?

"Are you insane?" Chynna said, her voice raising an octave. "Just go kiss him and get it over with. If your father finds out you stripped down in front of everyone, you won't have to worry about kissing anyone, ever! He'll lock you away until you're thirty."

Loukas and Krystina stood like two opponents in a boxing ring, assessing, watching, deciding their next move. "Oh, come on," she huffed, grabbing him by the wrist and dragging him in the direction of the cabana.

Loukas turned to the crowd and grinned, gesturing a thumbs-up.

They stepped inside and he shut the door.

"Don't think for one second that you won," she snapped. "We can just sit here for seven minutes."

"Nope. There has to be a kiss."

"But there's no rule that says it has to be on the lips." She crossed her arms with a smirk.

Defeat hung in the air. "I give up," Loukas surrendered. "All I wanted was for you to like me again. For me to show you I was sorry. That I miss my friend."

"You chose them over me. You did it once before, and you did it again." But the anger had left her. Now there was only hurt reflected in her voice.

Loukas ignored the hooting from outside as their friends teased them.

He took her face in his hands. "I would always choose you." Loukas leaned in, angling down to kiss her.

"But you didn't."

"I was stupid. I'm sorry," Loukas said sincerely.

"I don't know how to do this," Krystina whispered nervously.

"There's nothing to know. You only need to want me."

Softly, he brushed his lips against hers, careful to take it slow. Pulling back, he looked into her eyes, searching for consent. It came when she placed one hand on his shoulder and her other hand around his neck to pull him in for another kiss.

They were startled by several hands banging on the door. "Times up."

When they walked out, Loukas was on top of the world. Until Tommy went and opened his big mouth once more.

"So what happened in there? Did you get a peek at her panties again?" he joked. "Do they still have Minnie Mouse prints or has she graduated to Wonder Woman?" He snapped his fingers. "Oh, wait! Victoria's Secret, right?"

Krystina rounded on Loukas, flashing him a wrathful scowl. "I'm out of here."

"Krystina!" Loukas went after her. "That wasn't my fault."

She kept walking. "Just leave me alone. I played your stupid game. Now go kiss someone else."

Krystina swung open the gate and slammed it shut with force.

Loukas didn't move a muscle. Of all the freaking luck! He cursed Tommy under his breath. He had been so close. Frustrated and furious at his idiotic friends, Loukas left without even saying goodbye.

Chapter 17

Krystina

Present Day

"Don't make so much noise when you walk," Krystina complained, shoving Loukas with the little strength she had.

She had never experienced a hangover before, and God as her witness, she swore she never would again. All of her senses were on irritable high alert. The light burned her eyes, her hair hurt, and the tapping of heels against the marble floors as she and Loukas crossed the lobby was deafening.

"I'm wearing sneakers. Those are your shoes, Min."

"Okay, okay. You don't have to shout." She covered her ears.

Loukas shook his head, smirking as they entered the hotel café.

"Nice of you two to join us," Max jested. "Late night?"

"Not so late." Krystina rested her head on the table. "Does anyone have some Tylenol?"

"Hungover," Loukas mouthed.

"I heard that!" she grunted, whacking him on the arm.

"Krystina Markella Andarakis!" Mia pulled a pink designer pill case from her bag, shook out two white caplets, and handed them to her sister with reproving regard. "Just because there's no restriction on the drinking age here, it doesn't give you license to get trashed."

"It was an accident," Krystina said, covering her ears with her hands. "Now would everyone please just lower your voices?"

Kally giggled. "The liquor just happened to find its way down your throat?"

"She only had four," Loukas defended. "She kept saying they tasted like cherry soda."

"Eat something." Kally passed her plate of French toast over to her. "You'll feel better after a good meal and some coffee."

"I hope you feel well enough to enjoy your last day," Nicholas told Krystina. "Your flight leaves at eight-fifty this evening. A car will be here at six-thirty to pick all of you up."

Krystina narrowed her eyes suspiciously. "What do you mean by 'all of you?' What about you?" she asked, her voice grainy.

"Mia and I are heading to Monaco to direct a photo shoot," Nicholas said matter-of-factly.

Krystina popped her head up, her mouth agape. "I want to come!"

"You have school on Monday," Mia said.

"Come on! So not fair!" she complained. "I could post the work-in-progress on your social media accounts. I could be an asset."

"Not this time," Nicholas said. "I told you *if* school was on holiday and we had a shoot coincide, only then could you could assist, but not at the expense of your education."

"Math and science are not going to educate me on what I want to do in life," she protested.

"You'd be surprised at how useful those subjects will be in your future. The discussion is closed," Nicholas commanded firmly.

Krystina crossed her arms in front of her with a huff. Picking up the menu, she hid her face, deciding on what to order. She was famished. The few bites of Kally's French toast were just a starter. Her stomach grumbled angrily at the nutritional neglect.

When the server approached, she and Loukas gave him their orders and handed back the menus.

A suited gentleman from the front desk approached their table. "Mr. Aristedis?"

"Yes?" Nicholas replied.

"A package was left at the front desk for one of the ladies in your party. For a Miss Krystina."

Nicholas nodded. "Thank you," he said, rising to follow him to the front desk to collect it.

"It's not large. I can bring it to your table if you like," he offered.

"That's very kind. Thank you."

Nicholas frowned at his future sister-in-law. She shrugged, oblivious to what the package could be.

When the concierge returned, he handed Nicholas a thick manila envelope. Nicholas passed it to her.

Her name, scrawled across the front, was written by a shaky hand. By someone old or disabled, perhaps … or both? She sucked in a nervous breath, afraid to see its contents. The five sets of eyes on her didn't help to allay the knots in her stomach, either.

Opening the package, she peeked inside to find a stack of envelopes tied together by a worn blue ribbon. She pulled them out, noticing some letters were more frayed and yellowed at the edges than others. Then, a single sheet of paper fell onto her lap.

Picking it up, she scanned the letter. "It's from Panos!"

"Why did he single you out?" Mia asked, confused.

Krystina and Loukas looked at one another like two guilty parties hiding a not-so-well-concealed secret.

"We went to see him last night," Loukas admitted.

"My idea," Krystina confessed. "I thought I could talk some sense into him but instead I left frustrated and pissed off."

"Hence the drinking?" Nicholas asked with a raised eyebrow. "That's not a solution."

"It really was an accident! Sure, I was mad, and that took the edge off, but those *visinatha* martinis are addictive." She pointed to Kally. "You need to add those to your menu."

"I run a café, not a bar. I don't have a liquor license," she reminded her. "Now, would you please read that letter," Kally insisted impatiently.

Glancing down at the letter, Krystina felt her heart pounding in her chest. What could Panos possibly want to tell her? He had already made it clear he never planned to reunite with his wife.

Krystina exhaled, looking up at her captive audience as she read aloud.

Krystina mou,

These are letters I wrote to my Kalliope over the years but lacked the opportunity, and later the courage, to mail. I am not the heartless villain you think I am. When you return home, I only ask that you don't shatter her faith. Loving her was never a question. Hold onto these letters for a time until you see fit to show them to her. Maybe it would be best not to do so right away.

Krystina thumbed through the letters. They were dated in order, some not too long after he sent his wife to the States. Others from after his imprisonment had ended.

"He signed it '*Laying the past to rest, Panos.*'" Krystina sighed deeply and leaned back in her chair.

Everyone fell silent, taking in the enormity of what Krystina held in her hands.

"Should we read each letter before we give them to her?" Kally asked.

"No, that wouldn't be right," Mia answered. "What's in those envelopes is between our grandparents. It's private."

"We need to protect her, though," Kally said, nibbling on a thumbnail.

"My suggestion is that we don't tell her that we found him," Max said. "For now, anyway. We can say we hit a dead end. Letters or not, if we say we saw him and he refused to come home with us, it will break her."

The girls nodded in agreement.

"I'll hold onto these for safekeeping," Krystina said, slipping the letters back into the manila pouch. They were a heavy responsibility to bear, and she prayed she would recognize the appropriate time to share them with her grandmother. For now, though, she would have to put it out of her mind.

Krystina attempted a smile. "So, Nicholas, I'd like to revisit my coming to Monaco," she began, lightening the mood.

Nicholas and Mia stood. "Oh, look at the time," he said. "Your flight is leaving tonight but ours is leaving in a few hours We had better go." He began to escort Mia out of the café. Then turning, he said, "Have fun. See you back in the States." He grinned.

"Guess you're stuck with me again today," Loukas chuckled, obviously pleased with his situation.

"Stuck like a barnacle to the hull of a boat," she muttered.

Krystina's Visinatha Martini

Ingredients

1½ ounces cherry vodka

2 ounces visinatha or visinatha syrup

1 ounce ginger ale

Splash of lemon juice

Add all the ingredients into a shaker with ice cubes. Shake and then pour into a martini glass.

You can find visinatha at a Greek grocery, specialty store, or even on Amazon. (Search for Greek cherry preserves.) This delicious cherry preserve serves as a dessert on its own. Or add to a glass of water for a refreshing beverage. Visinatha is also available as a syrup. Either will work with this recipe. However, for best results, I recommend the visinatha preserves.

Chapter 18

Krystina

By the time Krystina arrived home the next day, she was so jet lagged she dropped her suitcase at the bottom of the steps, climbed the stairs, and flopped onto her bed. Within seconds, she was fast asleep.

A few hours later, she finally stirred, looking at the clock on her nightstand. After rubbing the sleep from her eyes, she padded to the bathroom to freshen up. It was only nine o'clock in the evening, though it felt like the middle of the night.

With both trepidation and anticipation, her chest tightened at the thought of facing her grandmother. Those letters might just hold the answers she was waiting for. But if she shared them now, what would her *Yiayiá* do? Hop on a plane to seek him out? Or would the revelations leave her too heartbroken to go on?

It had been decided to hold off on sharing them for now, but Krystina wasn't good with secrets or at concealing her emotions. And then there was the lie. A lie that included her mother. She had been a victim in all this, too, having been left fatherless her entire life. Pretending she hadn't met her long-lost grandfather would be the most challenging aspect of this whole charade.

Slowly, she made her way down the staircase, following the voices on the television leading her to her *yiayiá's* bedroom. A repeat of *The Golden Girls* was playing, one of the many episodes she could swear her grandmother could recite word for word. Peeking her head in the doorway, she smiled affectionately, watching her grandmother laugh while unwrapping Hershey's kisses and popping them into her mouth.

The room she occupied was more like a mini apartment—the result of an extension added to the house years ago to give *Yiayiá* private space as the family grew. A comfortable, old sofa covered in crocheted throws sat across from a large, flat-screen TV Krystina and her siblings had chipped in to buy for her birthday. The bedroom was separated by a doorway and decorated with furniture that had to be as old as Krystina's mother.

"*Koukla mou*, why are you standing in the doorway?" *Yiayiá* asked when she noticed Krystina. "Come and tell me everything."

Seeing the hope reflected in her grandmother's eyes made Krystina want to weep. Taking a seat beside her, she kissed her cheek. "Your country is beautiful, *Yiayiá*."

"I'm sure much has changed in all these years."

"It was all new to me, and I can't wait to go back."

"Did you ..." *Yiayiá* hesitated, her expression a mix of hope and fear. "Did you find who you were looking for?"

"No, unfortunately we didn't accomplish what we hoped to." That truly wasn't a lie, at least, Krystina thought.

"Oh," *Yiayiá* said, the disappointment palpable. "You tried. He's out there, somewhere," she mused.

Yiayiá attempted a smile but Krystina noticed it didn't reach her eyes. She knew her grandmother only too well. The woman was trying to regain some of the optimism she'd held onto for all these years.

"I heard a story once about an old couple," *Yiayiá* started. "The man would take his wife everywhere he went with a broad smile on his face, even though the woman never seemed happy. She always had a blank expression and appeared confused. It turned out that the woman had that Oldtimer's disease."

"Alzheimer's, not Oldtimer's." Krystina usually laughed at her language fumbles, but not today.

"Whatever." *Yiayiá* brushed it off. "Anyway, the woman didn't even recognize her husband anymore. *Kathólou.*" She smacked her hands together in a gesture she used to indicate there was nothing more to be done. "A friend of the man questioned him. 'Why do you take her with you everywhere? She doesn't even know who you are.' The man replied, 'She is the love of my life, and as long as she's on this earth, I will keep her by my side.'"

Krystina gave this some thought. "What point are you trying to make, *Yiayiá*? That maybe Panos is out there but doesn't know who he is? Or that you'll love him no matter what his reasons are for not returning to you?"

"Both *agápi mou*, both," she said, caressing her granddaughter's cheek.

They sat in silence for a few moments until *Yiayiá* turned up the volume on the TV and laughed at one of Sophia's wisecracks.

"How many times can you watch the same show?"

"It's funny, no? Tomorrow we watch *The Bachelor* together," she said, raising her eyebrows. "Those girls! *Po po po!*"

"You might just be the oldest woman in Bachelor Nation." Krystina laughed.

"Go get that bottle of ouzo and two glasses," her *yiayiá* instructed, pointing to the credenza on the adjacent wall.

Krystina crossed the room and poured ouzo into two shot glasses adorned with the Greek evil eye symbol.

"*Stin ygeía mas!* To our health!" her grandmother toasted before downing the shot in one gulp. "I wish I was in my twenties again to have sex three times in a Mykonos windmill."

"*Yiayiá!*"

"Maybe four times!" She held up her fingers and cackled.

"I'm going to ban you from that show."

"Eh!" She waved her off. "Now tell me, how did you and Loukas get along?"

"You went from windmill sex to Loukas?"

Yiayiá gazed at her with a not-so-innocent look.

"He was fine, I guess."

"You guess?"

"Okay, he was helpful when he wasn't on my heels like a puppy with separation issues."

"It doesn't go one way. You can't use the boy when you need him and then ask him to leave you alone when he might need you."

"I don't mean to. I never encourage him."

"You're young yet. But in time, you'll see things more clearly."

"This coming from the woman who wishes she could have windmill sex," Krystina mumbled. "Wait! Did you already do that once?"

Her grandmother formed a sly look on her face. "Noooo," she stretched out. "Not there, but … a boat cabin, a lighthouse, and maybe under the stars in an open field."

Krystina hurriedly raised her hand, stopping her grandmother from reminiscing any more. "I have school tomorrow. I'm going to bed now to try to erase those images from my brain." Krystina fondly kissed her grandmother goodnight and left the room, shaking her head, even though nothing she heard had actually surprised her. Not where her *yiayiá* was concerned.

* * *

The lunchroom was full of energy on the first day back at school after winter break. Favorite gifts, vacation stories, and all kinds of gossip to catch up on dominated the conversations.

"My parents bought me a new laptop for Christmas," Chynna said excitedly. "I've been playing around with all the new features."

"We had like forty people over on Christmas Day," another friend, Stacy, said. "It was a bit chaotic with all those little cousins running around. Other than that, I didn't do too much … except go ice-skating with James one afternoon." The girl grinned in a way that told Krystina there was more to this story.

"Spill! So I can lift my jaw off the floor," Krystina exclaimed. "Details, please."

"Yes! Please. Tell all," Jordyn, another friend sitting at their table, urged.

"It was unexpected," Stacy admitted. "I was at Starbucks and he got in line behind me and we started chatting. Honestly, I didn't think he knew I existed."

"Well, of course he did," Chynna said to the petite blonde. "You're so pretty."

"Thank you. That's sweet of you to say. Anyway, he asked me what I was doing the next day and wanted to know if I liked skating. The next thing I knew, we were making plans," Stacy stated as if it was the most unlikely thing to happen. "I swear, I didn't sleep a wink that night."

"So how did it go?" Krystina asked anxiously.

"Great! We even went to Prohibition for lunch the next day."

"So are the two of you a thing now?" Krystina inquired.

A smile and a shrug were all the answer she received. "But what about you? Tell us all about Greece."

Krystina didn't share the reason she and her siblings went on such short notice. She simply said it was incredibly fun. "We only had a few days but I packed in what I could. But guess what?! Nicholas, my future bother-in-law, promised I could use his house in Mykonos after graduation. And guess who I'm bringing with me?"

"Loukas?" Stacy teased.

Krystina gave her friend a playful shove. "No! The two of you! Won't it be amazing?"

"Oh, wow! Yes! I definitely want to go." Chynna confirmed. "But right now, I want to hear about Loukas! How did it go with him?"

"Pretty much how it always goes with him," Krystina said, offering no details. There were fleeting moments that were intimate, it was true. Moments that had her heart aching with confusion over her feelings for this boy. But she would never admit them out loud. Not even to her closest friends. Not even to herself.

Changing the subject, Krystina brought up James again. "You know, Stacy, prom is only five months away. What are the chances you'll be going with James?"

"Time will tell. I don't want to set myself up for disappointment." Stacy looked to Krystina. "What about you? Who do you have your eye on?"

There wasn't any particular boy Krystina was interested in dating but a few she'd consider going with as friends, should they ask.

"I can't think of a soul," she said on a shrug.

By the end of the week, the 'promposals' had begun, and they were getting more elaborate and ridiculous by the day. Krystina was caught off-guard when a boy she had known fairly well from some of her classes asked her to go with him. Thank the stars he didn't arrange a cheesy set-up, videoed it to post on Instagram, or organized a flash mob with her as the center of the pandemonium. Still, why couldn't he have found a private moment, somewhere away from spying eyes?

"So what do you say?" Noah asked anxiously. "If you don't already have a date, that is."

Krystina could feel her face flush. A nearby locker slammed shut, jolting her from her awkward daze. From the corner of her eye, she saw Loukas. The locker had swung back open from the force he'd hit it with. Again, he closed it furiously, pounding the door once with his fist before storming away. She winced at his reaction. If only he hadn't witnessed Noah's exchange with her. If he had just stayed long enough to see she wasn't accepting the date, she'd feel better. Now she had a pit in her stomach. Rallying, she smiled at the boy waiting for her response.

"Noah, it's a very nice offer ..."

"Oh, you have a date already. Sorry."

"No. Not exactly. You see, Chynna and I decided neither of us would go with dates. So she and I, and a few of our friends, are going together."

"Oh, okay. I get it."

Krystina wasn't sure he was convinced. "I'd love for you to come and hang out with us, though. Maybe save me a dance?"

"Sure thing. Let me know if the plans change."

"Oh, I'm sure some other girl will be lucky enough to snag that date with you, but if anything changes, you'll be the first to know."

After he walked away, Chynna approached. "You handled that really well. But why didn't you say yes to him? He's such a nice guy?"

"Because I really meant it when I said you and I are going together. Let's get the girls together and make a tentative plan."

"Tentative?"

"Sure. Plans change," Krystina said with a nonchalant shrug. "If one of you gets asked by someone you were hoping for then all bets are off!"

"Not gonna happen. At least not to me," Chynna assured her.

"Confidence, girl! Any guy would be lucky to escort you to prom."

* * *

"Krystina! Thank God!" Kally exclaimed when she walked into the café kitchen. "We're slammed out there."

"Where do you want me?"

"Egypt is running between coffee and the to-go counter. I think she's fine there but Katie and Loukas could use your help on table service."

"Okay," Krystina said, tying a Coffee Klatch apron around her waist.

Her sister wasn't exaggerating. Every table was full; patrons were hovering by the front door, waiting to be seated.

Outside, snow was gently falling, but the village still saw a steady amount of foot traffic even during the coldest months. It was lovely really. Like a postcard of a village from another era, or a small town nestled in a remote part of the country rather than a bustling town only a train ride from Manhattan.

Today, the Mexican hot chocolate was the clear winner, paired with buñuelos, a cinnamon puff of heaven that's a cross between a churro and a donut.

Hours later, when the crowd finally died down, Krystina flopped into a chair and put her feet up.

"This place gets busier by the day. How did you do it when we were away, Egypt?"

"With a lot of help and the promise of my own vacation."

"With Leo?" Krystina grinned.

Loukas cleared the last of the tables and headed for the kitchen. "I'm outta here. Goodnight," he called to Egypt.

"Goodnight, Loukas," Krystina called out mockingly. "What crawled up your ass? You haven't said two words to me all afternoon."

Turning, he flashed her a cold stare before disappearing through the doorway and out into the evening.

Krystina lifted her hands in confusion. "What did I do?" she asked.

"It's not fun having the tables turned on you, is it?" Egypt pointed out. "I love you, girl. You're like a sister to me. But you need to be a little more sensitive where that boy is concerned."

Katie, Kally's newest hire and an acquaintance of Krystina's from school, walked over to her. "Loukas saw Noah ask you to prom," she explained, placing a gentle hand on Krystina's shoulder.

"I know. So did a lot of other people. So what?" she asked defensively.

Both Katie and Egypt stared at her with admonishing expressions.

"Don't look at me like I did something wrong. First of all, I said no to the guy. In the kindest possible way, for your information. Chynna even said so herself. Second, it's not like Loukas asked me to the prom, so why does he care who I go with?"

"I'm going home," Katie said, throwing her hands into the air in defeat. "I'm Switzerland on this one."

"I'm going too."

"Oh, no. Plant your butt on this stool," Egypt ordered. "Loukas didn't ask you because he knows you would have only said no. You do nothing but shoot him down. Half the time it's like an amusing cat and mouse game, but that boy only laughs it off because there's nothing else for him to do."

"Why is everyone always on his side?"

"No one is taking sides," Egypt assured her. "You're a good kid. Deep down, you're kind and sensitive. You care about people. Don't be afraid to show that part of yourself to him. Stop acting like the brat I know you're not."

"What about everything he's done to me? Does that count for anything?"

"What? Made fun of your underwear when you were eight years old? Or pulled a dumb prank when you were twelve? Get over it! Boys do stupid ass things."

"You just don't understand. He was my best friend, and he sold me out. Twice! And then it came back to humiliate me one more time. And all for what? To impress his other friends. It was a betrayal."

"He was a child!"

"Okay. Whatever! But what do you want me to do? Apologize for someone asking me to prom?"

"You could tell him you said no to that guy and ask Loukas to prom instead."

"Maybe I could mention to him that I'm not going with Noah, but as for asking him to go with me …? Yeah, that's not going to happen," Krystina said definitively. That pit in her stomach was back. "I'm going home. I have homework."

Chapter 19

Loukas

With all the talk of prom everywhere he turned at school, Loukas couldn't avoid thinking of his own situation. There was only one girl he would even consider asking to go with him but he highly doubted Krystina would ever agree.

He had made some progress in re-establishing his friendship with her while over in Greece. Between the snide comments and jabs, they had enjoyed galivanting around Athens together. At least he had fun spending time with her, and he was pretty certain her walls had come down a time or two. But was that enough?

Maybe he made their whole bizarre dynamic worse by purposely annoying her, but it seemed the only way to get her attention. Through all the good-natured teasing, couldn't she see how much he cared for her? How much he missed the close bond they had formed from the time they were barely old enough to utter a few words?

Loukas had gone along with everything she had asked, even returning to Kostas' bar when he secretly thought it was a bad idea. He comforted her when it turned out badly, just as he'd expected it would, and later humored her even as she drank too much. Krystina had to know that he was on her side. He would forever be looking out for her. Surely he had proven that to her by now. If he could only take back his past transgressions.

As Loukas approached his locker pondering on what to do, he saw Noah approaching Krystina. He groaned in frustration. He was too late.

Noah Hartly didn't offer any grand gestures, although apparently, he still thought it was fine to ask Krystina to the prom for all to hear. That pissed him off more than he could ever express.

"Krystina," he heard Noah stutter nervously. "Um, prom is coming up. I thought it would be fun for the two of us to go together."

Loukas just stood watching, his stomach churning as he waited for Krystina's answer. But she only smiled sweetly at Noah.

"Would you want to go with me?" Noah elaborated. "As your date?"

Loukas' heart hammered in his chest. This couldn't be happening.

"So what do you say?" Noah asked again. "If you don't already have a date, that is."

Loukas wasn't about to stand by and listen to Krystina accept a date to the prom from someone else. Frustrated, he slammed his locker shut, punctuating his rage. Krystina turned in the direction of the noise only to see Loukas flash her a steely glare. He slammed the locker shut again, just to make his point clear. Then he stormed off before he completely lost his shit.

Later, at the café, he couldn't bring himself to speak to her or even look in her direction. Maybe it wasn't fair. Maybe he was acting immature. But right now, he didn't care. She had dished it out to him far too many times. Now it was his turn to show that he had feelings too.

Chapter 20

Loukas

Nine years earlier
Age 9

"Does she have to play with us?" Tommy complained.

"It's not Krystina's fault she's the only girl on the street," Loukas argued.

"That's not our problem," Phillip added. "Tell her to tag along with her sisters."

"Come on, they're so much older than she is." Loukas kicked a stone in the street with the toe of his sneaker. "And just so you know, she can outrun and out-goal all of you."

"You would know," Tommy said with a smirk. "You spend most of your time with her."

"Our moms are best friends," Loukas snapped back defensively.

"And Krystina is yours. *Loukas would rather play with a girl*," Johnny sing-songed.

"Ugh, here she comes. And in a skirt too!" Phillip warned.

Loukas didn't know what to do. He wanted to play with both the boys and Krystina. He didn't know what the big deal was.

"You can't play in that!" Tommy said when Krystina approached,

111

pointing his finger at her.

"Yes, I can, you big jerk." Krystina lifted the flap in the front of her skirt. "See, they're shorts. So there!"

"Let's just go in the backyard and play already," Kevin, one of the other boys, whined.

For the next half hour, Krystina proved Loukas correct. She could outkick all of those boys. But the more goals she made, the more aggressive the other boys became, ramming into her at every opportunity.

The so-called shorts Krystina had defended were more of a skort, and they were much looser fitting around the thighs than the average pair of shorts. When Phillip came charging at her to intercept the ball, he knocked her over, full force.

Loukas ran over, the other boys following. But whereas Loukas was concerned for his friend, the other boys began to laugh. Her skort had ridden high enough to see her panties peeking out. Panties printed with Minnie Mouse sporting a pink bow atop her head. The boys chanted, "Minnie Mouse, Minnie Mouse, go back to your little, pink house."

"Are you okay?" Loukas asked, helping her up.

"I'm fine. Really." She smiled, trying to ignore the boys.

"Minnie said she's fine," Tommy howled.

The boys continued to heckle her with their chant.

"Loukas, are you with us or against us?" Tommy challenged.

Loukas looked back and forth between his friends, all boys his age, and Krystina, his best friend. They didn't understand how close they were or how friendly their families were. He couldn't recall a time when he didn't know her. Yet he also wanted to be one of the boys.

"Say it or go home," Phillip ordered.

As soon as he did, Loukas knew he'd made the wrong choice. He was struck with regret the moment he looked into her wounded eyes.

Krystina brushed the grass off her knees. "You're all just a bunch of dumb boys. I don't want to play with you anyway," she shouted.

Krystina was trying to hold back her tears. Loukas could tell. Suddenly he felt sick to his stomach for what he'd done.

"And you!" She poked an accusing finger at Loukas. "Don't talk to me ever again. I mean it," she spouted vehemently before storming away.

Loukas watched in vain as she raced back to her house.

"That solves that problem." Tommy declared with a laugh, kicking the ball across the yard.

"Shut up," Loukas snarled. "I'm going home."

Chapter 21

Krystina

February 15, 2020

The Greek Orthodox Church of the Assumption, already blanketed in its ethereal beauty by the iconography painted on wall and ceiling surfaces, looked as though it had truly been elevated into the heavens. A white runner ran down the center aisle, and large bows of tulle and satin were draped over each pew, secured by gorgeous bouquets of white Chrysanthemums and blush pink garden roses.

In front of the altar, a wooden table had been placed to display a gold-encased Holy Bible and a silver tray. On the tray, the *stefana*, tied together by a single ribbon, sat atop a bed of *koufeta*—the traditional candy-coated almonds that would later be offered to guests.

Today was Kally and Max's wedding day. Krystina believed she was more excited than her sister, who seemed so utterly calm and composed for a bride-to-be. The bridesmaids had exited the limousine and were waiting patiently in the back of the church to make their entrances. But Krystina couldn't help but peek inside.

The four-foot candles adorned in layers of pink and white fabric were so beautiful standing on either side of the table displaying the *stefana*. And the floral arrangements on both sides of the altar entrance were breathtaking in soft shades of pastel pink. Her sister had chosen well, and everything looked exactly as Kally had planned.

Soon they were asked to line up, and Krystina's stomach fluttered with excitement.

"Are you nervous?" she asked Kally.

"Not at all," her sister replied, beaming. "I'm so ready to do this."

"I'm happy for you." Krystina took one last look at her sister before their father took Kally by the arm. She was grace and elegance personified, dressed in her classically styled wedding gown. The flowing crepe chiffon was cut in a refined sheath silhouette with a deep V neckline. But what made this dress simply dreamy was the sheer, long sleeves adorned with delicate lace appliques. A pink satin sash tied at the waistline completed the look.

The bridesmaids lined up in color coordinated dresses that ranged from powder pink to soft peony to rich magenta. Athena was the last to walk before the bride, sprinkling rose petals along the white path.

Krystina's eyes glistened with unshed tears as the priest exchanged the wreaths over the couple's head, uniting them as one in marriage. Across the marble platform, Loukas stole glances at her, and she'd quickly look away each time their eyes met. They had barely spoken for the better part of a month. By now, he knew she had refused Noah's offer, yet their interactions had only grown more strained than ever before. That was fine by her! Krystina had not forgiven him for making assumptions, and he, she presumed, had finally grown tired of her jabs. Still, it didn't stop him from spending most of his time at her home. Manny had kept up with his AA meetings, and she believed he was on the road to recovery. But she wondered if the relationship between father and son had already been too permanently damaged.

Krystina couldn't hold back her tears as Kally and Max began the Dance of Isaiah, her favorite and the most sentimental ritual of the wedding ceremony. At least, *she* thought it was. And to watch her sister take those first symbolic steps in marriage with her new husband while the priest led them around, chanting of sacrificial and unconditional love, was touching.

Kally smiled joyfully at Krystina as she and Max made the second pass around the table, Krystina wiping away the river of happy tears streaming down her face.

"*Na zísete!*" the wedding guests shouted, wishing the couple a long life and happy marriage as they began to come up the aisle.

Two by two, the bridal party followed, and as expected, Kally had matched Loukas and Krystina as partners.

He offered her his arm and bent down to whisper in her ear, "How about we call a truce for just one day? No insults. No ignoring each other."

They smiled and waved at friends and family as they made their way to the narthex.

"We're going to be thrown together all day for pictures and wedding crap," he continued.

She turned to glare at him. "I was about to agree until you said wedding crap."

He sighed loudly. "I didn't mean it that way. So is it a deal?"

"Deal," she agreed reluctantly.

Loukas had been right. They had been thrown together for almost the entire day. The ride to the Angelidis Vineyard was over an hour away, and Krystina had been wedged between Loukas and Egypt. Then there were the endless photos, the entrance into the ballroom, and her place card at the bridal table, which seated her right next to Loukas. But they had made a pact, and truth be told, it wasn't so bad.

Kally and Max took to the dance floor for their first dance as husband and wife. Halfway through Ed Sheeran's 'Thinking Out Loud,' the DJ asked the wedding party to join the newlyweds.

Loukas extended his hand to Krystina, and she graciously accepted.

Those flutters she felt earlier awoke, but this time they weren't from pre-wedding jitters on behalf of her sister. This time, it was because Loukas had taken her into his arms, and it was strange, and frightening, and pleasant, all in a weird way. A shiver ran up her spine, and she shuddered from the feeling of his breath tickling her neck.

"Is something wrong?" he asked softly.

"I'm a little cold," she lied.

Loukas released her to remove his tuxedo jacket. He placed it over her bare shoulders and pulled her back in against him, his hands disappearing under the jacket's material to run up and down her back to warm her.

Krystina looked at him in a way she never had before. What a sweet gesture, she thought. A genuinely caring one. She rested her head on his shoulder, settling into the crook of his neck, and she could have sworn she heard him sigh.

When the song ended, she reluctantly broke away from him and handed him his jacket. "I'm fine now. Thank you."

His warm smile was more genuine than it had ever seemed before, and for the first time in a long time, it seemed to light up his eyes with happiness.

At the end of the night, they sat side-by-side for the ride home.

"I like this truce thing. Maybe we can keep it up."

"We'll see," Krystina said with a small smile, resting her tired head on his shoulder.

Nothing is so painful to the human mind as a great and sudden change.
Mary Shelley

Chapter 22

Krystina

March, 2020

"One daughter comes home and the other takes off," George, Krystina's father, complained at the dining table. "When was the last time we all had a Sunday meal together?"

Melina rolled her eyes. "*Vre, Geórgios*, the girls aren't children anymore. They've grown and have lives of their own."

"And my son had to run off to England when there's an excellent college right around the corner." He waved his hands in disapproval.

"You have nothing to complain about, Dad," Kally laughed. "You live an ocean away from your parents. I'm only a few blocks from you. And yes, Mia lives in the city, but at least she's in the same state."

"I plan to travel the world," Krystina announced, cutting into her chicken.

"You're staying put, young lady," George said, pointing a pudgy finger at her.

"Forever?" she asked, defiance scored into her narrowed eyes. "I think not."

"That's enough," Melina interjected. "Right now, I'm a little concerned about Mia and Nicholas."

"Why?" Krystina wondered.

"I don't think they should be out of the country right now. Have you seen what's going on in China?"

"That's why they canceled the photo shoot in Singapore and relocated it to Croatia," Kally said.

"Not to alarm you but some cases of this virus are spreading throughout Europe now, particularly across Italy," Max said with a frown, rolling his veggies around on his plate distractedly.

"Mia said they were aware of a potential spread, and that's why they didn't take a crew with them," Kally added, glancing at Max in concern. "They plan to get in and out quickly. The models, photographer, and techs were hired by a local agency in Varaždin."

"Oh, I don't like it. Not one bit." Melina sighed, crossing herself in prayer. "Now I'm very worried."

"Let's change the subject," Kally suggested to take her mother's mind off Mia. "My latte flights have been a big hit. I had only ordered a small quantity of the mini glasses but I just ordered more to fill the demand."

"Good idea!" Krystina confirmed. "And we've been extra busy lately. You may need to hire more staff too," she suggested.

"Hold off on that," Max said, taking a pull from his beer. "There's buzz in the precinct, coming from higher authorities, that numbers are escalating in New York. Who knows what that will mean for all of us?"

Two days later, Mia texted Krystina and Kally to say they had left Croatia and had flown to Mykonos. Soon after, Greece and Italy went into lockdown. Mia begged her sisters to break the news to their mother gently before she called her. They would stay in Europe while Nicholas' sister remained in New York. The magazine's destination content would be nearly impossible to curate now that countries were locking down.

Krystina wasn't sure what all of this meant or how it would impact Nicholas' magazine. She tried to wrap her brain around a situation where business couldn't be conducted. Would the world come to a full stop? And for how long? Krystina had questions she wisely refrained from asking. Her mother looked paralyzed with fear. Mia was so far away, and one thing was for sure, Melina Andarakis preferred all of her children accounted for.

"Well, this is going to be fun," Krystina warned Kally. "Mom is already going into panic mode."

"Huh?" her sister asked, lost in thought.

"Are you on a different planet?"

"No, this one, unfortunately. Dealing with our mother's hysteria might be the least of our problems," Kally said with trepidation.

Her sister was correct to feel alarmed. Krystina never thought that situations oceans away could affect her own life. But now, only a week and a half later, Kally was told her business had to shut down for indoor dining, and to make matters colossally worse, classes transferred to remote learning only. That meant the end of Krystina's social life.

Suddenly, her little village looked like a grim ghost town. The few people she did spot walking around all wore surgical masks. It was strange enough when you couldn't see the whole of someone's face. But with fear of the unknown spreading, their eyes were as blank as the expression hiding behind the covering.

As soon as Kally got the order to shut down, she called a staff meeting. Every employee attended, willing to do whatever it took to keep her from losing the café.

"We have to stay relevant and current with the needs of customers in these difficult times," Kally said to the small group gathered before her. "I'm adding a small takeaway food menu. Nothing too crazy but I want to offer more than just dessert and coffee. I've already ordered a large quantity of takeout packaging."

Kally's usual optimism was gone, replaced instead by stress-induced enthusiasm. Worry etched lines into her brow. "I have to make this work. I can't lose this place. The powers that be say this will only be for two weeks but I can't see that small amount of time solving anything."

"We'll do anything we can to help," Krystina assured her.

"Thank you." She addressed Katie and Brittany, another waitress, first. They usually worked the dining room, but since that was now closed, she gave them another assignment. "The two of you will take to-go orders at the front counter." Then she turned to Loukas. "I'm going to have to add a delivery service. Would you be willing to drive?"

"Definitely," he said.

"Luis, Egypt, and I will handle the baking and cooking. But I might need help packing too. We can all pitch in where needed." She sighed. "Hopefully, we'll be that busy."

Max had already added a plexiglass barrier at the to-go counter as well as a barricade to prevent patrons from entering the dining section.

"One more thing. We'll be donating food to the local hospitals for the healthcare workers. That will be one of your runs each day, Loukas."

He nodded somberly.

"We'll be closed for the next couple of days. I can't do anything until I have my supply of masks, gloves, and containers. Thanks, everyone. I appreciate your support."

Krystina hugged her sister. "Do you need me to stay?"

"No, go home. We'll be working hard from here on in."

The March temperature chilled Krystina to the bone, the wind making it even more unbearable. She and Loukas couldn't run to her car fast enough. She turned the engine, waiting for the car to warm, looking out at the street beyond. Across the way was the dock. The sky above looked ominous, the clouds a gunmetal gray; it was hard to distinguish where they ended and the water began. An uncontrollable disturbance was brewing, in more ways than one, Krystina feared.

A shiver ran up and down her spine.

"What is it?" Loukas asked.

"Look at it out there? What do you see?"

He shrugged. "Nothing."

"Exactly." Her eyes grew wide. "Are we in an apocalyptic zombie nightmare? There isn't a soul out there. Did the walking dead ravage this town and now there's only a few of us left?"

Loukas chuckled. "You've been watching too much TV."

"I'm serious! What if this lasts longer than two weeks? What is our life going to look like? No more social life! When and how will we see our friends? What about prom, graduation, and senior cut-out day?!" The pitch of her voice rose with each question.

"I think we're on senior cut-out day every day now," he said with a laugh. His expression turned serious. "Listen, if they close everything up then there must be a good reason. This is no joke. People are dying," he added quietly. "I think prom is the least of our problems."

Krystina placed her arm on his bicep. "I'm so sorry. That was insensitive of me," she admitted. She knew he must be thinking of his mother and how so many others might lose their loved ones as well. And in that moment, she didn't feel quite so isolated.

Chapter 23

Loukas

4 years earlier
Age fourteen

Manny and Markella Mitsakis lived two doors down from the Andarakis family and often shared Sunday meals and holidays with George, Melina, and the family. The severed friendship between their children, Krystina and Loukas, hadn't gone unnoticed but the situation was dismissed by the adults as nothing more than a silly spat. It took a solid friendship to not let the children's squabbles affect the adult's relationships. And they all agreed not to interfere, for they believed Loukas and Krystina's little feud would eventually work its way out.

Loukas had tried numerous ways to make amends but the stubborn girl refused to give an inch. He had tried apologizing, offering her daisies, which were her favorite flowers, and had even sending apology notes through the crack of her slammed door. Eventually, he gave up and instead clung to her older brother, Theo, who he'd always looked up to.

"Loukas, would you tell Krystina to come down for dinner?" Melina asked.

"Sure," he said slowly, unsure he should be the one to summon her. There was little chance she'd listen.

He reluctantly climbed the stairs and rapped on her unwelcoming locked door. "Krys ..." He didn't dare call her Minnie. She'd surely not respond. Or maybe she'd open the door and punch him square in the face. No, goading her wasn't the right move. "Your mom wants you to come down for dinner."

He waited for a few beats, and when he heard no reply, he called out, "Are you in there? Did you hear me?"

"I heard you!" she replied snippily. "You didn't ask me a question so I didn't feel the need to answer."

Loukas was at a loss. To everyone else, she was friendly and kind. But to him, Krystina was a nasty little bitch. Maybe, on some small level, he deserved it, but was there ever going to be a time when she would just let it go? How many times did he have to say he was sorry?

"It's a good thing you're not like this all the time or you'd have no friends," he shouted.

The door swung open. "My friends don't throw me under the bus to impress their other friends," she countered with a furious glare.

"Get over it. I was twelve. That was two years ago," he defended. Turning, he waved her off in frustration. "I'm done apologizing."

"And your stunt last year by the pool? I haven't forgotten about that."

"I had to get you alone to work things out." He banged his hand against the doorframe. "It's not my fault Tommy had to open his big mouth."

"There wouldn't have been anything for him to say if it wasn't for you." She waved him away, annoyed. "We've been over this a hundred times. Go downstairs and leave me alone."

Loukas pushed his food around as the adults chatted on and on about subjects that didn't interest him. All he could think about was how

Krystina constantly threw the past in his face.

"What do you think, Loukas?" his mother asked, snapping him out of his own thoughts.

"About what?"

"About all of us taking a vacation together before school begins," Markella repeated. Turning to his father, she smiled affectionately.

"If the boy doesn't want to go, we'll just take a second honeymoon," Manny said, kissing his wife on the cheek.

"Don't cut us out!" Melina said, laughing. "Just because the kids aren't interested."

"I didn't say I wasn't interested. Can we go to Disney World?" Loukas asked, smirking. "I've always wanted to visit Minnie Mouse's house." Sliding his focus to Krystina, he searched for her reaction, hoping to annoy her. After all, she asked for it. He was satisfied when her brow knotted in irritation.

"No Disney World," George said.

"That's too bad," Krystina said to her father. "I was looking forward to watching Loukas cry on the kiddie rides." She smiled mockingly in Loukas' direction.

"Well, I hate to cut this short, but I have work tomorrow and laundry to catch up on," his mother announced. "We can talk about this tomorrow, Melina, and make some plans. I'd love to get away for a few days."

Standing, Manny offered his hand to his wife as she rose from her seat. "Whatever makes my wife happy. You ladies make the plans," he said.

Double-cheek kisses were offered all around. Loukas was aware of how much his parents loved Krystina. Of course, they loved all the Andarakis children, but Markella had a soft spot for Krystina. Maybe because she was the youngest and the closest to her son's age. And of course, Krystina's middle name was Markella, an honor given by Krystina's mother, her closest friend.

An hour later, Loukas was in his bedroom, engrossed in *Grand Theft Auto*, frenetically mashing the controller's buttons as though his life depended on it. The volume from the soundbar connected to the flat-screen TV drowned out all external noise.

So when his mother took a tumble down the stairs and screamed for help, Loukas didn't hear her. Nor did he hear the panic in his father's voice as he yelled for him. Instead, what Loukas heard, or rather felt, was the vibration coming from his pocket. Before he could say hello, his father's voice came frantically from the other end.

"Get down here! Your mother is hurt," Manny lashed out in alarm.

Loukas threw aside the controller and was on his feet in a second.

His mother was lying at the bottom of the stairs, laundry strewn about. She seemed to be shaken up more than anything.

"Where does it hurt, Mom?"

Speaking in a breathy, clipped manner, she answered, "I tried to break my fall with my arm. My wrist hurts most of all. And ... my head. I think I banged it against the wall."

"Let's help her up, and I'll drive her to the ER," Manny said.

"I'm coming with you," Loukas insisted.

"No, stay here. I'll call you when we know something. Unfortunately, they only allow one person into the ER with the patient at a time."

Loukas wanted to argue but his father cut him off.

"Go tell George and Melina what's going on."

"Okay," Loukas relented. "And I'll clean up all of this," he added, referring to the garments scattered at the bottom of the stairs.

They helped her into the car but not without difficulty. Markella's injuries were more significant than she originally thought. Her ankle was swelling, and she couldn't put any pressure on it. Bruises were beginning to bloom on her arm, thigh, and by her temple, where a large bump had risen. The pain in her wrist was so severe, she felt as though she would vomit at any given moment.

Once his parents had driven away, Loukas sprinted down the

street to the Andarakis' home. Frantically knocking twice on the side door leading to the kitchen, he let himself in. He found *Yiayiá* alone in the kitchen, pouring herself a cup of tea and preparing a slice of *portokalopita*, a syrupy orange cake. She took one look at Loukas' sheet-white face and shuffled over to him.

"*Pethí mou*? My child, what's wrong?"

"Dad just took Mom to the hospital. She fell down the stairs."

"*Panayía mou*! Melina!" She called out to her daughter.

"*Ti! Ti!*" Melina said, running into the kitchen, George following closely behind.

"It's Markella. She fell down the steps."

"Oh my God!" Krystina exclaimed, catching up with the events as she hurried down from her bedroom.

Melina grabbed Loukas by the hand. "Let's go."

"They're already on their way to the hospital," he said, stopping her. "Dad asked me to let you know. She fell while taking down the laundry. I didn't even hear when it happened. I had the volume on my game up so loud," he said on a strangled sob. "If I had taken the basket down for her this wouldn't have happened."

"This is not your fault," Melina affirmed. "Come, I'll help you pick up the clothes while we wait to hear from your father."

"I'll come too," Krystina said stepping in by Loukas' side. "She's going to be fine," she tried to assure him.

"I don't know." Loukas met her gaze with fear in his eyes. "I hope so. You should have seen what she looked like. I think I'm going to be sick."

"Sit down and take a deep breath," Melina ordered. "Krystina, get Loukas a cold glass of water."

"Your mother is a strong woman." *Yiayiá* took him into her embrace.

It was well after midnight before Loukas' parents returned home. Markella's wrist was fractured and had been placed in a cast.

Fortunately, her ankle wasn't broken and had only suffered a severe strain. And other than a headache from the bump to her head, the rest of her bruises were minor.

"Thank you for staying," Loukas said to Melina and Krystina gratefully.

They had not only picked up the laundry but had washed, dried, and folded it as well. Any dishes left in the sink were placed in the dishwasher, and Krystina made sure the rest of the house was tidied up before Markella arrived home.

"You call us if there's anything you need." Melina hugged Loukas affectionately before she and Krystina departed.

The next morning, Melina came to check on her friend. Loukas was biting into a warmed Pop-Tart and grabbing his backpack as she entered the kitchen.

"How is she this morning?" Melina asked.

Loukas shrugged, shaking his head. "Not sure. She's a little off-balance, but I don't know if that's because of the painkillers or the headache she's complaining about."

"I'll keep an eye on her while you're at school."

"My dad took the day off from work. He's worried." As much as he tried to conceal his own concerning thoughts, the trepidation in his eyes gave him away.

Melina cupped his cheek. "You know he dotes on her more than he needs to. Go to school, *agori mou*. She'll be fine."

But Melina was wrong. During sixth-period math, the school secretary's voice came over the loudspeaker asking Loukas Mitsakis to head to the front office.

Alarmed, Krystina's troubled eyes met his. She immediately jumped from her seat to leave the class.

"Miss Andarakis? Where do you think you're going?" Ms. Anderson asked sternly.

"I have to go with him. It might be his mom," she rattled off before rushing out.

Wordlessly, they sprinted to the front office. The secretary met him at the door, her expression sympathetic.

"Your mother was taken to the hospital," she said.

"But she was fine this morning." His words were strangled as his throat constricted. It wasn't a surprise that his mother was still in pain with all the bruises she had endured and the break on her wrist. But the hospital had checked her out thoroughly, he was told. So what had changed? For the second time in less than a day, Loukas felt like he was going to vomit from fear.

"Is she at Mather or St. Charles?" Krystina asked, taking control.

"Stony Brook."

"I'll call my mom to take us," Krystina offered, snatching her phone from her back pocket. She made Loukas sit down, patting gentle circles on his back to calm him until her mother arrived.

According to Manny, Markella had grown more confused, disoriented, and dizzy as the day progressed. Her words slurred, and he feared his wife had suffered a stroke. By the time the ambulance arrived, she had slipped into unconsciousness.

Melina immediately took Loukas to the hospital. When they saw Manny waiting outside his wife's room, they rushed to him. Getting any information from his father was a near-impossible task. The man was inconsolable; he could barely form words between his sobs. In a few short hours, he looked as though he'd aged ten years.

Loukas looked through the glass window into his mother's room. A nurse was checking her, and they had to wait before they could go inside. She was hooked up to so many machines. Too many for his comfort. Fear crept through his being like an unsettled ghost possessing his body. A chill ran up his spine, and he wished he could shake the dread from it. He understood the wires and IV drips connected to his mother's still body were the only things keeping her alive.

Even in her unconscious state, he sensed her love wrapping around him like a warm blanket on the coldest of days. "Mom," he whispered in a strangled sob, hugging himself before collapsing to the floor. All he wanted was for her to open her eyes and smile at him.

Later that evening, Markella passed away. She had suffered an epidural hematoma when she fell down the stairs. As a result, she was now brain-dead. Loukas didn't know if it was his mother's choice or God's, but she had been taken into his realm without forcing the family to decide whether or not to remove life support. Loukas could never have lived with himself if he had been forced to make that decision, and with complete certainty, he knew it would have destroyed his father.

* * *

Why was it that it always seemed to rain at funerals? In the movies, it was used for dramatic effect. Loukas would pull a face each time the camera panned over a funeral scene blurred by a torrential downpour. Especially when it was a cheesy love story. Now, here he stood, at his mother's gravesite, his drenched shoes sinking into the muddy earth. Rain poured around his umbrella like a waterfall. Through the haze, he watched his broken father, barely able to stand on his own, supported by George and Melina.

Up ahead, the priest, dressed in his black garment and gold-threaded stole, censed the casket, reciting prayers in Greek. Smoke mingled with the rain, its scent uniquely identifiable to the Greek Orthodox Church.

The moment the mourners began to sing the memorial hymn, Loukas lost it. The umbrella fell from his grasp, blowing away with the wind. Covering his face with his hands, he bent over, sobs wracking his body.

Krystina, who was standing several steps behind him with her sisters and brother, ran to his side. Taking his hand, she intertwined her fingers with his. Little did she know, or maybe she did, that it was precisely what he needed at that very moment. Feud or not, Loukas loved her. She was his best friend. Krystina was the first person he thought of when he awoke in the morning and the girl he dreamed of at night. His lifeline. His everything. And although he'd never accept their bond was severed for good, Loukas understood it was damaged and frayed by his own mistakes.

Loukas wrapped himself around her, bending down to cry into the comfort of her sweet-smelling neck. A torrent of rain soaked their clothing, hair, and faces. Krystina didn't seem to care. "We'll get through this together," she whispered. "I'm right here," she added. "I'm not leaving your side," she vowed.

Krystina held tight to those words. She stayed with Loukas through the *makarea*, the memorial luncheon, held at George's restaurant. And later, her hand was firmly clasped in his while the family went back to Loukas' home, now empty and cold without the woman who had filled it with such laughter, love, and food.

When it was time to leave, Loukas begged her to stay, so she did, foregoing sleep to binge-watch *Game of Thrones* with him.

Loukas had lost his beloved mother, but he had his Krystina back, if only for a short while. And it was short-lived. It only took one of Loukas' wisecrack friends to remind her of what he'd done. One step forward and ten steps back. Little did he know that his existence as he knew it was about to change even more than he ever thought possible.

Chapter 24

Krystina

Present day

By the middle of April, the situation had grown grim. New York had been deemed the epicenter of the COVID pandemic. Hospitals were at capacity, and the number of positive cases was through the roof. But what was more frightening, were the daily announcements marking the deaths caused by this mysterious virus.

It was now official. Schools would remain remote for the remainder of the year. No prom, no graduation. Birthdays became quick drive-by celebrations, and churches closed for services, even for the major holidays. Krystina only saw her immediate family, Loukas, and his father, for whom she was concerned.

Since the lockdown started, Manny had to attend his AA meetings online, and she was worried he wouldn't follow through. Her mother was the only one she had confided to about driving him to those meetings. Now she had to tell Loukas so he could ensure Manny logged on and continued with the program.

She found Loukas where she'd expected. In Theo's room, engrossed in a video game.

She entered the room and sat down beside him in the unoccupied beanbag chair. "Loukas, can you pause the game for a minute. I have something I need to discuss with you."

"Is something wrong?" he asked, concerned.

"No, not really." She didn't know where to start or how Loukas would take it. He'd all but distanced himself from his father, and she worried he'd be indifferent regarding his care. "A few months ago, I talked your dad into committing to AA meetings. As you're well aware, his license is suspended, so I've been driving him there each week."

"Why didn't you tell me? I could have taken him myself."

"I don't know. He was embarrassed … and I thought it was best to keep it under the radar for a few reasons. I pretty much gave him an ultimatum, so I felt it was my responsibility." Krystina didn't elaborate further.

"You did that for him? Why?" Loukas asked, surprised.

"He's family," she simply stated. "He couldn't go on that way. He needed help. And I was happy to do it."

There was no way she'd admit she did it just as much for Loukas as for his father. Krystina had barely confessed it to herself. Plus, as much as she always loved Manny, if he laid one more finger on Loukas, she would have beaten the ever-loving crap out of him herself.

"The meetings are remote now, and I'm worried your father won't follow through," she said on a sigh. "That's why I'm telling you now. I'll need you to make sure he logs on once a week and attends the meetings. I'll write down the details for you as to when they meet."

"I can do that," Loukas agreed quietly.

"Good." She paused. "This is a good thing," she added.

"I know." Loukas lowered his eyes. "Krystina. Thank you."

She nodded. The lump in her throat stifled her ability to speak. That went better than she had anticipated but she sensed some level of conflict in Loukas. Was he ashamed someone other than himself had tried to sort out his father's addiction? She hoped that wasn't the case. She had done what she had in good faith, not to lay blame on someone who already blamed himself far too much already.

"I have to go or I'll be late for my shift at the café," she said quietly. "You're not on today?"

"No but I'm working all day tomorrow."

Standing, she left Loukas to his thoughts.

Working at The Coffee Klatch kept Krystina sane. It was the only proof that humanity still existed in her little town. They were busier than ever with takeout orders. So much so that it was hard to keep up with the increasing demand.

Krystina was happy for Kally, who had feared she would lose her café when the lockdown was ordered. But if they kept up at this pace, she'd not only meet her sales goals, she'd surpass them. Unfortunately, that wasn't the case for so many other establishments, especially those in the city that depended heavily on the influx of lunchtime business.

Krystina pulled into her driveway after her shift. The blackened sky was illuminated by the full moon shining down on the frosted lawn. From the corner of her eye, shadows danced explosively through the air like a silhouette in a silent black and white film. Suddenly it registered that the movement beyond was Manny and Loukas fighting it out.

Krystina ran to intervene when she heard them shouting. "What are the two of you doing?"

"He thinks he's walking into town," Loukas snarled, holding a tight grip on his father.

"You won't give me my keys," Manny slurred as he stamped out a cigarette. "So I'll walk," he argued, pushing himself from his son's confinement.

"Hey!" Krystina shouted, her hands planted on her hips. "Have you been drinking?"

"Just a little," Manny said, closing one eye and pinching his thumb and forefinger together.

"That wasn't part of the deal. No drinking." Krystina schooled her features into a stern glare.

But it was more than that. Frustrated and deeply concerned was how she actually felt. Now that Manny was out of work due to the COVID lockdown, what did he have to do all day but dwell on what made him start drinking in the first place? She had to tell her parents. Drastic measures might need to be taken.

"A little something to take the edge off," Manny said pathetically.

He was such a broken man. Unfortunately, Krystina had failed to help him or save Loukas from the man's abuse.

"I've got this," Loukas said quietly. "Go home."

She looked at him with uncertainty, her feet planted in one spot, reluctant to leave Loukas to contend with his father alone.

"Go," he said assuredly.

"No!" she insisted, making her decision. "I'll help you get him inside."

She secured Manny by the arm, Loukas supporting him on his other side. But Manny was more inebriated than they thought, and he jerked to remove himself from their grasp like an entrapped feral animal.

Krystina yelped when his arm cracked against her jaw.

"You worthless piece of shit!" Loukas shouted, grabbing his father by the collar of his shirt and yanking him away from her. "Touch her again, and I'll kill you myself."

"I didn't mean it," Manny sobbed, crumbling to the ground.

"Are you okay?" Loukas asked, turning to Krystina. "Let me take a look."

"I'm fine," she said, rubbing at the side of her face. "I was more startled than hurt."

"Please go like I asked. I'll deal with him."

Krystina didn't move. Leaving him alone with his father was not a good idea. The man became violent when he drank too much, and Loukas was his punching bag. She stared at him, pleading silently.

"I've got this," Loukas assured her.

And then she remembered Leo had trained him. This was what it was for. To protect himself and subdue his father when necessary.

"Okay. But I'm going to tell my parents what's going on, so if you need them, just call."

Melina groaned. "My poor, dear friend. He's unrecognizable from the man he used to be," she told Krystina after hearing what had happened. "I'm working from home from now on, so I'll check in on him throughout the day tomorrow."

Krystina's father remained silent until she finished recounting the altercation. "I understand you've been taking him to AA meetings," George said. "Your mother told me," he confessed. "You're a good girl, Krystina *mou*."

Before she could reply, her phone signaled an incoming call.

"It's my dad," Loukas said frantically when she answered.

Krystina hit the speaker button so her parents could hear what Loukas was saying. "What's wrong? Is he still attempting to leave the house?"

"No. He's coughing up blood," Loukas said in a panic.

"How much?" Melina asked.

"I don't know, but it looks like a lot. He's in the bathroom, and I can still hear him coughing. Should I call an ambulance?" he asked in a rush.

"We'll be right over," George said. He ran out the front door, not even bothering to change out of his slippers. Krystina and Melina hurried along close behind.

"He's always coughing. It's those damn cigarettes," Melina complained, panting as they ran up the block. "I keep telling him to stop."

When they got to the house, George headed straight for the bathroom. "Call an ambulance," he shouted when he saw how much blood was in the sink and splattered on the floor.

"We're getting you help, my friend," George promised, trying to stay composed. But Manny seemed disoriented and didn't answer. He remained leaning over the sink, bracing himself on the counter to combat his lightheadedness.

Krystina pulled her cellphone from her back pocket, punched in the emergency number, and gave the dispatcher all the necessary information. When she hung up, she found Loukas by the bathroom door, sheet-white and frozen in place.

"Oh my God!" she exclaimed. Blood was everywhere. On the rim of the toilet, the sink, and the floor. "The ambulance is on its way," she told Loukas, her heart pounding. "Come away from the door." Gently, she took his arm, leading him over to the couch. "My dad will take care of him until they get here." She was fearful Loukas would pass out from the shock of it all.

A shiver raced through her, a cold chill taking residence in her body. The nervous shaking was uncontrollable, and the chattering of her jaw made it impossible to string another sentence together.

Melina came up behind her, embracing Krystina and Loukas while offering up prayers for Manny.

"George, have Manny sit in a chair by the kitchen sink, and I'll clean this up," Melina requested.

"No, leave it," Loukas said, walking back over to the bathroom. "The EMTs should see how much blood there is," he explained in a shaky voice.

Melina nodded. "You're right. Go stand by the front door and wait for the ambulance." Melina nudged him in the right direction. "And breathe. There are many reasons for this. Not all of them are as serious as it looks."

Within ten minutes, the ambulance had arrived. Manny's blood pressure was dangerously low, but although he was still coughing into a handkerchief, little blood stained it.

"I'm coming with him," Loukas said when they strapped his father to the gurney.

"I'm afraid that's not possible," one of the uniformed professionals said regretfully. "New rules due to COVID. Patients only in the hospital."

"What about visiting hours?" Krystina asked.

"All suspended. No one goes in or out except patients and hospital personnel."

Manny reached for his son's hand. "It will be alright. You can call me."

"Where is his phone?" Krystina asked. Spotting it on the coffee table, she snatched it up and handed it to him. "Don't lose this. It's the only way we'll be able to get in touch with you."

Once his father was out of his sight, Loukas crumbled onto the sofa, his head in his hands.

"At least he's conscious," Melina comforted him. "The doctors will know what to do."

"Can you tell us what he was doing when this all happened?" George asked.

Loukas laughed humorlessly. "We were arguing. What else is new?"

"About the drinking?" Krystina asked.

"Yes. I told him everyone was going out of their way to help him and that he was an ungrateful bastard because he broke the faith and trust his friends had in him."

"Alcoholism is an illness," Melina said sympathetically. "He can't control it." She slid onto the couch beside him, stroking his hair. "He was a good father and husband. Try to remember that. He hasn't been able to cope with your mother's death."

"I lost her too," Loukas cried angrily. "But when I said that to him, he took a swing at me."

It wasn't until she touched his cheek that Krystina noticed the bruise blooming under his eye. It wasn't the first time Manny had struck Loukas. She had hoped that by attending AA and dealing with his grief it would never happen again.

"You're coming home with us tonight," Melina insisted. "Tomorrow, I'll go to church, light a candle, and pray for your father."

"You can pray," he spat bitterly. "I need to punch something."

Chapter 25

Loukas

It was days like today that Loukas was thankful he had a key to Leo's gym. Channeling his rage on a punching bag helped to burn the resentment and anger out of him, if only temporarily. The solitude was what he needed. There was no one to ask him questions. No one to push his emotional boundaries. Yet as he looked at the empty boxing ring elevated in the middle of the industrial-styled space, he longed for the chance to fight. To take his aggression out on another human being.

But if hurting someone was the goal, Leo, an ex-military man, would have reprimanded him and probably made him practice meditative Tai Chi exercises until he got his head screwed on straight.

Each punch relieved the frustration, and he kept them coming, pummeling the bag in a manic rage. His entire existence changed after his mother died, and now, the whole world was in a state of chaos and uncertainty. Loukas felt trapped by his circumstances, further subjugated by an invisible germ running havoc on the population. Fear clawed at his sense of survival. Who would he lose next? What would life look like a year from now?

Loukas finally sauntered back into the Andarakis home about the same time the rest of the family was beginning their day.

Yiayiá was standing at the stove, pouring a cup of freshly brewed coffee from an ancient percolator.

Sitting at the kitchen table, Melina looked up from her laptop in relief. "I was worried about you when I didn't find you in Theo's room this morning."

It had been a long time since anyone cared enough to keep a close watch on him, and Loukas felt tears prick at the back of his eyes. He turned away. "I went to the gym," he muttered awkwardly.

"I called the hospital but there's been no word yet," Melina said. "They'll run some tests today."

"Here," *Yiayiá* offered, handing him a cup of coffee. "Can I make you breakfast?"

"No, it's okay. Thanks, but I have to go to 'school.' Loukas air quoted, twisting his lips in annoyance. "What a waste of time."

"Knowledge is never a waste of time, *pethi mou*. Be grateful you have this option. Others are not so fortunate."

Loukas didn't argue. Instead, he headed up the stairs. Last night he wasn't in the mood to see a soul. Now he hated the thought of being alone and isolated from his peers. He grabbed his laptop and walked down the hall to Krystina's room.

"It's me. Loukas," he said, rapping two knuckles against the door. "Can I come in?" He didn't wait for her to answer. "Hi. Can I stay in here and do class with you?"

Krystina stared at him, waiting for a beat before answering. She must have seen the darkness pooling in his blue eyes like a raging storm.

"Sure." She slid over to one side of her desk, making room for him.

Her workspace seating was a plush, upholstered bench that ran the length of the desk. There was more than enough room for both of them to sit, albeit the close proximity allowed for him to feel the heat emanating from her body. Or was that his temperature rising?

Krystina was clad in sweatpants and a matching top cropped just above the belly. Comfort clothing seemed to be the garments of choice these days. No more tight jeans or mini-skirts. But Krystina would make his heart race even if she'd been wearing a nun's habit.

"How's your eye?" Krystina asked, turning to Loukas.

What was he to say? "Compared to the rest of the shit going on, it's not bad." He shrugged, trying to make light of it.

She reached up and touched the swollen area. "I'll get you an ice pack."

Covering his hand over hers, Loukas kept her in place. "I don't need one. Being next to you, knowing you don't hate me, is enough."

Krystina sighed wearily, her hazel eyes unsure. "I don't hate you. I never have."

"The opposite of hate is love," he said, looking deeply into her eyes. "Do you love me then?" he asked softly.

"I wouldn't go that far," she said unconvincingly, mesmerized by the pull of his gaze.

"How far would you go?" Loukas asked, hoping the moment would present itself to kiss her. But by the glint in her eye and the slight curve of her mouth, regrettably, her mood had changed.

"Cheesy," she laughed, playfully slapping him on the arm.

And just like that, another opportunity was shot to hell.

＊ ＊ ＊

Later that afternoon, Melina knocked on the door. "Am I interrupting school?" she asked.

"No," Krystina said. "We're doing homework now."

Melina took Loukas by the hand. "Come sit with me for a minute," she said, directing him to the edge of Krystina's bed. "I spoke to the doctors a little while ago. The results of your father's tests came through."

By the expression on Melina's face, Loukas suspected the news was bad. "Is he going to be okay?" His throat had suddenly gone dry and his heartrate sped up as he braced himself for his father's diagnosis.

"There are treatments, and the doctors will put him on a scheduled routine as soon as possible."

"Treatment for what?" Loukas asked nervously.

"I'm afraid your father has lung cancer."

Krystina gasped at the news. Her eyes flew to Loukas, waiting for his reaction.

Loukas felt as though the floor had collapsed beneath him. He resented Manny for what he'd become. For a relationship gone to hell. But he was still his father, even if he was no longer a man he recognized. Once he had been a man Loukas looked up to, respected, loved. He already felt as though he had lost his dad, but despite everything, there was always a glimmer of hope that things could get better. Now Loukas was in peril of losing another parent.

"They can cure him, though, right?" he asked desperately.

"Many patients have survived cancer. But he also has a case of pneumonia and is running a fairly high fever. So they have to address that first," Melina explained.

Krystina rose from her seat and joined Loukas and her mother on the bed. She wrapped her arms around him, and he held onto her tightly, sobbing into the crook of her neck. No one said a word as Loukas absorbed the gravity of the situation. Krystina tenderly rubbed her hand up and down his back in comfort. "It will be alright," she cooed, resting her head against his. "It has to be."

Forgiveness isn't approving what happened. It's choosing to rise above it.
Robin Sharma

Chapter 26

Krystina

April was sliding into May, a time of the year when the world around Krystina usually became brighter. The days grew longer and the weather warmer. But this year, the season hadn't sprung forth with a sense of renewal. Instead, it was nearly as bleak as the grayest days of winter.

This Easter was the most depressing of her life. The churches were closed. During Holy Week, large gatherings of worship and the partaking of ancient rituals were forbidden unless you watched it via livestream. The midnight resurrection service, traditionally performed outside the church, garnering record attendance, was anticlimactic viewed on her computer. It was saddening to see rows of empty pews. As she listened to the priest performing liturgy to an empty church, his words echoing off the silent walls, she had to remind herself that these measures were being taken in an effort to preserve the public's health and safety. Still, no matter how practical the rules were, Easter was usually Krystina's favorite holiday of the year, and not only couldn't she attend with the masses, but her entire extended family was separated as well.

Yiayiá and Melina cooked all the usual favorites for the

fast-breaking meal—traditional *Mayritsa* soup, *pastitsio*, stuffed *dolmathes* with *avgolemono*, and a leg of lamb—in an attempt to make the holiday festive.

Krystina had to admit that it was fun driving to her aunts' and cousins' homes to drop off the food and, in turn, bring home their offerings.

But when evening had arrived and she found herself watching the service on television while Zooming with her relatives, her jubilance fell flat. It served as a poor substitute for the celebration she was used to. Under the circumstances, though, it was the best they could do. So they ate, drank, and laughed, pretending they were all together, as always. And at least they felt blessed they were all healthy and able to celebrate even this compromised version of their holiday.

Loukas' father still remained in the hospital. Unfortunately, the cancer was advanced, and now his immune system was weakened further by his bout of pneumonia. With COVID cases escalating every day, the hospitals were overloaded. Though infected patients were isolated, this insidious evil invader spread like a fog blanketing a forest on a dreary autumn morning. Sadly, Manny was now its latest victim. After already spending two weeks in the hospital battling cancer and pneumonia, now he had to fight COVID too. It had all taken a heavy toll on his system, and, as a last resort, the doctors had no choice but to place him on a ventilator.

"Forgive him," Krystina heard her grandmother say to Loukas.

Krystina had crept inside from the back door of the house through the garage. Upon hearing Loukas' dismay, she remained in the shadows, eavesdropping on what ranged from deep lament to inexorable bitterness.

"I'm scared," he admitted. "Scared it's too late to repair our relationship. Scared of what might happen if he dies. It will hurt so much more to leave things on good terms only to lose him." Loukas lifted

145

the collar of his shirt over his face to wipe away his tears. "I can't go through this again."

Tears welled in Krystina's own eyes as she listened in.

"No!" *Yiayiá* declared adamantly. "If you don't forgive him, your grief will be so much worse. It will eat you from the inside out," she added.

Krystina found herself nodding in agreement, though no one could see her.

"Now get your labtop or your phone and FaceTalk with your father," she ordered gently, kissing his cheek.

Krystina stifled her chuckle. Her grandmother had a funny way of mixing up words and phrases.

"Laptop," Loukas corrected, smiling sadly.

Krystina crept inconspicuously into the kitchen.

"And it's not ..." He shook his head. "Never mind."

"No never mind," *Yiayiá* insisted. "You forgive but that doesn't mean you forget. Do this for yourself."

"Hi." Krystina walked into the kitchen gingerly. "She's right, you know. Do it for the father he once was. Tragedy has a way of changing people. Be stronger than he was, for both your sakes."

He kept his gaze trained on hers. With an imperceptible nod, Loukas agreed, but Krystina could see the tumult of emotions running through him. Turning, she knew he wiped away a tear he was too embarrassed for her to see.

"Okay. Let's do this," he said resolutely, squaring his shoulders. Then, exhaling, he shook out his nerves.

Krystina made several attempts at calling the hospital. Each time reception told them Manny was not awake. Finally, his attending nurse brought an iPad bedside, and Loukas could finally see his father.

"Dad! Dad?" Loukas said louder than he usually spoke. "Can you hear me?"

"Hear you. See you," Manny labored.

The nurse intervened. "His voice will sound different because of the ventilator. Also, when the machine cycles, he won't have the air to speak. Bear with him."

Krystina held Loukas' hand for support. Seeing Manny in this condition was upsetting for her, but for Loukas, it was far worse. She felt his hand clenching hers and noticed the tensing of his jaw. He was hanging on by a thread.

"I'm sorry, Dad." Loukas choked on his words. "I'll be here for you when you get out of the hospital."

Manny shifted his head from side to side, the exertion evident.

"No, no," he forced. "I'm sorry. Your mom … you … everything to me. Love you."

A sob broke free from Loukas' chest.

It would have been easier to harbor hate, Krystina thought. Now he'll mourn for what could have been and what might never be.

His father fell silent, his eyes closing.

"He fell asleep," the nurse interrupted.

Loukas wasn't in a state to respond.

"Thank you," Krystina said. "Hopefully we can speak to him again in a day or two?"

"We'll see what we can do," she answered kindly.

But that was never to be. Manny had spoken his last words to his son, and later that evening, he took his last breath. He'd drifted into the next world, no doubt guided by his beloved Markella, joining her in a peaceful existence.

Melina's dolmathes stuffed with meat & rice

Ingredients

1 jar grape leaves, rinsed and drained

1 pound ground beef or lamb

1½ cups rice, uncooked

1 large onion, grated

2 tablespoons fresh mint, chopped

2 tablespoons fresh dill, chopped

2 tablespoons fresh parsley, chopped

1 tablespoon salt

1 teaspoon pepper

2 tablespoons olive oil

1 quart chicken broth

Avgolemono Sauce

2 lemons, juiced

2 eggs, scrambled

Method

Thoroughly rinse and drain the grape leaves. Set aside. Prepare a large pot or Dutch oven by placing several grape leaves on the bottom to form a layer. In a large bowl, combine all the ingredients except for the chicken broth. Starting with a single grape leaf, place a tablespoon of the mixture at one end of a leaf, leaving a little at the top edge of the grape leaf to fold over the meat mixture. Fold in the sides and roll. (The method is similar to folding an eggroll.) Place each stuffed grape leaf seam-side down in the pot. Continue in a single layer, and when there is no more room, build another layer. Once all the dolmathes are in the pot, pour the chicken broth over them until they are covered by the liquid. Cover the dolmathes with a flat plate that's just the right size to fit in the pot. This will help to keep them intact while they cook. Put a lid on the pot and bring to a boil. Then lower to a simmer and cook for approximately 50-60 minutes.

To prepare the avgolemono sauce, place the two eggs in a blender for a minute or so until they become frothy. Add the lemon juice and blend for another minute. Slowly add some of the liquid from the pot to temper the egg/lemon mixture. Turn off the heat on the dolmathes and add the frothy egg mixture to the pan. Place the lid back on the pot and let it sit for five minutes before serving.

Chapter 27

Krystina

Krystina helped Loukas drag the sidewalk tables into the café entranceway. Then she locked the door behind her.

"I'm glad it's closing time," Krystina said. "It's such a beautiful evening. Maybe I'll ask Kally if I can take Emma for a walk on the beach."

"That little pup is so tiny, she'll sink in the sand," Loukas said with a chuckle. "You could take me instead."

But before she could banter back, her phone beeped, indicating a text message had just come through. Naturally that was not unusual. Texts for Krystina came in all day. But this time, every phone in the room signaled an incoming message at the exact same moment.

"That was odd," Kally said, pulling her phone from her apron pocket. "It's from Mia!" she exclaimed.

The list of people attached to the text was surprising. Aunts, uncles, cousins, and close friends were all included.

"What is that girl up to?" Egypt asked.

As Krystina scrolled through the detailed message, she found it curiously mysterious, like some kind of strange covert mission.

On Sunday, May 17th, at twelve-thirty p.m., Mia had instructed them to gather at her parents' home and connect the Smart TV to

FaceTime. In a separate text, she informed them there would be more details to follow.

Krystina calculated that in Mykonos, that time would be about 7:30 p.m. Just about sunset on the island, she figured, wishing she could see it for herself. Now she was insane with curiosity. What was Mia planning? But she hadn't offered even a hint of what she was up to.

She was dying to know when she and Nicholas could finally come home, or if they weren't planning to, whether she could visit them over the summer? But she always got the same old answer from Mia every time, reminding her that travel into Greece was closed, especially to Americans.

With that, she digressed, barraging Mia with text messages instead, prodding her for more information about her big secret. No one else pressed Mia for answers but Krystina was relentless. She only hoped the plan lived up to the hype. She'd had enough doom and gloom to last a lifetime.

The morning of the highly anticipated day, Krystina and Kally received another text message from Mia with explicit instructions. No sooner than she finished reading it, the doorbell rang. When she opened the door, a young man pushed a clipboard toward her, asking her to sign for a delivery.

But before she could finish writing her name, a flurry of activity erupted as transportation personnel began to unload chairs, floral arrangements, and various equipment, carrying them through to the backyard.

"You better come here now!" Krystina exclaimed, frantically calling for Kally.

Turning, she ran into the house to find her parents, but before she could make it upstairs, the doorbell rang again. This time, an impeccably dressed woman with a broad smile stood on the front step balancing five dress boxes in her hands.

"Hello. Mia Andarakis ordered these to be sent over this morning.

Each box is labeled as to who they are for."

"Thank you," Krystina said in awe, speculating what on earth was happening. Maybe Mia was coming home and throwing a party to surprise everyone. But no, that didn't quite add up with her instructions to set up FaceTime on the TV.

"Mom!" she called out, confused. "You better get down here!"

The backyard was being transformed before her eyes. Technicians were hooking up a television on the patio. Chairs adorned with floral garlands were being set in rows facing the screen.

"What's going on?" Melina asked in confusion.

"Our backyard is being transformed into … I don't know what. Plus, these dresses were just delivered to us." Krystina opened the box labeled for her. A gasp of delight punctuated her adoration for the blush-colored satin gown contained within. Ruched at the waist, with a plunging neckline, the formfitting garment befitted Krystina's slim figure.

When she lifted the dress to hold it up against her body, an envelope fell to the floor. Swiping it up, Krystina opened it, her eyes growing wide as she read.

"You are cordially invited to witness the wedding of Mia Andarakis to Nicholas Aristedis at the Greek Orthodox Church of Agios Nikolakis in Mykonos on May 17th, 2020, at twelve-thirty p.m. eastern standard time." Krystina looked up at her mother, her mouth agape. "I can't believe she's doing this to us!"

"This must be a joke," Melina pronounced with irritation.

"Why?" *Yiayiá* asked as she came into the living room. "Why are you surprised? She never wanted all the fuss of a big wedding."

"But I wanted to plan it with her."

"You already did that with Kally." *Yiayiá* stroked her daughter's face affectionately. "But Mia wants something different. *Melinitsa mou*, it's her life."

Melina nodded, resigned, her expression revealing her disappointment.

"It's a happy day," *Yiayiá* added. "Be happy."

"*Yiayiá*, this is for you." Krystina handed her grandmother a dress box.

"For me?"

"Of course! Mia would never forget you."

Accepting the proffered box, *Yiayiá* kissed her granddaughter's cheek before excitedly scurrying to her bedroom with it clutched in her arms.

Krystina checked her phone when it signaled another incoming text from her sister. This one grouped her in with just Kally and Egypt, explaining there were bouquets for each of them. During the ceremony, they were to stand by the arc of peonies Krystina had watched the florist assembling over by the television the technicians had set up outside. Three rows of flowers formed the seven-foot arc in variegated shades of light pink. As she continued reading Mia's instructions, Krystina let out a whoop of joy. Mia had appointed her as maid of honor. And to think, she thought her sister was going to cheat her out of the experience with this unconventional wedding! It wasn't quite how she envisioned her titled responsibilities or her walk down the aisle ahead of the bride, but it sure was unique.

Relatives began to arrive one by one. As the guests found their seats, many complimented Krystina and Kally on how they had converted the yard into a floral wonderland.

"That was all Mia!" Krystina admitted. "She arranged every detail."

"I'm not surprised," her Aunt Thalia said. "She's my goddaughter. She gets her creative side from me."

Shaking his head, Uncle Markos rolled his eyes.

"I saw that!" Thalia said to her husband.

"Saw what, *vre*! I'm behind you."

"I have eyes in the back of my head," she snapped, glaring at him.

Krystina excused herself. If she had stayed a second longer, she would have burst out laughing. "It's almost time. Kally and I need to check ..." She had to think quickly before the giggles she was holding back burst out. "... the Wi-Fi," she lied, dragging Kally away from her aunt and uncle.

"What's wrong with you?" Kally reprimanded as Krystina pulled her behind a rose bush and exploded in a fit of delight.

"I'm giddy with excitement! And those two are ... those two ..." Krystina shrugged, gathering herself together. "Bickering must run in Mom's family."

"Really?" Kally stared at her incredulously. "Pot, meet kettle."

Krystina's mouth hung open. "Me?" she asked, offended.

"Think about it," her sister said, patting her shoulder before walking away.

Finally it was time. At exactly twelve-thirty, an image of the tiny church in Mykonos, proudly footed at the edge of the pier, appeared on the screen. It reminded Krystina of all the breathtaking postcards and travel advertisements she'd seen of the island. She dreamed of seeing it all in person one day. The stark, whitewashed structure with the vivid blue dome and Greek flag waving high above made for the most romantic setting.

Even if Mia had wanted guests to witness the ceremony, Krystina doubted any more than ten people could fit inside the tiny structure.

The door to the church opened and oohs and aahs of anticipation sang out. The camera's perspective mimicked the view of a guest entering the fourth-century sanctuary. Nicholas, handsome in a tuxedo, stood waiting at the ancient altar with a young, bearded priest dressed from head to toe in a black inner cassock. Over it, his white stole, running down the length of his garment, was intricately embellished with gold embroidered crosses.

Krystina furrowed her brow at the couple standing beside Nicholas. They were both strangers to her.

"*Kalispera*," Nicholas said, wishing the virtual guests a good evening.

"Or good afternoon for you. It's a beautiful evening here. Sunset is less than an hour away, and we hope to capture it for you. Thank you for supporting our decision to wed so far away from all of you."

"Did we have a choice?" Melina muttered.

Krystina stood under the arc by the large screen, yet she could still hear her mother's complaint from several feet away, and she swiftly shot her a reproving glare.

"It's been a trying few months for all of us, and after so much sadness, Mia and I realized that time waits for no one. We wanted to share our love and joy now. Not a year from now."

The camera panned to the entryway again as Mia came into view, floating down the short aisle. The guests oohed and aahed once more, admiring her elegant, one-shouldered gown that, at first glance, appeared white. But on closer inspection, they noticed it was the palest shade of shimmering rose with delicate organza flower petals sewn into the bodice, attached by seed pearls in the center of each bud. Mia was a vision of loveliness, beaming with joy as she approached Nicholas and smiled up at him.

Once the ceremony began, Krystina watched through misty eyes. She had to compliment the camera person for capturing every fine detail of the service rituals. They zoomed in on the couple's hands as the *koumbaro*, the male sponsor or best man, exchanged the rings on the couple's fingers three times. She had a much better view of what was happening than if she'd been standing on the altar with them. And the expressions on Nicholas' and Mia's faces while this important moment occurred were unforgettable. There was so much love and devotion in their countenance.

Krystina watched her mother pull a tissue out of her sleeve. Tears streamed down Melina's cheeks. All her dissatisfaction over not planning the wedding had been forgotten. Instead, her mother was genuinely struck by the treasured rituals of the ceremony as her middle child embarked on her next phase in life.

The female sponsor, the *koumbara*, stepped up behind the couple after the priest placed two silver wreaths covered in rhinestones and connected by a satin ribbon on their heads. Krystina sighed deeply in admiration and affection. The crowning was one of her favorite traditions in the wedding ceremony. Leave it up to Mia to find the most unique pair of *stefana*. Usually the wreaths were fashioned of silk flowers. Someday, fifty years from now, when she decided to settle down, Krystina would find a similar pair, she decided.

The *koumbara* exchanged the wreaths over the couple's heads three times, symbolizing the glory and honor bestowed on them by God during the sacrament.

Krystina imagined, had she been there, it would have been she performing this honor, and although she was glad the family was able to participate in some small way, she couldn't help feeling just a bit sad that her sister was doing this, thousands of miles away, without them.

It wasn't until the priest led Mia and Nicholas around a small table three times for the Dance of Isaiah that Krystina's tears welled with emotion.

Together, the *koumbari* followed behind, their fingers holding onto the satin ribbon connecting the wreaths in symbolism of uniting the couple as one in the eyes of God. Soon the ceremony was over, and although the couple couldn't hear their guests, they all still shouted out wishes for a long, happy life together. Krystina now had two married sisters, she realized, as she passed around the bundles of candied almonds her sister had sent over from Greece.

Turning when she heard Mia's voice, Krystina squealed with delight when her face came swimming into view on the screen.

"Hi, family!" Mia spoke excitedly to the camera. She and Nicholas were now standing outside the church in front of the white structure, under the bluest sky.

"We wish we could have flown all of you here to be with us, but unfortunately, it would have been impossible. Still, we can feel your happiness and love for us." Mia suddenly choked up and her next words came out in a croak. "I miss you all, and I can't wait to come home to hug every one of you. In the meantime, please enjoy the rest of this day and celebrate as if we were there with you. I love all of you!" She blew kisses to the crowd. "And I love my new husband!" Mia grabbed him, kissing him passionately as the camera came in for a closeup. The crowd clapped as Nicholas waved goodbye with a broad grin. Dipping his bride, he planted a long kiss on her before the camera cut out.

Soon caterers arrived with a buffet set up for appetizers and a cocktail hour. A magnum-sized champagne bottle popped, and glasses were filled. Then a server rolled out a three-tier wedding cake. Krystina just couldn't believe her sister had pulled all this off. From so far away, no less.

"Dance?" Loukas asked, holding out his hand.

Krystina's shoulders slumped a little. She was hungry and ready to devour every bite she could fit on her plate. But how could she refuse Loukas, much as she wanted to? He had been through so much lately. The least she could do was make an effort to be kind and tell her stomach to shut up for five more minutes.

"Sure, as long as you promise to do-si-do me over to the food when the song ends."

Loukas laughed. "I'm pretty sure the song playing is 'When a Man Loves a Woman' not 'Cotton Eye Joe,'" he teased.

"I'm aware," she deadpanned. "But if you want to dance, it better be right this second, because the only thing this woman and her appetite wants is a big pile of food."

"Woman, eh?" he whispered, wriggling his eyebrows as he took her into his arms.

"Ugh! You are a pain in my ass."

Chuckling, he pulled her in closer. "Nice wedding, considering the circumstances. Hopefully, by the time we get married, this virus will be long gone."

"Oh, don't worry. It will have because Hell will have frozen over too."

Outer beauty pleases the eye. Inner beauty captivates the heart.
Mandy Hale

Chapter 28

Krystina

July 4th, 2020

Independence Day held a whole new meaning this year. Just about everything had been taken away from Krystina over these past several months. There was no prom, senior trip, or in-person graduation. What a way to finish twelve years of school.

Still, with lockdowns lifting, friends and family were finally coming out from the shadows. And although gatherings were still restricted, her town was slowly coming back to life. Almost. There would be no parade this year. No crowds lining Main Street or waving flags. No bar crawls. But at least restaurants were now allowed to open for more than just takeout, as long as they could provide outdoor seating.

This improvement, Krystina loved, and she hoped it would last long after it was no longer necessary. Tents were erected in parking lots, string lights hanging from the frames, casting an almost romantic mood. Lanterns set on picnic tables added extra illumination at night, and tables for two lined the sidewalks.

The Coffee Klatch was busier than ever, and Kally offered Krystina's friend, Chynna, a waitstaff position. After a ten-hour shift, the girls plopped themselves down in a chair, exhaling exhausted breaths.

"Wearing this thing all day makes my throat sore," Krystina said, ripping off her mask.

"I don't mind wearing it. I prefer it, to be honest," Chynna said.

"Seriously?" Krystina asked, knitting her brow. "Why?"

"No one can see my imperfection," she explained quietly, lowering her eyes. "With the mask on, I'm just like everyone else. No one stares at me."

"Chynna," Krystina whispered sympathetically, leaning in to hug her friend. "When I look at you, I see my best friend. My beautiful best friend. I don't think you realize how pretty you are."

"You have to say that."

"No. I could say nothing at all. Look, I don't walk in your shoes, so I can't pretend to fully understand how you feel. But instead of looking at your birthmark as a flaw, think of it as something that makes you unique." Krystina pulled out her phone, searching for an article she had read in a magazine. "Look at these photos. I want you to scroll through each one."

Chynna took the phone from her friend. Scrolling, she shrugged her shoulders in confusion. "What's your point?"

"Each one of these people is a model."

Chynna's brows practically lifted to her hairline.

"That's right. They took what others might think of as a flaw and proudly proved the world wrong. This woman"—Krystina pointed to the screen—"doesn't have just one stain around her mouth. She has hyperpigmentation. Her entire face is covered in spots, making her skin tone uneven. But look at her fierce stance. Her confidence."

"How do I get that?"

"Confidence? You own it. You look in the mirror and zero in on your almond-shaped eyes, silky hair, and high cheekbones. And then you tell yourself you're worth more than you allow yourself to believe. You stop picking apart your features. Your beauty shines from within. I know because I've never met a kinder person."

Chynna's eyes glistened with emotion. "You're the best."

"I'm only telling the truth. Besides, I see how the boys ogle you when they come in."

Chynna rolled her eyes. "Now you're just making things up to make me feel better."

"No, I'm not. There's one guy in particular who keeps coming in," Krystina told her knowingly. "I have no idea who he is but I plan on finding out."

"You're too funny. I think your imagination has run wild," Chynna laughed.

"With a figure like yours, it's no surprise to me that you'd have many admirers."

"You really are an ego-lifter," Chynna said, hugging Krystina.

Krystina only hoped she had convinced her friend to look at herself in a more favorable light.

"You might want to think about a career as a motivational speaker," Chynna joked.

Krystina picked her goals off one by one on her fingers. "Blogger first, then mega-influencer, world traveler, and then maybe I'll think about your suggestion."

"Right now, I'd like you to exhibit your superstar mopping skills," Kally ordered. "Let's clean up and go home. It's been a long day."

The next morning, Krystina caught her parents and *Yiayiá* as they walked out the door.

"Where are you all going?" she asked.

"To the restaurant," her father replied. "Thanos, my chef, tested positive for COVID. So we need to go in and cook before opening."

"Oh, no! Is he going to be okay?"

"So far he's only lost his sense of taste and smell, but for a chef, that's not good. Not good at all."

"Tell him I'm thinking of him when you speak to him. And Dad, don't overwork my *yiayiá*."

"Ba!" The old woman waved her off. "I could run circles around all of you."

"I'm sure that's true." Krystina grinned, shaking her head. Her grandmother was like no one else on Earth.

After they left, she stepped onto her front porch to see what kind of day it was. Sunny and warm. No humidity, thank the heavens. The few clouds scattered in the sky were low and as white as enormous cotton balls.

Last year, at this time, she was out exploring shops and restaurants to feature on her blog. This year, with people shying away from crowds and Krystina trying to stay safe, what was there to write about? A lot, actually, she thought as she brainstormed new ideas. She'd ask to interview the owners of places she'd featured in the past and blog how they'd adapted to their new set of circumstances and restrictions. It was a win-win for all concerned. The owners could regain business through exposure while the customers were reassured of safety precautions.

Krystina felt invigorated for the first time in months, but as she followed the sound of the thrumming of a lawnmower, her heart sank a little. Loukas. Last week he had cleaned out the gutters. Today he was mowing. She didn't know how he managed the upkeep of the house, especially financially, along with all of his other responsibilities.

These days she barely saw Loukas unless their shifts at the café crossed over. He didn't even have time to pester her or follow her every move like a puppy at her heels. Observing him from a distance, she frowned. His situation bothered her more than she expected it would. It just didn't seem fair; forced into adulthood when he didn't even have a chance to play out his teens.

With purpose, Krystina walked across the lawn. With all the responsibility thrown upon Loukas, she had decided he needed some downtime for the day.

Quickening her stride to catch up with his steady pace as he mowed row by row, she tapped him on the shoulder. "Loukas," she shouted above the noise of the motor.

Caught off guard, he jumped. Once he saw who it was, Loukas set the mower to idle. "Hey, what's up?"

"Are you almost done?" she asked.

"Just about."

"Do you want to take a ride out east with me?"

"You're asking me? Why? Where's Chynna?"

"I don't know. I didn't call her. I'm asking you. Now do you want to go or not?" she bristled, placing her hands on her hips.

"Sure," he answered suspiciously. "What's your angle? Last time I had to practically beg you to let me come along?"

"Could you please not read into it and just say yes?"

"I did say yes."

"No. You said 'suuure' like you weren't sure at all."

"Now who's making a big deal out of nothing?"

"Forget it!" She threw up her hands and stomped away.

"Krystina!" Loukas ran after her. "I want to go with you. I'm just surprised. Besides, if I don't get out of here, I'll just spend another day fixing things around this house."

Krystina's features softened as she turned to face him once more.

"How do you do it?" she asked suddenly. "Manage it all? And afford it?"

"I get by." He shrugged it off. "Come on, let's get out of here."

Chapter 29

Loukas

Krystina sat quietly in the car, staring out the passenger window. Her phone was nestled in her lap but she didn't once pick it up to scroll through Instagram as she often did. To Loukas, Krystina seemed a million miles away.

"Are you okay?" he asked, taking his eyes off the road for half a second to glance at her.

"Uh-huh," she said on a preoccupied sigh. Then, after several minutes of awkward silence, she asked, "What did you mean by 'I get by?' A house is a huge responsibility for someone your age."

Stealing another glance her way, he trained his focus back on the road before replying. "The house was paid off, and my dad had some money in the bank. More than I'd expected. So I'm able to handle the bills."

"But you can't stay there forever, managing it all alone. Can you?"

Krystina was asking Loukas the same questions he'd been grappling with ever since his father had passed away. Should he keep the house so he could stay in his neighborhood or sell it and find himself an apartment? Going away to college wasn't even an option right now what with classes only being held virtually. And although there was money left in the bank, was it wise to spend it on an education? The cost would drain his account. What then? Loukas needed guidance, and he would seek it eventually. Right now, the manual labor of working on the house kept him too busy to dwell on all he'd lost.

But Loukas was lonely. The house was too quiet. Even though his relationship with his father had been virtually non-existent, the awareness that he wasn't the sole occupant kept him from feeling a complete sense of isolation. But that was only part of it. He was now entirely on his own. Both of his parents had been only children. There were no cousins, aunts, or extended family of any kind. The Andarakis family was as close as it came for him, but they weren't blood.

It was unsettling to be orphaned, even at the age of eighteen—to realize no one connected to him by blood was left in this world. Unsure of his place now, fate had once again screwed him over.

"Loukas?"

He snapped out of his solemn contemplation. "I don't know. I have to give it some thought," he said coldly, keeping his eyes trained on the road. "Maybe I'll skip college altogether and train to fight."

"What? You can't be serious. Training for exercise or to work out your frustrations is one thing but to put yourself in a ring, for the sole purpose of becoming someone else's punching bag, is another idea altogether," Krystina lectured very animatedly with her hands, her voice rising in pitch. "Have you lost your mind?"

"Tell me how you really feel."

"I just did, *malaka*."

"Resorting to name-calling now?" Loukas chuckled. "It was only a thought."

"Unthink it."

Changing the subject, Loukas turned up the music, singing along with his favorite classic rock tunes. Def Leppard, Led Zeppelin, Black Sabbath. Krystina had enough when Pink Floyd started playing. Disconnecting the cable from his phone to hook in hers, she chose the next several songs.

"It's only fair," she defended when he groaned.

A fan of Harry Styles and Taylor Swift, he was not. But he'd suffer through it … for her.

Krystina decided she'd feature the north fork town of Greenport on her blog. She was surprised when Loukas asked her why she was doing a feature on a town she had already written about.

"I've read every entry," he confessed.

"Oh. I had no idea."

This girl could be so damn frustrating. Did Krystina purposely turn a blind eye or was she completely unaware of his feelings for her?

"The piece I wrote was pre-COVID," she explained. "I want to revisit all the towns I've featured to see how they've adapted and write about what they have to offer visitors in our current situation."

"That's a clever idea for content."

"I thought so," she agreed. "I had to come up with something. I haven't blogged in months."

As they turned down Main Street, Loukas was pleased to see the town was full of life. Unfortunately, he'd read many articles on how stores and restaurants all over the island had closed for good.

They parked the car and began to stroll down the side streets; many of them narrowed down to one car lanes to accommodate for outdoor dining. Main Street bustled with vendors selling everything from sunglasses and personalized dog scarves to empanadas and gourmet pickles.

"Before you start interviewing shop owners, can we grab something to eat? I'm starved."

"Yes! Me too. I'm famished," Krystina agreed. "And I know just the place!"

They walked to a restaurant called First and South. At first, Loukas thought they were trespassing on someone's property. The old, white Victorian home had been converted into a restaurant. Situated on one side of a residential street, nestled between other homes built during the same era, the wraparound porch was open for seating and offered a beautiful view of the boats in the distance. Periwinkle hydrangeas surrounded the seating area, giving the place a garden-like atmosphere. But due to COVID restrictions, only staff was allowed inside the building where he could see the bar and indoor seating were cordoned off.

They sipped ice tea from mason jars and devoured the signature 'Really Good Burger' loaded with gruyere, Applewood bacon, grilled mushrooms, and onions topped with a fried egg.

"This was a good idea," Loukas mumbled through a mouthful of food.

"What?" Krystina asked with a laugh.

He swallowed. "Good idea," he repeated. "I'm glad we did this."

Feeling more alive than he had a few hours ago, he smiled. The sun warmed his skin and the light breeze sifting through his hair was comforting. For the first time in a long while, he felt relaxed.

"Today the world almost seems normal again," Krystina said, her chin propped on her hand as she observed passersby. "Except for the masks, that is. Do you think we'll ever be able to hug a friend we run into on the street or see a stranger's full face again?"

"Who knows?" Loukas wiped his mouth with his napkin. Now that his mood had shifted, he didn't want to entertain any subject that was the least bit negative. "Let's get the check and take a walk down by the water. I need to work off this burger."

To the right of the pier stood a carousel on an open grassy area. "When was the last time we rode one of those?" Loukas asked.

"I can't remember. I'd say we were probably in grade school."

"Let's go on!" he proposed.

"Okay!"

Loukas grabbed her by the hand and they ran across the lawn to find the ticket booth. He bought two tickets and, as soon as the ride came to a stop, they hopped on excitedly. Choosing side-by-side horses, they laughed as they spun around.

"This was faster than I thought it would be," Krystina said with a laugh. "Not exactly a thrill ride, but fun all the same."

When it was time to dismount, Loukas held her by the waist, helping her off the horse until her feet were planted on the floor. But the ride jolted, coming to a sudden stop. Krystina fell forward and braced herself against his chest. Instead of letting go, she remained frozen in place, her palms cupping his muscular pectorals, and he swore he heard her breath hitch.

With his heart hammering, he wondered if he should take this opportunity. But did he dare? He bent down to meet her gaze. Krystina's lips were but an inch from his. But the second their eyes locked, she slipped under his arm and jumped off the ride's platform.

"Come on." She waved him over, ignoring what she had to have felt pass between them. "I have work to do."

The disappointment that had washed over him at her escape was quickly forgotten when he watched her interview several shop and restaurant owners. Krystina handled herself in a confident, professional manner that was well beyond her years. He was in complete awe of her. She'd make a great journalist one day, he thought.

And as she interviewed, Loukas played his part, snapping photos of different foods, the gelato they devoured, and the various vendors at the street fair. In addition, he photographed dozens of pictures of Krystina in action so she'd have plenty of content for both her blog and her Instagram.

When she had everything she needed from Greenport, Krystina and Loukas headed back to the car.

"Loukas, are you in a rush to go home?" she asked.

"No, not really. Why?"

"I was just thinking. Would you mind if we went to the Lavender field? It's only a few miles away. I did a piece on them a few years back, and since we're all the way out here, I thought I could revisit there too," Krystina explained.

167

"Sure. Lead the way," Loukas said, happy to take her anywhere she wanted to go.

Lavender by the Bay attracted many visitors during the summer season. Guests could purchase pots of lavender or instead walk the fields and pick it themselves. But it was also one of the most stunning photo spots on the east end.

Loukas took picture after picture of Krystina amidst the tall sprigs until a middle-aged couple interrupted him.

"Son," the older man said. "Go stand next to your girl; I'd be happy to take a few pictures of the two of you."

Loukas was about to thank him and politely refuse when the wife chimed in. "Go on." She nudged him. "The two of you make such a handsome couple."

Tentatively, Loukas hesitated. What the hell. He put his arms around Krystina's shoulders. Then, in the next shot, he held her by the waist. By the last pose, he felt bold, kissing her on the cheek while praying it didn't result in a punch to the stomach. Or somewhere worse.

Breaking from his hold, Krystina thanked the couple, taking the phone back from the man.

"What do you say we head home?" she asked, her voice sounding a little strained.

"Sure." Loukas sighed. She had to feel the electricity passing between them. It was impossible not to.

"Can we stop at Hellenic Snack Bar on the way and get some lemonade?"

"Okay," he agreed with little enthusiasm.

"Have you ever tried it?" she asked, oblivious to his sudden change in mood.

"Nope."

"It's the best. Made with fresh lemons and super frothy. It has the perfect balance between tart and sweet."

"Sounds great," he replied, but his thoughts were elsewhere. Loukas' disappointment in his ability to penetrate Krystina's heart was getting to him. Every time he thought he'd made progress, something pulled her back.

"You okay?" Krystina asked.

"Yup. Fun day." He blew out a breath. "Why'd you ask me to come with you today?"

"That again? Don't overanalyze it. We're friends, I suppose. Right? And I thought you could do with a day away from the grind."

Loukas sighed as he watched Krystina walk back toward the car. Friends. Not what he was hoping for. But it was an improvement from 'Leave me alone and get out of my face.'

Chapter 30

Krystina

The following day, Melina left the house with George to help him out at the restaurant again. *Yiayiá* had been a little under the weather the night before and, after some debate, she had finally agreed to stay home.

"I'll stick around to keep an eye on her," Krystina offered.

She tiptoed into her grandmother's room only to discover she was sound asleep. *Yiayiá* was usually up before the rest of the family, dressed and at the stove, whipping up breakfast for everyone or getting a head start on the evening meal. Krystina couldn't recall a time when she was ever ill, not even when the flu ran through the entire house.

Krystina was seated at the kitchen table, tapping away on the keys of her laptop, when she heard her grandmother stirring in the suite she occupied off from the kitchen. A deep, dry cough captured her attention.

Rising, Krystina called to her. "*Yiayiá?*"

The old woman had propped herself up against her headboard. "Krystina *mou. Fére mou éna potíri neró.*"

Krystina nodded and hurried to the refrigerator to pour her

grandmother the water she requested. She really must not be well. Her *Yiayiá* never asked for help.

Scurrying back, she handed *Yiayiá* the water and tried to help her prop herself up more comfortably.

"*Efharistó, koúkla.*" She drank the water in one large gulp.

Palming the side of *Yiayiá's* neck, Krystina exclaimed with alarm, "You're burning up!"

"I'm fine. I'll sleep now."

"I'm going to make you chicken soup *avgolemono*."

Krystina left the bedroom, returning a few minutes later with two Motrin and a thermometer.

"Take these," she ordered. "I'll check back on you in a little while."

Although her grandmother fell asleep right away, it didn't stop Krystina from checking in on her every fifteen minutes to assuage the unsettling feeling that was suddenly washing through her stomach.

Without warning, Loukas entered through the kitchen door. "What are you cooking," he asked, pulling Krystina from her thoughts.

"Don't you ever knock?" she snapped.

"No. Your mom said I should come and go as I please."

Turning her attention back to the stove, she rolled her eyes. Of course, her mother did. She always gave Loukas free rein here.

"To answer your question," she said as if he had no right to ask, "I'm making soup for *Yiayiá*. She's not feeling well."

"What's wrong?" he asked, coming up behind her and snatching a carrot from the cutting board.

"A cough. One hundred and two fever." There was concern in her tone.

"You need to get her COVID tested," Loukas stated seriously.

"Oh my God! You think?"

"Definitely." Loukas pulled his phone from his back pocket. "I'll find out where we can take her."

171

"Take her! She can't go out in her condition."

"How do you think they do it? We have to get her in the car and go to one of those drive-thru sites. Unless you think we should take her to the hospital?"

"Absolutely not. That place is overrun with COVID patients."

"Here." He showed Krystina his screen. "I can make an appointment online for later today."

"Okay," she agreed. "Book it."

* * *

Seventy-two hours. That's how long it took to obtain the positive COVID result. In the meantime, Krystina and Loukas wondered if they, too, were now infected. And what about her parents, who had worked side-by-side with her grandmother the day before? So now everyone had to be tested.

"Do you want the good news or the bad news first?" Krystina asked Loukas.

"Doesn't matter," he said with a sigh. "Until your grandmother recovers, it's all bad news."

Over the last three days, *Yiayiá* had weakened. Krystina had to force fluids into her and could only keep her fever down by overlapping doses of Motrin and Tylenol. But the cough had exhausted her, and Krystina grew more concerned as her breathing became labored.

"The good news is that my mom and dad are negative," she told Loukas, relieved.

Her parents planned to stay at Loukas' home until the test results came in. But now that they knew they were negative for the virus, they had to remain there until *Yiayiá* was no longer contagious. So now it was up to Krystina and Loukas to monitor *Yiayiá's* symptoms.

"My parents will need more clothing than they brought over to your house. I'll pack a bag. Can you take it over for me? But just leave it at the front door. Don't go in."

"Sure," he agreed. "But why?"

"Because I didn't tell you the bad news yet. You and I both tested positive."

"Are you sure? I feel fine," Loukas questioned.

"So do I. I don't have even one symptom. But it doesn't matter. I already received a call from a CDC contact tracer checking to make sure we've quarantined."

"I guess you're stuck with me then," Loukas said, sounding almost gleeful.

"I've always been stuck with you," she retorted, brushing past him.

"*Pethiá.*" *Yiayiá* summoned Krystina and Loukas. "Come sit with me." She looked so frail sitting up in her bed, her face pale and drawn. "I've never been one to be afraid," she began. "I always believed you face what you have to and somehow manage to get through it. But I'm a little frightened now."

"Don't be," Krystina reassured her. "You feel that way now because you're weak, but I bet in another few days you'll be back in Kally's café telling her how to roll the *kataifi* properly.

Yiayiá extended her hand to her granddaughter, patting it gently. "I hope so, *koukla.*" A tear dripped from the corner of her eye. "These are the times when I miss my Panos the most. He gave me the strength to go on when my parents died. He loved me and your mother, and he protected us. Provided for us and sacrificed so much so we might have a better life together."

Sadness washed over the elderly woman like a cloud blocking the sun's golden rays; *Yiayiá's* bright spirit and optimism dimmed.

"Wherever he might be now," she said in a whimper, "I only wish I could say goodbye."

Fearfully, Krystina looked at Loukas. Loukas locked eyes with Krystina. Then, simultaneously, they nodded as they both came to the same conclusion. This was the right time to present her grandmother with the letters she'd been holding onto. Her stomach flipped, and Krystina exhaled a shaky breath, nervous to show them to her, though, in her heart, she knew this was the right moment. The stack of unsent letters Panos had entrusted to Krystina were meant to be shared at her discretion. And it was finally time for her grandmother to learn the truth. To know that Panos was alive and living in Athens.

"*Yiayiá*, please don't say things like that. You'll be as good as new very soon. But hold on, I have something I need to show you." She rested her hand affectionately over *Yiayiá's*. "I'll be right back," Krystina promised.

A few minutes later, she returned with a stack of worn letters tied by a blue satin ribbon. "I have something to tell you, *Yiayiá*, and I need you to hear me out before you say anything."

Her grandmother's eyes flickered between her granddaughter's and Loukas' serious faces.

"When we went to Athens with Mia and Nicholas, we told you we didn't find Panos." Krystina sucked in a nervous breath and took her grandmother's hand. "That wasn't entirely true."

Suddenly there was panic reflected in her grandmother's eyes. "His grave?"

"No, no! Nothing like that," Loukas answered quickly. "Panos is alive," he assured her, taking *Yiayiá's* hand in his. "He's just not the same man you remember."

"Take a look at me," she said, coughing through her words. "Neither am I."

"Not like that," Krystina explained. "He's not the person you knew. The man you once loved."

"That's for me to judge," she argued, confused at their confession. Suddenly realization dawned across her face. "He doesn't love me," she cried weakly.

"He loves you very much," Loukas said. "That's why he stayed away."

Upon hearing this, the devastated expression clouding over her eyes immediately changed to one of fury. "*Sahlamares!* Nonsense!" she fired off, anger flaring within her even in her weakened state. "I had faith, waiting and waiting for him to return." She fisted her hands and shook them in outrage. "He had a choice, and he didn't choose me." She turned her head from them in shame, hiding the tears that were now rolling down her face. "What a stupid woman I've been."

"No, you aren't. You were right to believe in him. He gave me these." Krystina hurriedly held out the stack of letters, still tied in the satin bow. She presented them to her grandmother, setting them down on her lap.

Yiayiá looked at Krystina with a curious expression.

"They're letters Panos wrote to you. He told me to give them to you when I felt the time was right."

"You've had them all these months?"

"Yes. I've been waiting for … I don't know … a sign, maybe."

"Some of the letters were written to you while he fought in the Resistance, when it was too risky for him to send them. The ones from later years, he was either unable or too afraid to send," Loukas explained.

"This top letter he wrote recently though." Krystina held up a crisp white envelope that looked out of place among the other yellowed and frayed letters. "He wants you to read this one first."

"You read it to me," *Yiayiá* said, squeezing her eyes shut to prevent more tears from spilling.

"Are you sure? It might be private."

"You read, Krystina *mou*."

Clearing her throat, she seated herself in the kitchen chair she had dragged in earlier. Once Loukas carried one in for himself, she ripped open the envelope with her forefinger, gathering the courage to read its contents.

Kalliope mou, agápi mou,

Not one day has passed that I have not thought of you and our Melina. I keep my love for you in my memories and in my heart, but that is all I have to offer. That and my long list of regrets. I've failed you.

My dreams and visions of you kept me alive during a most unbearable imprisonment. I owe everything to you yet gave you nothing in return. Please believe me when I say that I wanted to return to you more than I could ever express. But I am not the man you married and promised to devote your life to. Holding you to those vows would have been unfair. Forgive me for what I've done. I wear my shame in my soul and as my disfigurement, a daily reminder of my misplaced priorities.

    Eternally Yours,

    Panos

"*Vlakas*," *Yiayiá* cried through her tears. "I love that man with everything I have."

Leave it up to her grandmother to call the love of her life an idiot. She was right, though. Panos didn't understand that *Yiayiá* couldn't care less what he looked like, and she would have forgiven him for anything. But maybe this was all the betrayal she could handle.

"At least you understand his reasons now," Loukas said softly. "It has to help a little."

"It helps nothing," she spat. "I knew he was alive. I told all of you. I felt him in here." She laid her hand over her heart. "I knew he was still alive," she repeated. "But I made up every excuse in my head. Dementia. Amnesia. Some reasoning that explained why he forgot me. I could never accept he'd choose not to come back to me, but that's exactly what he did."

"If you saw him, you might understand," Krystina said. "He's crippled. I believe his leg has been crushed. He has scars all over his face, and he's missing an ear. And that's just on the outside."

Her grandmother wept. "I would have nursed him back to health."

"I know. But maybe he felt he couldn't be put back together."

"I'm tired," *Yiayiá* stated suddenly.

"Okay. We'll let you rest. I'm just going to take your temperature before I leave."

Krystina aimed the temperature gun in front of her grandmother's forehead. It was still on the high side so she asked Loukas to bring her some Tylenol and a fresh glass of water. She scooped up the bundle of letters but her grandmother stopped her.

"*Ásto*. Leave the letters with me. Tomorrow you can read them to me."

Krystina looked to Loukas, uncertain what she should do.

"She'll be okay," he whispered. "Don't underestimate her. She needs a chance to absorb what she's just learned, but I think she's ready to hear whatever is in them." He took her hand, leading her out. And this time, Krystina hoped he was right.

Chapter 31

Krystina

The repetitive ringing of the doorbell roused Krystina from sleep. Or what little sleep she had managed to snatch, anyway. She had barely eked out a few solid hours the night before, tossing and turning as she worried over her grandmother's condition. Every hour or so, she'd wake up and check on her, making sure her breathing wasn't labored or her color too pallid.

"I'm coming, I'm coming. Where's the fire?" Krystina complained.

Opening the door, she found Egypt, Kally's best friend, standing on the porch.

"It's seven o'clock in the morning. Geez, Egypt." Krystina ran her hand through her tousled tresses.

"I thought the iPhone was a permanent genetic appendage to you Gen Zs. I've been texting and calling."

"I shut my ringer off to get some sleep." Krystina put her hand up as Egypt stepped closer to her. "Six feet apart, remember?"

"You're in my pod," Egypt reminded her. "We work together. But I'm glad you're being responsible. How is *Yiayiá*?"

"Hanging in there, but I'm worried."

"Listen, my parents advised that you shouldn't bring her to the hospital unless her situation grows dire, but they felt you needed to have some vital equipment," Egypt explained.

Egypt's parents were physicians, working tirelessly at Stony Brook University Hospital. They'd expressed their hopes that their daughter would follow in their footsteps but Egypt had nearly flunked science in high school, and worse, she detested biology class. Much to the Basu's dismay, Egypt was a creative free spirit who preferred making jewelry and adorning Kally's pastries with intricate designs instead.

Egypt placed a small shopping bag on the front step of the house and backed away. "Supplies are short these days but my mom gave this to me for you to borrow. It's an oximeter to measure your grandmother's oxygen level. Mom wrote down the operating instructions. If the number dips below a certain level, you'll have no choice but to take her to the hospital."

"Thank her for me. That's so kind!" Krystina was truly appreciative. This would help to ease her mind from the constant worry.

"We all love her. She's a great lady," Egypt said with a sad smile. "If you need advice or help, just call my mom or dad."

"You're the best. Thanks for bringing this over."

"Virtual hug," Egypt offered with a smile, gesturing.

Krystina made every excuse to put off reading the letters. Though she was curious about their contents, her concern was in how they would affect her *yiayiá*.

She heated up broth and tea, feeding it to her grandmother slowly. Then she changed the sheets on her bed, asking Loukas to help carry *Yiayiá* to the chair while she stripped and remade it.

Krystina combed her hair and helped her brush her teeth before delving into the bag Egypt brought over. First, she checked her blood pressure, which read on the low side. Then she clipped a small apparatus onto *Yiayiá's* forefinger and waited for the readout. Thankfully, her oxygen level was not in the danger zone.

"*Paidí mou, arketá! Diávase éna apó ta grámmata se ména,*" *Yiayiá* ordered.

Krystina could stall no longer. *Yiayiá* had just made it clear she was done waiting for her granddaughter to sit her butt down and read her one of those letters.

Loukas stifled his laugh. Barely. "The boss has spoken."

Reluctantly, Krystina untied the blue ribbon from the stack of letters and took a seat. Then, steeling herself, she removed a yellowed sheet of paper from the manila envelope.

May 17, 1968

Dear Kalliope mou,

It has been two months now since I sent a letter to you. I pray you received it and I can only hope it eased your mind. For now, I am safe. But more importantly, I want to reassure you of my love for you. It is all going well here, and we are working diligently to restore freedom in Greece. My two loves will return to their beautiful homeland as it should stand, as a free and independent nation.

I love you too much to risk not returning to you. So I must take careful precautions. For this reason, I don't know if or when this letter will reach you.

Keep me in your heart and prayer always. I will see you soon. I know this because I must.

With eternal love,

Panos

"Nine months without him. Nine months fighting that crusade, and nothing had changed," *Yiayiá* lamented weakly.

"Men go to war. They get drafted or enlist," Loukas said. "Wasn't that the same in his case? How is it different than any other war where the men had to leave their families to go fight for their country?"

"Loukas is right, *Yiayiá*. What about all those old 1940's movies you love so much where the husband goes off to war? What made you like them so much?"

"It's not the same. He sent us off to a foreign country. And he promised he would come for us. But he never did. He left us by choice."

"He loved you so much," Krystina maintained. "You always had faith. You held onto it all these years. Don't let these letters rob you of that now."

"He loved Greece more."

"And you don't?" Krystina joked. "All you talk about is how everything is better in Greece. 'The oranges are juicier. The tomatoes are plumper. The fish is fresher,'" she mimicked in her grandmother's accent.

Loukas chimed in. "'The ocean is bluer, and the olive oil is the best in the world.'"

"*Alítheia!* Truth!" She shook a finger at them, suddenly finding the energy to defend her homeland.

But for all their jesting to get her spirits up, *Yiayiá* had a single focus.

"Another letter," she croaked through a raspy cough.

Krystina patted her grandmother's arm affectionately. She pulled the second letter from the envelope and set it on her lap before reading it. Removing the hairband she had wrapped around her wrist, Krystina twisted her long locks into a messy bun.

Hours before, *Yiayiá* had asked to have the air conditioner turned down and, although she was still chilly despite being covered in a blanket, Krystina felt like a pillar candle melting down to a waxy puddle.

June 5, 1968

Kalliope mou,

Nothing has changed since I last wrote except that my heart aches for you even more. It's only been a few weeks. I know you haven't received my last letter because I still have it in my possession. Someday I will be able to mail each one I write so you will understand the full depth of my love and my deep despair. I miss you more than words can reveal.

We continue the fight. More citizens join our cause every day. And as much as I miss you and our Melina, I know I made the right choice for our future. I had to send you to a place of safety until Greece is free from this tyranny.

Bursting with love for you both,
Panos

"See! You were right to believe in him, *Yiayiá*. He loved you so very much."

"For so long I waited for the mailman, hoping for one of these letters," *Yiayiá* said sadly. "So many years have passed, and he had them all this time," she added weakly. She gestured for Krystina to continue.

The next three were each dated approximately two weeks apart. And they all said pretty much the same thing. Panos missed her and would come for her as soon as the fight was won.

When Krystina's throat grew hoarse from reading aloud, Loukas took over.

September 1, 1968
My Sweet Kalliope,
We had a close call. Members of the Junta stormed into the flower shop asking too many questions and throwing accusations around. They even inspected a copy of Seeds of Prometheus, but thankful, they tossed it aside as nothing more than a magazine of worthless gardening tips. I'm not sure how long we held our breaths, but we all sighed with relief when they left.

This reality struck me with great fear. Pray for me that I make it back to you. These people are evil. Citizens caught resisting the new regime have been arrested and imprisoned, or even executed.

My sense of reality doesn't allow for an ending to this mess where I don't come back to you and our daughter. Melina must be growing

before your eyes, and I'm missing it all. Give her a kiss from her Babá.
   Dreaming of you,
   Panos

Krystina tried to hold back her tears as Loukas finished reading. When a sob escaped from her constricting throat, Loukas clasped her hand. Accepting it gratefully, she rested her head on his shoulder for comfort. They were both painfully aware after meeting Panos that his fear had been realized.

"I begged him not to get involved," *Yiayiá* whispered, tears rolling down her face.

"I think that's enough for one day," Krystina said softly. "I'm going to bring your medicine. I want you to rest now."

But before she even finished her sentence, her grandmother had already drifted off to sleep.

A hundred hearts would be too few to carry all my love for you.
Henry Wadsworth

Chapter 32

Loukas

Ominous low clouds rolled in, shadowing the sky with varying shades of ash gray and deep pewter. The impending storm veiled the Andarakis home in solemnity, matching Loukas' mood.

This last letter had rattled him. He tried to put himself in Panos' place. In what scenario would Loukas ever consider leaving the love of his life? He now knew Panos had regrets. The man had no idea how much he would sacrifice for his country at the time of his writing. *'My sense of reality doesn't allow for an ending to this mess where I don't come back to you and our daughter.'* That's what he'd said.

Loukas had no one, only the Andarakis family. Only Krystina, if someday she'd accept his love. *His* sense of reality wouldn't allow him to abandon her for any reason.

But it was for Krystina, and especially for *Yiayiá* that Loukas slipped into a melancholy mood. *Yiayiá* was like a grandmother to him, and he hated to see her so despondent. She'd spent years believing her husband would come back to her. Now, in the face of an uncertain recovery, her faith had been shattered.

And what of Krystina? Loukas could read the sadness and frustration in her eyes. The powerless remorse of her failed efforts. Nothing she'd said to her estranged grandfather had shifted his misguided conviction that his wife was better off without him.

Once Krystina was assured her grandmother was sound asleep, they rose quietly and left. Carefully, she closed the bedroom door behind her, leaving it ajar so she could hear her grandmother if she awoke.

Loukas called to her but Krystina crept up the stairs wearily, ignoring his plea. For once, he refrained from their usual banter. Instead, he'd afford her time alone with her thoughts.

But as more time passed, Loukas grew concerned. Standing on the other side of her bedroom door, he debated whether or not to rap on it. Instead, he headed to Theo's room, where he usually slept when he stayed over. In no mood for video games or TV, Loukas laid down on the bed and stared at the ceiling, lost in his own thoughts.

But for faint rumblings from afar and the pitter-patter of raindrops hitting the window, the house was utterly silent. Loukas couldn't remember an instance when this home wasn't bellowing with noise and laughter, music and the clinking of dishes. Without the family bustling about within its foundations, it no longer felt warm and comforting.

He popped up suddenly when a flash of bright light followed by a thunderous boom struck. The house shook from the vibration, and when another crash of thunder immediately followed in its wake, he heard a deafening shriek rip from Krystina.

Running out of the room, Loukas met her by the staircase.

Krystina's eyes were wide with fear, and her face had paled. "Did you hear that?" she asked in a shrill voice.

"I think the whole island heard that," Loukas joked, making light of it.

Screeching, she practically jumped into his arms when another thunderbolt struck like a discharged missile hitting the earth.

"I need to check on *Yiayiá*," she said in a panic.

"I'm right behind you."

But *Yiayiá* had remained fast asleep during the entire cacophonous storm, which, apparently, had no plan to blow out to sea any time soon.

"You think she's okay?" Krystina rested her palm on her grandmother's forehead.

"I think COVID has exhausted her. Her breathing sounds fine, though. She's just in a deep sleep," Loukas reassured her.

When they headed back up the stairs, Krystina turned to him. Her hazel eyes, which usually shimmered with tenacity, suddenly reflected a state of uneasiness. "Loukas, I don't want to be alone."

Nodding, he followed her to her room. Then grabbing the remote off her dresser, he asked, "TV?"

"Sure." She propped the pillows up against the headboard of her full-sized bed.

"*Walking Dead*?"

"No! Not tonight. Nothing scary."

"You're not going to make me watch one of those chick flicks, are you?"

"Since when do I watch chick flicks? I'm sure we can find something we both can agree on," she said with a sigh.

"*Outer Banks*?"

"Okay," she agreed, snuggling in next to him.

Each time they thought the worst of the storm had passed another series of lightning strikes flashed across the sky followed by devastating claps of thunder.

"Do you remember when we were really little and we were both afraid of the thunder?" Loukas asked softly.

"We must have been about five or six years old," Krystina mused. "We were terrified. But then our mothers told us that it couldn't hurt us because it was farther away than we thought."

"My mom sat us on the couch by the living room window and taught us how to measure the distance between us and the lightning."

Krystina smiled. "One one thousand, two one thousand." She

chuckled. "We couldn't do the math but we counted all the same."

Loukas put his arm around her. "I miss her. My mom."

"I know," she said, turning to face him. "I do too."

They fell silent as Loukas thought of his mother. And that brought him around to thinking about everything else that had happened recently.

"Do you think Panos did the right thing?" Loukas asked softly. His thoughts jumped from one person to another. His mother. His father, for all his faults. Panos. And even Krystina's father, who'd affected his whole family by his indiscretion. Yes, he knew of what no one talked about. Theo had once told him that Melina was not his birth mother but instead the result of his father's affair during their separation.

"Do you think it's okay for a man to leave his family? Even if it's for a good cause?" Loukas' voice was barely a whisper.

Krystina sucked in a deep breath. "I don't know. Maybe? Hasn't it happened since the beginning of time? Men and women choose to serve this country and enlist in the army all the time."

"But my question is why? To protect their family or their country?"

"Both, I guess. I'm sure each person has their own reason." She paused for a beat. "I think Panos didn't like what was happening and wanted to make sure his country remained as the homeland he knew and loved. And he wanted that for his wife and child too. He wanted them to live a free life and to prosper in the Greece he believed in. And even now, in some crazy, uber-frustrating way, he's still thinking of her."

"But it's hurting her."

"I know." She yawned. "I'll have to think about what to do there. But tonight, my brain is fried, and I'm tired."

"I'll let you sleep." Loukas pointed the remote at the TV, shutting it off. He went to slide off the bed but Krystina clasped his hand.

Her eyes locked with his. "Stay with me. I'm afraid to be alone."

Wordlessly, he let her pull him back onto the bed. She didn't know what she was asking of him, but he would stay, for her.

"Thank you," she whispered, rolling onto her side.

"I'm here for you." Loukas spooned her, his front to her back. "Whatever you need."

When he thought she'd finally drifted off to sleep, he ran his fingers down the length of her hair, pushing the soft tresses away from her face.

"Loukas?"

He hesitated, worried she may snap at him. "I thought you were asleep."

"No, I'm just very relaxed."

"Good. It's been a rough few days."

"Loukas?"

"Krystina?"

"Are you okay?"

"That depends on what you mean by okay."

"With this, I mean," she clarified with uncertainty.

He laughed, burying his face into her hair. "No, I'm not really okay. I'm a horny eighteen-year-old guy in bed with the girl I've been in love with since I was old enough to walk, and you expect me to be okay?"

Krystina flipped onto her back to face him, her eyes wide. "You love me?"

She sounded stunned. Stunned! How did she not know?

"But you make fun of me. You basically live to annoy me. For years you've found ways to irritate and embarrass me."

"Annoying you is the only way I can gain your attention." He frowned, puzzled at her reaction. "But I'd rather capture your attention in better ways. Do you think we can bury the hatchet? It all happened so many years ago? I was just a dumb kid playing along with my friends. I can't tell you how much I regret what I did back then but kids do stupid shit. Do I have to pay for it forever?"

"I suppose not," she agreed. "And honestly, I don't know what I would have done without you here with me through all of this."

"I should go now that you know how I feel."

"No, just stay. It's totally innocent. After all, we were practically raised like siblings."

Well, that statement deflated more than just his ego.

"Right," he said with resignation. "Goodnight, Minnie."

The next morning, Loukas awoke before Krystina. He didn't have the heart to rouse her from her deep sleep so he went down to tend to *Yiayiá* by himself. He found her propped up in her bed looking irritated.

"Good morning, *Yiayiá*. How are you feeling?"

"Weak and bored. I want to get out of this bed," she complained. "*Varéthika pia!*"

"And you think you can do that?" Loukas grinned. "I'll tell you what—if you can get out of this bed and walk to the kitchen, I'll take you to the gym with me, and we can go a few rounds."

"Don't get smart with me," she countered, pointing a shaky finger at him.

"I'm trying to make you laugh." His expression turned serious. "I know this isn't fun, but soon you'll be as good as new and ordering Kally around at the café."

The old woman crossed herself three times in succession. "May *O Theos* answer my prayers."

"Let's start with getting some food into you."

Yiayiá waved off the idea.

"I have to insist. I'll put on some tea, but you need some protein too. An egg, maybe?" Loukas took the thermometer off the nightstand, aiming it at her forehead. "You still have a fever, but I want you to eat before I give you something to bring it down." Placing the oximeter on her finger, he was relieved to find her oxygen level no worse than the day before.

Ten minutes later, Loukas re-entered the bedroom with a tray of tea, scrambled eggs, and a blueberry muffin.

"You're a good boy," *Yiayiá* said, patting his cheek as he bent down to place the tray in front of her. Sipping her tea, she looked him over, nodding her head contently.

"Try the eggs before they get cold," he suggested.

"Very good, *agori mou*. At least I can still taste. I heard some people can't."

"That would be the worst!" he teased her with a grin.

She tried to laugh but only a cough erupted from her throat, resonating deep from within her chest. "The way you like to eat, yes, I suppose it would be," she murmured once she got her breath back. She took another bite of food, and Loukas handed her a couple of pills to swallow with a glass of water.

"But believe me, there are much worse things. Time is not our friend." Grief was written all over the old woman's face. "Tell Krystina you love her."

Loukas opened his mouth to speak but snapped it shut. Dumbstruck, words escaped his grasp. Instead, he only managed to form a series of grunts.

"Don't look so surprised. I see what's in front of me."

Finally Loukas found his voice. "It doesn't matter. I finally told her last night." Loukas hung his head. "She doesn't feel the same way."

"*Vlakeía!* She just doesn't know it yet."

"Yet?" He laughed, more at his own frustration than at the self-assured, old woman before him who he couldn't have loved more if she was his own grandmother.

"Each of my granddaughters is like me in some small way. All of them good girls, but Kally has that little bit of fire and rebellion, like I do. Mia can be stubborn, and, well, we all know I insist on getting my own way. And Krystina has a kind heart, but she has, how you say? A sassy mouth."

Loukas grinned. "Yeah, she sure does."

She pointed to the pitcher of water on the nightstand and Loukas poured her a glass.

Sipping before she continued, *Yiayiá* handed the glass back to him. "But she hurts as much as she loves, and that gets in her way. Give her time. You're both so young. It took me a while to warm up to my Panos. But once I did, there was no turning back. He became my world." Her eyes misted over at the memories.

Loukas didn't think the situations were comparable but he nodded and smiled to appease her. "You should rest now."

"That's all I've been doing," she complained. "I'm bored."

"Would you like me to turn on the TV? Maybe the Greek channel?"

She shook her head. "I'll try to fall asleep. Maybe I'll dream of better days."

Chapter 33

Kalliope

Kalamáta 1963

Kalliope opened the oven door, inhaling the fragrant aroma wafting up from the roasting pan. She'd taken great care in preparing dinner for Panos. Unbeknownst to him, tonight marked a very special occasion.

Psari a la Spetsiota was one of his favorite meals. The baked fish topped with garlic, parsley, fresh tomatoes, and breadcrumbs was finally ready. Kalliope covered the pan with a ceramic platter to keep the fish warm while she fixed the rest of the meal.

With a dreamy expression, she absentmindedly shaved more *kefalotyri* cheese than she needed to top off a fresh salad of tomatoes, Kalamáta olives, red onion, and peppers. Kalliope happily sang along with the radio as she bustled about the small kitchen. She loved the upbeat tunes of American Rock n' Roll. Dancing her way to the oven, she removed the potatoes and artichokes roasting in olive oil and lemon juice.

Now that the oven was free, she slid the *portokalopita* onto the middle rack and set the countertop timer to fifty minutes. If Kalliope timed it all accurately, she'd have just enough time to pour the simmering orange-infused syrup over the cake once it cooled, before they had to sit down to supper.

When Panos finally came through the door, Kalliope's enthusiastic greeting nearly knocked him over.

"I'm happy to see you, too, *agápi mou*," he chuckled, picking her up at the waist to meet his height. His kisses were always as passionate as their first, but with an added element of desperation, as if it might also be their last. He awakened all of her senses with a simple touch, and she knew that would never change. Life with Panos was an adventure with his strong convictions and unending optimism. This was a man who had an appreciation for each time the sun rose, treating every day as if a miracle had taken place.

"What smells so good?" he asked. "I'm so hungry; I could eat all the fish in the sea."

Kalliope laughed. "You'll have to settle for just one." Then, taking his hand, she dragged him over to the table.

"What's all this?" he asked, eyeing the elaborate place setting.

Flowers from the garden had been placed in a vase and sat atop her mother's delicate linen tablecloth. On either side of the arrangement, a pair of taper candles flickered brightly, their color complimenting the blue Greek key design rimming her mother's fine china.

"Is it a special occasion?"

"Can't I spoil my hard-working husband?"

"With this delicious meal? Oh, yes. But then ..." He pulled her onto his lap, and she squealed with delight.

Panos skimmed his fingers down her face, trailing them along her neck and continuing to the swell of her breast. Then, sliding one sleeve off her shoulder, he pulled her dress down enough to expose one already aroused nipple.

Kalliope rocked against him as he flicked the puckered nub with his tongue, moaning out his name until she finally regained her senses.

"Panos." She tried to pull away but had little resistance when it came to her husband. "Panos, I've been cooking all day."

"I needed a little taste to hold me over." He gave her a wicked grin, those gray eyes of his penetrating her own, making it almost impossible to refuse him.

Kalliope pulled the straps of her dress up and delivered a playful slap to his arm. "I knew you were trouble the second I laid eyes on you," she giggled, extricating herself from his lap.

"And that's why you couldn't resist my charms for too long."

She shook her head, amused by his mock conceit.

"Besides, your efforts aren't wasted. I'm going to enjoy every last morsel of this meal; I'll be devouring it in record time."

"I made dessert too."

"That can wait for after." Panos raised a provocative eyebrow, smirking at her deviously.

Kalliope watched as her husband kept his promise. He consumed everything she put in front of him. Granted, he worked long hours and was most likely famished, but the speed in which he ate amused her, until she remembered her news.

"I have something to tell you, Panos," Kalliope began after he had consumed his last bite of food. "I had to wait to be sure, and now I am."

Kalliope's serious tone alarmed Panos. It was written all over his face as he jumped to her side. "No! It's happy news," she assured him. Stroking the sides of his face, she met his eyes. "I'm pregnant."

"You are?" Panos smiled but his eyes showed not a hint of delight.

Kalliope was confused. "Aren't you happy? Don't you want a baby?"

"More than almost anything."

"Almost?" Her lips quivered. She tried unsuccessfully to hold back her tears.

He took her in his arms. "Don't be upset, *agápi mou*. But having a baby isn't worth it to me if it's at your expense."

"Panos," Kalliope whispered sympathetically. "Many women have miscarriages. Don't assume the worst."

"That day is burned into my mind. I thought you might die. There was so much blood …"

"I know, but it's not uncommon, especially for how far along I was."

Panos raked his fingers through his hair. "I had to watch you day after day, refusing to eat, to get out of bed … It nearly broke you."

"I was sad, and a part of me will always ache for the child we lost. But I want this baby, and I need you to be happy about it."

Panos wiped a tear from her cheek. She stared into haunted eyes. Eyes that revealed everything to her. She saw there the longing of a boy who'd been motherless by fault of his own birth. And the terror of a husband whose wife might see the same fate. But Kalliope could also see the unwavering love he had for her and the fierce protectiveness he possessed. He'd sacrifice his life to keep her safe.

And her own devotion was as unconditional as his. She would draw the fear from him even if she had to fight the devil himself. Kalliope had no intention of ever leaving him, and this time, she was determined to hold their healthy child in her arms.

Panos rested his hand on her belly and smiled. "Our child." He bent down on one knee and unbuttoned the front of her dress. "Be good to your *mamá, mikroúla*," he whispered, kissing the bare skin of her belly.

"What shall we call him or her?" Kalliope asked relieved at his acceptance.

"Anything you like, as long as it's not the name we had chosen for our boy."

Kalliope sighed. "I will think about it then. But if it's a girl, I'd like to name her after my mother."

"Who also just happens to share the same name as one of your favorite movie stars." He winked at her.

"Yes," Kalliope confirmed with a smile. "And if it's a girl, she will brighten the stars in heaven. We will call her Melina. Melina Nikopoulos."

Kalliope's Portokalopita

Ingredients

I package phyllo (16 ounces)

4 large eggs

1 cup sugar

Juice and the zest from two oranges

1¼ cup Greek yogurt

1 tablespoon vanilla extract

1 tablespoon baking powder

1 cup vegetable oil

Syrup

1½ cups sugar

3 cups water

Juice from 2 oranges

2 cinnamon sticks

Method

Preheat the oven to 350° F.

Remove the phyllo from the package and shred it into thin strips. Spread it out on a large baking sheet and place it in the oven at 200° F until the phyllo has dried.

Grease an 8x13 inch dish with vegetable oil or oil spray.

Combine the eggs with the sugar in a large bowl. Beat with an electric mixer until pale and frothy. Add the orange zest, juice, Greek yogurt, vanilla extract, and baking powder. Beat on medium speed until well combined. Slowly add the vegetable oil while continuing to beat. Crumbling the dried phyllo with your hands, add it to the batter and whisk it carefully until fully incorporated.

Pour mixture into prepared dish and bake for 45-50 minutes.

While the cake is baking, prepare the syrup. In a saucepan, bring the sugar, water, orange juice, and cinnamon sticks to a boil. Lower to a simmer for 10-15 minutes. Remove from the heat and set it aside to cool. Pour the cool syrup over the hot *portokalopita*. Let the cake sit for at least an hour to absorb the syrup. Cut into squares and serve cold.

Chapter 34

Krystina

Present Day

Krystina rubbed the sleep from her eyes as she descended the stairs. She hadn't meant to sleep in so late. It had been an exhausting last few days. Still, she was solely responsible for her grandmother's care. Padding to her bedroom, she stopped short of entering. *Yiayiá* was sound asleep. In fact, she had a curiously peaceful look on her face, as if she was in the middle of a pleasant dream.

Krystina's eyes landed on a half-empty cup of tea on the nightstand. With a puzzled frown, she realized the blood pressure cuff and thermometer were on the edge of her bed, not where she'd left it the night before.

"Loukas," she whispered. He must have already attended to her grandmother. But where was he? A knot twisted her insides as she thought of his confession and the way she had made light of it. He couldn't possibly have meant it, could he? But the wounded timbre in his tone made her question everything. They were spending far too much time together as it were, quarantined in the house with no other company aside from her sick *yiayiá*. And he must have been lonely and scared after all that had happened. That must explain his fleeting moment of sentimentality.

Yet there was heat between them, an unexplainable pull, an electrifying consciousness as his body lay next to hers. It was all too confusing for her to deal with right now and Krystina found it easier to dismiss it as nothing of great importance.

Loukas was nowhere to be found, so Krystina stepped out onto the back porch to look for him. There he was, off in a distant corner of the property, punching the air as if he was hitting an enemy target. Right jab, left jab, right, left. Roundhouse kick. She started for the lawn then changed her mind. What would she say to him? Besides, from what she could tell, Loukas was in no mood to be disturbed. She turned back for the house with an uneasy feeling gnawing in the back of her mind.

A little later, when her grandmother finally awoke, she asked Krystina for one thing, and one thing only. Not food. Not pain medication. She only wanted the letters.

Krystina took a seat and pulled the next one from the stack. "October 3, 1968," she began. She turned around when *Yiayiá* waved Loukas in.

Leaning on the door frame with a blank expression, Loukas didn't move past the threshold. Krystina beckoned him to look at her but he addressed *Yiayiá* instead.

"Maybe you and Krystina want some time alone."

"No," her grandmother stated in too firm a voice for a woman in her condition. "You sit."

Krystina stifled a laugh.

"An order is an order," he agreed with a chuckle, his features softening somewhat.

"Thank you for taking care of her this morning. I didn't mean to oversleep," Krystina said, reaching for him.

But he pulled away when she placed her hand over his. "I'm happy to help."

Clearing her throat, Krystina began to read, glancing at his cold expression as a worried frown played across her brow.

Dear Kalliope mou,

Not much has changed here. We struggle to fight the evil that has taken over Greece. I take comfort in knowing that both my girls are safe. I dream of the day when we will all be together again. In the meantime, I see you in my dreams. I think of the life we were building and the one I hope to have again one day soon.

With all my love and devotion,

Your Panos

"How nice it would have been had he mailed these to me," *Yiayiá* said sorrowfully.

"It was too much of a risk," Krystina explained, trying to keep her grandmother from feeling so hurt. "But you have them now."

"Maybe. But I still don't have my Panos." She turned her head away.

"Panos loved you. The letters prove that," Loukas assured her. "But the man we met in Athens was not the same man who wrote these letters."

"Look at me. I'm not the same. Yet I still want him." She motioned for Krystina to take another letter. "Read, so I can dream of my youth."

November 2, 1968

Sweet Kalliope,

I have terrible news. Papandreou is dead. You may already know from the newspapers. One less leader standing for democracy. The funeral is tomorrow, and protests are planned all over Athens. I'm not sure when I'll be able to write again. Keep me and all of Greece in your prayers.

Eternal love,

Panos

"It's like peeking into a time capsule!" Loukas exclaimed in wonder. "Who was the man who died?"

"He was the former Greek Prime Minister. There was to be an election, and Papandreou's party was sure to win. That's when the Junta overthrew the government," *Yiayiá* explained. "He and his son were arrested."

"Did they kill him?" Krystina asked.

"No. He died from a stroke, if I remember correctly. But the people held the dictators responsible."

Krystina now felt as though she was reading so much more than simple love letters. History was written on these pages. Curious, she opened another envelope.

"This one is only a few days later!"

November 6, 1968,
My dear, beautiful Kalliope,
War is a series of both triumphs and sorrows. The people have spoken. They shouted; demanding freedom, condemning the regime, and chanting for democracy. Papandreou was laid to rest with honor and dignity. Thousands mobbed the streets, following his casket to the church. It was a hopeful sight to behold. Until the police could no longer control the crowd and took measures to stop the protesting. The authorities were brutal. Bashing heads with batons. Dragging women away by their hair. Stomping on bodies to silence them. Many citizens were arrested, some from our own organization.

I am safe for now, but I fear for our future here. This is not our Greece.

Keep me in your prayers,
Your loving husband

Krystina had to hold back the tears as she read, the words sticking in her throat. The emotions conveyed in the letter were too much for her to bear. Loukas took the letters from her when she could go on no longer, reading the remaining sentences in a subdued voice.

The room fell silent but for their solemn sighs adding a heaviness to the air. Outside, a drifting cloud covered the sun, darkening the atmosphere. Even the heavens reacted to the somber memory.

Yiayiá was the first to speak. "Four hundred years of Ottoman occupation. Then Hitler and Mussolini marched their forces in during World War II. How often would the Greeks have to say 'Never again?' This time, it was Greeks fighting Greeks. A sin." Weakly, she crossed herself in prayer.

The subsequent few letters didn't hold much more information. Panos asked for her patience and testified his love for her. Their Resistance group held back, lying low and growing more cautious. Apparently, there was a mission planned, but Panos wasn't ranked high enough to know the details. That all changed with a letter dated October 28, 1969.

"Why is that date so familiar?" Krystina wondered.

"Seriously?" Loukas mocked. "Weren't we taught this every year in Greek School? It's *Óxi* Day."

"Oh, right."

Óxi Day, pronounced Ó-hee Day, is a Greek holiday commemorating the day in 1940 when the Greek Prime Minister stopped Mussolini from crossing the border from Albania into Greece. The citizens of Greece took to the streets shouting, '*Óxi!* No!' The day has since been looked upon as one of bravery and solidarity.

Pausing a beat, she read the first line to herself and then handed the paper over to Loukas. "You read this one. I don't have a very good feeling about it. There's a reason they chose that particular date."

Agapiméni mou,

I don't wish to worry you, but for the first time, my optimism has diminished. It's the early morning hour, and I'm about to perform a mission I don't fully support. We are in desperate times, and the

202

Resistance leaders are taking drastic measures. My role is to create a diversion. I'll be far from the actual event, or dare I say, attack. But fear has taken hold of my senses. I pray I'll be able to write again tomorrow saying all is well, but I need to be extra careful now. This and the rest of my letters will be entrusted to a friend along with some money I've put away for you in case of an emergency.

Please know, whatever happens, you are in my heart. My soul cries out for yours. Time and distance will never separate us.

Always and forever devoted to you,

Panos

Loukas folded the letter and hung his head in despair. "This must have been the mission that went terribly wrong."

Her eyes glazed with tears, Krystina took *Yiayiá's* hands in hers. But her grandmother's reaction surprised her.

"*Psémata.* Lies," *Yiayiá* murmured. There was no vehemence in her voice. Only disappointment at her husband's broken promises.

"I think he meant every word of it, *Yiayiá*. The mind and body can only take so much trauma. He probably suffered from PTSD and was never the same again."

"I agree with Krystina," Loukas said. "None of us, not even you, can begin to understand what he went through."

"I would have nursed him. He could have been my Panos again."

"That might not have been possible, *Yiayiá*."

Loukas unfolded the letter again. His brow creased as his eyes scanned the page.

Krystina eyed him with interest. "What is it?"

Yiayiá had drifted off again. In a whisper, Loukas began to think out loud. "The letters materialized after all these years, but what about the money? Where did it go?"

"What money?"

"Right here." He poked the page. "The money Panos said he saved for her. If he loved her as much as he said he did, when he was finally able to retrieve the letters, he should have at least found a way to get the money to her."

"He did!" *Yiayiá* exclaimed suddenly, her eyes popping open.

Krystina jumped. "I thought you were asleep." She shook a finger at her in admonishment.

"My ears were awake."

"I bet. Like spy radar."

"Wait," Loukas said. "What do you mean by 'he did?' You said you never heard from him."

"I didn't. Or at least, I thought I didn't," she pondered. "Years ago, I received a check in the mail from a Greek bank for a little over five thousand dollars. I tried to find out what the money was for. I wrote to the bank but I was told the money had been sitting in an account made for me for some time and they needed to close it."

"Five thousand must have been a lot of money in those days," Loukas said.

"He must have saved every penny he earned," *Yiayiá* whispered on a sorrowful sigh. "Why, Panos? Why?" She spoke nearly inaudibly, a faraway look misting over her eyes. "So many lost years," she murmured wearily. *"Eímai kourasméno."*

"Of course, you're tired. You're ill, and these letters are emotionally draining you. Sleep now, *Yiayiá*," Krystina said, patting her hand gently.

She pulled the covers up to her grandmother's chin before drawing another letter from the bunch.

"What are you doing?" Loukas reprimanded. "You can't read that until she wakes up."

"I just want to look at the date, that's all." Krystina's eyes widened in realization. "It's just as I suspected. The date jumps to almost six years later."

"That must mean ..." His eyes flew up to meet hers.

"He was arrested soon after that last one." A shiver crept up her spine. "It was as if he predicted it."

"And took measures to protect the only valuable thing he had," Loukas added.

"These." Krystina sighed, holding up the letters.

Chapter 35

Krystina

Mother Nature had reared her fickle head again. The storm the night before felt like the wrath of angry gods on Mount Olympus until the sun came out in the morning. Krystina could practically see spry little fairies prancing around from flower to vine. But dusk invited another deluge, along with an unseasonable chill in the air.

Loukas barely uttered a word to Krystina for the remainder of the day. Instead, he busied himself with video games and martial arts podcasts. So she organized her closet, and later, found a cozy corner in her bedroom to read the latest Stephen King novel.

Thunder rattled the house. Startled, the book flew out of Krystina's hands. "Maybe now's not a good time for this particular book," she mumbled to herself.

Loukas knocked on the ajar door before opening it all the way. Hovering by the threshold, he dug his hands into the front pockets of his jeans. "Um, a bunch of our friends want to Zoom chat tonight. They feel bad we're stuck in the house."

"You're speaking to me again?" she asked sardonically.

"I'm just giving you space," he admitted. "After all, who wants their brother up their ass all day."

"Loukas." She sighed, closing her eyes. "I only meant—"

"No need to explain," he grumbled. "You made yourself perfectly clear. In or out?"

"What?"

"Zoom. In or out?" Loukas tapped the door frame impatiently.

"In," she said with resignation.

He offered a curt nod and walked away. Before he disappeared from view, he turned to face her once more. "I'll hang out in Theo's room and use my own laptop."

So this is what it was like to have the tables turned—on the other side of one's animosity. It wasn't a nice feeling. But wasn't that what she had always wanted? For Loukas to leave her be? It *was* what she wanted, right? Then why on earth did she suddenly feel so empty inside?

When the time came to log on and talk to her friends, Krystina did not possess her usual enthusiasm. So much was weighing on her mind. Her grandmother, the letters, and the dread of what they'd discover in the next one … And then there was Loukas. What was it about him that disturbed her the most? Krystina couldn't quite put a name to it.

"You're awfully quiet, Krystina," Chynna commented. "Are you feeling ill?"

"I'm fine. It's just been an emotional week taking care of my grandmother. But Chynna, can I ask why you're wearing a mask on a Zoom call?"

Chynna felt the mask as if she wasn't aware she had it on. "Oh, I think I've just gotten used to it."

Krystina picked up her phone while the others chatted. She typed a text to her friend.

Krystina: *You're not fooling me. Take the mask off.*

Chynna: *I feel better with it on.*

Krystina: *Everyone knows you. They all know about your birthmark. They—*

But she stopped and looked up from her phone when an exchange between Loukas and their friend, Jordyn, silenced the rest of the group.

"So what do you say?" Loukas asked her. "When I finally get cut loose from COVID prison, do you want to hang out? See a movie or something?"

Jordyn laughed nervously. "Loukas," she scolded. "You're putting me on the spot, doing this in front of all our friends. What if I said no?"

"Are you going to? Say no?"

Jordyn twirled a lock of hair around her finger. Then, batting her lashes, she answered, "No." She wore a sly smile. "I wasn't going to say no."

"Okay," Tommy interjected. "Now that this episode of *Bachelor in Paradise* is over, and lover boy here has handed out his rose, can we talk about something else?"

Please, God, yes! Talk about anything else. Krystina was about to be sick. WTF! Thank Tommy, who she usually thought was a tool, for steering the focus in another direction. It was probably her imagination but Krystina swore several sets of eyes were staring directly at her.

Shaking inside, she concealed the hurt, the anger, and the confusion with a forced smile. Krystina blinked back the tears before they could embarrassingly spill out in front of all her friends. Just like the adults in an old *Charlie Brown* cartoon, the conversation was a muffled noise to her ears. Emotion clogged her brain, and the only thing she managed to conjure up was an exit strategy.

"Hey, guys," Krystina interrupted, putting on a brave face. "I'd love to chat longer but I need to check on my grandmother." She formed a heart with her fingers. "Hope to see you all soon. Bye."

Sitting cross-legged on her bed, she closed her laptop before collapsing over it, finally letting the tears spill.

It took a good half hour to pull herself together and venture from her room. With a puffy face and red-rimmed eyes, Krystina tiptoed down the hallway. Peeking over, she saw that Loukas' door was still closed. The coast was clear for her to quietly head down the stairs. Then, realizing that he was unbothered and enjoying himself while she suffered, she felt upset all over again. No. It made her angry. Angry and bothered. And really, freaking hurt.

"*Yiayiá?*" Krystina stepped into her room. "Can I get you anything?"

"*Neró,*" she answered, her voice coarse.

Krystina scurried to the kitchen, pouring a glass of water from the refrigerator dispenser.

She positioned *Yiayiá* up into a sitting position, fluffing her pillow to make her comfortable. With her emotions running high, it didn't escape Krystina's notice that her grandmother's already slight frame seemed thinner and more delicate. Tears clogged her throat as she tried to conceal her mood.

"You need to eat, *Yiayiá.*" Worry etched her brow. "I could read you another letter while you sip some soup."

"Maybe tomorrow. I'll sleep now."

"Okay. Just let me take your temperature first."

Before Krystina left the room, *Yiayiá* had already fallen asleep. She had slept a good portion of the day, which was beginning to concern Krystina greatly.

She lumbered up the stairs feeling tired, worried, and sad. Already isolated from the outside world with this temporary quarantine, she felt even more alone as she passed Loukas' closed door.

So what was that telling her? To be careful of what you wish for?

Krystina crawled under her covers and wept. Not just for Loukas, but for everything that had changed in the last few months.

"What?" Krystina croaked when she heard a knock on the door.

"Are you crying?" Loukas asked from the other side. But before she had a chance to answer, she heard the doorknob turning. "I'm coming in," he declared.

Krystina felt the depression on her bed from the weight of his body as he sat down beside her. Stroking her hair, Loukas willed her to turn around, but she didn't lift her face from the pillow.

"Talk to me."

Tears burned her throat, making it hard for Krystina to form words. "I think *Yiayiá* is getting worse."

"Do we need to take her to the hospital?"

She shook her head, her face still buried in her pillow.

Gently, he turned her around by the shoulders. "Look at me," he demanded. "Tell me what's really bothering you."

She burst into sobs. That was the last thing she wanted to do in front of him, but her emotions could no longer be contained. She was like a dam whose flood gates had just broken free.

"Are you mad that I asked Jordyn out?"

"What do I care?" she wept.

"It seemed to me like you did. You got off the Zoom chat awfully fast after that."

"It was cringeworthy," she accused. "That should have been done in private, just between the two of you."

"It didn't seem to bother anyone else." He lifted her chin, forcing her to meet his eyes.

Those damn blue pools could make the Caribbean Ocean envious.

"It was uncomfortable. You're staying here with me and asking someone else out."

"You said I was like your brother." He lifted an eyebrow in challenge.

"I didn't mean it that way," she mumbled, averting her gaze.

"No? Then what did you mean?" There was a bitter edge to his voice. "Tell me where I stand with you. Do you like me? Hate me? Love me? Or do you hope I cross the street and get hit by a bus?"

"I don't hate you." She sighed wearily. She tried to speak but her lips quivered and the tears began to flow again. "You were my best friend, and you sold me out over and over again." She pointed a finger at him accusingly. "I know you said you were young and stupid, but it hurt. At eight, it was forgivable, but not so much after the last couple of times."

"I thought we already got past this." Loukas blew out a frustrated breath.

"You were my person. The one I always thought I'd be able to count on," she admitted reluctantly. "You hurt me so I hurt you back."

"When someone is your person," he started cautiously, sounding a bit confused, "that means you love them."

Their eyes locked. What she saw reflected in his was a glimmer of hope although she also detected a sense of ambivalence emanating from him. Boys are clueless, she thought.

Chapter 36

Loukas

Their eyes locked. What Loukas saw reflected in Krystina's eyes was fire and exasperation. Her irises were a kaleidoscope of browns, greens, and gold. It was too much of a mystery to decipher what was churning in that brain of hers.

"Of course, I love you, you idiot," she fired off. "Do you think anyone I didn't care so deeply for could get under my skin the way you do?"

Speechless, Loukas had to take a beat to decide what to react to—the 'I love you,' or the 'you get under my skin' comment.

Tenderly, he took her face in his hands. "You love me?" Man, that sounded pathetic even to his ears. "What a romantic way to tell me," he followed up, a bit stunned. Of course, he realized Krystina had been just as surprised as he was now when he had told her he loved her. Maybe they were both idiots.

"I call it like it is." Reaching for a tissue on the nightstand, she wiped her tears.

"Let me," Loukas said, brushing his thumbs over her cheek. He smiled softly at her. "I'm going to kiss you now." He leaned in closer. "And it won't be for a dare. Or to prove a point."

Krystina grasped his t-shirt. "Stop talking," she demanded, pulling him in for a kiss.

The blood in his veins thrummed. This was the kiss he'd been waiting for. She spoke volumes; the way she played with the hair on the nape of his neck. Tongues collided, hands explored; he thought his heart would explode with joy.

"Love you," he panted. "Love you so much."

"Me too. I love you." She leaned her forehead against his. "Please don't date Jordyn."

He chuckled. "I think that's a no-brainer."

But what he didn't say was that he and the girl had set the whole thing up. Once Krystina had sent him into the 'brother zone,' he came up with a drastic plan to find out once and for all how she truly felt. It might have been a bit sneaky, but Loukas couldn't go on like this anymore. Krystina had to figure it out for herself, and had it gone the other way, and she didn't care who he dated, he'd decided that he would finally cut his losses and give up.

Loukas' heart raced as he laid down beside Krystina. They kissed for what could have been five minutes or an hour. He lost all sense of time, drowning in this girl. His Minnie. She was like a ramekin of the crème brûlée her sister made at the café; delicate and smooth once you cracked through that first hard outer layer.

Finally, they pulled apart from each other, their foreheads still touching. Her cheeks were flushed and he smiled, enjoying the effect he evoked in her. "Stay with me." Krystina tenderly brushed the hair from his forehead. "I won't be able to sleep tonight. I wasn't lying when I said I was worried about *Yiayiá*."

Loukas rolled onto his back, his arm remaining around Krystina, hugging her close, feeling her warmth against his body. He sighed. "Do you think she's depressed? Maybe the letters are upsetting her."

"I was wondering the same thing. What would you think if I called Panos and told him how sick she is? Do you think he'd come around and agree to at least speak to her?"

Loukas leaned in and brushed his lips over hers before answering. "We have nothing to lose. Of course, he could say no again, but we'd be no worse off than before."

"We?"

"Yes, we. It's you and me, Minnie. And I call you that only with affection, just to be clear."

"I'm kind of used to it now," she giggled.

When Krystina finally fell asleep, Loukas was still wide awake. He brushed the hair from her face and kissed her cheek. He couldn't remember the last time he felt so happy. Finally something good had come out of the current situation. *She loves me.* He wanted to play those words over and over in his head. For him, their fate was forever sealed.

"It might be a long time from now," he whispered in her ear, "but someday I'm going to marry you."

Chapter 37

Krystina

"Really? He won't speak to me?" Krystina held the phone in the palm of her hand. It was set on speaker so Loukas could hear. "You tell him his wife is sick. Very sick with COVID." She was livid. "For a man who claimed to be so brave in the name of his country, you're telling me he has no spine to face his wife?"

Cradling her from behind, Loukas rubbed soft circles into her back to calm her down.

"How bad is she?" Kostas asked from the other end of the line.

"She's not in the hospital but she's declining. Loukas and I have been reading Panos' letters to her. We thought it would help but it seems to be having the opposite effect. Can you please appeal to his conscience?" Krystina pleaded. "If she could finally see him, I think it would lift her spirits."

"Hold on," he groaned.

She waited, and waited, and waited. Several minutes went by before she heard a gruff voice address her. It was Panos.

"Read the rest of the letters to her. I won't speak to her until then."

"She's very sick and there's still several more to read," Krystina said. "There's no time to waste."

"Which letter are you up to?"

"The last one before you were arrested, I think."

Heavy breathing came through the line. "Finish them and call me back. I'll talk to her then, if she is still willing to speak to me." Panos hung up without another word.

Krystina felt like screaming. Why was this man so damn stubborn! She threw the phone onto the couch in frustration.

"We better get started," Loukas suggested.

Together, they prepared her grandmother's breakfast and tended to her needs. Then she looked over to where Loukas was loading the dishwasher. Forgiveness felt good for the soul. The truth was even better. Free from the metaphorical walls that had encapsulated her in resentment and insecurities, Krystina could finally replace those emotions with optimism and hope.

She would convince Panos to speak to her *yiayiá*.

All these years, Loukas had always championed her, even when they argued. Even when she pushed him away, insulted him, rejected him. Their frenemy banter had become a habit, one she was now happy to kick.

When they finished cleaning the kitchen after a messy attempt at preparing breakfast, Loukas flipped her around, stripping her of the dishwashing gloves she wore to preserve her over-sanitized, dry hands. As he pressed his body against hers, her lower back smacked against the counter with a jolt. But she didn't care. All she felt was arousal as Loukas claimed her mouth, kissing her deeply, like a man taking his first drink after being lost in a desert.

What happened to the boy she'd known all her life? Loukas kissed her with the hungry passion of a starving man. As he pressed against her, Krystina was caught in a bubble of electricity; the atoms entwining them charged with volts of power rivaled only by the thunderbolts that had shaken the house. Her body thrummed from the sheer nearness of him. Cirque du Soleil must have taken residence in her body, judging by the flips and flutters in her belly.

"Who are you and what did you do with Loukas?" she panted.

"This is me making up for lost time," he murmured. "Get used to it."

Nodding in satisfaction, Krystina grasped his neck, dragging him down to her level. "No argument from me," she agreed before pressing her lips to his with even more passion than before.

"That's a first," he teased, mumbling against her mouth.

She nipped at his bottom lip in a playful act of revenge, but Loukas had the last laugh. Swooping her up, he threw her over his shoulder and smacked her on the ass. "Come on, we have some letters to read."

In side-by-side chairs, arms linked, Krystina's head resting against his shoulder, Loukas read at *Yiayiá's* bedside. Panos' letter was dated many years after his last, and Krystina surmised why. This will not be easy, she thought. She only hoped it didn't take a further toll on her beloved grandmother.

August 30, 1974

My sweet angel,

It's with a heavy heart that I write this letter. As you can see, it's been too long since I last wrote. Since I was last able to write. Maybe it's for the best I never mailed the other letters. I dropped from your sight once before. To sentence you to that horror twice would be cruel and too much to expect you to endure. I will bear the pain for you, even though that suffering is greater than any physical torment I've lived through these past years.

Please know that this shell of a man is alive only because of you. The memory of your smile. The feel of your skin as I once caressed you. The sound of your sighs, knowing I pleased you as no man ever had before. My desperate need to return to all we'd once shared was my only salvation, and it fed my soul, though my battered body had been nearly depleted of all life.

You deserve better than to care for a broken, disfigured man like myself. I refuse to burden you. I'm sorry but I cannot come for you. The man who made those promises so long ago no longer exists.

Forgive me. Forever in my soul,

Panos

Through labored breaths, *Yiayiá* whimpered. "He abandoned me for what? All I needed was to look into his eyes, and I'd have known he was my Panos. No amount of scars could conceal who he was. I would've recognized his beautiful soul."

The effort of speaking sent *Yiayiá* into a fit of exhausting coughs.

"*Yiayiá*, please," Krystina begged. "Please don't upset yourself or I'll have to stop reading."

"There's only one letter left," Loukas informed.

"We can save it for another time," Krystina said with concern.

Yiayiá waved her hand, dismissing the idea. "Read," she croaked.

Loukas looked at Krystina, waiting for her approval. When she nodded for him to continue, he unfolded the last yellowed sheet of paper.

"This one isn't dated," he said. He scanned the page and shrugged. "It almost seems like he wrote this one on impulse. There's no point of reference as to how long after the last it was written."

"What does it say?" Krystina asked.

Kalliope,

Forgetting you has proven impossible. You are in my heart forever. I dream every night of what we once had, and it's those memories that sustain me. But that life no longer exists for me. Yet I cannot forget you. But please, I want you to forget me and make a good life for your-self. I need to believe that you can be happy.

Panos

"This one hurts more than the rest," *Yiayiá* said sadly. "No more 'I love you.' No terms of endearment. No warmth at all. He dismissed me."

"He wanted you to move on. Can't you see?" Krystina pointed out. "The only way he could survive this life was to let you go."

Loukas laced his fingers with Krystina's. "He loves you. Panos sacrificed his own happiness for you." Loukas was likely thinking of how his own father had wallowed in grief and self-destructive pity when he lost the woman he loved.

"I want to sleep now," *Yiayiá* said, leaning her head back and closing her eyes.

With a heavy sigh, Krystina leaned over, kissed her grandmother on the cheek, and signaled for Loukas to follow her out of the room.

With eyes narrowed and lips tightly pressed together, Krystina's mind raced.

"What's going on in that brain of yours?" Loukas asked suspiciously.

"We went through every letter, exactly as Panos requested. So now, I'm calling him, and he better damn well get on that phone, Skype, FaceTime, or whatever the hell he prefers. But either way, he will speak to her." Her conviction was strong enough for her to lift a tractor-trailer all by herself.

Loukas reached around Krystina, pulling her iPhone from her back pocket. "Go for it," he encouraged, handing it to her. "If I ever need someone to fight for me, I want you on my side."

Slipping her hands around his neck, she whispered, "I've always fought for you. I just never let you see it."

The brilliance of Loukas' azure eyes clouded over with memories. Krystina could see it. His mind took him to the same dark corner as hers; she knew he was remembering his father's neglect, and later, abuse. It just seemed so tragic now that Manny was gone. To grieve for the dead through self-destruction was such a pitiable waste when the living still craved love and attention. Krystina had tried to get Loukas' father to see that. In the end, he did, but the clock had run out. Now time was ticking away at her grandmother's chance to reunite with the man she had longed for all these years.

Steeling herself, Krystina inhaled deeply. Then, exhaling slowly, she tapped on the number for the bar in Athens, which she'd saved in her contacts.

"*Kostas? Eímai egó, Krystina. Kalimera.*" Stuttering, she corrected herself as it was already evening in Athens. "I mean, *kalispera*. I need to talk to Panos. It's urgent."

She could hear the frustration in Kostas' sigh. "*Éna leptó.* One minute," he said with disapproval.

"Krystina," Panos greeted her emotionlessly.

"Yes, it's me, and before you say anything, we read all the letters to her, just like you asked." Not giving him a chance to respond, she went on. "She's not doing well. *Yiayiá* is still home but COVID is beating her up. She needs something to hope for. She needs you. And if you refuse to speak to her, I'll hold you personally responsible if she dies."

"Are you done?"

"That depends on what you say."

"All my life, every choice I made was to protect her." There was a moment of silence. "I'll speak to her."

"Thank you," Krystina said with relief. "Can we do a FaceTime call?"

"No. I don't want her to see me as I am."

"She's old and sick in bed. How good do you think she looks?"

"She may have aged but she hasn't been maimed. I don't want to disgust her."

"You didn't disgust me, and I'm your granddaughter. I don't even know you, but still, you're family all the same."

"You're asking too much of me. I only agreed to a call."

"*Yiayiá* is aware of your injuries. She doesn't care. Do you want to know what she told me?"

"Krystina ..."

"She said she only needed to look into your eyes. To see into your soul. That as soon as she did, she would know you, and you would be the most beautiful sight."

Panos fell silent but for the nervous clearing of his throat. Then, after a pause, he spoke, his voice gravelly. "Give me until tomorrow to compose myself. Call me at four o'clock."

"My time or yours?"

"Mine."

Chapter 38

Krystina

Bright sunlight streamed in through the slats of Krystina's window shades, irritating her tired eyes. Squinting, she jumped out of bed, pulling at the cord to darken the room. The anticipation for this morning's call had kept her awake most of the night, thinking, pacing, dreaming up wild scenarios in her mind.

At some point, she must have fallen asleep, but from the pounding in her head, Krystina assumed her slumber had been brief. She was exhausted. The last thing she remembered was spouting off a string of 'what ifs' to Loukas.

"It's nine-thirty. Almost time," Loukas announced as he sauntered into her room.

Rubbing at her temples, she asked, "Did I fall asleep on you last night?"

Loukas chuckled. "Yup. At about four a.m., mid-sentence, explaining yet another theory on how badly today might go. And I have to tell you, each version was grimmer than the last."

Krystina groaned. "What if I've made a disastrous mistake and it all blows up in my face?" She flopped backward onto her bed. "What if it ends up making things worse instead of better?"

"That's not going to happen. Besides, how much worse can it get? They've been separated for fifty years." Then, taking hold of her wrists, Loukas pulled her up. "Now let's get some coffee in you before we make that call."

"Are you ready?" Krystina asked Panos.

He looked more put together than when she'd met him in Athens. Clean-shaven, his hair neatly combed and parted to the side, Panos had made an effort to look presentable despite the visible scars and self-described deformities.

Yet the jump in his jaw and the tremble in his voice as he answered her call made her wonder if he could go through with it.

"Does she know? Is she expecting me?" he asked anxiously.

"No, it will come as a surprise. I couldn't take the chance in case you changed your mind and disappointed her."

"Your lack of faith in me is justified but I'm here now." His eyes reflected his regret.

"This has to work. I think it's the only option that might will her back to health. I believe she is finally recovering from COVID. Now it's her mental state I'm more worried about."

Krystina kept the iPad at face level as she walked from the kitchen to *Yiayiá's* bedroom. She nodded to Loukas, who went to her grandmother's side, fluffing her pillow and helping her to sit upright.

"*Yiayiá*, we have a surprise for you," Krystina said in a sing-song voice, praying this was the right thing to do. She hadn't even consulted her mother, and if this didn't go well, she'd have a lot to answer for.

Loukas squeezed *Yiayiá's* hand. "Someone is on the iPad screen and he would like to see you."

With shaking hands, Krystina turned the tablet around to face *Yiayiá*. At first, she didn't think it registered with her grandmother. Until she grabbed the device from Krystina and drew it closer to her face, shock marring her features.

"*Agápi mou, karthoúla mou.* My love, my sweetheart, it's me—"

"*Panos? Panos mou?*" she wept, touching her fingertips to the screen as though she were stroking his face.

With Loukas standing by her grandmother's bedside blocking her view, Krystina scurried around the bed to the other side.

"*Eímai hália kaíého yerásei*"

Panos laughed through his welling tears. "We've both aged, *agapi-meni mou*. But if anyone is a mess, it's me. I'm distressed for you to see me this way."

"You are a beautiful man, my Panos. Forever my handsome husband."

Tears the size of rain droplets fell from Krystina's eyes, her throat constricting with emotion. Already, she could see the color returning to her grandmother's face, and her voice was stronger than it had sounded in weeks. Loukas motioned for Krystina to leave the room with him.

Leading the way, he turned back to whisper, "Let's give them a few minutes alone."

With a deep sigh of relief, Krystina collapsed into Loukas' arms as soon as the door closed behind them.

"You did a good thing," he whispered in her ear.

"We did. I couldn't have pulled this off without you." She relaxed into his embrace. "That could have gone in one of many ways."

After approximately ten minutes, they gingerly tiptoed back into the bedroom, careful not to interrupt a private discussion.

"I need you to get well," they heard Panos say. "As soon as this lockdown is over, I will get on a plane, if you want me to."

"I've always wanted you. I've waited my whole life for you."

"You understand from my letters that I'm not the same."

"I look into your eyes, and I see the same man. The only man I've ever loved."

"Rest, my love." His voice cracked with emotion. "I will speak to you again in a few days, and I want to find you stronger."

When they closed the chat, *Yiayiá* pressed the tablet to her heart. "Thank you," she said, overcome with emotion. She returned the device to her granddaughter. "Sit, *pethia mou*," she commanded, patting the bed. "Thank you so much. I never thought I'd see his face again. All those years of worry. Not knowing. Then letters. And now, this gift."

Krystina took her grandmother's hand. "We weren't sure how it would turn out, but at the very least, we wanted you to have answers. To at least have closure."

"Closure." *Yiayiá* smiled. "Today everyone looks for closure. Someday you'll learn there is no such thing as closure, only acceptance."

"So if you didn't get this chance to speak to him, like ever, you'd accept that?"

"You read the letters, *koukla*. We may want what we want, but let's not forget that every person has their own … how you say? *Myaló*."

"Mind, point of view," Loukas confirmed.

"With what he went through, he had his reasons for not coming to me. I always believed there was a reason."

The corners of Krystina's mouth turned up. "You did. You always had faith."

"That doesn't mean I approve. We lost too many good years, but I now have to accept it was what he had to do. What he thought best. And even if I had never found out what happened, I still knew in my heart he loved me. See, it's acceptance, not closure."

"You're very wise, *Yiayiá*," Krystina said.

"I've lived a long time," she said with a deep sigh.

"Can I get you anything?" Loukas asked. "How about something to eat?"

"I will rest now." She pointed to her dresser. "Give me my *icona*. I want to pray now and thank *Panayia*."

"So what now? She could be asleep for hours," Krystina said. "When do you think this quarantine will end for us?"

Wrapping his arms around her waist, Loukas nuzzled her neck. "Can't wait to kick me out of the house?"

"No!" She pushed at his chest playfully. "But I'd like to see our friends. Go work at the café. Take a ride out east before the summer ends."

"Come on. You didn't get any sleep last night. Take a nap while you can." He led her up the stairs and into her room.

"Are you staying?"

"Only if you want me to."

"*Yiayiá* isn't the only one who has to make up for lost time." She yanked him by the shirt, pulling him onto the bed with her.

Straddling him, Krystina kissed Loukas deeply, and before she realized it, she was rocking into him. Her mind raced, thinking of the everlasting love between her grandparents. They were once young and on fire for each other. They had laughed, planned, shared ideas, and made love. How could she not want that for herself? A love that never burned out. That stood against the test of time and tragedy. Krystina didn't wish to live cloistered like this. She dreamed of travel, adventure, new experiences—she craved it all. And love and lust were on that checklist too.

"Hold on, Minnie! Do you have any idea what you're doing to me?"

"I think I might have an idea," she giggled, pressing into him.

"Then we need to pull it back a little," he said, panting.

"Why?"

"Min, please. I'm trying to do right by you."

"Good. That's what I want too," she agreed. She dipped her tongue into the hollow of his throat and smiled when a soft groan rumbled from his chest.

"You're killing me, Minnie."

Chapter 39

Loukas

Loukas felt what little restraint he had slipping away. This wasn't just any girl. This was Krystina. His Minnie. He'd secretly loved her his entire life, even while they jabbed each other with insults. Her parents treated him as one of their own and gave him emotional support through everything he'd endured. She meant the world to him; the whole family did.

His head was rationalizing while his body and heart were screaming at him to ravage every inch of her. Could he ignore all the arguments as to why he shouldn't and instead listen to the reasons why he should? They both were, after all, adults now. Eighteen years old. Isn't that the age you got to make your own decisions?

"You're killing me, Minnie."

"Me, too, and it will be a sweet way to go." Her voice was muffled as she peppered him with kisses. "We have a lot of time to make up for. And if there's anything I've learned over these last few days, it's that time isn't guaranteed."

"I promise, we have a lifetime."

"You can't know that." Krystina took his face in her hands, worry etched into her brow. "You don't want me?"

Looking into hazel eyes that revealed a jumble of emotions, Loukas knew he was done for.

"You know I do." He sighed. "I love you, Minnie. I always have. And I always will."

Crushing his lips to hers, he stripped off his t-shirt, the heat of his desire flowing through him like liquid lava. There was no turning back now. His mind was lost to his senses. The feel of her skin as she shed her tank top. The smell of her lemon shampoo as he tangled his hands through her hair. And the sight of her eyes clouding over with need—for him. If this wasn't heaven …

Unclasping her bra, Loukas discarded it carelessly over his shoulder. Brushing his thumbs over the hardening nubs of her breasts, Krystina moaned, throwing her head back in ecstasy.

Desperately, they shimmied out of their shorts. Now body to body, skin to skin, no barriers between them, Loukas reveled in every explosive sensation until the warning bells in his mind went off. No barriers! "Wait! Condoms. We need a condom."

"Don't look at me," Krystina countered, wide-eyed. "I don't have any."

"I do. One. In my wallet."

"Saving it for a rainy day?" she teased, one suspicious eyebrow raised.

He answered her with a playful smack on her ass before bolting out of the room to find the one thing keeping him from making love to her.

Seconds later, Loukas returned and clumsily picked Krystina up, laying her onto the bed with a thump.

"I guess you've done this before," Krystina said, a slight tremor in her voice. "I … haven't."

"You are the only girl I've ever loved. But yes, I've had sex before." He could see the uncertainty in her eyes. "We are the only two who exist right now. I want to know what it's like to make love to you."

"Like in a cheesy romance movie?" she joked nervously.

Wasn't that just like his Krystina to banter when she felt out of her depth? Well he could give it right back to her. "FYI, I only had sex with the others to practice while I was waiting for you."

Krystina's laughter came out in snorts reminiscent of a content piglet rolling in the mud. "I'm sure that was such a great sacrifice for you."

"Enough talk." Loukas quietened her, pressing his lips to hers. Then drinking her in, he raked over her with a heavy-lidded gaze. Running his fingertips down her shoulders, over her ribcage, and finally to the small of her back, he smiled against her skin when she shivered beneath his touch. His need for her was too intense, and it took a Herculean effort for this to not be embarrassingly over in the next five seconds.

Quickly, he sheathed himself. "I'll be careful," he panted. "Tell me if I hurt you."

"I'm ready," Krystina said, wrapping her legs around him.

She was tight, and Loukas took care to ease into her gently, but God, he'd never been this connected to another human being. She was everything he'd waited and hoped for, and from her reaction, he believed Krystina felt the same.

Save for the grip Krystina had on his back and her nails digging into his skin, she gave no verbal indication she was in any kind of discomfort.

"Are you okay?" he asked.

"A little uncomfortable but I'm adjusting." Krystina brushed the hair from his face and kissed him. "It feels good to feel you inside me."

"I-don't-think ... I can't last ... much longer," he grunted.

"Don't hold back. I want this."

Loukas came, shattering into a thousand pieces. Blissfully exhausted, he rolled onto his back, breathing heavily.

"I'm sorry." He roughed his hands over his face. "I wanted that to be as amazing for you as it was for me."

"It was," she said, rolling onto her side to face him. "It was only my first time. And I can't wait to do it again." She giggled.

"We can't until I get more of these babies," he laughed, referring to the discarded foil packet.

"Amazon?" she laughed.

"Good idea. In the meantime, there are other ways to please you," he whispered, mapping her body with kisses.

Chapter 40

Krystina

Up to this point, *Yiayiá* had survived only on broths, tea, and the occasional bite of toast. She was getting thinner by the day, and Krystina was worried she wouldn't have the strength to fully recover from this virus with so little food in her system. Her mother was driving her to the brink of insanity, calling several times a day with advice and orders. Rightfully so, she supposed. If Melina couldn't be there to care for her mother, she was going to make darn sure her youngest daughter was doing her best in her absence.

After her delightful 'love romp' with Loukas, Krystina floated down the stairs as if she was a spirit drifting among the ether. It was time for *Yiayiá's* next dose of medicine, and hopefully, she could convince her to eat some solid food.

Much to her surprise, Krystina found *Yiayiá* sitting up in her bed, her features brighter than they had looked in days. Panos' old letters lay on her lap, her reading glasses perched on the end of her nose.

"You're awake! I would have come for you sooner had I known."

"Ba!" She waved her off.

Krystina picked up the thermometer and took her grandmother's temperature. "Normal. That's good news!" She snapped the oximeter onto her finger. It also read within the recommended levels.

"I feel better but still too weak to get out of bed by myself."

"Of course, you can't. This virus kicked your butt. Plus, you haven't really eaten anything."

"I'm hungry now."

"That's a good sign." Krystina was relieved. "Let's start with something light. Eggs, perhaps? Maybe some potatoes?"

"I think lamb chops and *horta*, yes? With plenty of *lemóni*."

She looked at the old woman in amazement. "I'll check to see if Mom has any lamb chops in the freezer. But we definitely don't have any *horta*. I can see if any of the supermarkets have those kinds of greens, and if they do, we can have them delivered. But for now, I think you should start with something plainer."

"You mean food with no taste." She wrinkled her nose in disdain.

"And my *Yiayiá* is back." Krystina laughed. "I've missed you."

"I missed you too!" Loukas agreed, walking into the room and looking a tad rumpled.

"You forget to comb your hair? Or too busy kissy kissy my *engoní?*"

Loukas turned a deep shade of red. Or was that purple? He should be used to her grandmother's irreverence by now. Krystina found it amusing, but poor Loukas looked as though he had been caught stealing from the house's petty cash jar.

"Oh, you are feeling better. You're embarrassing Loukas."

"*Sahlamáres!* Nonsense!" *Yiayiá* waved a finger at him. "You kissy kissy all you want. Panos and me—we kissy so much, the next thing I knew, Melina was born."

If Krystina's jaw wasn't attached to her skull, it would have cracked to the floor. Stunned, she turned to Loukas, who wore a mischievous grin. "*Yiayiá!* Are you saying what I think? Were you … pregnant with my mom …?" She waved her hands as though they could replace the words she was struggling to convey. "…before you were married?"

Sensibly, Krystina knew this happened all the time, especially today. But in her mind, her grandmother had lived in another far more innocent era.

"It was the sixties, not the Victorian era," Loukas whispered in her ear, holding back his laughter.

"You think you kids invented the sex?" *Yiayiá* removed her glasses. "We were getting married soon anyway." She shrugged.

Krystina made a gesture mimicking an explosion. "Mind blown! After everything you have ever told me, you leave this part out?"

"It wasn't important," she said matter-of-factly.

"Changing the subject," Loukas started "why don't you make something for *Yiayiá* to eat while I make some calls to find out how and when we can get her tested again."

"No one is going to make a house call, and I really don't want to put her in the car and wait in one of those long lines again."

"So what do you suggest we do?" he asked.

"The CDC says she has to quarantine for fourteen days after the symptoms end," Krystina said. "I'll ask the contact tracer when she checks in again."

"So fourteen days from now, if her fever stays down and the cough is subsiding, we can leave the house?"

Krystina lifted her palms. "I guess? Maybe I'll call Egypt and have her ask her parents what we should do."

That evening there was a knock on the door. Krystina looked out the window and saw Egypt's mother, Dr. Alvita Basu, double-masked and clad in scrubs and surgical gloves, standing on the doorstep.

"Dr. Basu!" Krystina greeted when she opened the door. "I didn't expect you. I only asked for Egypt to get your advice."

"I don't want our Kalliope sitting in a car for God knows how long in her weakened condition," Alvita said warmly. "I only wish I could do the same for everyone. I brought tests for all three of you to see where you stand. I can document the results and send them to the CDC."

Krystina escorted Egypt's mother to *Yiayiá's* bedroom. "She finally ate a decent meal. Would you believe she had lamb chops after hardly eating for almost two weeks?"

"Nothing surprises me where Kalliope is concerned."

"Hello, Kalliope," Dr. Basu greeted warmly. "How are you feeling?"

"Alvita? Is that you?" *Yiayiá* asked.

"It's me! What gave me away? My fashion?"

They both chuckled.

"I know that voice from anywhere. How are you managing at the hospital?"

"I'm tired. Tired and sad. I'm grateful you've been able to recover at home though," Alvita admitted. "I'd rather you were nowhere near the hospital. It's far too risky. Now let me examine you, and after, I'll test you for COVID to check your status. Krystina, would you mind stepping out of the room?"

"Sure."

After exiting the room, she sought out Loukas. At the top of the stairs, she heard him on the phone talking to Leo.

"I've been training in the backyard every morning as best I can without any equipment. I can't wait to get back to the gym."

Krystina shouldn't have eavesdropped but Loukas' increasing interest in fighting concerned her.

They'd been binging episodes of *Cobra Kai* on Netflix together while in quarantine, and as entertaining as the show was, Loukas' comments and references alarmed her. 'That will be me one day.' And 'I can't wait to fight in a tournament.' His statements filled her with anxiety. With a great amount of difficulty, Krystina kept her opinions to herself. Instead, she shoved handfuls of popcorn and red M&Ms in her mouth; she wanted to pretend the possibility didn't exist. If she ignored him, she could believe he was just getting caught up in the edge-of-your-seat drama. Drama she didn't want to see played out in real life. Or on Loukas' body.

"I know the gym is closed," she heard him say. "But who knows how long this could go on for. Maybe just the two of us could go in.

Couldn't we both use a good sweat session?" Then, after a pause, he sighed. "Ok. Let me know."

"Hey, I was looking for you," Krystina said, walking over.

"Oh, yeah?" Loukas smirked, leaning against the doorframe cockily. "Can't live for a second without me, huh?"

Twisting her mouth, Krystina cocked her head. "You're awfully confident all of a sudden."

"Maybe because you allowed me to have my wicked way with you."

She shot him a disgusted look. "Keep talking like that, caveman, and it won't happen again." Krystina planted her hands on her hips. "Besides, maybe it was me who had my wicked way with you," she added with a smirk.

"I like the sound of that," he chuckled, pulling her in by the waist. "You smell so good," he murmured, kissing her just under her earlobe. "Is Egypt's mother still here?"

"Yes. She kicked me out to examine *Yiayiá*. We should probably go back down. She wants to give us COVID tests too."

"Sure. Why not," Loukas complained, his voiced laced with sarcasm. "I'd always choose having a stick jammed up my nose over staying up here with you."

"How is she?" Krystina asked Dr. Basu as she stepped out of *Yiayiá's* room and into the kitchen.

"She definitely seems to be improving. Her oxygen level is good. Her lungs sound clear. Get more protein into her, though. And plenty of liquids."

"She ate her first solid food today," Loukas shared.

"I heard. I'll let you know her test results as soon as I get them back. Now let's swab the two of you."

"Just try not to remove any of my brain cells. I don't have many to spare," Loukas joked as he took a seat.

Krystina punched him in the arm. "Don't be an idiot." She giggled.

"I can see the two of you are getting on the same as usual," Alvita said dryly, a smirk playing at the corner of her mouth.

"We're getting on just fine," Loukas said under his breath.

Glaring at him, Krystina stomped on his foot under the kitchen table.

"Ouch! What was that for?" Loukas complained.

Alvita looked back and forth between the two of them. "I'm going to throw out a wish to the universe you're all now negative so you can leave this house before the two of you kill each other."

"Thank you, but we're actually getting along just fine," Krystina assured her with a bright smile. "But it would be nice to see the outside world again." The next day or two were going to be a tense waiting game.

The secret of change is to focus all of your energy not on fighting the old, but on building the new. Socrates

Chapter 41

Loukas

Lying in bed, Loukas whispered in Krystina's ear, "I'm going to miss this."

Slivers of moonlight snuck through the slats of the window shades, casting a celestial glow on Krystina's sun-kissed body.

"Tomorrow we get the test results, and as much as I want a negative result, I'm disappointed this won't be possible anymore." Lightly, his fingertips circled one breast and then the other.

Shuddering in response, she said with a sigh, "We'll find a way."

"We're finally on the same page, the way I'd always hoped, and now everything is about to change."

"Not everything."

Loukas rifled his fingers through his hair. "Your dad called me. He wants to have a serious discussion with me when our quarantine is over."

"About what?"

"Money. The house. My dad put him in charge of it all."

"You mean he made him executor?"

"Yes, that's what he said. He told me he had let some time pass before approaching me about it but now he feels it's time to make some important decisions."

"Okay." Krystina propped herself up on one elbow. "It will get sorted out, and everything else will pretty much remain the same."

"No, it won't," he argued. "We may have not have said goodbye to high school in a cap and gown but we still graduated. So that's off to college for you, and who knows what for me."

Krystina narrowed her eyes. "Wait! You were at the top of your class. You didn't apply for college?"

"I did. But what is the point in attending anywhere with all this uncertainty? Everything is such a mess. Anyway, I don't have that kind of money to spend when they haven't even figured out how to run the schools properly in this unusual circumstance."

"That's a cop out. Thousands of students are taking classes remotely."

"But that's not what I'd call a real college experience," he muttered.

"Oh, so what are you looking for? Frat parties, beer pong, and random hookups?"

"Come on, Minnie. Don't give me the stink eye. That's not what I'm saying."

"What are you saying?"

"I don't know." He sighed. "Like you know exactly what you want to major in, right?"

"Yup. Media management." She furrowed her brow. "You don't?"

"No. I only know that I prefer to spend my time at the gym honing my skills." He lowered his voice. "Fighting."

"No," she said adamantly.

"No?"

"That's right. I don't want you doing that. I can't stand the thought of it."

Loukas' face clouded over. "So if that's what I decide to do, if I'm in a fight, I can't count on you to support me?"

"I'll support you in anything you want to do. I'll always stand by your side. For anything. Anything, except that. I can't. I just can't."

The muscles in Loukas' clenching jaw jumped. He waited for a beat before attempting a rebuttal. "I would encourage you in anything you wanted to do. Anything at all. And I expect the same from you. This is important to me."

"Really? Anything? If I told you I wanted to be a stripper, you'd cheer me on?"

Sitting up, he reached down for his boxer briefs and slid them on. "That's a stupid comparison. There's no getting through to you, though, is there? You're the most stubborn girl I've ever met."

"I'm not stubborn. You're the one being stupid and reckless. If it's the *Cobra Kai* thing, just remember, it's only a TV show!" she shouted. "I like *The Walking Dead*, but I have no desire to be a zombie."

"Now who's being stupid?" He began to leave the room.

"Not me! So now you're running off to sulk because we have a disagreement? Because I care about what happens to you?" Krystina growled. "Fine," she spat.

When a woman says fine, it's anything but. It's one of those fundamental things every guy instinctively knows if he has any brain cells at all. She was pissed, but too bad, so was he. Leo and Max had pulled him through some very dark times with his father. Max had given him a place to stay when he needed an escape and saved him from running with the wrong crowd. And Leo had taught him a way to channel his anger in a more positive manner. Loukas had learned discipline and self-reliance while building muscle and strengthening his body from the inside out. He owed them everything. The gym was like a second home.

It was the first place he had felt a sense of belonging since his mother died. Sure, Melina and George treated him as one of their own, and he came and went from their home as he pleased. But he was never quite sure if he was just an obligation; a promise Melina had made to her friend to protect her only son. Krystina didn't understand what she was asking him to give up.

He slipped into his bed. Well, Theo's bed really. But while Theo was away and Loukas was homebound by the fast-spreading virus, this was now his room. He punched at his pillow in frustration until it molded to his comfort. So he and Krystina were back to square one. Again. Well that was just fine with him.

For the next two days, Loukas and Krystina did their best to stay out of each other's way. She tended to her grandmother, cleaned the house, ordered groceries, and when Loukas wasn't outside working out, he could catch a glimpse of her reading on the patio, sunning herself.

It was torturous being in the same house with her and not speaking. But he had to hold his ground. He would do anything for her. Had he not proven that? Why couldn't she do the same for him.

When the call came in from Dr. Basu, Loukas sidled up beside her to find out the news. Krystina slapped him away when he tried to put his ear close to her phone as they listened for the results.

"Thank you. Will do." She closed off the call. In a flat tone, she gave him the news. "You and I are negative, but *Yiayiá* is still testing positive. Dr. Basu recommends we stay in the house a few more days and get tested again." She shrugged. "Since you're negative, you can go if you want. I can handle this."

"Is that what you want?"

She shrugged. "I don't want to force you to stay."

"You're not. I'll see this through but I'll stay out of your way."

"*Pethia?*" *Yiayiá* called out from her bedroom.

Loukas and Krystina looked at each other.

"See? She wants both of us here," he maintained.

"Are you okay?" Krystina asked as they entered her room.

"Help me up. I need to get out of this bed."

"Do you feel strong enough to walk?" Loukas asked.

"*Ne, ne!* Of course. Enough lying down."

As she began to pull herself up, Loukas rushed to her side, afraid she'd fall. Carefully, he helped her to her feet.

"I want to take a *tsower* and fix my face. Maybe you take me *gyro*, *gyro* outside to get a little sun."

"Sure, *Yiayiá*."

"After, we call Panos on the Facething. Maybe this time I'm not *éna hália*."

Krystina laughed. "You're always beautiful. I know for a fact, Panos thinks so too."

"I'll make her something to eat while you help her in the shower." Loukas nodded. "This is good. She's getting her strength back."

"Thanks." Before walking away, she laid her hand on his bicep for just the briefest of moments. Yet that was all it took to make his heart skip a beat. His body warmed at the contact, his need for her never wavering, even for a second. But he had to remind himself that respect should be reciprocal. Their life dreams had to align. He had always held onto the faith that they could connect once more. Only this time, he held little hope they would.

* * *

Loukas was seated at the kitchen table with George. *Yiayiá* had finally recovered, and all three of them had tested negative for COVID. So, finally, Melina and George came home, and Loukas could now return to his own house, if he chose to.

"We have a lot to discuss," George started one evening before Loukas had left. "As you know, your father trusted me to make the best decisions for you, but you are eighteen and a young man who can make his own choices. So I won't do anything without weighing in with you first."

"I appreciate that," Loukas said relieved. There was a lot to consider and, from what he knew, George had always been good with finances.

"A word of caution though. I remember how I was at your age."

241

George laughed. "I knew it all, and I didn't want to hear what anyone else had to say. The truth is, I knew nothing. It would serve you well not to make the same mistakes."

Loukas nodded. "What are all these papers?" he asked, gesturing to the documents strewn about on the table."

"Mortgage, life insurance, 401K. That sort of thing." George rubbed at his brow. "Your dad had his problems, it's true, but I have to hand it to him; he didn't leave you with a mess. The mortgage on the house is almost paid off. The life insurance policy and 401K were changed in the will to name you as the beneficiary after your mother passed away. And he left you a decent sum of money to live on. But trust me, money runs out quickly. The taxes on the house alone will put a dent into your funds."

"What do you suggest? Sell the house? And if I do, where will I live? If I get an apartment, won't that money disappear down the drain too?" Loukas' mind was running through a hundred different scenarios at once.

George sighed. Leaning back in his chair, he rolled a pen between his palms as he thought. "That's what we need to decide. You can keep the house and live in it." He rocked his head back and forth. "But if you don't have a full-time job, it will be hard to maintain, even once it's paid off."

"What if I rented part of it out?" Not that he wanted to share the house, but he might not have a choice.

"That's a possibility, and it will give you income, but being a landlord is not as easy as you think. If something breaks, you'll be responsible for getting it fixed. You'll also have to make sure you find tenants who are reliable and responsible."

Loukas' heart sank. "Right. I've heard some brutal stories."

"Listen to me. Right now, with COVID locking everyone up in their homes, people are leaving the city in droves. Working from home in cramped apartments just isn't working for a lot of people, especially if they have kids who are remote schooling too." George

242

lifted the mortgage papers and dropped them back on the table. Stabbing the pen to one of the documents, he emphasized, "This is a goldmine. The price of housing is going through the roof. If I were you, I'd sell now. Who knows how long this crazy rush will last."

"Okay. If you really think that's what I should do …" Worry etched the lines in his brow.

"What is it, my boy?"

Loukas shook his head. "I've lived on this street my whole life. I can't imagine being anywhere else." He sighed, resigned. "So much has changed already. This is just one more thing, I suppose," he said quietly with a frown.

George patted Loukas on the back. "There will come a time when you'll ache to spread your wings. You won't always live on the same street you grew up on. One day, whether it's now or in the future, you will move, for one reason or another. But that time has not yet come. Melina and I would like you to stay with us. You know we've always considered you as part of our family."

"That's a kind offer, but once Theo comes home, there won't be room for me."

"*Ba!*" He waved him off. "There's always Kally's old room. But I think you like Theo's better." George chuckled. "And it doesn't look like he's coming home anytime soon. Stubborn boy," he muttered. "He refused to come back when this coronavirus struck. Now he can't come home at all." He blew out a frustrated breath.

Loukas was relieved the focus was diverted away from him. He didn't know where he would live or what he'd do with his father's house, but one thing was clear: he couldn't live here under the same roof with Krystina no matter how much he wanted to. No doubt, he would always love her, but he had his limits, and if they had any chance at all of making it as a couple, they had to have each other's backs.

"*Vre*, Loukas? I asked you a question."

Loukas shook his head, bringing himself back to the present.

"Sorry. I'm with you. I was just thinking about Theo."

"What about him?" George asked impatiently.

"He's in love," he blurted. Oh crap! He wasn't supposed to say anything yet. "He said he wasn't about to leave her alone what with everything going on."

George narrowed his eyes, examining Loukas' expression. Then, after a beat, he burst out laughing. "You're good," he said, shaking a finger at him. "You didn't even crack a smile."

"That's because I'm not joking."

"Theo? In love?" George chuckled. "That boy goes through more girls than a sugar addict goes through gummy bears."

Loukas stood. "Brace yourself. Theo might decide to stay in London after he graduates. As for me, I'll think about everything you said, and I'll let you know what I decide."

The single biggest problem in communication is the illusion
that it has taken place. George Bernard Shaw

Chapter 42

Krystina

"Take me to the café," *Yiayiá* insisted.

Krystina had just taken her to the doctor for a complete checkup and now they were on their way home.

"Let's not overdo it. One step at a time."

"The doctor said I'm in good health."

"But she also said to take it easy," Krystina warned. "You were out of breath just walking from the car to the doctor's office."

"I changed your diapers. Don't forget that!"

Stopped at a red light, Krystina turned to face her. "That has nothing to do with anything. Maybe I'll be changing your diapers one day," she added to get a rise out of her.

"I'd rather go to my grave first," *Yiayiá* huffed, crossing her arms across her chest.

"*Yiayiá!*"

Naturally, Krystina relented, turning right onto East Main Street, heading in the direction of The Coffee Klatch. There was no point in arguing when her grandmother insisted on something.

She found a spot a few shops down from the café and parallel parked the car. But before she could open her door, *Yiayiá* laid a hand over hers, stopping her.

"Tell me, what has you so sad?"

"Nothing," Krystina lied. "Hasn't the last few months been enough to tie us all in knots?"

"This is something different." Her grandmother took her by the chin, forcing her to look at her. "The eyes don't lie. The story of your soul is written in them."

"You wanted to come to the café. Let's go inside."

"No. We talk first. I'll start. Tell me about Loukas."

Krystina rolled her eyes, sighing. "What about him?"

"You know. Now you tell me."

"It doesn't matter. It's over," Krystina supplied in an emotionless tone.

"You kids have been fighting most of your life. Finally you figured out what everyone already knows, and now, it's over already? *Malakia!*"

"You wouldn't understand."

"After what I've been through, I know I would."

She was right, of course. "Loukas wants to fight," she finally said.

Krystina rushed to clarify when she saw the look of confusion on her grandmother's face.

"At the gym, with other fighters. Like on the show, *Cobra Kai*."

"He fights with snakes?"

"No," Krystina answered, laughing. She thought for a moment. "Like *The Karate Kid*."

"Oh!"

"He can get seriously hurt. He's pretty new at all of this, and I told him I don't want him to do it."

"Ah! I understand. I begged Panos to keep out of the politics. I pleaded with him not to send your mother and me away. But he did what he needed to do."

"And look how that turned out. He nearly died in a prison camp."

"I know. But if he hadn't done what he thought was best, it might

246

have ruined us."

"But it did ruin you!" Krystina insisted.

"No. Nothing could break our love. But in the end, had I forced him to remain out of it, he would have resented me." She stroked her granddaughter's cheek. "You still young girl," she said in her halting English. "You maybe have many boyfriends. I don't know." She shook a finger. "No, I know. That boy loves you. In here." *Yiayiá* pressed a hand over her heart. "Deep. *Stin psyhí tou.* In his soul. That will never change." She nodded resolutely. "I see it in you too. Let him do what he needs."

Krystina shook her head in irritation. "Let's go. I can't think about this now." But that was a lie. Loukas was the only thing occupying her mind.

Supporting her grandmother by the arm, Krystina helped her from the car, but the feisty, old woman wriggled free from her hold. "I'm not ready for a walker yet," she scolded. "I can get by on my own."

"You're awfully crabby today."

"Only when my family treats me like a rickety, old lady," she complained, stepping into the café entrance.

The place was as busy as before COVID. The café was still surviving on mostly takeout orders but they had been able to place a few tables out front along the sidewalk. Kally and Luis, her baking assistant, mixed and kneaded, whipped and poured, all with systematic efficiency. Katie, one of their part-time servers, Egypt, and Loukas bustled in and out of the kitchen, gathering orders for delivery.

Krystina worried her lip, her heart plummeting into the kaleidoscope of butterflies thrashing around in her stomach when she spotted Loukas. Picking up a large order for delivery, he didn't so much as glance her way when she greeted her sister.

"Hey, Kally! *Yiayiá* and I just got back from her checkup. She got the all-clear. And the first thing she wanted to do was come here to help you bake."

247

Krystina was pacing back and forth, following Kally's steps as she busied herself about the kitchen. "I told her it was too soon but she insisted."

"It's fine. I'll try to keep an eye on her," Kally said hastily while icing some cupcakes. "She can work at her own pace. Get her an apron and set her up over there," she instructed, lifting her chin in the direction of a corner workspace.

"Do you have an apron that says 'Talk to me at your own whisk?' Because that's the one she needs to put on today."

"That ornery, huh?" Kally giggled.

"Something like that."

Krystina waved her grandmother over. She had already found an apron and had decided to make individual *bougatsa* pies.

Once *Yiayiá* was settled, Krystina sought out Egypt. "Got a minute?"

"For you? Always. Katie," she called over to the to-go counter. "I'm going to take a quick break."

They stepped outside, away from the outdoor dining tables, and leaned up against the window of a clothing shop two doors down.

"I was wondering if you could give me Leo's number."

"Why? You want to date him?" Egypt joked. "I have to warn you, he's not the most emotionally available guy."

Krystina frowned. "What's going on? I thought the two of you were solid."

Egypt huffed. "Solid as a loofah sponge."

Krystina winced. "Did you guys break up?"

"Nope. We just are ... are us, I guess."

She shrugged it off but Krystina could see something was bothering her friend. She motioned for Egypt to continue.

"He and I met at the same time as Kally and Max. You know that, right?"

Krystina nodded.

"We've been dating a couple of years now, and I've watched both your sisters get married. Hell, next it will be your turn, and I'll still be single!"

"Bite your tongue! I'm only eighteen. But geez, Egypt. I've never heard you talk like this before. I didn't think getting married was on your agenda."

"That's not the point. A woman would like to know where she stands with her man. That's all."

"Okay." Krystina rested her hands upon Egypt's shoulders. "Then you need to talk to him."

"It's hard when he tells me 'I love that we're on the same page, baby' in that deep, sexy voice of his. It just makes me want to jump him on the spot."

Egypt was trying to brush it off but Krystina was having none of it. "You are the one person I know who is never afraid to speak her mind. Well, you and my *yiayiá*. You both know how to let your words spill freely without regret or hesitation."

Egypt closed her eyes, shaking her head in self-disgust. "I know. But when it comes to him, I hold back." She was silent for a beat before remembering Krystina had asked for his number. "What did you want from him anyway?"

"I want to ask him a few questions. About Loukas. He wants to fight, and I need to know what Leo is filling his head with."

"Leo wouldn't be filling his head with anything. And I can assure you, he wouldn't let anyone fight in his gym if they weren't ready." Egypt pulled her iPhone from her back pocket, bringing up her contacts. "I just shared his number with you. But keep an open mind, Krystina. Martial arts can be as mentally healing as yoga."

"I'll try," Krystina agreed. But she wasn't convinced.

"I have to get back. Good luck."

"Thanks, Egypt."

* * *

Gravel crunched under the tires of Krystina's car as she pulled up to a steel-gray industrial building. As luck would have it, Leo was off duty and had told her to meet him at the gym in an hour.

"Hello? Leo?" Krystina's voice echoed around the open gym.

"Back here." Leo popped his head out from his office, waving her over.

"Wow, Leo. I had no idea this place was so immense."

"Yup. Lots of space, but as you can see, it's empty."

"Hopefully not for too much longer."

"I'm working on a schedule where I can have a limited number of members train at once." He blew out a breath. "And hopefully get some new dates scheduled for the fights I had to cancel."

"Right," Krystina said with little enthusiasm. "That's kind of what I want to speak to you about."

Leo leaned back in his office chair, his hands cradling the back of his bald head, the smirk on his face barely concealed. "You looking to sign up?"

"Me? Fight? No, no, no."

"Didn't think so."

"I want to talk to you about Loukas. I'm worried about him."

"Loukas? The boy you generally ignore except when you throw insults at him? That Loukas?"

"I'm not all that bad," she argued, punching his bicep. "Crap! That hurt. What are you made of? Granite?"

"I work out," Leo deadpanned.

"For your information, Loukas and his friends have humiliated me more times over the years than I can count."

"Considering you were stuck alone with him for weeks, I'm shocked you're both still alive."

"Now you're just playing with me." She glared at him. "I'll have you know, Loukas and I got along just fine. Better than fine. In fact, I couldn't have been happier stuck in the house with anyone else."

Leo raised his eyebrows in incredulity. "Strong statement. Are you trying to convince yourself or me?"

"Ugh!" she groaned in frustration. "I came to talk to you about the matter of Loukas' safety. This is serious."

Leo gestured for her to continue.

"Let me first start by saying it's great that Loukas can come to you and Max for anything. He's had a rough go of it, and the two of you have been there for him when he needed you the most."

Krystina was suddenly nervous, afraid she might offend Leo. But what was suitable for Leo wasn't necessarily good for Loukas.

"You've had a big influence on him, and it's great that he likes working out here. But that's where it should end. Now he's talking about fighting in tournaments, and I think he's going to get his ass kicked. Or maybe even worse."

A smile curved at the corner of Leo's mouth. "I've had my ass kicked more than once. That's the way it is."

"But look at you! Six foot and then some. Muscles as hard as stone. Loukas is lean. I mean, he's definitely toned up real nice since he's been working out, but he can't compete with someone who looks like you."

"That's why there are different weight classes. Krystina, do you think I would ever put Loukas, or anyone else in my gym, in harm's way?"

"Not intentionally."

"You need to trust that I know what I'm doing. Yes, Loukas has been pushing for a chance to fight, but I keep telling him he isn't ready."

Krystina threw her head back and blew out a breath. "What a relief."

"Hold on." Leo raised a hand. "I promised to train him harder so he can get ready for the lowest level of an amateur match."

She snapped her head back down to face him, stunned. "Seriously?"

"Why are you so opposed to this? Have you ever even been to a fight?"

"No, and no offense, I don't want to."

Leo massaged his chin, collecting his thoughts. "Have you considered Loukas' reasons for wanting this? For needing this?"

Krystina lifted her shoulders. "Absolutely! It's obvious. You took him under your wing, and now he wants to be just like you."

"Wrong. All I did was give Loukas a coping mechanism when he was angry or upset," Leo explained. "Instead of going home and taking his father's abuse, he could stay here, safe, and let out his frustration on a punching bag. If he was too far out of control, I had him practice meditative Tai Chi exercises to center himself."

Krystina hesitated. "I didn't realize."

"Martial arts can be brutal in some cases, but it's also an expressive art form. And it teaches discipline. Loukas needs this. You can't take away a man's—or a woman's—choices. If you do, nothing good will come of it. All you'll accomplish is in erecting a divide between the two of you."

"I've already done that," she admitted regretfully.

"Then fix it," Leo advised.

"I want to but I don't know if I can." Krystina sighed. "Why couldn't he have taken up something else like golf or bird watching?"

"Bird watching? You'd be interested in a guy who spends his days looking through binoculars, mimicking bird calls?"

"Good point." She laughed before her expression turned serious once more. "So basically, Loukas is going to do what Loukas is going to do, and most likely, he'll break a few bones along the way. Fine! But I won't be on the sidelines rooting for him."

"You might want to rethink that. It means a lot to a guy to have his woman nearby for moral support."

She rolled her eyes. "I'm not his woman."

"No?" Leo cocked his head to one side.

She decided to change the subject. "Speaking of which, what's going on with you and Egypt?"

He looked puzzled. "Nothing. Status quo. What makes you ask?"

"Status quo?" Krystina's tone shifted to one of annoyance. "Are we talking about your girlfriend or a job application?"

"It's all good," Leo said impatiently. "What do you want to hear? Egypt is Egypt and I'm me."

"What in the hell does that mean?"

"Just that Egypt is a free spirit. You know how she is. Nothing ties her down, and that's fine for me. I keep things cool and easy; the way she wants it."

Krystina stared at him completely speechless, which was rare for her. Were all men idiots? Did they have no clue what a woman thought or felt? How did Leo not understand he was Egypt's exception to her no-commitment rule?

"What is wrong with you? You and that *free spirit* have been dating for almost two years. Get your act together and decide what you want. Talk to her. And be direct. No one wants limbo status forever." Krystina stood. "Thanks for the chat, Leo."

"Don't you dare take one step out of this office."

Leo's commanding police officer voice stopped her dead in her tracks.

He stroked the stubble on his chin. "I'm assuming Egypt said something to you. Not that it's any of your business, but I do care about her." He leaned forward in his chair. "For your information, women aren't the only ones who get hurt. I've been burned more than once so I tread lightly. Egypt means a lot to me, and if I have to keep our relationship uncomplicated so I don't stifle her then that's what I will do. But that doesn't mean I'm not going to protect myself from history repeating itself."

"So instead you put up an impenetrable barrier around your heart?" Just like she had, Krystina realized. "Read the signs, Leo. She's never been with anyone for this long. A guy was lucky to get a third date out of her. The only reason she is going along with this whole 'everything is cool' vibe is because she's too scared to tell you how she feels for fear you don't feel the same way."

Leo laughed humorlessly. Then, steepling his fingers, he sat pensively for a moment. "Thanks, kid. You're right. Men are idiots."

Maybe so, but Krystina was a coward. Leo had given her some clarity regarding Loukas' need to fight, but still, she couldn't be a part of it. The idea of seeing him hurt was too much to bear. She just couldn't deal with it. But was she willing to lose him for her own convictions? It was all just a bit too much at that moment, especially after everything else that had happened. Yet Leo's words hung in the back of Krystina's mind. 'It means a lot to a guy to have his woman nearby for moral support.' Conflicting emotions roiled within her and she just didn't know what to do about it.

Yiayiá's Bougatsa

Ingredients

4 tablespoons unsalted butter, melted

½ cup granulated sugar

4 cups milk

½ cup fine semolina

3 large eggs

½ teaspoon vanilla powder

1pound phyllo

1 cup unsalted butter, melted for brushing the pastry.

Cinnamon and powdered sugar for dusting.

Method

Preheat oven to 350° F.

In a large pot, over a medium-high heat, combine the melted butter and the sugar. Mix until combined and then slowly whisk in the milk. Add in the semolina and vanilla while continuing to whisk. Cook for about 5 minutes, stirring regularly.

Beat the eggs and then very slowly add them to the pot, stirring continuously. Continue to cook for about 10 minutes until the custard has the consistency of a pudding. Remove from the heat and set the custard aside. Unroll the phyllo so the sheets lay flat. Cut the stack of phyllo sheets in half to a size approximately 8x13 inches.

Lift three sheets of phyllo together at once, setting them on a cutting board. Brush melted butter on the top sheet. Place a little more than ¼ cup of custard at the shorter end of the phyllo, leaving about 1½ inches from the edge. Fold the edge of phyllo over the custard and then fold in each of the sides. The custard should be fully covered by the phyllo. Fold the phyllo and custard over and over until you reach the other end. Use a spatula to help flip the bougatsa pie if needed. Brush both the top and bottom of the pie with butter. Then, using a spatula once more, carefully transfer the pie to a parchment-lined baking sheet. Repeat the steps until all the custard and phyllo are used.

Bake for approximately 20 minutes or until the phyllo is a light golden-brown. Remove from the oven and cool on a baking rack. Dust with cinnamon and powdered sugar.

Chapter 43

Loukas

Two weeks had passed since Loukas moved back into his home. George had given him a lot to consider. And it was way too much for an eighteen-year-old who'd basically been raising himself since his mother had died.

Loukas contemplated his options as he bulldozed his way through the house, one room at a time, trashing years of unnecessary possessions he no longer had any need for. With ninety-nine percent certainty, he was sure he'd sell the house and move on. But it was for that strong one percent clawing at his heart that he resisted letting go.

After cleaning out his father's closet and packing the clothing in donation boxes, he frowned at the empty space. And so it began. Poof! Just like that, he had expunged all traces of his childhood, one room at a time.

He thought of the sweet years of his early youth and the darker days of his recent past. Though he'd like to forget the latter, it was sewn into the fabric of who he was, and it couldn't be erased.

Loukas opened a drawer in his parents' bedroom expecting to find clothing to add to the donation box. Instead, he came across something far more priceless—photo albums, his old report cards, and the academic awards he'd earned at school over the years.

Taking a seat on the floor, he leaned against the bed and opened one of the albums. The page was filled with pictures of himself. He looked to be around three years old. Photo after photo depicted a happy family. His father, kissing his mother; Loukas between them at their feet; Loukas on his father's shoulders; his mother, rocking him to sleep …

This was his life until death stole his mother away and grief claimed his father. Now he was all alone in the world, left with nothing but an empty house void of the warmth and love it had once possessed. And he only had enough money to survive for a short while.

He laughed humorlessly, knowing none of that was really true. Stop the pity party, he berated himself, rubbing the dark circles under his eyes. He had Max and Leo. And the entire Andarakis family. Well, except for one, maybe. Unfortunately, she was the one who counted the most.

Turning the page only evoked more memories. These photos cataloged his youthful days with the only girl who had always occupied his heart. There they were as a pair of three-year-old children, locked in an embrace on Christmas day, cheek to cheek, flashing their innocent grins for the camera.

A single tear plopped onto the photo's clear protective plastic. Quickly wiping away the others that were about to fall from his cheeks, Loukas got ahold of himself, stood, and found an empty box in the corner of the room. Carefully, he placed the contents of the drawer stuffed with mementos into the box, marking it 'important to save.'

It occurred to him that leaving the house wasn't what made him sad. After all, it was merely an unoccupied structure. It no longer breathed the life that made it a home. No, it was the neighborhood he'd miss. His childhood friends, the comfort of the Andarakis family nearby, the benefit in knowing every bumpy crevice in the road and every branch on the trees he'd climbed to sneak into friends' rooms late in the evening.

Loukas hadn't put the house up for sale yet. But once he finished cleaning it out and repairing the walls and doors, collateral damage from the scuffles he'd had with his father, he'd list it. It bought him a little time to make some critical decisions.

The impatient sounds of a successive pounding on his front door drew Loukas out of his reverie. "Hold on!" he shouted, straightening himself out. "I'm coming."

When he opened the door, he found *Yiayiá* standing on the porch with her cane lifted, ready to thwack again.

"*Yiayiá!*" Loukas exclaimed, looking around to see if anyone was with her. "What are you doing here unescorted."

"I can walk two houses down the road," she argued with exasperation. "This!" She shook her cane. "Is going in the garbage soon."

No sense in challenging her. She had a will of iron, and if anyone could make it happen, it was her. If only she'd admit that COVID had left her weakened.

"Come inside and sit down," he offered. "Is there something I can do for you? Do you need a ride someplace?"

"What I need is for you and Krystina to come to your senses."

Loukas sighed, leading *Yiayiá* to the sofa. "I have come to mine. You should speak to her."

"Tell me, is it more important for you to get kicked in the head than be with the one you love?"

"It's not that simple, *Yiayiá*. It's about believing in me enough to let me make my own choices. It's about trust and encouragement."

"I did all of that for my Panos, and yet we were apart for fifty years." She patted Loukas' cheek sadly. "There are sacrifices and regrets in every choice. But you must make the one that gives you the most happiness."

After *Yiayiá* left, Loukas mulled over her advice. After a while, he pulled his phone out from his back pocket. With his finger hovering over her name, he contemplated texting her. Finally he tapped out a message.

Can we talk?

He waited for the dancing bubbles to appear, signifying an incoming reply, but his phone remained unresponsive. Shaking it off, he went back to work, applying Sheetrock putty to a gaping hole in the wall.

A half-hour later, his phone signaled an incoming text.

Krystina: *I don't think that's a good idea.*

Loukas: *I miss you.*

Krystina: *Me too. But I want you to live out your dreams, and this is one I can't be a part of. I'll be rooting for you in spirit but I can't stand by and watch. I'm sorry.*

The phone dropped from Loukas' hands as the finality of her words set in. With his back to the wall, he slid to the floor, crestfallen. Loukas didn't bother to respond. She'd made herself clear. Krystina had cut ties with him once again.

Chapter 44

Krystina

"Mia's on the phone!" Krystina ran down the staircase, waving her cell phone in the air. "Mom! She and Nicholas are coming home!"

"Let me have the phone," Melina said, snatching it from her daughter's hands. "When? I'm so happy. I want you to come straight here so I can see you for myself."

"Put her on speaker," Krystina prodded, jumping from foot to foot in excitement.

"I can't wait to see you, too, but we'll go to the apartment first," Mia said, laughing at the other end of the line.

"I want to meet you in the city when you arrive. I can freshen up your place before you get there. Please, please," Krystina blurted out in one breath.

"That's not necessary. We have a cleaning service for that," Mia said. "But I promise we'll have a girls' weekend soon."

"Are you flying to Athens before you come home?" Melina asked.

"Yes. We're flying home from Athens International Airport."

"Can you do me a favor and check in on Panos … my father?" she corrected. "Maybe you can even bring him here with you?"

"I'll talk to Nicholas. It's not that simple though. He'll need a passport and a visa."

"See what you can do. *Yiayiá* isn't getting any younger, and COVID took a toll on her."

"What about you and Dad?"

"We're fine. We've managed to keep the restaurant open, and so far, we haven't contracted it. We get tested weekly."

"That's a relief," Mia said. "I've been worried about all of you."

The muffled sound of Nicholas' voice was heard calling to Mia in the background.

"I have to go. Nicholas is calling me. I'll see you soon. Kisses." Mia signed off.

* * *

With Mia coming home, Krystina finally had something to look forward to. She was lying on her bed, staring at the ceiling, dwelling on Loukas when he unexpectedly texted her. Hearing from him hit her hard. After all, he was the one who walked out on her. But now, here he was saying that he missed her and wanted to talk. Her mind was reeling in a state of confusion. Krystina sat up, not knowing what to do. She was tempted to run down the street and resolve their conflict. But was it resolvable? Loukas was entitled to live his life in a way that fulfilled him. Who was she to give him ultimatums? No one had that right. Not even her, regardless of the fact she loved him.

It took her a good long while, sitting cross-legged, staring at the phone, balancing on her knee before she answered Loukas. Then, with tears of sorrow swimming in her eyes, she set him free and prayed for his safety.

"I want to talk to you," Melina said, stepping into her bedroom.

"Is everything okay?"

"Yes. Well, with everyone except perhaps you and Loukas."

"I don't want to talk about him," Krystina said through a sniffle.

"I'll tell you about Markella instead then," her mother maintained, taking a seat on the edge of Krystina's bed. "Do you know why I gave you her name as your middle one?"

"Because you were close friends?"

"Yes … but there was more to it than that. I had asked her to be your godmother, but she declined."

Krystina frowned in confusion.

"Let me explain. Loukas was a few months old when you were born. She was thrilled you were a girl. So with our families spending so much time together, she figured you kids might also become close. She didn't want to take the chance in case one day the two of you became more than just friends."

"I'm totally not following you."

"Godchildren and the children of the godparents are considered siblings in the eyes of the church and are not allowed to marry."

"Oh. Okay. I see now. So instead you gave me her name to honor her in another way."

"Exactly."

"How is this relevant to me now?" Krystina asked, feigning disinterest.

"You said you didn't want to talk about Loukas so …"

"So you decided to tell me how his mother hoped from the day we were born that we'd get married?" She stared at her mother in annoyance.

"I thought it was something you should know."

"Well, thank you. As if I don't get enough pressure from everyone else, now I have the added weight of disappointing a dead woman watching from above."

"Krystina," her mother said in a reprimanding tone.

"Mom, let it go. Loukas and I are taking different paths. It's just the way things happen sometimes."

Melina patted her daughter on the leg, sighing in resignation. "Okay. You're so very young though. Boys will come and go, and if you and Loukas are meant to be, it will happen in its own time."

Once her mother left the room, Krystina sank her head into her pillow, muffling her sobs. Until now, she had held back the tears she'd rebelliously refused to shed in front of her mother.

Collecting herself, Krystina tried to formulate a plan for her sister's homecoming. But it was in vain. She just couldn't shake the sadness from her soul.

Three days later, Mia called again. Unfortunately, this time the news was not good. Switching the call over to FaceTime, she asked Krystina to gather the family together.

Chapter 45

Mia

Mia and Nicholas checked into the hotel as soon their plane landed in Athens, eager to call the bar and speak to Panos. But after several unsuccessful attempts to dial through, Mia grew frustrated.

"Let me see what I can find out," Nicholas offered, opening his laptop. Kostas' bar wasn't the kind of establishment updated with a consumer-tempting website though. In truth, the place was somewhat dilapidated, and the technology had unlikely been upgraded over the last several decades.

Mia came up behind Nicholas, wrapping her arms around his neck. "Find out anything?"

"According to this listing of local bars, it should be open. Try the number again," Nicholas suggested.

"Nothing," Mia said after letting the phone ring several times.

"I'll arrange for a taxi. Maybe their phone is out of order."

But when they arrived, the bar was pitch black. Even the battered neon sign was eerily unlit.

"This doesn't make sense," Mia said, frowning.

"Maybe the bar couldn't survive the lockdown," Nicholas speculated.

"Doesn't Kostas and Panos live in the back rooms?"

Nicholas asked the cab driver to take them around back. *"Perímene,"* Nicholas said, asking the driver to wait. He handed him fifty euros to ensure the man stayed. The street was completely desolate, and it wasn't the best part of town.

Gravel crunched under their feet, and Mia held onto Nicholas to steady herself as they blindly negotiated the dips in the road.

"Panos! Kostas!" Nicholas banged on the metal door.

From the other side, a gruff voice complained, *"Oríste. Poios eínai?"*

"It's Mia and Nicholas," Mia called out. "Open the door."

"No. I have the coronavirus," came the muffled reply.

"Is that you, Kostas?" Nicholas asked with a worried frown.

"Yes."

"Open the door. We have our masks on, and we'll stand away."

As the door creaked open, Mia stifled a gasp. Like Panos, Kostas had suffered many permanent scars during his inhumane internment. But now he looked twenty years older than the last time they saw him. Though the weather was warm, the haggard man was wrapped in an ancient flannel robe riddled with dime-sized holes. The dim lamplight did nothing to hide how difficult it was for him to stand as he supported himself against the doorframe. "Kostas! You look awful," Mia exclaimed as she took in the pallor of his skin and the sweat dripping down his forehead, his matted hair plastered to his face. "You need to go to the hospital!"

"No. I'm not as bad as I look," he labored. "I feel like I have the flu but my fever hasn't broken yet."

"Is Panos sick too?" Mia asked, craning her head around Kostas to look for him. "Where is he?"

"I'm afraid he's at the hospital," Kostas said through a cough. "He was having trouble breathing. He and your grandmother had another FaceTime call a couple of days ago. He wasn't feeling well but he didn't tell her. Later that day, he grew worse. So I called for the ambulance," Kostas explained, breaking out into another fit of coughs.

"Why didn't you go too?" Mia asked with concern.

"I was still fine at that point."

"We can arrange for you to go to the hospital now," Nicholas offered.

"I don't need to." Kostas fell silent for a beat. "Panos is much worse." Distress coated his words. "Much worse," he trailed off.

Mia glanced soberly at Nicholas, her eyes reflecting her worry.

"You need to rest," Mia told Kostas. "What can we do to help you?"

"Nothing. I'll get by."

"I'm going to arrange for cooked meals to be delivered here daily," Nicholas said with authority. "And I'll contact the local pharmacy to deliver any medications or supplies you may need."

"I wish I could wrap you up in a hug," Mia said. "When this is all over, that's just what I'm going to do."

"*Koukla.*" Kostas blew Mia a kiss.

Nicholas asked Kostas which hospital Panos was admitted to. They said their goodbyes and then instructed the cab driver to head there immediately.

"It's too late, Nicholas," Mia sighed. "They'll never let us in at this hour."

"*Agápi*, we aren't getting in at all. Hospitals aren't allowing visitors."

"That doesn't seem fair," she complained. "He's all alone and probably scared." She dabbed at the corners of her eyes. "Maybe we should call and let the staff know that he has family nearby."

"No. We need to get an update on his condition now and make it clear that you are to be notified if anything changes."

"When we get back to the hotel, we'll have to call the family," Mia said with dread.

Nicholas agreed. "But not until we have information."

"She's his granddaughter. And the only relative he has in Greece." Nicholas argued with the woman handling the hospital lobby front desk.

267

"We are under the most critical restrictions. There is nothing I can do," the receptionist said firmly.

"You can get me an administrator," Nicholas demanded. "I understand the dire situation here but this is an unusual circumstance. Mr. Nikopoulos needs to know he has family here, caring for his wellbeing."

"We are doing our best to treat all our patients," the woman countered wearily.

How many times a day did this woman get verbally abused by frustrated relatives? Mia wondered. She didn't envy the receptionist one bit and regretted that Nicholas was contributing to her unpleasant evening.

Nicholas was about to challenge the woman again but Mia gently placed her hand on her husband's arm.

"I only ask that you update me regularly on his condition and let him know we're here," Mia said calmly "I think it would help lift his spirits to know he has family looking out for him."

"I can do that."

"Thank you." Mia smiled graciously.

"We'll be back tomorrow with an iPad for him to FaceTime with family. His wife is in the States, and they've been separated far too long," Nicholas explained.

"I'm sorry to hear that," the receptionist said sincerely. "I'll be here all day tomorrow. I'll make it my personal mission to make sure he gets the device."

Nicholas pressed fifty euro in the palm of her gloved hand. "Thank you. We would appreciate it. Good night."

"Nicholas," Mia scolded as they walked through the automatic glass doors. "You can't keep throwing money around at everyone to get them to do what you want."

"Sure, I can. And I just did."

"I believe she would have followed through regardless."

"Now we know for sure she will," he stated with utter confidence.

"Smug bastard." Mia laughed. But she loved him all the more for caring for her family as he would his own.

Chapter 46

Krystina

Krystina gazed out her bedroom window, ruminating on Mother Nature's remarkable ability to commensurate the gloomy sky with her current state of being.

Today was going to be one of those days when Krystina would have to rummage through the back of her closet in search of a warm sweater. Every year, at the end of August, there were a few days when the temperature dropped and the precipitation rose, the sudden chill penetrating her to the bone.

And although the warm days were sure to return, it was a devious little reminder that summer would soon slide into fall, and not far behind that was winter. Ugh! That was one season she could live without.

Maybe the heavens were as angry as she was, hence, the impending storm. So this was the payoff after all those years of separation, prayers, hope, and survival of torture? It just didn't seem fair.

Like a punch in the gut, Mia's news felt like things couldn't be any worse. But she knew that wasn't true. *Yiayiá* had recovered from the virus, and now Panos had to as well. After all the beatings and humiliations he'd endured in the past, a germ invading his body couldn't be his undoing. It was simply unacceptable.

Descending the stairs, Krystina heard the typical clamoring in her home that had been absent while quarantined with her grandmother and Loukas. Pots and pans clanging. Her parents arguing over something inane. The deafening sound of her father's coffee grinder. Ordinarily, she would have silently begged for quiet during these early morning hours. But now it was music to her ears. Funny how she, and people in general, had little appreciation for what they have until it's been stripped away.

Sadly, that thought regrettably brought her mind back around to Loukas. After pushing him away for years, she was somehow only able to hold onto him for a fleeting moment in time. Maybe it was a sign. Maybe it proved they simply weren't meant to be after all.

Krystina wanted to slap herself silly. There was no room in her brain to dwell on this now. Instead, she had to keep her focus on figuring out a way to reunite her grandparents.

"Hey, Mom, is *Yiayiá* awake yet or ...?" Krystina didn't finish her sentence as she rounded the corner into the kitchen. It was her grandmother making the racket with the frying pans on the stove.

"Shouldn't you be resting?" Krystina asked.

"No!" *Yiayiá* waved the spatula in her hand as if it were her weapon of choice. "I called Panos on that *micró* TV and the nurse say he sleeping. So I cook and I wait."

Krystina whispered in her mother's ear. "She doesn't seem too worried. That's good."

"She's a wreck," Melina muttered back. "You're in the way, *vre, Giorgio*. Get out of the kitchen," she added in a louder voice, gesturing for her husband to move out of her way.

"Can't a man make a decent cup of coffee in his own house?"

"*Katsé.* Sit!" *Yiayiá* insisted. She nudged Krystina and her parents over to the kitchen table. "I made Panos' favorite. Fried eggs cooked with *pastrouma*." She used a pancake flipper to carefully serve sunny-side-up eggs onto each plate. Then she placed thin slices of the cured,

271

spiced meat alongside the eggs.

Her mother was right. *Yiayiá* was a wreck if she had made them the favorite meal of a husband who was in a hospital five thousand miles away.

After two hours passed and no call had come in, Krystina took matters into her own hands. Once again, the attending nurse answered the iPad.

"Hello? I'm Panos' granddaughter. We've been waiting for a call back. Is he able to speak yet?"

"I haven't had a chance to call you. I'm so sorry. We are handling too many patients at once," she explained while adjusting the drip on his IV. It was hard to fully tell what the nurse looked like or how old she was, protected as she was in what looked like a hazmat suit.

"I understand. I don't mean to bother you," Krystina apologized.

"He's awake now, but he's very weak. So please keep it brief."

"Thank you. Give me a second to get my grandmother."

Krystina's heart bled when she stepped into *Yiayiá's* bedroom. With tightly closed eyes, her grandmother was counting off knots on a black prayer rope, her words inaudible; the petitions were meant for God's ears only.

"*Yiayiá?*" Krystina interrupted quietly. "Panos." She handed her the tablet.

"*Panos, agápi mou, ti épathes?*" The distress in her voice was evident. "I had the corona too, you know. So don't be stubborn," she rattled off in her native tongue. "Listen to the doctors so we can be together when you recover."

"I'll swim across the ocean if I have to," Panos promised, his voice barely a whisper. "Don't worry. I've been through worse."

"I worry. I just found you." Her eyes glistened with unshed tears. "I want to hold your hand. And touch your face," she said, the words lodging in her throat. "I need you."

"You have me." He began to drift off. "Always."

"That's all for today," the weary nurse stated, her bloodshot eyes revealing her level of exhaustion.

"Thank you," Krystina said, taking the tablet from her grand-mother. "We'll call back tomorrow." She walked out of the room and lowered her voice. "In the meantime, if my grandfather's situation changes, please call me."

"I will."

Krystina felt sick. Physically sick. And helpless. She crept up the stairs, one hand on the banister, the other wrapped around her stomach for support. As soon as she reached her room, Krystina flopped face down onto the bed and wept. She needed to cry the myriad of emotions out of her system.

She knew she shouldn't, but she couldn't help herself. Tapping out a text to Loukas, she hesitated before pressing send.

Krystina: *Panos is in the hospital with COVID. He's not doing well. Thought u should know.*

Loukas: *I'm sorry. What can I do?*

Krystina: *Nothing to be done from here. Mia & Nicholas are in Athens handling it.*

Loukas: *How's Yiayiá?*

Krystina: *Pretending to be stronger than she is.*

Loukas: *Mind if I come by to see her?*

Krystina: *Of course. No matter what, you'll always be family.*

Krystina watched the jumping dots on her phone until they suddenly disappeared. Then, after a long pause, they appeared again. Once again, they stopped. Whatever Loukas had written, he must have erased. She was just about to put her phone away when a new text came through.

Loukas: *Thanks. I'll be over later today.*

Yes, he would, she thought with a deep sigh. But Loukas was coming for her grandmother, not for her.

Chapter 47

Loukas

Loukas covered his head with his hoodie and ran from his car to the gym door. Rain pelted him from every which way, soaking him to the bone in a matter of seconds. Fumbling with the key, he turned the lock, stamping his feet dry as he entered. The place was silent but for the deluge of raindrops pummeling the aluminum roof, rivaling the sound of alarming gunfire.

He'd do a little pummeling of his own. If anyone wanted to understand why Loukas needed to channel his aggression, all they had to do was watch and learn. And, of course, he was mainly referring to her. Krystina. His Minnie.

Everything had gone to shit. His life, the world, even the people he loved had their own problems. And he was powerless to do anything to change it.

Loukas' fists made impact with the punching bag with such velocity, it was as though he'd waged war with it.

Thwack. Thwack. Thwack.

"Yo! Hold on there."

Turning, Loukas found Leo standing with his arms crossed, a disapproving grimace on his face.

"How long have you been there?" Loukas asked, panting.

"Long enough to see you expel every last drop of energy way too quickly."

"I'm building up my stamina." Loukas wiped the sweat from his brow.

"That's not how it's done." Leo narrowed his eyes. "What's your deal today?"

"My deal is I want in on the next tournament," he almost shouted with conviction. "I need to win at something, and this is my focus right now."

Leo rubbed at the scruff on his chin. After a long pause, he said slowly, "I'll make you a deal. I'll train you, and I'll train you hard. I'm looking to open the gym now that the COVID case numbers seem to be under control. I need to recoup some of my lost revenue, and a tournament will help."

Loukas listened with wide-eyed anticipation.

"I think I have someone who would be a pretty even match for you, and he's in your weight class."

"And you'll let me go up against him?" Loukas asked hopefully.

"Yes, but there are conditions. You train the way I tell you with no arguments."

"Got it," Loukas agreed.

"Not so fast. You have to enroll in school. I don't care what you do. Go to the community college and major in liberal arts or culinary arts. Go learn a trade like plumbing or mechanics. It doesn't matter. But you will do something more than just train."

"I don't know what I want to do, though. It's such a waste of time until I figure it out," he argued, dismissing the idea defensively.

"Yeah," Leo stretched out his response. "That's not gonna fly. Figure it out. I know from reliable sources your grades were high enough to get you into a good college." Raising an eyebrow, he waited for an answer.

Exhibiting his frustration like a cranky toddler about to throw a tantrum, Loukas moaned. But once Leo pinned him with his unrelenting stare, he complied. "Okay," Loukas reluctantly agreed.

"Not just okay. Say 'Yes Leo, I'll put as much effort into school as I will training.'"

Loukas dragged through the repetition like a petulant child. If he wanted to be mature about it, he'd admit Leo was right. But he'd had to be mature since the day his mother died, and honestly, it was freeing to let go of it all, even if only for a few hours. And with Leo, there was a line of trust that allowed him to be himself.

* * *

"I miss you," *Yiayiá* told Loukas when he found her sitting in her recliner in front of the TV with a blanket draped over her feet.

"I miss you too," Loukas admitted as he dragged in a kitchen chair, taking a seat beside her.

"Why you no come for dinner anymore?"

"I've been busy cleaning out the house."

"I don't believe you."

"Have you spoken to Panos today?" he asked, purposely changing the subject.

"No. We can try him now, though."

"That would be nice. Is he doing any better?"

Anguish clouded over the usually mischievous sparkle in her eyes. "No. He very weak."

"I'm sure he'll recover. It takes a while."

"I'm scared, *agori mou.*" *Yiayiá* took his hands, gripping them tightly.

Loukas leaned in to hug her, whispering words of comfort in her ear. He noticed Krystina glimpsing him as he embraced her grandmother. The second their eyes met, she jumped out of sight.

The exchange wasn't lost on *Yiayiá*. "Time is not our friend. Don't waste it," she whispered back purposely.

Loukas' chest constricted. "Let's make that call."

After five rings, the masked and shielded face of a woman in scrubs answered.

"*Kalispera*, Maria," *Yiayiá* greeted the attending nurse. "How is my Panos today?"

"I'm afraid he's had a rough day. I'm sorry, Kalliope. We have him on full oxygen."

"Is he awake?"

"No. He's finally getting some much-needed rest."

"Can I at least see him for a minute?"

Maria, the shift nurse assigned to Panos, turned the camera toward his face. A bulky mask covering his mouth and nose was strapped around his head, pumping oxygen into his lungs and obscuring his face from view. But what didn't fail their notice was the pallid color of his skin.

Loukas grasped her hand with his free one in support when *Yiayiá* stifled a cry.

"Is he critical?" Loukas asked with concern.

"He's not at the point where we feel the need to intubate him. We've seen many cases where the increase of oxygen is enough."

"When can I talk to him?"

The look on Maria's face didn't offer any encouragement. "Maybe in a couple of days."

Loukas couldn't see her face but the nurse's voice rang of compassion. "Thank you," Loukas said quietly, squeezing *Yiayiá's* hand. "Take good care of him."

"We will." She closed the call.

"I don't have a good feeling. *Panayia*, help him," *Yiayiá* muttered, crossing herself in prayer.

Loukas wasn't sure if calling for the Holy Mother would help or not. It sure as hell didn't work for his mother. But if it made *Yiayiá* feel better, that's all that mattered.

"Why don't you watch something funny on TV to get your mind

off of your worries."

"Only if you stay," she countered.

Today was a day of ultimatums. First Leo and now Krystina's grandmother. Naturally, he complied. Loukas wouldn't deny this woman anything, especially not now, not when she needed him the most. She wasn't his blood, but in every other way, she was his grandmother.

And this is how Loukas found himself spending the remainder of his day sitting through a marathon of *The Golden Girls*.

Memory ... is the diary that we all carry about with us. Oscar Wilde

Chapter 48

Kalliope

Present Day

Three days later, Kalliope spoke to Panos again. Maria had called via FaceTime, informing the family he was agitated and kept trying to pull his oxygen mask off. Frustrated, he threatened to yank all the wires from his body unless he was granted permission to speak to his wife.

Finally, when her face appeared on the screen, Panos sighed in relief, touching the glass as though he could caress his wife's face through the screen.

Panos spoke with great difficulty, stopping after every few words and gasping for air. "*Kalliope mou, agapimeni, mou,* always remember, you are my life and forever close in my heart."

His labored breathing told her this was draining him of all his strength. And this time, his confession of love offered her no comfort. 'Always remember.' Those two words altered a meaningful sentiment promising a lifetime of devotion to a heart-crushing goodbye.

Yiayiá wanted to shout, 'I don't want to remember. I want to live in the present with you!' But instead, she blinked back her tears and forced a smile for her husband's sake. "Save your energy. You don't need to speak. I know," she assured him. "I know and I've believed in you and waited all these years to see you again. Soon we'll be together." But as much as she tried to say the words with conviction, a chill still crept up her spine.

His expression remained grim, and Kalliope surmised it took too much energy for him to form a smile.

"Is the family there?" he asked.

"Everyone is in the house. Yes."

It was Sunday and Melina had asked the family to gather together for dinner. Since the start of the pandemic, family gatherings had been rare. Now, with everyone here, Panos would finally have a chance to see all of his family. This would surely lift his spirits; surrounded by so many people who love him.

"I want to see them."

"*Pethia! Élla ethó*," *Yiayiá* summoned.

Melina ran in first. "What's wrong?"

"Your *babá* wants to talk to all of you."

"Hi, *Babá*," Melina said, trying to sound cheerful. "Are you feeling any better?"

"They are doing what they can for me," Panos answered slowly. "*Koritsi mou*, forgive me," he pleaded though his wheezing. "I love you so very much."

"I love you too," Melina said, her voice thick with emotion. "You already asked for my forgiveness the other day and I gave it. Please don't ask again." Tears overtook her and Melina couldn't continue. She sucked in a calming breath to compose herself and went on. "You did what you thought was right for us. Keeping your family safe was more important than your own happiness. I understand that now." She exhaled a shuddering breath. "I'm the one who is sorry, and I want you to know I love you and I need you."

Yiayiá leaned against her daughter and ran her shaking hands up and down the length of her arms in comfort. Melina had always resented the faith *Yiayiá* had in her husband. She argued that he'd abandoned them. Now her daughter finally saw the truth. But would she ever have the chance to hug her father? The fear of losing Panos again clawed at her insides.

Soon, everyone had crowded into *Yiayiá's* bedroom, each person taking a turn to pop their face on the screen to offer their greetings.

"Love to all of you," Panos labored. "My family …" He trailed off. "Look at my family," he said softly to his attending nurse.

"They seem wonderful and they obviously care about you," she said sincerely.

"Thank you for bringing my Kalliope back to me," he struggled to say when his granddaughters' faces filled the screen once more.

"He's getting very tired," *Yiayiá* whispered to Melina in despair. "He needs to rest now."

"We love you," the girls said simultaneously.

"We'll come for you as soon as you're better," Nicholas added.

"Melina *mou, sagapó*," Panos choked out with emotion.

"I love you, too, Babá."

"*Kalliope mou*," Panos uttered on a hoarse whisper.

Yiayiá laid her hands over her heart and mouthed her 'I love you.' The love and longing in his eyes told her all she needed to know. Now if she could only shed the sense of dread running through her veins then she could finally have some peace.

"I think that's enough for today," Maria said with regret. "Continually pulling off the oxygen mask is not helping his condition."

"Melina, Kalliope." Panos reached for the tablet. "I love you forever." His hand touched the screen desperately, as though he could really touch them.

The screen went black. And suddenly, so did everyone's moods. Normally, *Yiayiá* would scold the group for their somber dispositions. But not today. Today her heart felt like a ball of yarn, unraveling little by little, falling to pieces around her.

"Come on, let's have dessert," Kally said, forcing a cheerful lilt to her voice.

Suddenly feeling older than she'd like to admit, Kalliope preferred solitude to the raucous ramblings of her family over coffee and cake. But she sat at the table for what she believed was an acceptable amount of time before quietly retreating to her room.

* * *

Kalliope found the respite she craved in the comfort of her bed, drawing the coverlet up over her small frame and hiding away from the world. Time and memories had a unique relationship. The fifty years that had passed seemed so distant now. It was as though two lifetimes had come and gone. Yet there were other occasions when Kalliope could close her eyes and swear she was still a young woman in Kalamáta. Her mind tricked her senses into believing she smelled the salty sea air and felt the breeze brushing across her face, just as she had when she and her Panos walked the pier together. As her eyes grew heavier, she contemplated. If time was merely a concept and impossible to truly measure then who was to say she couldn't experience it all again?

* * *

Kalliope's modest home hadn't been filled with so many guests since her parents' funerals. But unlike the somber mood of those occasions, the women in her village were now giddy with excitement.

With the absence of a mother to dote on her on this particular day, Stavroula, her mother's closest friend, offered to step into the role. Since Kalliope and Panos had no family, and she was still in mourning, they had planned a small wedding. They had only asked Demos, her employer at the taverna, to attend to act as the *koumbaro* for the couple. But Stavroula would have none of that, and so she had gathered up the local women to organize a day Kalliope would never forget.

Kalliope felt like a princess, or at the very least a Hollywood movie star. Her friend, Argi, fussed with her hair while another young woman applied a touch of makeup to her face. Never in her life had she been so pampered.

"My dress is hanging on the back of my door," Kalliope told Argi.

"You're not wearing that!" her friend argued.

"But it's my Sunday best."

Argi held up a finger, signaling for Kalliope to wait. Then, as quickly as she had scampered away, she returned, carrying a tea-length white dress. Save for the delicate lace trimming adorning the V neck and the cap sleeves, the garment was simple.

"I don't understand," Kalliope questioned, her brow creasing with confusion. "This was your wedding dress."

"And I'd be honored if you'd wear it today."

"But—"

"No buts! If you don't use it, it will sit in my closet for years only to be food for the moths."

"Well, when you put it that way," Kalliope giggled.

"Come on. I'll help you into it."

As she shed her robe, no less than six other ladies stormed into her tiny bedroom, buzzing about her all at once. A young girl around the age of fifteen nimbly fastened the many buttons running down the back of the dress. Once the girl was done, Stavroula tied a satin bow she'd adorned with tiny iridescent seed pearls at her waistline.

"Oh! Did you make this sash?" Kalliope asked with admiration.

Stavroula nodded proudly and Kalliope threw her arms around the woman in response. She was overwhelmed with emotion for what these women had done for her. Her eyes swam with gratitude as the tears welled. She dabbed the corners with her pinkies so as not to ruin the applied cosmetics.

Your mother would be so proud of you today," Stavroula said affectionately offering up a double-cheek kiss. "You're a vision."

The tender moment was broken by a young woman, still in her teens, holding a pair of white shoes in one hand and a pen in the other. "You know what to do with these!" she boomed eagerly. "Write my name first!"

Kalliope had almost forgotten about this tradition. She was to scribble the names of every single woman attending the wedding on the bottom of her shoes. Then, at the end of the night, whoever's name had not worn off would be the next to marry.

"Don't be in such a rush to get married," Kalliope advised.

"I'm only two years younger than you," the girl confirmed.

"Panos was unexpected. I wasn't searching for a husband," she admitted. But Kalliope complied and wrote Antonia's name first before taking a mental inventory of the other single women in the house and adding their names to the soles.

"One last touch before we walk you to the church," Kalliope heard someone say.

The crowd fell away like the parting of the Red Sea as an older woman approached, her delighted expression revealing the pride in the garment she gingerly held in her hands.

"For you," the old woman offered.

Kalliope gasped. The tulle veil was trimmed with seed pearls identical to the ones Stavroula had affixed to the sash. This must have been a difficult task for the woman with her arthritic hands and poor eyesight. Overcome, Kalliope tried to hold back the tears, but despite all her efforts they flowed freely.

"Thank you so very much." She hugged the woman tightly. "I'll treasure it."

Kalliope looked about the room. "Thank you, all of you, for making this day so special for me. I know in my heart that my mother is smiling down on your kindness."

Stavroula came up beside Kalliope, draping an arm around her shoulder. "She was my best friend. I miss her terribly. She would want us to do this for you."

Kalliope nodded, attempting to ebb the flurry of emotions.

Argi clapped her hands. "Let's get this girl to the church!"

Singing a joyful wedding tune, the women filed out of Kalliope's home, escorting her down the path leading to the church. As they continued to stroll along, the crowd following behind them grew. By the time they reached the stone courtyard outside the entrance to the narthex, over one hundred villagers were waiting to see the bride and groom in this special ceremony.

Demos appeared amid the crowd and offered his arm. "You look lovely." He smiled warmly. "Thank you for this honor."

"My father would be happy I asked you."

Demos kissed each cheek affectionately. "Are you ready to meet your groom?"

"Yes. I can't wait a minute longer."

"You won't have to," he said with a laugh as Panos appeared from behind a cluster of onlookers.

"You are a vision," he cooed, his voice thick with emotion. "The most beautiful woman I've ever laid my eyes on."

Kalliope suddenly felt the heat of a flush rise on her cheeks.

"These are for you." Panos handed her a small bouquet of white peonies tightly bound at the stems by a white satin ribbon. "These I did not yank out of the ground," he said with a twinkle in his eye.

Kalliope laughed. "I would love them all the same even if you had."

"Are you ready?" the priest interrupted.

"We are," the couple said in unison.

Holding a gold-bound bible, the elderly clergyman led the way, his white and gold vestments blowing with the breeze as he walked. Forming the sign of the cross with the holy book as he entered the nave, he began the procession, each guest crossed themselves as they filed into the church.

* * *

Kalliope sighed in her sleep, a smile drifting across her face as she dreamed. Visions of the ceremony flashed before her mind—the crowning, the Dance of Isaiah, the *koufeta* thrown over them in a shower of celebration as they walked back up the aisle.

In a semi-conscious state, her clouded mind entertained the possibility none of this was real. At least, not in this time and place. But if that were so, she wished for nothing more than to remain here in her most blissful of moments.

* * *

"Are you nervous?" Panos asked.

Demos had thrown a reception for the couple at his place. Now, after a long day, they were finally alone.

"I'm not sure," Kalliope admitted. "I want you so very much, but ..."

"But you're afraid? Don't be, *agápi mou*. I promise it will be easier than the first time."

"No, that's not it." She reached up and stroked his cheek tenderly, her eyes wide and nervous. "But I do want to please you."

Kalliope didn't often let her vulnerable side show. But Panos was her husband now, and suddenly she was aware she was very much out of her depth.

Panos took her face in his hands and kissed her. "You already do. Our passion will carry us through."

Panos looked at the bed and frowned. "What do we do about this, though?"

Before they did anything else, they needed to empty the bed from all the superstitious items placed onto it by the single women in the village. Rose petals forming two hearts decorated the center of the bed. Money for prosperity and rice for putting down roots were scattered about.

"At least they didn't leave the baby with us," she laughed.

"Baby?"

"Yes. A baby had been set down onto the bed in the hopes we'd soon have a child of our own. It's tradition."

The expression of horror on Panos' face made her laugh nervously. "Don't you want children?"

"Of course, I do. But could we have a moment or two alone before we take on that responsibility?"

"I agree. We have plenty of time."

"I think these women are expecting me to knock you up tonight."

Kalliope yanked on the end of the duvet, pulling it and all the contents off the bed. "That takes care of that," she said with determination.

Panos motioned her over with his forefinger. "Come here," he demanded.

If his expression held any more smolder, Kalliope could stuff him with firewood and warm the house all winter long. She could feel herself burning up from his gaze alone.

Mapping kisses down her neck, Panos slid the straps of her dress off her shoulders. Then, turning her tenderly, he unfastened one button at a time, his fingertips seducing her as he grazed her back.

Kalliope shuddered in response; the hundreds of butterflies that had taken flight in her belly must have escaped and scattered throughout her trembling body.

"You're exquisite," he moaned, turning her around to face him as her dress cascaded to the ground. Then, swiftly, he shed himself of his clothing until he was down only to his briefs.

Taking her in his arms, he lifted her, laying her gently onto the bed. Like the first time they had made love, Kalliope wasn't sure what to do. Her hands remained palms down on the bed. Willing herself to relax, she hoped it didn't hurt as much this time. But then she reminded herself she was with her Panos. Her understanding, tender-hearted husband. The man she trusted with her life. Knowing this calmed her mind, although her heart still raced. With anticipation. With need. With all the love she had for this man. She wrapped her arms around him, running her hands up and down his sun-bronzed back.

Every inch of Panos was solid muscle—his arms as she grasped hold of them, his chest pressing against her as he kissed his way down her body, and his legs as they spread hers apart to make room for him.

After Panos shed Kalliope of her bra and panty, he trailed soft kisses down her body until he reached the apex of her thighs, arousing her in a most unexpected way. She didn't know what to make of him kissing her *there*, but her body reacted, writhing with pleasure as she grew even more desperate for him.

"I want you to be ready for me," Panos panted.

If ready meant rapturous in a way she had never known before, Kalliope was more than ready.

"Panos, please." She could barely choke out the words, running her hands through his hair in a frenzy. "I want you."

Lifting his head, Panos looked at his wife through heavy-lidded eyes and inched his way up her body, stopping only to draw a hardened nipple into his mouth.

Kalliope cried out, clutching his back as she rocked into him, hoping for release. Panos tugged at his briefs, kicking them off in a rush. As he lined himself up with her entrance, Kalliope sighed with passion. She was more than ready, and if there was pain again, it would be worth it. Right now, nothing could outweigh her desire to feel him move inside her. To fill her with his body. With his love. She wanted, needed, now more than ever, for them to be joined in body and soul.

Panos was a considerate lover, taking it slow until she adjusted to his girth. But there was no pain this time, only ecstasy as she pleaded for more of him. Finally, she reached her peak, her world detonating around her in a blinding explosion of brilliant lights and colors. Kalliope's body thrummed in pleasure as her inner walls pulsed around him. Grabbing his bottom, she urged him to thrust harder, and that was all he needed to find his own release.

As their first glorious night as husband and wife gave way to the break of day, the lovers remained entwined, exploring and worshiping each other's bodies, and whispering professions of devotion.

Kalliope stirred. A soft caress grazed her cheek like a whisper in the wind. "Panos?" she murmured sleepily.

"Yes, my love. One day we will be together again."

* * *

Kalliope awoke lying in a tear-stained pillow. A sense of dread had seized her entire being. If someone had yanked her heart from her chest and drained it of every last drop of blood, she couldn't have felt emptier than she did at that moment.

"*Yiayiá?*" Krystina rushed into her room. "I heard you crying. What's wrong?"

"He's gone," she wailed. "My Panos is gone."

"No, no," Krystina assured her as she wrapped her grandmother in her arms, gently rocking her. "You must have had a bad dream. That's all."

"I had a beautiful dream, and now he's gone." She pulled away to look her granddaughter in the eye. "I can feel it in here." *Yiayiá* pressed her hand to her heart, her small frame shaking with her sobs.

"Krystina." Mia stepped into the room, a solemn expression on her face. "Can I talk to you for a minute?"

"Now? Can't it wait?" Krystina asked irritably.

"No, I'm afraid not."

Krystina sighed. "Rest. I'll be right back and then we'll call the hospital to ease your mind." She kissed her grandmother on the cheek, hurrying from the room.

But Kalliope knew what her granddaughter didn't. There would be no good news from the hospital. And her heart was breaking.

Chapter 49

Krystina

October 2020

"What is it?" Krystina snapped at her sister after exiting *Yiayiá's* bedroom.

"Nicholas just got a call from the hospital."

That caught her attention. Krystina's heart skipped a beat when she saw the grief reflected in her sister's eyes.

"There was a complication." Mia's voice trembled as she continued, "Panos … our grandfather, passed away."

"No, no, it can't be." But Krystina knew it was true. She covered her face with her hands, weeping as she thought of the deep sadness reflected on her grandmother's face. "They truly were connected at the soul," she whispered, wiping away her tears. "She knew," Krystina murmured. "She knew."

"Who knew?" Mia asked, pulling Krystina's hands from her sister's face.

"*Yiayiá*. I was just consoling her." Krystina was astounded. "She told me he was gone. She just … knew," she trailed off.

* * *

"I'm marking off the days on my calendar until this year is over," Krystina whispered adamantly as she and her sisters filed solemnly into the church.

Forty days had passed since Panos had died, and the family had come to memorialize him. Nicholas had arranged for a proper Orthodox funeral for him, but no one except the priest was allowed to attend due to the current restrictions. Even if Kostas had wanted to go, the man was still too weak from his own bout with COVID. But at least he was recovering.

Today, the entire assembly of Andarakis family and friends was there to remember Panos and to pray for his soul. It didn't matter that most of the mourners had never met him. They were there to offer comfort to her grief-stricken grandmother.

In the narthex, Krystina lit a thin beeswax candle and secured it in the bed of sand holding it in place. The ornately carved wooden table meant to hold the candles parishioners lit as they entered the church stood between glass-encased icons for worshipers to venerate. Silently, she prayed for life to return as it once was while making the sign of the cross. Quietly, they walked to the front row pew, smiling sadly at the others who had also come to pay their respects.

During the entire liturgy, Krystina distracted herself, examining each life-size icon painted on every wall in the church, admiring the chandeliers, and staring at the bright beams of light shooting through the dome windows above.

Anything was better than looking at the inconsolable expression on her grandmother's face. Dressed in black like an old village woman, *Yiayiá* seemed to have aged twenty years in the last month and a half. For a lady who preferred bright colors and a touch of lipstick, seeing her in drab clothing and gray hair was a devastating turnaround. There were wrinkles on her face that Krystina had never noticed before, and even her posture had taken on the form of a woman older than her years.

When the liturgy had ended the priest walked over to a table in front of the altar. Two altar boys holding life-size candles followed the clergyman. On the table stood a cross, a framed photo of a much younger version of Panos, and a beautifully decorated platter of *kollyva*. *Yiayiá* had insisted on preparing it herself rather than asking the church to arrange for it. The sweet offering, prepared to remember the dead and pray for their souls, contained wheatberries, cinnamon, nuts, raisins, and parsley. The mixture was then blanketed with a thick layer of powdered sugar and adorned with silver candies.

Krystina's parents held *Yiayiá's* hands throughout the memorial prayers and the censing and blessing of the *kollyva*. But Krystina could no longer hold back her tears when the priest began to chant the memorial hymn. *May his memory be eternal. May his memory be eternal. May his memory be eternal.*

A sob escaped from deep within her, but when she saw *Yiayiá* crumple to her seat, her resolve finally shattered altogether. Krystina turned when a hand squeezed her shoulder in support. Loukas looked at her with so much grief in his eyes, they pierced her soul. She acknowledged him with a sad smile and felt another stab to her heart as she met his gaze.

"What happens now?" Loukas asked, coming over to Krystina at the memorial luncheon.

"That's an odd question," she said wearily. "What's to happen? *Yiayiá* will probably mourn for the rest of her life. We're living in limbo. The world is at a standstill, yet everything, absolutely everything, has changed."

She looked in Egypt's direction, shaking her head imperceptibly. She was sitting with Leo but the vibe between them was off. "Even Egypt is thinking of moving on to get out of this rut."

"What do you mean by 'moving on?'" Concern was etched into Loukas' face.

"She's thinking of moving to L.A. Her jewelry designs have been selling well, and she was offered an exclusive contract with a department store there. But she hasn't told anyone yet, so keep it to yourself."

"What about Leo?"

"So far, he hasn't given her any reason to stay. She could design from here and travel to Cali when she needs to, but Egypt thinks maybe it's time to distance herself from Leo."

"She can't do that!" he exclaimed. "He loves her."

"What? How do you know?"

"He told me. The only reason he keeps it casual between them is because that's what he thinks she wants."

Krystina groaned. "He told me the same thing when I asked him about it. Leo said he *cared* about Egypt but he never used the L word in our conversation. And as far as I can tell, he's done nothing to make his feelings clear. She has no idea."

She looked back over to the couple and saw no outward sign of affection between them. No handholding or comforting arm around Egypt's shoulder. Nothing to indicate they were anything more than friends. It was as though the spark was gone.

"Egypt never wanted anything serious with the other men she dated in the past," Krystina explained. "But right from the start, Leo was different." Krystina chewed the inside of her cheek thoughtfully, her brow furrowed. "We have to do something about this, or else!"

"Or else, what? This is between the two of them," Loukas supplied.

"But what if they have their signals crossed. If we don't intervene then ..." Krystina sighed, slumping her shoulders in defeat.

"They miss a chance that may only come along once in a lifetime," Loukas said thoughtfully.

Their eyes locked, and suddenly Krystina had the feeling Loukas was no longer talking about Leo and Egypt.

"You'd think at their age they'd have it all figured out," she said, thinking out loud. Her focus blurred. Krystina was lost in thought.

Loukas snapped his fingers to break her concentration. "I can see the wheels turning in that brain of yours."

"What if I set up a girls' night? You know, a sleepover, with boy talk, and all that. I'll get my sisters to work on her until she agrees to come clean to Leo about her feelings." She waited for a beat before going on. "You do the same. Get the guys together to knock some sense into Leo."

"And then what?" Loukas asked.

"I don't know!" Krystina threw her hands up. "Either one of them spills or we get them both in a room together and restrain them until they admit their feelings."

* * *

"I can't remember the last time we've had a girls' night," Kally said.

Her stepdaughter, Athena, was spending the night with Melina and *Yiayiá*. The plan had worked out for everyone. There was no better way to put a smile on their grandmother's face than by letting her spend time with that sweet child.

"I can't believe it's chilly enough for a fire and flannel pajamas," Krystina complained. "I didn't even get a chance to post any summer Insta photos. My *Island Trotting* blog is practically dead. All I keep doing is reposting old articles."

"Girl, you need to learn to adapt," Egypt suggested. "Come up with something new. Reinvent yourself."

"Is that what you're doing?" Krystina challenged. "By upping and moving away from us?"

Egypt cocked her head to one side. "I'm not moving away from *you*. I'm considering an opportunity."

"Yes, designing jewelry that you can make over here and ship there."

"Ease up, Krystina," Mia reprimanded. "If this is where Egypt needs to go to further her career then we need to support her."

Kally handed Krystina a mug of hot chocolate. "I'll have a glass of wine instead," Krystina huffed irritably.

Kally laughed. She took a sip from her stemless goblet. "No."

Krystina sneered. "No fair. It sucks being the youngest."

"You'll appreciate it when we have wrinkles and you don't," Mia joked.

Pivoting, Krystina turned her attention back to Egypt. "Tell me the real reason you want to flee the island."

"Flee! You certainly have a flair for the dramatic," Egypt laughed. "I'm not running from the law."

Krystina cupped Egypt's shoulder. "Aren't you, though?"

"Hmm, she has a point," Kally agreed, amused.

"What? Who? You mean—"

The sisters all shot her the same pointed glare, one eyebrow raised, arms crossed over their chests.

"Leo? You all think I'm running from Leo?" Egypt's voice rose two octaves.

"The jig is up," Mia said.

"You really should stop watching those old black and white flicks," Egypt griped. "Okay, okay. I'll admit that where Leo and I stand factors into my final decision. But he's not the only consideration."

"What else then?" Kally asked.

"My parents." Egypt sighed. "They never let up on me. And now, with the greater need for healthcare workers, they're constantly reminding me it's not too late to enroll in school."

"But you know, parents can nag you on the phone too," Krystina reminded her. "There's no escaping it."

Egypt poured herself another glass of wine. "Isn't that the truth?" She nodded, her faced scrunched up in annoyance.

"So that brings us back to Leo."

"Krystina, why can't you just leave it at the fact that I need a change of pace?"

"Because it isn't true. You love Leo, don't you?"

"What difference does it make if he doesn't feel the same way?"

"How do you know he doesn't?" Mia asked. "Have you talked it through?"

"No! No way. He's made it clear he likes us just the way we are. I mean, it's not like I'm asking him for a stroll down the aisle."

"Oh, E ..." Kally sighed. "You may not be asking, but is that what you really want?"

"I don't know. It seems to be working for the two of you," Egypt grumbled.

"But you've always been more of a free spirit than we were," Mia remarked.

"That's exactly what Loukas said," Krystina blurted out before slapping her hands over her mouth.

Egypt's sage-colored, cat-shaped eyes narrowed in suspicion. "What does Loukas have to do with this?"

"Nothing."

Egypt jumped on top of her, pinning her in a headlock. "Tell me, or I will tickle-torture you."

"No! Anything but that," Krystina shrieked.

"Then start talking," she threatened.

"Okay, just let go of me." Krystina closed her eyes and took a deep breath before spilling all the details in one long, endless sentence. "Leo and Loukas were talking at the gym, and Loukas asked what the deal was with you two, and Leo said everything was cool, just the way Egypt liked it, and Loukas asked 'are you sure about that' and Leo said 'Egypt'"—she pointed at her—"'is a free spirit and he doesn't want to stifle you, but if he had it his way, things would be different.'"

"Huh! Well, I'll be damned," Egypt said, looking utterly confused. "And Loukas told you all of this?"

"Every bit of it." She didn't want to tell Egypt they had discussed it while plotting to get the couple back on the same page. "So now you can go to Leo and tell him he has it all completely wrong and that you love him and want to stay in New York with him." Krystina nodded enthusiastically.

"I can do that, you say?"

"Yup. Here's your phone." She retrieved it from the coffee table and handed it to her with a smug expression on her face.

"The hell I will!" Egypt roared in defiance, tossing the phone across the sofa.

"Ouch! That hurt," Mia complained when it landed on her lap. "You want me to call him instead?" she teased.

"Big ass cop," Egypt mumbled. "Tough guy, martial arts fighter. And he's afraid to tell a woman how he feels about her?"

"Now you've done it," Kally rebuked her sister.

"Get over it. They're no worse off than they were before," Krystina defended. "Besides, Loukas is working the other end of this over at the gym."

Kally's mouth fell open. "Is that why all the guys are at the gym tonight?"

"Uh-huh. Loukas arranged it."

"Maybe the two of you should work on patching up your own relationship and leave Leo and Egypt to solve their problems without your interference," Kally suggested with an admonishing glare.

"Loukas and I are only eighteen," Krystina replied smugly. "Time is running out for them at their age."

"I heard that." Egypt scowled. "And I'm going to find a way to make you pay for that statement."

Chapter 50

Loukas

"As much as I appreciate all of you including me in this," Nicholas said when Leo threw him a pair of boxing gloves, "I'm more of a fencer." He looked around the gym's high ceilings before his eyes came to rest disdainfully on the boxing ring dominating a large portion of the room.

"As a rule, do you pull out your sword before or after your polo match?" Max wisecracked, grabbing his brother-in-law in a chokehold.

"How about we keep the sparring in the ring?" Leo suggested with a laugh.

Throughout the warm-ups, Loukas had wracked his brain on how to segue Egypt into their conversation. Anything he said would come out sounding forced, so he decided just to go for it, and whatever happened, happened.

"I have to ask," Loukas started. "You guys have way more experience with women than I do."

They all laughed.

"Just a little," Nicholas said. "Although, if you're going to ask us the secret to understanding how a woman's mind works, I don't think any of us can help you with that."

"Yeah, yeah." Loukas pulled a face. "Venus, Mars, and all that crap. What I want to know is if you think it's a turn-on for women to see their guy fight it out?"

Max shook his head, uncertain. "Nah, I don't think Kally would go for that. She gets nervous when I have to go to the scene of an altercation let alone seeing me actually fight."

"That's a hard no for Mia too," Nicholas said with assurance.

"What about Egypt?" Loukas asked.

"E? She's cool," Leo said.

"Huh," Loukas said. "You sure? You keep saying she's cool about everything but is she really?" he asked accusingly.

Leo, Max, and Nicholas each stared at him with the same curious expression on their faces. For a second, Loukas became a little nervous that the 'Three Musketeers' had banned together, their arms crossed over their chests as they evaluated him. Swallowing, he pictured himself up against a firing squad—Nicholas with his sword, Max with his gun, and Leo with his fists. Krystina and her big freaking ideas.

"Just what are you driving at?" Leo asked carefully.

"Um, it's just that I don't think Egypt wants things as cool and casual as you think she does."

"And what makes you think that?" Leo inquired quietly.

Loukas remained silent, not sure how much to divulge. After a long pause, Leo motioned with his hand, impatient for Loukas to speak. Man, he loved this guy, but he could be damn intimidating when he wanted to be.

"Krystina. She said Egypt is considering a move to L.A. because nothing is happening between the two of you and a change might be good for her."

"What the fuck!" Leo slammed his bare fist into the uppercut barrel punching bag suspended from the ceiling. "Why wouldn't she discuss something this important with me?"

"Calm down a minute," Nicholas said. "Leo, have you told her how you feel?"

"Not in so many words. I didn't want to put any pressure on her," Leo defended himself. "She's not exactly traditional like Kally or Mia."

"She might be more traditional than you think," Loukas said.

"Kid, you better tell me everything you know, right now." Leo stepped in line with Loukas, getting in his face like a drill sergeant reprimanding a recruit.

Loukas stepped far enough back to reclaim his personal space. "The girls are over at your house, Max, trying to convince Egypt to tell you, Leo, that she loves you before she makes her final decision."

"She loves me?"

"Shit, are old people dense? What do you think? She's been dating you, and only you, for two years."

"Call me old again and I'll separate your teeth from your jawbone. Got it?" Leo threatened him with a murderous look in his steel-gray eyes.

"If you're so wise, why are you and Krystina on the outs?" Max asked.

"Aw, hell. That's a completely different situation."

"We have time," Max said, slapping Loukas on the back.

"I'm all for talking this out," Nicholas agreed. "Better than getting thrown around by that guy." He cocked his head in Leo's direction. The dude was pacing the room with a vengeance, muttering indistinguishable words to himself.

"Well, aside from trying to steer the focus onto Leo and Egypt, I really do want to know if it's a turn-on for a woman to see a guy fighting. You see, Krystina refuses to date me if I pursue this, but if she had a chance to watch me in action, maybe she'd change her mind." Looking hopeful, he asked, "You think?"

"Can't say, but I wouldn't count on it," Nicholas said. "Look, you have your whole life ahead of you. You need to consider that if you can't support each other's dreams then maybe it's too soon for a relationship. Or maybe the two of you aren't right for each other."

"No, I love her. I've always loved her. Even when I tortured her as kids."

Max closed his eyes, massaging them with the tips of his fingers.

"Sometimes we fall in love with the idea of a person rather than the actual person."

Loukas had no idea what that meant. And it showed on his face.

Max held up his hand before he was barraged by questions. "Let me explain. When I met my first wife, I thought she was smart, beautiful, and sweet. We wanted the same things, and we were happy. Or so I thought. But I was only taken by her beauty and the parts of her she allowed me to see, the parts I allowed myself to see. So I created an ideal of who I thought she was. It turned out she was selfish, greedy, and irresponsible. The ugliness she hid inside eventually came out, and I finally saw her for what she was."

"He's right," Nicholas chimed in. "My first serious relationship was back in college. At first, Devalina seemed like the most incredible woman. However, she proved to be nothing like who I thought she was."

"Why are you two slamming me with your dating disasters? It's not like that with Krystina. She's a sweetheart," Loukas barked. "Most of the time, anyway. When she's not telling me to get out of her face."

Max laughed. "You two." He shook his head. "Don't get us wrong. We love her. She's our sister-in-law. All I'm saying is maybe you've put her on a pedestal, and that your expectations are unrealistic. What she wants her life to look like might be very different than what you see for your own future."

"If that's true then there's no hope," Loukas said, deflated.

"What I think Max is saying is that you should let the future play out naturally, as it's meant to," Nicholas interjected.

Loukas exhaled. "I set this night up to deal with Leo, not my problems. Now, tell me, what do we do with him?" He glanced over at the raging man as he paced back and forth muttering to himself. "He looks like he's going to blow a gasket."

"We?" Nicholas asked, raising an admonishing eyebrow. "This was your idea."

"No, it wasn't. Krystina put me up to it."

Nicholas pinched the bridge of his nose. "I don't even want to know."

"Hey, man," Max called over to Leo. "The floor is going to wear out."

"You know, Egypt is at Max's house. You can go there right now and tell her not to go to L.A.," Loukas suggested.

"Why would I do that?"

"To tell her why you want her to stay. You love her, right?"

"Nope. Not gonna do it. If she can't even give me the courtesy or consideration of talking to me before making a decision that affects both our lives then she can go ahead and make her plans without me. Why should I stick my neck out?"

Nicholas and Max shook their heads in vain as Loukas groaned. Krystina would have to come up with a Plan B. But this time, she could leave him out of it.

Chapter 51

Krystina

Two days had passed since Krystina's and Loukas' bungled missions to get Leo and Egypt to admit their true feelings for one another.

Claiming she had jewelry orders to complete and ship to California, Egypt hadn't visited the café in that time. But from what she told Kally, neither she nor Leo had so much as texted each other.

Finally, Egypt made an appearance. Grumbling a word of greeting, she picked through Kally's personal collection of aprons instead of grabbing a standard one with The Coffee Klatch logo. Instead, her apron of choice simply read 'Talk to me at your own whisk.'

"We have to do something," Krystina whispered to her sister.

"Haven't you done enough already?"

"I can fix this," Krystina assured her. "I have a plan."

"Since you think so highly of your matchmaking skills, maybe I should take this off and let you wear it." Kally's apron read 'A legend in the baking.' "No! Wait." She rummaged through a clothing rack of neatly pressed aprons. "Put this one on instead."

"Ha-ha. You're such a comedian." But Krystina took the proffered garment anyway, slipping it over her head and tying it back behind her. "Easier bread than done," she muttered in complaint. "You'll take back those words. But seriously, I need your help."

"In case you haven't noticed, I'm trying to run a business here."

"I'll tell you what I think we need to do while we ice those cupcakes," Krystina offered, following Kally over to a batch Luis had set on the working station.

By the time Krystina had finished explaining her plan, the cupcakes were decorated. And so were her frosting-covered hands and the sticky ends of her hair.

"Will you do it?" Krystina pleaded.

"We can give it a try." Kally sighed, reluctant to interfere again. "But if this new plan of yours goes south then you have to promise me this will be the end of it."

"I promise," Krystina vowed, crossing her heart and leaving a trail of icing now on her apron too.

"They're adults, after all, and it's up to them to communicate without third parties interfering all the time."

"Okay. I get it," Krystina squawked. "But can you text Max now and find out whether Leo is working or not?"

Max replied right away. He was on shift, but Leo was not.

While Krystina looked over her shoulder, urging her on, Kally sent out a message to Leo.

Kally: *Hi Leo. I need a favor if you're not too busy.*

Leo: *I'm around. What do you need?*

Kally: *You know how tiny my office is. I'm trying to make more room. I need a file cabinet moved. Can you come over?*

Leo: *Be there in ten.*

Kally: *Thanks* ☺

"Shit, shit, shit!" Krystina shook her hands like they were on fire. "How do we get Egypt in the office before Leo gets here?"

"It's your plan!"

"I didn't think that far ahead," Krystina admitted.

"I'm beginning to wonder if you just sit at home and study episodes of *I Love Lucy*. Are you auditioning for a remake?"

"Enough with the sarcasm. We have about seven minutes."

"It's a good thing one of us is level-headed," Kally said with a smirk. "I'll tell Egypt that I'd like a few more Halloween decorations cut out. I'll ask her to go into the office and use my Cricut to punch out some pumpkin shapes and laminate them."

"That will work." Krystina eagerly nudged her sister in Egypt's direction, smiling like it was all her idea.

Krystina kept her eye trained on the door, waiting for Leo to enter so she could quickly usher him into Kally's office. So far, all her ducks were lining up. Egypt had been taken off the to-go counter and sent to work on the decorations. Now she just needed to get him in there.

"Leo!" Krystina jumped when she saw him walking in through the front door. "Hi! Thanks for coming. Kally asked me to show you where she wants it."

"Okay. How are you doing?" Leo asked suspiciously, his eyes narrowing as he approached. "You seem a little on edge."

"No. Just another busy day at the café." She pointed to the closed door. "Go on in. I'll follow behind."

Suspicious, Leo followed her lead. As soon as he entered, Krystina shut the door and locked it from the outside.

"Now you two talk things through," she shouted through the door. "And when you're done, I'll come back for you."

Chapter 52

Egypt

Sitting behind Kally's desk in the cramped space of the small office, Egypt looked up at Leo in confusion before she realized what had happened. With an equally shocked look on his face, Leo stared back at Egypt.

"Krystina Markella Andarakis," Egypt shouted. "You unlock this door right now, or I'm going to beat the ever-loving shit out of you."

"Let me know when you both have come to an understanding that I can live with, and I will." Krystina's muffled reply came from the other side of the door.

"That *she* can live with?" Egypt and Leo exclaimed simultaneously with the same measure of incredulity in their tone.

After a minute of dead silence, Leo resigned to his fate and took a seat on the opposite side of the desk. "What are you working on?" he asked.

"Pumpkins for the window, or some kind of bullshit." Egypt pushed what she'd completed out of her way. "Kally didn't really need these. It was all just a setup."

Leo roughed his hands over his face. "Why would they set us up? Tell me." He looked at her with fury in his eyes. "We were doing fine until I found out from Loukas that you were planning to leave the state. From Loukas! A kid!" he punctuated.

Leaning back in her chair, Egypt looked up at the ceiling. What could she say that wouldn't make her sound like a weak, pathetic female? She blinked back tears, determined to stay strong.

"I haven't made my final decision yet. I would have told you once I did."

"And I don't get to weigh in? I don't factor into your life's equation at all?" Leo lashed out in anger. But it was evident from his expression that an undertone of hurt lay beneath his harsh words.

"I wasn't sure it mattered to you," she said quietly. "You never gave me any indication that it would."

Leo stood. Turning, he raised a hand in fury. She thought he was about to put his fist through the wall, but then he dropped it and turned back to her, his expression unreadable. The vein in his neck was bulging like it was about to explode. If it wasn't for the hurt reflected in his eyes when she glanced his way, she would have thought he hated her.

"Two years. Do you know how many women I've been with for that long?" He didn't wait for her answer. "One. You. No other women but you for the last two years. What does that tell you?"

"Really, Leo." Now it was Egypt's turn to get angry. "I can best you. Not only have I been with you, monogamously, I might add, for two years, but you are also the only man I've ever let into my life on a personal level. Most men couldn't even get a third date out of me, much less any sort of commitment."

"Don't you think I know that? It scares the crap out of me knowing that one day you'll turn around and tell me you're bored with me. That's why I have been trying to give you all the space you need. So you don't tire of me and dump my ass!"

"Men! How is it you've been allowed to rule the world? You're all a bunch of idiots," she ranted in frustration.

Egypt stood and walked over to his side. Her five-foot two-inch frame couldn't measure up to his six-foot three-inch height, but what she lacked in size she made up for in moxie.

"Do you really think giving me space will ensure I won't grow bored?" She fisted her hands on her hips. "Did it ever occur to you that maybe I've considered that your behavior reflects a lack of interest on your part? So, why would I consider you in my life choices?"

"Let me make something clear," Leo said firmly. "I am not bored of you. I am not interested in anyone else. Nor will I ever be. If you don't want me, that's one thing. I won't stand in the way of your happiness or future plans. But in no way will I have an easy time living without you. Ever!"

Misty-eyed, Egypt took two steps closer to Leo and took his face in her hands. Awestruck by the sincerity she saw in his eyes, she stepped up on her tippy-toes and kissed him. To think she almost walked away from him.

When she broke the kiss, Leo's face softened. With a smile, he murmured, "I love you, E. I'm in love with you."

"Like for real love? Not the 'We just had great sex, and I love you for that' kind of love?" She bit her lip nervously.

Kissing her, he laughed. "You're a bit certifiable, you know?"

"I know. But apparently you're drawn to women on the brink of insanity." She looked into his eyes. "I'm insanely in love with you, and I thought you were pulling away from me."

"And I thought I'd completely lose you if I asked you for a commitment," Leo admitted. He shook his head, laughing at himself. "You love me," he repeated in awe. "Maybe I won't strangle those teenagers after all."

"So what do we have to tell her to get out of here?" Egypt asked.

"Do we have to go just yet?" Leo slipped his hands under Egypt's t-shirt, skimming the edges of her lacy bra with his fingers.

"Leo! The walls are thin in here. It's Kally's office!" she exclaimed with a giggle.

He picked her up, seating her at the edge of Kally's desk. Wedging himself between her legs, he pressed himself against her. "When do you get off?"

"Just as soon as that conniving teenager lets us out. Those sisters owe me a day off."

"I think it's us who owes them," Leo said.

"Have I told you that I'm crazy in love with you?"

"Let's get out of here and you can show me," Leo suggested.

Jumping off the desk, Egypt ran to the door and banged her fists against it. "Krystina!" Egypt shouted. It was time to go home.

Chapter 53

Krystina

"I've never seen so much candy!" Athena sat on a blanket, which was spread out on the Andarakis' living room floor. Treat-sized packets of candy surrounded the child.

"Now take a treat bag and fill each one with four different candies," Krystina instructed. "There's no reason we can't have some fun. If not as many trick-or-treaters come knocking at our door, I'm going to hunt them down and pass the bags out myself."

Athena giggled. "Are you going to wear a costume?"

"Sure! What should I be? Something creepy like an unraveling mummy? Or a cute baby Yoda, perhaps?" She unwrapped a mini bag of M&Ms and poured them out into her hand. Picking out the red ones, she returned the rest of the colors to the package.

Athena looked at her curiously. "Why do you do that? Only eat the red ones?"

Krystina shrugged. "I don't know. It's something I started doing it when I was even younger than you. They're just my favorite." She spilled out the contents of the bag again and held out the palm of her hand. "You can choose a favorite color of your very own, if you'd like."

"What if I want red too?" Athena proposed.

"You're out of luck, kid. I already called a claim."

"Okay. I guess I'll take blue then."

"What's the big debate here?" Max asked, strolling into the room.

Krystina sifted through the candy-coated chocolates and handed Athena all the blue ones.

"I'm choosing my favorite flavor, like Krystina," the little girl replied happily.

"Let me tell you a secret, Athena. You can eat the blue ones if you like, but all the colors taste the same," Max said with a smile. "Try not to corrupt my daughter to your irrational line of thinking," he told Krystina, chuckling as he walked away.

One by one, the rest of the family arrived for Sunday dinner. Even Mia and Nicholas took the trip in from the city. After dessert was served, the men grabbed a couple of six-packs of beer and left to sit by the outdoor fireplace in the backyard.

"You need to stop being so rude to Loukas," Mia told Krystina curtly, taking her by surprise.

All the women were sitting around the table nursing hot cups of tea.

"I'm not being rude. Rude would be if I was making snarky comments to him all the time." Krystina held her ground. "I just avoid speaking to him at all."

It wasn't as though she planned it this way. It was just easier. Once Egypt and Leo had straightened out their differences, she realized that she and Loukas couldn't do the same. The thought should have given her some closure. Instead, it just made her feel dejected.

"Hasn't this gone on far enough between the two of you?" her mother reproved. "And you were doing so well while *Yiayiá* was sick. I thought, finally, you were both back to how things should be."

Yiayiá, who had not uttered a single word throughout dinner, suddenly found her voice. "Loukas and Krystina are in love, just like Kalliope and Panos." She spoke as though in a trance, referring to herself in the third person. Her comment lacked her usual zeal, though, and Krystina could tell she was stuck in a distant memory.

"Loukas and I—" Krystina started to protest but her mother silenced her. Krystina complied immediately when her mother gave her 'the look.' The one that breathed fire.

Once again, her grandmother fell silent. Krystina wished she could do something to heal her grandmother's soul, just as she had when she tended to her body during her bout with COVID.

"*Mamá?*" Melina took her mother's hand. "Do you want to rest in your room?"

Without replying, *Yiayiá* began to rise. Melina helped her up and escorted her away.

"She's still so weak," Egypt whispered.

"I think it's more her mental state than the lingering side effects from the virus," Kally explained.

"We have to figure out some way to cheer her up," Egypt decided.

"Nothing has worked so far," Mia said on a sigh.

"I think we could all use a little cheering up. And I have something that might be fun for the four of us."

"What?" Krystina nearly jumped out of her seat. "I need some fun. I'm bored to tears. My Instagram is looking extremely drab these days."

"Well, what if I told you there could be some sun and palm trees in your near future?" Egypt asked with a satisfied grin on her face.

"In my future?"

Egypt nodded with a grin.

"Yes!" Krystina fist pumped. "The Caribbean? Hawaii?"

Egypt shook her head to both guesses.

"So it won't be until after the New Year, but I actually do need to go to L.A. for business, and I thought we could make it a girls' trip."

"I'm in! I'm in!" Krystina practically shrieked, raising her hand like she was in class.

"Oh, E." Kally sighed with disappointment. "I don't think I can.

Who will run the café if we're both away at the same time?"

"It would be a stretch for me too," Mia added. "But I'll see what my schedule looks like."

"But I can still go without them, right? Because I'll be on break."

"Yes, you can still go." Egypt laughed.

"I have two months to plan my outfits and scope out the best photo locations."

"If you were smart," Mia suggested, "you would have told her the night before you left, as parents do with children when they're heading off to Disneyworld."

Completely ignoring her sister's remark, Krystina got up from the table. "I have to call Chynna!" Then, wrapping her arms around Egypt, she hugged her excitedly. "Thanks, Egypt. You're the best."

"That's so exciting!" Chynna said. "I've been to L.A. with my family. You'll love it."

Krystina had immediately gone upstairs and called her friend via FaceTime. "I don't have all the details yet but I know it will be epic. I can't wait to just get off this damn island for a few days."

Chynna scratched at her nose under her mask.

Frowning, Krystina snapped, "Would you take that thing off? You're in the house."

"I forgot it was on. I just got in from picking up takeout," Chynna explained. "I'm kind of used to wearing it now."

But she didn't fool Krystina. Chynna had taken to wearing it even when it wasn't necessary. If Chynna were a superhero, her mask would be the costume that emitted powers her everyday life couldn't.

"Anyway ... you know that guy who keeps coming into the café?" Krystina asked, changing the subject. "I swear, he's going to drown himself in coffee just for a chance to speak to you."

"What are you talking about?"

"Don't play dumb with me. You know exactly who I'm talking about. Every time he tries to approach, you either run into the kitchen

314

or help another customer."

"I don't do that. And I don't know who you're talking about," Chynna defended herself indignantly.

"Yeah, right," Krystina said dismissively. "I did a little digging, and Stacy told me that he's related to Andrea's boyfriend. You know who I mean, right? Andrea Walker from school?"

Chynna nodded. "I know Andrea."

So, anyway, he's the first cousin of Andrea's boyfriend. He's from Iowa, or was it Idaho? Well, no matter." She waved it off. "Anyway, he's a sophomore at Stony Brook University but renting an apartment off-campus at a house right here in Port Jeff."

"Wow. You should become an investigative reporter," Chynna said sarcastically. "And why is all of this important?"

"Chynna," she drawled out in frustration. "He *likes* you! That's why. Now"— her tone suddenly turned serious—"what are we going to do about it?"

"Nothing. Seriously. Stop. I love you, Krys. You're my best friend, and I can't think of anyone I'd rather have in my corner. But I need you to stop pushing me out of my comfort zone." Chynna sighed. "For all we know, the guy heard about my deformity and is just wondering what lurks under the mask. I'm probably just some freak show to him."

"Okay," Krystina whispered as her exuberance died on her lips. Suddenly she realized her insensitivity. Imagining herself in Chynna's shoes, Krystina relented. "Okay," she repeated quietly. She held up a finger, staring firmly at the screen before Chynna could object. "But you are never to refer to your birthmark as a deformity. Ever. And I don't think that's the case with Daniel. That's his name, by the way."

"You know, I find it interesting how you try to mend everyone else's relationships and fix up anyone who isn't in one, yet you're not willing to deal with your own."

"I'm not in a relationship."

Chynna took off her mask, staring at the screen in all seriousness. "Read my lips. Ignoring it won't make it better, Krys. You want everyone else to be happy, but what about you?"

Krystina covered her face with her hands. It was much easier to occupy her mind with other people's relationships. "I don't know," she answered softly. "I just don't know."

Look out for those who look out for you. Loyalty is everything.
Connor McGregor

Chapter 54

Loukas

November 2020

"How are you holding up, kid?" Leo asked, slapping Loukas on the back.

Loukas exhaled. "Nervous. Excited. A little scared." Sitting on a bench in the locker room of Leo's gym, he jiggled his legs. The roar of the crowd had him pumped as spectators cheered and yelled from the stands outside. It was exhilarating until he realized he'd soon be the next one out there. What if he wasn't the one they rooted for? Or worse. What if he lost the fight before it even began? Loukas had heard of that happening before. One move, and it was all over. He would never be able to show his face in the gym again.

"It's normal to be a little nervous," Leo said. "That adrenaline can work in your favor though. Use it. Remember, be confident but don't get cocky," he warned. "If you're too relaxed, chances are your attitude is way more confident than it should be. Now, are you ready to go out there?"

"Yeah, I think so." Loukas breathed heavily, his heart pumping as the nerves swam to the surface, threatening to overwhelm him.

"No. What have I taught you?" Leo asked sharply. "This takes as much mental skill as it does physical. Lose your focus, and you're done."

"Got it," Loukas said, slipping on his fingerless fighting gloves.

Leo rattled off a list of last-minute instructions as they watched the event from the corner of the gym, waiting for Loukas' turn to compete.

Leo bumped elbows with him. "Take a look out there." He pointed to a particular section in the stands. "You have your very own cheering section."

Everyone was there—Kally and Max; Max's brothers and his father; even Mia and Nicholas had come out from the city just to see him compete. Egypt, some of the girls from the café, and even Luis from the bakery were all there too. Loukas spotted a bunch of his friends from school grinning and jostling about in the stands. Even Melina and George were watching excitedly, and they had brought *Yiayiá* along too, which pulled at his heartstrings even more, especially since she rarely left the house since Panos had died.

Catching Loukas' attention, George gave him the thumbs up. The night before, he had presented Loukas with a pair of Aegean blue shorts the color of the Greek flag to wear for tonight's occasion.

But *she* wasn't there. Loukas sighed. Krystina's absence was as apparent as a white smoke message written on a clear, blue sky. It pained him more than the rapid pricks recently applied to his skin when the tattoo artist inked over his pulsating heart.

After what seemed like an eternity, his name was finally called. Loukas shook all extraneous thoughts from his mind, just as Leo had taught him to.

"Focus," Leo ordered, cuffing his shoulder. "You got this."

Loukas took in a deep breath, inserted his mouthguard, and crawled into the cage to face Aldo, his opponent.

Leo had made sure to match Loukas with someone of similar experience and stature. For both young men, this was their first fight. A series of attempted jabs started the round. Neither Loukas nor

Aldo made contact until his competitor grew impatient. Going in for a roundhouse kick, Aldo foolishly aimed for a middle kick, placing him in a vulnerable position. Loukas distracted him with a jab while attempting a sweep.

Whistles and shouts of encouragement sent Loukas' euphoria on a high. But he knew he still had to work for his win. First, Aldo hit him with an uppercut, and it took Loukas a few seconds to recover. Aldo decided to take advantage, charging Loukas like a bull in the streets of Spain would.

But Loukas quickly got his wits about him and almost laughed at Aldo barreling toward him, arms flailing, unknowingly exposing himself to repeated punches. Knee kick to the stomach. Under hook. Jab, jab.

But then Aldo managed to grab ahold of Loukas in a clinch, though Loukas still had the advantage. Loukas passed under and around his opponent's arm, gripping him at the waist from behind. Pressing his head against Aldo's back, he straightened his leg and placed his foot behind the heel of Aldo's.

The tension and anticipation in the room were palpable, but Loukas kept his concentration. While maintaining his grip, Loukas fell to the mat, bringing Aldo down with him.

The referee called a one-minute break. Leo shoved a towel and a bottle of water in his hand, a broad grin spread across his face. "Keep it up, kid."

The bell went again and they were back at it. Loukas and Aldo circled the mat until Aldo grabbed onto Loukas' arms and the young men grappled. Aldo tried to come in close enough to trip him but failed, and Loukas was able to break free, placing him in the perfect position for a roundhouse kick. He'd aim low, just as Leo taught him. But as he turned to execute the move, something caught his eye. There, in the stands, he recognized the blurred image of Krystina. Distracted, he hesitated. Aldo jumped on the opportunity and grabbed his extended leg, knocking Loukas to the ground and pummeling into him.

Chapter 55

Krystina

Krystina had spent the last three days moping around the house. She had no interest in her Instagram account or in adding anything to her blog. She barely listened when her sister gave her orders at the café. Her mind churned, working overtime, and it was occupied with only one subject. Loukas.

Mulling over everything Yiayiá had advised, Leo had shared, and her sisters had admonished her for, Krystina's mind was in overdrive. She couldn't forget the censure she'd received from Egypt and Chynna either, as they defended Loukas. Did everyone think she was wrong? Why couldn't anyone see her side of this?

But as the day of the fight arrived and the guilt set in, she started to wonder how she could possibly stay away. If he did well and came out proud of his accomplishment, she wanted to be there to witness his moment of triumph. But if it went the other way, and he came out injured either in body or spirit, Krystina had to be the one there to heal his wounds. She shuddered at the thought of him hurt and alone.

And this is how it came to be that Krystina called Chynna at the very last minute to attend the event with her. Loukas had just begun his match when the girls made their way to the stands, squeezing in next to *Yiayiá*, who had suddenly become quite vocal, shouting out her support. If this is what it took to bring her grandmother back to life then she was all for it.

Krystina didn't know whether to watch her grandmother fiercely mimicking Loukas' moves or watch Loukas himself. One was comical; the other scared her to death.

Each time his opponent struck Loukas' beautiful face, Krystina had the urge to yell out a string of curses at the guy. But Loukas was holding his own, and very impressively too. So, after a while, she began to relax, if only marginally.

"You did right," *Yiayiá* said, patting her thigh fondly. "You love him," she whispered in her ear.

"I suppose that's true," Krystina relented.

She didn't realize she was holding her breath until the competitors took a short water break.

"What's that?" Krystina leaned forward in an attempt to gain a better view. She had zeroed in on Loukas' bare chest. "Did he get a tattoo?"

She tapped Chynna on the arm. "See what I mean? First the fighting, now he's inking his body. What is happening?"

"I really worry about you," Chynna said with a roll of her eyes, the expression made even more obvious as it was the only part of her face Krystina could see above the mask she was wearing. "Stop jumping to conclusions. It's only one, and ..." She laughed, lifting her brows knowingly. "I thought that's what it was." She nudged Krystina's elbow. "You better take a closer look."

Krystina leaned forward again, squinting to better make out the design. "Oh my God!" she exclaimed, her jaw dropping in surprise.

The cartoon character indelibly marked over his heart was Minnie Mouse, adorably bending down to pluck a daisy from the ground, a hint of her pantaloons showing. And she thought Loukas was so angry over her lack of support for him that he had forgotten her. Tears brimmed in her eyes and she wanted to shout out his name, if only she hadn't lost the power of her speech.

Once the match resumed, Loukas and Aldo grew more aggressive in their attacks. Krystina cheered for Loukas when he landed a punch and screamed when Aldo tried to take him down. But Loukas had the upper hand. Then, for one brief second, his eyes locked with hers, and he hesitated, surprise flashing across his face. That brief moment was all Aldo needed to take him down.

The fight was called and the winner named. Krystina felt awful, blaming herself for his loss. It had only taken that one second for Loukas to lose his focus, and it was all her fault.

Loukas exited the cage, escorted by Leo. Impulsively, Krystina jumped from her seat, excusing herself as she descended the bleachers. Without thinking, she entered the men's locker room, calling out Loukas' name.

"You can't be in here." Leo blocked her from walking any further into the forbidden zone. "You should have warned him you'd be here." He glared at her, enraged, regarding her with crossed arms. Leo was angry with her, it was true, but no more than she was at herself.

"It's okay, Leo," Loukas said, emerging from within. "I'll step out into the hall." He ushered her out of the room.

"You came," Loukas stated, staying rooted in place near the entrance of the locker room.

Competing thoughts reeled through Krystina's mind as she desperately tried to decide what to do next. Keep her distance, as he had? Turn and run away? No! She had been cowardly enough already. Krystina's emotions decided for her. Bursting into tears, she rushed to Loukas and threw her arms around him.

"I'm-so-sorry," she cried, gasping for air. "You would have won if it wasn't for me."

She buried her face in his chest. Loukas was completely soaked in sweat, from the hair on his head to the drenched shorts her father had gifted him. But she didn't care. Despite all she had done to him, Loukas didn't turn her away. Instead, he embraced her, murmuring in her ear.

"Don't cry," he said soothingly. "You being here means more to me than a win. It's all I ever wanted."

She looked up at him. "Really?" she sniffled.

"Yes. And I had decided that, one way or another, I was taking you into that cage with me."

"This?" She laid her hand over the tattoo covering his pectoral muscle. "You shouldn't have done it."

"I wanted to, and I had to, so I could prove that my love for you is as permanent as the ink on Minnie Mouse's panties."

"Just her panties? The rest is temporary?" she countered with a small giggle.

He kissed the palm of her hand then placed it over his heart. "No. Forever and unending."

"I've been so stubborn," Krystina admitted.

"Yes, you have," he said with a small smile.

"You're not supposed to agree with me."

With his eyes trained on her, Loukas erased what little space was left between them. Then, cupping her butt cheeks in his hands, he lifted her off the ground.

Supporting herself with her arms around Loukas' neck, Krystina wrapped her legs around his waist and stared into his piercing blue eyes. Worry deepened the lines in her furrowed brow as she examined his face. She wiped away the rivulets of sweat dripping down his forehead and brushed her fingers carefully over the nasty bruise blooming across his left cheek. Even beat up, she could admire his full lips, the dimple of his chin, and his perfectly straight and unharmed nose. Had that Aldo person damaged it in any way, she would have had to exact some sort of awful revenge on him.

"How long are you going to stare at me before you kiss me?" Loukas asked with a twitch of his lips.

Krystina ran her thumb over the purple mark circling his right eye. "Long enough for me to see that you weren't hurt too badly."

Turning so that Krystina's back was against the wall, Loukas held her up by her bottom, pushing her against the hard surface. He brushed his lips softly over hers with a teasing graze.

That was all Krystina needed. A spark ignited the second their lips met. Electricity rippled through her like a downed powerline sitting in a puddle of water. She grabbed his face and kissed him as though her life depended on it.

"I love you," she breathed into his mouth.

"I've always loved you," Loukas said.

"I'm glad you kids finally worked things out," Leo interrupted. "Now take it out of my gym and someplace private."

Krystina giggled, climbing down from Loukas' hold. Leo didn't fool her. He could act short-tempered and stern all he liked, but she knew better. He was a big softy, especially where Loukas was concerned.

"We're heading out," Loukas said.

"You okay, man?" Leo asked, gripping his shoulder affectionately.

"Absolutely fine." Loukas grinned.

"Better luck next time," Leo said.

Next time. The thought made her insides twist. But Krystina had made a decision that day, promising herself to stand by Loukas no matter what. She wouldn't go back on her word. She loved him. It mattered not that they were still teenagers; she knew her heart. Their feelings would grow and mature as the years went by. And if there was one thing she felt with great certainty, it was that he was embedded in her soul forever. Just like *Yiayiá* and Panos, Krystina and Loukas belonged with one another.

The future belongs to those who believe in the beauty of their dreams.
Eleanor Roosevelt.

Epilogue

Krystina

December 2020

"Who here is happy to see the end of 2020?" Melina asked her daughters with a wry smile, raising her glass of wine.

Without hesitation, each one of them picked up their glasses, toasting to the end of a harrowing year.

It was the Sunday before Christmas, and Melina had asked the family to gather for an early dinner. Theo was finally coming home from England. Of course, it was only for the holidays, but Krystina couldn't wait to see him. Judging from the way her mother was scrubbing down the house, she wondered if the Prince of Wales was accompanying him.

Theo was bringing home someone special, too, which might explain all the primping and fussing on her mother's part. She'd cooked enough food to feed a small island too. But that was hardly unusual in her home. Melina was excited when she learned that Theo had a steady girlfriend. She surmised it must be someone important for him to bring her all the way home from England. But Krystina knew her brother hadn't yet told his parents everything. This year might still go out with a bang, she thought.

"I for one hope that the new year brings a fresh start, our lives back to normal, and the disappearance of this virus," Kally declared.

"Maybe we can throw a mask burning party," Mia joked.

"And you think a date change is going to rid us of a spreading killer germ?" Krystina asked.

"Not everything about 2020 was all bad," Loukas interjected as he came into the kitchen. Looping his arms around Krystina's waist, he rested his head on her shoulder. "Considering Minnie finally admitted she didn't hate me after all, I'd say the year ended up okay for me."

"Just okay," Krystina bantered, punching him in the bicep in mock anger.

Loukas chuckled. "Ouch," he teased, rubbing the spot. "You'll pay for that." Playfully grabbing her by the arm, he twisted it behind her back. With his other hand he grabbed her by the waist, lifting her off the floor. "Can I steal you away for a few minutes?"

"Go, go." Melina waved them away. "Before you wrestle each other to the ground. Just make sure you're back before Theo gets here."

"We're only going upstairs." Loukas led Krystina up to her room and took a seat on the edge of the bed, pulling her down beside him. "I have a little pre-Christmas gift for you. But before I give it to you, I've been doing a lot of thinking, and I want to ask you something."

"Okay," she said hesitantly, draping her legs over his. Now that he was hers and they'd finally mended old wounds, Krystina couldn't keep her hands off him. The little girl who had once followed him everywhere, insisting he play with her at every moment, had returned. Only this time, kickball and tag wasn't what she had in mind.

Holding his breath, he took her by the hand, fiddling with the rings on her fingers. "Where do you see yourself in ten years?"

Krystina looked at him with puzzled amusement, her brow creasing. The question had thrown her. "Is this a job interview?" she laughed nervously.

"I'm serious," he maintained. "I mean, what do you expect your future to look like, and where do I fit into it?" Loukas quickly clarified, tripping over his words. "Like when we're, I don't know, twenty-eight or so?"

Krystina took a few seconds to think before she answered. "I don't know that I've thought all of that through yet," she admitted. "I want to finish college, I guess. Then maybe get a job at Nicholas' magazine, if he'll hire me as a travel writer. I'd love the opportunity to recommend locations, resorts, and restaurants for features in each issue. Or at least, I want to travel in some capacity, even if it doesn't end up being a part of my career."

"And me? Where do I fit into all of this?"

This conversation was getting heavy. For the last couple of months, they had been living day-to-day, dealing with only the most imminent problems. And now, suddenly, he was asking her about a time so far away in her own mind. She didn't even know what tomorrow would bring. Krystina exhaled the breath she didn't realize she was holding. "I suppose that depends on your plans," she said. "I only know that we just figured us out, and now I can't imagine my life without you in it." She brushed away the hair falling over his face, which had been hiding his worried eyes. "Why all these questions about the future?"

"I've been doing a lot of thinking lately, and you know how I said I didn't know if I should even go to college because I don't know what to major in?"

"Yes, and I think I told you to just take some classes locally, which you did, and that maybe you'd figure it out."

"Well, now I know what I want to do, and what I hope for our future. I'd like to know how you feel about it though, and if it works for you."

"Okay. Go on." Krystina braced herself, silently praying he didn't want to fight professionally.

"I'm going to stay in college and major in computer science."

She smiled in relief. "Wow, I think that's a great fit for you. So fighting is off the table?"

"It was never my intention to make it a profession, but I'd like to keep training." He shrugged. "Maybe enter a fight here and there."

"I think I can live with that," she agreed reluctantly. "What do you want to do with your degree once you graduate?"

"My first thought was to get a position as an analyst. I heard the money is great. But I want our lives to fit together. That's way more important to me because, without you, there's no point to any of it."

Krystina leaned in and kissed him. There it was. That completeness of being she'd missed without him. Could a heart really swell with love? Because she could swear hers was about to burst from her chest.

"You're distracting me," Loukas mumbled through her kiss.

"I'm sorry, but are you finished with your life plans yet?" Krystina taunted, mapping kisses down his neck.

"I'm serious, Minnie. This is important," he stated. "I'm going to double major in education and teach computer science," he continued. "That way, I'll have the summers off, and we can travel during those months, if you like."

"You've really thought this through," she said, sobering. "I'm impressed."

"So what do you think? About us and our future?"

"I think we've come a long way, and together, we can go all the way."

"All the way?" Loukas wiggled his eyebrows.

"You know what I mean. I thought you said you were serious."

"I am. About our careers, building a life with you, and very, extra serious about going all the way with you as often as possible."

Krystina shoved him playfully. "You're such a boy."

"Glad you noticed."

"Have you made any decisions about the house?"

"I did. That's another thing I wanted to talk to you about," Loukas said. "After many conversations with your father, I've decided to sell the house."

"Are you sure?" Krystina was surprised and just a little sad. It was one more chapter closing in their lives. "I thought you wanted to hang onto it."

"I thought I did, but I really have few good memories there," he admitted. "With my mother's fall, leading to her death, and my father changing into someone I no longer recognized only to also leave me, I feel no sentimental value for it anymore. It just harbors bad memories now."

"So you'll sell it and live with us?"

"No. I don't want to live with you under your parent's roof. I'll get an apartment or live on-campus. Later, you and I will get a place of our own."

Krystina's eyes widened as she broke out into laughter. "Have you met my parents? They'd kill both of us."

"Well then," he started, leaning in and running his nose down the length of hers. "I might just have to rethink that ten-year plan and ask you to marry me sooner."

Krystina ran her hands through his hair and kissed him. "One step at a time. As long as I'm with you."

"Always."

"Hey, did I pass?" Krystina pulled back, suddenly remembering she was being tested.

"Pass what?" he asked in confusion.

"The test. You said you had something for me if I answered your questions."

"Oh, that. Hold on," he said, raising a finger.

Loukas jogged from the room, rushing back in not five seconds later with a plain, white bag in his hands. "For you." He proffered the bag with a sly grin.

Krystina peeked in, opening her mouth in surprise, looking up at him in amazement. Inside was a cellophane bag of red M&Ms!

Proudly, he instructed, "Take one out. I had them inscribed."

"Inscribed? I didn't even know that could be done." She untwisted

329

the package tie and took one from the bag. "Forever my Minnie," she read aloud. "Loukas. This is the most thoughtful gift ever!" Nearly knocking him over, she jumped into his arms, her eyes sparkling with happiness. "I'll have to savor these so I don't finish them off too quickly. And I'll have to keep at least one as a souvenir."

"Oh, don't worry. There's more. Plenty more," he assured her. "I had to make a minimum purchase to customize the order so I bought a five-pound bag."

"My love meter for you just ticked up five times higher for that."

"That's all it took?" Loukas slapped his forehead. "I could have saved myself so much grief all these years, if I only knew."

"But it wouldn't have been as much fun," she teased, dragging him off the bed. She could say that now that they were solid. But in actuality, constantly snubbing him had never been fun.

"As much fun as this?" Loukas walked her backward until her back hit the wall. He pressed into her, claiming her mouth with a deep kiss as he slid his hands under her sweater.

"Loukas," she moaned. "We can't. Theo will be here soon. We need to tell my parents what we know about his girlfriend before they arrive. The poor girl doesn't know what she's walking into."

"And why is that our job?"

"Because you and I are the only ones Theo confided in about Mackenzie. He's not sure how they'll react to her, and he asked me to break the news to them gently." Krystina blew out an anxious breath. "I could kill him for putting this on me. But I'm the fixer, right? Isn't that what everyone says about me?"

"Meddler, matchmaker, busybody. Those might be better words," Loukas joked, holding his hands up protectively before she slapped him.

"Say what you want, but if it wasn't for me, *Yiayiá* would have never seen Panos or had the chance to say goodbye to him. Egypt would be halfway to California, and both she and Leo would be miserable. And if I hadn't intervened and finally introduced café boy to Chynna, she wouldn't have a date with him this week."

"Now that you have everyone else settled ..." he said, turning her face gently by the chin to face him. "I'm all you need to focus on now," he whispered, claiming her mouth again. The intense heat of his desire spilled into Krystina, bleeding through her very pores, igniting every cell in her body until she was completely overcome by the deep connection she shared with this boy.

Finally, she could fully grasp the depth of her grandmother's faith and unconditional love. Now she truly understood for herself that love was worth fighting for.

The end

Continue reading for an excerpt from

Love in Plain Sight

Theo's story

Book four in The Meraki Series

Chapter 1

Theo

September 2019

Foot traffic moved at a steady pace on the streets of London by the Holloway campus of the London Metropolitan University. The masses hurried to reach their offices on time while students walked briskly to their classes, either chatting with classmates or alone, occupied by the music playing from their AirPods.

Theo ducked into The Rocket building for a coffee and a scone before heading to class. By day, students caught up with friends, absorbed a bit of sun in the courtyard, if it ever decided to come out from behind the clouds, or quietly tapped away on their computers at the café. But before the night's chill set in, this campus venue transformed into a loud and vibrant bar.

Taking a seat at an empty table, Theo answered an incoming text before pausing to spread the clotted cream on his chocolate chip scone. Finally putting his phone down, he took his first satisfying bite and couldn't help thinking of his sister, Kally, who made very similar ones at her café back home on Long Island.

As he sipped his coffee, Theo looked around to see if any of his friends were around, but there wasn't a familiar face in the crowd. But to his right, at an adjacent table, he spotted a young woman. His head snapped back toward her. She was absolutely beautiful. It was the dazzling color of her hair he noticed first—cinnamon with luminous golden strands highlighting her waist-length tresses. The smattering of freckles across her delicate nose on her otherwise flawless, creamy skin drew his attention to a pair of eyes so light blue they were nearly translucent.

She looked up from her laptop and stared in Theo's direction. But when he smiled at her, she didn't react. No smile back at him. No flip of the hair. No turning away to avoid him. He had the urge to pat himself to make sure he hadn't disappeared.

Gaining a woman's attention had never been a problem for Theo. Usually, they approached him first, and he couldn't remember the last time he was the pursuer. Shrugging it off, he finished his scone and took his coffee to go. But each day, for the next few days, Theo returned to the student café looking for her. She haunted his dreams, and he was beginning to wonder if she was just an apparition.

* * *

It was five minutes past nine o'clock in the morning and Theo was late for his event management class. Sprinting into the building, he slowed down to a jog as he rushed down the hallway. Unfortunately, the seat he usually took in the back row was taken, so instead he quietly headed to the front of the room, where he noticed an open spot.

After settling into his seat, Theo pulled out his laptop to take notes.

"I'll be assigning a group project next week," the professor explained. "I'll detail it all out by then, but in the meantime, you need to find a partner." The stylish, middle-aged woman declared, "Once you've found your teammate, I'll expect an email from each group stating who you're working with."

The year had only just begun, and Theo hadn't seen any familiar faces on the first day of class. Turning to look over his right shoulder, he glanced at the students behind him. As Theo came back around, his elbow clipped the edge of his mobile and it slammed to the floor. When he bent down to retrieve it, he accidentally bumped into the girl on his left and did a double-take when he lifted the phone off the floor. It was *her*. The delicate beauty with the aquamarine eyes was in his class. How had he not noticed her before?

"Excuse me," Theo whispered.

"It's fine," she replied, though she never turned to face him. Instead, she kept her eyes trained forward in the professor's direction.

Finding her behavior a little odd, he continued, "I saw you at The Rocket last week. Maybe you noticed me?"

"I'm afraid not," she whispered back, pointing a finger to her lips and shushing him silently.

Theo wasn't sure if he was being snubbed or if the girl simply wanted to focus on the lesson. She hadn't even bothered to look his way.

When class was over, Theo slipped his laptop into his messenger bag and stood. "I'm Theo," he said, introducing himself.

"Hello, Theo," she replied distractedly, turning her head in his direction but still not actually meeting his gaze.

"I didn't realize you were in my class when I saw you at the café." Theo tried his best to engage her in a conversation but she seemed uninterested and aloof.

"I'm often overlooked," she said with little emotion as she slipped her laptop into her tote bag."

"I find that hard to believe." He paused for a beat. "Now that you know my name, can I have yours?"

"Mackenzie," she answered, smiling for the first time. But as she secured her laptop into her bag, she pulled out another contraption.

Suddenly, realization struck when she expanded a rod that was collapsed into four sections. Mackenzie was blind! She hadn't ignored his friendly smile at the café. She couldn't see it. And here he was asking her if she noticed him. Now he was a little embarrassed and at a loss for words.

Mackenzie gathered her things without another word, ready to exit the classroom.

"Wait," Theo said. "Can I walk you out?"

"I'm quite capable on my own," she replied with a smile that didn't quite reach her eyes.

Theo raked his fingers through his hair, contemplating whether or not to pursue her. But, he had to admit, the revelation stunned him, and he was a bit ashamed of his reaction. He was only glad she couldn't see the stricken look in his eyes when the cane had materialized.

"That's quite apparent," Theo said, striding up alongside her. "But I thought we could talk about class."

"What would you like to discuss?" Mackenzie asked as the cane guided her along.

"Well, I need a partner for the project, and I'm assuming since it was just assigned, you do as well. Maybe we could team up," he suggested cautiously, unsure she'd be interested. So far, she hadn't engaged with him, answering his questions with only the barest minimum of replies.

"It would solve my problem as no one else will probably offer." She stopped and turned to face him. "Why me?"

Theo stumbled on his words. He was a little taken aback by her directness. "I don't believe either of us knows anyone else in the class," he started, trying to formulate the words to articulate his motives without raising suspicion. "And I think we could be friends." That would have to do for now until he figured it all out for himself. But there was something about this woman that drew him to her. Something that separated Mackenzie from the many others he'd dated before. And her vision impairment had nothing to do with it. Theo only knew he had to learn more about her.